"Jamie, you remember
ange

The one you haven't co

"I haven't completed it? I've more than completed my assignment. I didn't just find the boy a mentor; I became his mentor," Caine said. "I've updated regularly with his academic performance until he's eighteen."

Evie didn't bat an eye. Between the black-framed glasses and the knot she'd twisted in her dark hair, she looked like an uptight professor. And why that made him want to back her against the wall and kiss her until her glasses fogged and her long, silky locks escaped from the knot to fall about her shoulders, he didn't have a clue.

"So, that's how you think it works? Hand over some cash and sign a few papers and the deal is done?" She stepped into his space and inched up on her toes. "That may be how it's done in your world, Mr. Elliot. But it's not how it's done in mine."

Wrapping his hands around her biceps to lift her off her feet, bringing them eye-to-eye, nose-to-nose, mouth-to-mouth, he said, "Be careful, Ms. Christmas. You know what they say about playing with fire."

"Are you the fire?"

PRAISE FOR DEBBIE MASON'S
HARMONY HARBOR SERIES

THE CORNER OF HOLLY AND IVY

"[A] delightful return to a small town that I adore. Frankly, I've never met a Debbie Mason story that I didn't enjoy, and this one is no exception. I had fun with Connor and Arianna, cried a bit, laughed out loud, and experienced the magic of a small-town Christmas season. If that doesn't equal a great Christmas romance, then I don't know what does."

—KeeperBookshelf.com

"Mason takes her romances to a whole new level with plenty of content to make for a more action-packed romance than just two people falling in love. So again this was another fun trip to Harmony Harbor that I'm sure romance readers will enjoy."

—CarriesBookReviews.com

SANDPIPER SHORE

"Hurray for SANDPIPER SHORE, a Cinderella story loaded with intrigue."

—FreshFiction.com

"Quirky, funny, sweet, and overflowing with a colorful cast."

—*Library Journal*

DRIFTWOOD COVE

"Mason rolls out the excitement in the fifth book in the Harmony Harbor series."
—*RT Book Reviews*

"I love second-chance romances, and Debbie Mason has written another good one in her Harmony Harbor series, with some pretty significant obstacles between our hero and heroine and their happy ending."
—TheRomanceDish.com

SUGARPLUM WAY

"4 Stars! Harlequin Junkie Recommends! An amazing addition to this sweet and sassy series."
—HarlequinJunkie.com

"I really enjoyed this story...it had a lot of elements that put together made for a Christmas where dreams really do come true."
—RomancingTheBook.com

PRIMROSE LANE

"4 Stars! This is a book worth savoring as it has all the elements of a fantastic read."
—*RT Book Reviews*

"Wow, do these books bring the feels. Deep emotion, heart-tugging romance, and a touch of suspense make them hard to put down, while the humor sprinkled throughout keeps the emotional intensity balanced with comic relief."
—TheRomanceDish.com

Christmas in
Harmony Harbor

ALSO BY DEBBIE MASON

The Harmony Harbor series

Mistletoe Cottage
"Christmas with an Angel" (short story)
Starlight Bridge
Primrose Lane
Sugarplum Way
Driftwood Cove
Sandpiper Shore
The Corner of Holly and Ivy
Barefoot Beach

The Christmas, Colorado series

The Trouble with Christmas
Christmas in July
It Happened at Christmas
Wedding Bells in Christmas
Snowbound at Christmas
Kiss Me in Christmas
Happy Ever After in Christmas
"Marry Me at Christmas" (short story)
"Miracle at Christmas" (short story)
"One Night in Christmas" (short story)

Christmas in Harmony Harbor

DEBBIE MASON

FOREVER
New York   Boston

Copyright © 2019 by Debbie Mazzuca
One Night in Christmas copyright © 2019 by Debbie Mazzuca

Cover illustration and design by Elizabeth Turner Stokes. Cover copyright © 2019 by Hachette Book Group, Inc.

Forever
Hachette Book Group
1290 Avenue of the Americas, New York, NY 10104
read-forever.com
twitter.com/readforeverpub

One Night in Christmas first published as an ebook in May 2019.

First Edition of *Christmas in Harmony Harbor*: October 2019

Forever is an imprint of Grand Central Publishing. The Forever name and logo are trademarks of Hachette Book Group, Inc.

The publisher is not responsible for websites (or their content) that are not owned by the publisher.

The Hachette Speakers Bureau provides a wide range of authors for speaking events. To find out more, go to www.hachettespeakersbureau.com or call (866) 376-6591.

ISBNs: 978-1-5387-3171-0 (mass market); 978-1-5387-3169-7 (ebook)

Printed in the United States of America

OPM

10 9 8 7 6 5 4 3 2 1

This book is dedicated with much love to my daughter Jess for reading my first drafts, answering my endless questions, heading up Team Mason, and for loving the holidays and happily-ever-afters as much as me.

Acknowledgments

Heartfelt thanks to my editor, Alex Logan, who works tirelessly on behalf of my books, whether it's searching out a new promo opportunity or editing when she's supposed to be on holidays. Her dedication is much appreciated, as is her attention to detail. She never fails to make each book better.

To Beth DeGuzman, Amy Pierpont, Leah Hultenschmidt, Madeleine Colavita, Cristina Lupo, Jodi Rosoff, Estelle Hallick, Monisha Lakhotia, Tareth Mitch, Penina Lopez, Elizabeth Turner Stokes, and the dedicated sales, marketing, production, and art departments at Grand Central/Forever, thank you so much for everything you do on behalf of my books.

Many thanks to Pamela Harty for always being there for me. Thanks also to the members of Pamela's team at the Knight Agency: Deidre Knight, Eileen Spencer, and Jamie Pritchett.

To Perry, April, Jess, Nick, Shariffe, Sara, Lilianna, and Gabriella, thank you for all your love and support. I couldn't do what I do without you guys. I wouldn't want to. You are my world.

Many thanks to all the wonderful and supportive writers I've met through ORWA (Ottawa Romance Writer Association), especially: Ludvica Boota, Cynthia Boyko, Ellen Bruce, Christine Enta, Lucy Farago, Vanessa Kelly, Joyce Sullivan, Randy Sykes, Allison Van Diepen, and Teresa Wilde.

And last but not least, a very big thank-you to the readers and reviewers who take time out of their busy lives to hang out with me in Harmony Harbor and Christmas, Colorado, and on social media. Your messages, FB comments, tweets, and reviews mean the world to me. Thank you for sharing your love of the Gallaghers and McBrides with your family, friends, and followers.

An extra special thanks to members of my readers group, Robin Whitaker and Cindy Hetherington LeMay, who named Max.

Chapter One

♥

A power outage on Black Friday was the last thing Evangeline Christmas needed. As the owner of Holiday House, a year-round Christmas store located in the town of Harmony Harbor, Massachusetts, Evie had been planning for this day for months.

She'd scrimped and she'd saved and she'd begged and she'd borrowed (from her tight-fisted mother), pouring every nickel and dime into making this the biggest kickoff to the Christmas season yet. She'd spent more on advertising for this weekend than she had for the past year's holidays combined.

She wasn't alone. Her fellow shop owners along Main Street were also pulling out all the stops to get customers through their doors and turning over their credit cards once they had them there. Although Evie more than anyone needed those customers today. Her entire future hung in the balance. She wasn't being a drama queen or a Negative Nancy.

Evie was a thirty-year-old woman who typically saw her glass as half-full rather than half-empty. But after the week she'd had, her optimism was flagging. Now, as she stood in the dark an hour before customers should be clamoring to get into her store, that glass was bone-dry.

If only she could pick up the phone and call her dad. He'd had a way of making everything better. She could practically hear him in her head. *There's always tomorrow, Snugglebug.*

"I wish that were true, Daddy," she murmured, her fear of the dark causing her heart to race as she blindly edged her way past the display tables to the sales counter with only the light on her cell phone to guide her. She caught movement near the front window and whipped around to confront the shadow in the corner.

Show no fear. *Show no fear,* she repeated in her head with more force, as if that would vanquish the panicked emotion freezing her to the floor. She pictured herself in combat boots instead of the Naughty and Nice knitted booties she wore and with a fierce, don't-mess-with-me expression on her face. She held up her cell phone. "You better get out of here. You've got two minutes before the police arrive."

Hoping to blind her would-be assailant, she aimed the light where she guessed his eyes would be. It hit him dead-on, right in his painted black eyes that didn't blink. A small, mortified groan escaped from her. She had nothing to fear from the blow-up Santa Claus.

She wished her fears for Holiday House's future were also in her head, but they weren't. Three days before, her circumstances had become as dire as George Bailey's in *It's a Wonderful Life*. Just like poor old George and the savings and loan, she had a conniving schemer trying to bring her down—billionaire developer Caine Elliot.

His glass-and-steel office tower would not only destroy the seafaring charm of Main Street, but the national discount chains destined to be housed in the tower's street level would put the future of Harmony Harbor's mom-and-pop shops at risk.

With some help from Harmony Harbor's Business Association and some really good friends, Evie had managed to stall the development of the three empty lots beside hers for more than a year. But this past Tuesday, she'd learned Holiday House was in imminent danger.

Harmony Harbor's town council would vote on Monday whether or not to take her land to accommodate the parking spaces required by a long-forgotten bylaw for a development the size of the office tower. A bylaw she herself had brought to the town council's attention in a last-ditch effort to quash the development.

"And look how that worked out for you," she said as she tried first the landline and then the credit-debit machine on the counter, neither of which worked.

Turn your frown upside down and sit a spell, Snugglebug. Let those endorphins do their work. You'll have your answer in no time.

Despite feeling like the dark cloud hanging over her was about to burst and bury her under a mountain of debt, Evie couldn't help but smile at her dad's favorite refrain. Taking his advice, she lowered herself onto the stool behind the counter, once again wishing he was a phone call away. He'd know what to do. He always had.

If wishes were horses . . . The cell phone's light glinted off the tarnished gold cash register. It was almost as old as Holiday House. At least she'd be able to ring sales through and accept cash, she thought, giving the antique register a grateful pat and her dad a silent thank-you.

She glanced over her shoulder at the three generations of her father's family looking at her from the framed photos on the wall. Each of them had successfully run the store before her. She wondered what they would have done had they found themselves in her position.

"They wouldn't have been in your position. The three stores beside you wouldn't have burned down, leaving the lots ripe for development. And Caine Elliot wouldn't have been born." The reminder helped, she decided, getting up from the stool on a wave of determination. It wasn't entirely her fault she was days away from losing a business that had been in the Christmas family for a century.

Chewing the peppermint-flavored ChapStick off her bottom lip, she moved the light on her cell phone to the stairs leading to the second level. A redbrick three-story with classic wood beams and plaster interior, Holiday House had been the family home before her great-great-grandparents had turned the front rooms on the main floor into a Christmas store. The wooden Christmas ornaments her great-great-grandfather made back then had been the biggest draw.

Last year Evie had taken up residence in the attic, converting three of the second-floor bedrooms into showrooms for the other popular holidays. If she roped off the stairs and found a way to light up the main floor, at least customers could shop in relative safety.

She bent to open the cupboard under the sales counter, moved aside two boxes of bags, and found a flashlight. It wouldn't provide enough light until the sun peeked through the window by mid-afternoon, but the fieldstone fireplace across the room would help. Candles too. Lots of them. She'd have time to make more to fill the orders, especially if... No, she wouldn't lose hope.

All she had to do was walk into Monday's town council meeting with a sack full of this weekend's sales receipts and the testimonials she hoped to wrangle from customers to prove that Holiday House was an integral part of the community, a much-loved piece of their history that they couldn't allow Caine Elliot to destroy for his modern-day eyesore.

She forced her lips into another smile in hopes the action would release a bunch of stress-reducing endorphins. Then again, there probably weren't enough endorphins in all of Harmony Harbor to reduce her level of stress. It was Caine Elliot's fault.

Almost a year ago to the day, she'd picked up the phone and a velvet-smooth deep voice had come over the line. As annoying as it was to admit now, she'd initially been seduced by his dreamy Irish accent. She'd even begun to fantasize about the man behind the voice. A lovely, mildly erotic fantasy that had been rudely interrupted as soon as Caine Elliot got the social niceties out of the way.

She didn't care about his statistics and facts, his company's success, or his many business degrees. No matter that he presented his development as the best thing to happen to Harmony Harbor since the advent of electric lights, she knew exactly what would happen to the small town she loved if no one stood up to him.

At the time of that first call from the Ogre of Wicklow Developments, Evie had been running Holiday House for only two months. But she had a long history with the small town. Every year, she and her dad would leave her mom and the sweltering heat of New York to stay with Evie's great-aunt Noelle and help out at Holiday House for the entire month of August.

They'd visit in the fall and winter too, but it was the month-long summer stays that Evie treasured most as they readied the store for the holiday season. Some of her best memories had taken place in Holiday House.

She'd felt safest here, happiest here, and no way was she letting some hotshot developer steal that from her or anyone else, which she'd told him that day. And he'd told her she was allowing her emotions to color her decision and that sentimentality had no place in business. The call had devolved after that as emotions got heated. Her emotions at least. As far as she could tell, Caine Elliot didn't have any. The man was coolly unflappable and arrogant. Their conversations over the last year had only served to validate her initial opinion of the man.

"Okay, enough. Time to get this show on the road." Her voice sounded odd, higher-pitched than usual. She kept talking to herself anyway. She needed the distraction as she made her way around the tables and out of the shop, heading for the storage room and boxes of candles. "Only an hour until the doors open and all those Christmas-loving customers pile..." She trailed off as the darkness swallowed her whole.

Her *It's okay. You're okay. There's no one here but you and Santa Claus* was interrupted by a rap on glass from the front of the store and her friend Mackenzie's voice calling to her through the door. Evie ran from the back hall into the main room, almost knocking over a display table.

Relieved to hear dull thuds and not the sound of shattering glass as several items fell to the wood-planked floor, she held on to the edge of the pedestal table until it stopped wobbling. Once it had, she rubbed what felt like a bruised thigh and limped her way to the front of the store. Thanks to her trembling fingers and sweaty palms, it took longer than it should to unlock the three dead bolts and open the door. Evie smiled as she stepped aside to let Mackenzie in, hiding her hands in the pockets of her knitted green-and-red sweaterdress.

"Are you all right?" Mackenzie asked, looking around the shop with a frown while closing the door behind her. Gorgeous, with long caramel-colored hair, the owner of Truly Scrumptious handed Evie a bakery box.

"Other than the power being out, I'm fine, and these gingerbread cookies smell amazing. They're still warm," she said, praying Mackenzie didn't notice the box trembling in her hands. "Isn't your power off too?"

"No." Mackenzie glanced out the window. "It looks like everyone has power but you. The streetlights are still on."

Something Evie had failed to notice. Clearly nerves had messed with her powers of observation. Of course they had. She'd thought Santa was about to run across the store and attack her.

"Right. I..." She trailed off as the consequences of Holiday House being the only business without power hit her. What if Tuesday's payment to the electric company had bounced? Could she have forgotten to make it after learning Holiday House might very well be bulldozed into the ground to create a parking lot? She checked her banking app for a notice or payment receipt.

"Evie, are you sure you're all—"

She smiled. "My payment went through."

"Oh, okay, that's good," Mackenzie said in a halting tone that seemed to indicate Evie's smile appeared more manic than relieved. "You probably just have to change a couple of fuses."

And there went her profound relief, right out the front door. The fuse box was in the basement. A basement that hadn't been updated since the early 1900s and could be a stand-in for the basement in *The Evil Dead*. The closest Evie had come to going down there since she'd taken over the store was opening the basement door for the furnace repairman.

At the thought of descending the wooden stairs into the dark, unfinished cave-like space with only the flashlight to guide her, she cleared the ball of terror from her throat. "You know, I think I'll leave the lights off. The customers will feel like they've been transported back in time. I'll light the fire, put candles all around. I even have an oil lamp I can use. I'll put it over here." She gestured to a table that held a collection of Fitz and Floyd tea sets and Christmas dinnerware. Behind the table sat an artificial fir tree decorated in antique ornaments of red and gold. "I'll set out your cookies on one of the platters. Did you bring me more business cards?"

Not only was Evie showcasing Mackenzie's ginger-bread cookies, each of her tables displayed items from the shops on Main Street. The other stores were doing the same for her. Mackenzie had two of her Fitz and Floyd Christmas cookie jars on display at the bakery.

"I do, and I need more cookie jars. I sold yours yesterday." She pulled an envelope from her jacket pocket, handing it to Evie.

"You didn't buy them, did you?"

Less than an hour after Evie had been informed about Monday's vote, her friends had begun arriving at the store, declaring they absolutely had to have whatever their eyes landed upon. Their gazes had landed on a lot, but Evie was more grateful for their friendship than the sales. She didn't want them buying her merchandise just to help her out. She had a special connection with nearly every piece in the store, and she wanted her customers to feel the same.

"I bought one and my sister bought the other one, but we love them. Honest. Give me the singing Christmas tree cookie jars to display. I promise I won't buy them."

Evie understood why. Listening to "Rockin' Around the Christmas Tree" every time someone opened the lid on the plastic tree got on her nerves, and she'd celebrate the holiday year-round if she could. Which she supposed she already did.

"All right." She moved the cell phone light around

the room. "Now I just have to remember where I put them."

A muffled *ping* came from Mackenzie's pocket, and she pulled out her cell phone. "It's Julia. She's opening Books and Beans early and needs her cupcakes. Drop the cookie jars off whenever you get a chance," Mackenzie said as she walked toward the door. She turned back, digging around in her pocket. "I almost forgot. We've been collecting signatures for Monday's meeting. So far we have a hundred names on our petition to save Holiday House." She handed the papers to Evie. "I'm sure we'll double that this weekend."

Evie looked from the list of signatures to Mackenzie. "I don't know what to say."

"Don't say anything. This is what friends do for friends." Mackenzie hugged her. "I've gotta go. Let me know if you need more cookies."

"I will, and thanks. Thanks for everything. I don't know what I would have done this year without all of you in my corner."

"It's us who are grateful to you, Evie. You're the one who's led the fight against Wicklow Developments from the beginning. You've done all the heavy lifting, and it was for our benefit as much as yours. Now it's our turn to fight for you and Holiday House. And we've got a secret weapon. Rumor has it that Theia Gallagher is like a sister to the CEO of Wicklow Developments, and *he* can't refuse her anything. We've got this, girlfriend." Mackenzie gave Evie a fist bump. "Have fun this weekend and forget about Monday."

Surprisingly, it was easy. With so much to do

in such a short amount of time, her mind was kept occupied. And while hauling the candles from the pitch-black storage room took longer than it should have, she'd gotten the job done. It was better than making the terrifying descent into the basement of horrors. Eventually she'd have to ask someone to help her with that. She could play the helpless-little-woman-who-didn't-know-how-to-change-fuses card, something she hated to do. But if it meant she saved face while at the same time saving herself a trip into her own personal nightmare...

She took one last look around the room, from the candles that flickered on every available flat surface to the flames dancing in the fireplace. Despite being unable to plug in the Christmas lights on the three decorated trees, the room was not only well and safely lit, the ambience was as warm and as inviting as she had hoped. She just needed some music to put her customers in the Christmas shopping spirit. As she went to pull up the holiday playlist on her phone, *The Grinch*'s theme song, her mother's ringtone, shattered Holiday House's happy vibe—and Evie's.

She was tempted to hit Decline—her morning had been difficult enough—but instead she did what her dad would expect her to. "Happy Thanksgiving, Mom!"

"You're a day late."

"Well, I know, but remember I told you I'd be busy getting everything ready for the Thanksgiving dinner at the community center yesterday. I did text though."

"Texts don't count; nor does a video of dancing turkeys."

Her dad would have loved it. "I'm sorry. I should have called. Did you have a nice time at Auntie Linda's?"

"How could I? Her grandchildren were there. They're spoiled and have no manners."

Her cousin's children were adorable and well behaved. It was just that her mother subscribed to the adage that *children should be seen and not heard*. Evie wondered if she should text an apology to her aunt and cousin. It used to be her dad's job.

"But that's not why I called. I received a registered letter from Wicklow Developments regarding the offer they made to buy Holiday House last month."

Evie's heart banged against her rib cage. "I don't know why they sent it to you. It must have been a mistake."

"I have a fairly good idea why they sent it to me, young lady. They've obviously learned that I own shares in Holiday House and wanted to be sure I was apprised of the situation. The situation in which the majority shareholder doesn't have a shred of business sense. You're just like your father. Too soft and sentimental. Honestly, I don't know what possessed me to loan you the money. Now, as soon as I hang up, you are going to call Wicklow Developments and accept their offer."

"Mom, you don't understand. They don't want to buy Holiday House. They want to bulldoze it into the ground." And that offer would no longer be on the table since they had a ninety-five percent chance of getting their wish without paying a penny, which wasn't something she would share with her mother.

"So let them. You're barely eking out a living. Your last quarter—"

Evie hummed *The Grinch* theme song in her head. Her mother wasn't shy about sharing her opinion of Evie's and Holiday House's shortcomings and did so on a regular basis. Neither of them measured up to her mother's exacting expectations.

Evie knew it was her own fault for hiring her mom to do her books, but the thing was, if anyone could teach her how to manage inventory, cash flow, and pricing, it was her mother. Lenore Johnson (she'd refused to take her husband's last name) was a highly regarded accountant who'd won New York's Outstanding CPA in Industry Award three years in a row.

But more than her mom's business acumen and advice, Evie had hoped Holiday House would give them something to bond over. Because of course glass-half-full Evie had been positive that she could turn around the family business. And make her mother proud, she thought with a sigh.

"Mom, Holiday House has been in the Christmas family for more than a century. Daddy would want me to do this. You know he would."

"Of course he would. He was up for any lame-brain scheme you came up with. Remember when the two of you got it into your heads that you'd make a fortune selling candles for the holidays? There's still a box of them in the spare bedroom. Or what about the time you and your father took up knitting Christmas stockings? Noelle sold them for less than it cost for the wool."

Evie looked around the shop, wondering if her mom had a spy cam installed. "I was twelve, Mom."

"Your father was old enough to know better than to encourage you like he did. It's time you admit defeat and rejoin the real world. How you could up and leave New York and your job at the hospital to run Holiday House, I'll never know. You have a doctorate in psychology, Evangeline. You were making a decent living. You had benefits and a 401K, and now what do you have? Nothing but—"

At the mention of her old job, Evie headed straight for the front door, unlocked it, opened it, and reached under the Santa attached to the outside of the door to flip his battery to On. Then she began opening and closing the door with Santa *ho, ho, ho*-ing as she did so. "Sorry, Mom. It's getting busy. I've gotta go. I'll call you later." As soon as she disconnected, Evie looked at Santa. "I love you. I really do."

"Probably a good thing, considering you own a Christmas store," said a smooth-as-silk male voice.

A tiny shiver of awareness danced inside her. Some women had a thing for handsome faces; she apparently had one for sexy baritones. She turned slowly as she worked to smooth the reaction to his voice from her face. Unlike people who wore their emotions on their sleeve, Evie wore hers on her face. At least that's what her friends told her.

Whoa. His voice had nothing on his face. Which, if she was reading the slight uptick of his lips that were half-hidden by his beard correctly, he knew exactly what she was thinking. Unless she'd said *Whoa* out loud instead of in her head. She snorted at herself. The stress must be getting to her. She wasn't a fan of men with beards. Except he kind of had her revaluating that opinion.

She had a feeling that, with one look from those incredible blue eyes and that sexy half smile of his, he'd have her reevaluating her opinion on just about everything: like not dating a man until he had a psych evaluation (given by someone other than herself), not sleeping with a man until she'd dated him for at least three months, or like chocolate was better than sex.

Okay, so maybe not everything.

Not that it would matter because he was out of her league. And no doubt, with the length of time she'd been staring at him, she'd now embarrassed herself not once but twice. Possibly three times if she'd said *Whoa* out loud. She needed to say something, some witty remark to redeem herself.

"Ha ha, yeah, I love my men with beards... White beards, I mean, and jolly. Jolly with big bellies." What was wrong with her? She should have simply smiled and walked back inside the store. Wait a minute. When had she walked outside?

"Brr, chilly out, isn't it?" She wrapped her arms around her waist and pretended she hadn't responded to the siren call of his voice and face and had instead come outside to check her window display. "Okay, everything looks good from here." She tapped the glass. "I'd better get back inside. Nice, ah..." It had been a one-sided conversation, and she couldn't say *looking at you*, even though it was true. "Have a good day."

The corner of his mouth twitched as he walked around

her to hold open the door. She glanced at the Red Sox
ball cap he wore with a gray knitted scarf, black leather
bomber jacket, and jeans. He wore the hat rather low
and the scarf rather high, almost like a disguise...

"Um, thanks." Her heart bumped against her ribs
when he followed her inside. He hadn't seemed as in-
timidating outside as in. Maybe because being this close
to him she noticed how big he was compared to her. He
had to be at least six foot four to her five foot three.

"Sorry. I didn't realize you wanted to come inside.
Are you looking for anything in particular?" Nerves
caused her voice to come out a little high and a little
breathy.

"Yeah, you."

Chapter Two

♥

Evangeline Christmas's heart-shaped face lost its rosy glow, and she took two steps back. "Me?" she asked, her voice pitched so high it squeaked.

Brilliant. Caine had managed to terrify the owner of Holiday House, exactly what his grandmother had been planning to do to ensure the woman complied with the council's decision to take her property. They had it on good authority that Monday's meeting was more for show than anything else. However, since the owner of Holiday House was the most uncompliant, contrary, pain in the arse he'd ever had the misfortune of dealing with, he agreed with his grandmother's concerns.

If anyone could find a way to scuttle the council's decision, it would be Evangeline Christmas. But while the office tower was as important to him as it was to his grandmother, perhaps more so, there were lines he wouldn't cross. Frightening women was at the top of that list, which was why, fifteen minutes after ending the call from his grandmother last night, he'd boarded his private jet and flown directly here to protect the owner of Holiday House. The woman who'd caused him no end of grief and tens of thousands of dollars in delays this past year.

Evangeline backed into a table, staring at him through wide hazel eyes. "Why are you looking for me?"

Unless he'd allowed his irritation at what she'd put him through this past year to show on his face, he didn't understand her obvious panic. He was positive her reaction had nothing to do with him personally. They'd never met face-to-face, and even had she bothered to Google him, there were no photos of him with a beard, and he'd made sure to conceal his accent.

"Just relax, okay. I...Do you smell something burning?" He scanned the candlelit shop, wondering if she planned to burn the place down and collect the insurance.

"No. I..." She sniffed, glanced over her shoulder, and gasped. "My Santa collection!"

Spotting a flicker of flame, Caine reached into the window display on his left to grab a tall red vase that held an elaborate floral display. Tossing the red and white roses from the vase, he nudged Ms. Christmas aside and dumped the water on the table. A table that didn't appear to be on fire, he noted a nanosecond before dousing it completely. He glanced at the candle in her hand and a singed Santa bear on a wood floor in need of repair.

She looked from him to the table. "I can't believe you just did that! My entire Santa collection is ruined, and so is the floral arrangement from In Bloom. What were you thinking?"

Did she just stamp her silly green-and-red knitted bootie at him? "I was thinking I was saving your shop from going up in flames. What were you thinking having candles sitting within inches of flammable material? It's a bloody fire hazard."

Her eyes narrowed. "Who are you?"

Bollocks. His accent had come through. He reached inside his jacket and held up the envelope she'd returned to him last month, and not very professionally or appreciatively, he might add, recalling what she'd told him to do with the offer. An offer that was five times above the appraised value of her Christmas shop. "Messenger," he said.

"Really. You don't look like a messenger." She glanced out the front window as though searching for his mode of travel. "Where's your car?"

Hopefully in the back lane where he'd told his uncle Seamus to park. An uncle who Caine had assumed was dead up until two weeks ago.

"I parked across from the florist. A white Honda Accord. Would you like my license plate?" She looked like the type to ask, so he handed her the envelope. "I just need a signature and I'll be on my way."

And while he did a bang-up job of keeping his emotions from showing, Evangeline Christmas did not. She looked at the envelope with his company's logo as if she wanted to tear it into a thousand little pieces. He reached in his pocket for his smartphone and was about to pull up the signature app he'd downloaded earlier in order to stay in character when she tried to do just that.

"You can tell your employer exactly what I think of
his offer," she said, struggling to rip the bulky envelope
in half.

"He's not my employer. I was simply hired to deliver
the envelope to you. Would you like a hand?"

"No, I would not like a hand. I'm perfectly capable
of doing this on my own," she said through gritted
teeth, her face flushed. "And if you're just a messenger
for hire, how did you know that I was Evangeline
Christmas?"

The woman was sharp, something he should have remembered from their previous conversations. Although
conversations weren't an apt description. They were
more like lectures on the evils of big business destroying the beauty of small towns with a total disregard
for the lives they ruined, a complete evisceration of his
company and himself in particular. Granted the woman
was the emotional type, but the tears in her voice at the
end of their last conversation had been his undoing. It
was why he'd quadrupled his initial offer.

"I knew you worked for him," she said when he
didn't immediately respond.

"No. I don't. I was just trying to remember who gave
me your description." He scrolled through the e-mails
on his phone as though looking for the source, holding
back a sigh when texts from Seamus, his grandmother,
and Theia Gallagher popped into his feed.

Out of the three, Theia's most concerned him. Because
not only was she his best friend and former employee,
since her move to Harmony Harbor, she'd become
Evangeline Christmas's biggest fan and champion. It

was bloody annoying. And the last thing he needed was for Theia to catch him here.

She'd blow his cover, and once she had, she'd try guilting him into backing out of the project, which he couldn't. Saying no to her was easier over text or phone than it was in person. It was time for him to leave. He'd obviously overreacted to his grandmother's remark that she'd ensured Ms. Christmas would be only too happy to leave Harmony Harbor after today. The woman seemed perfectly safe.

He checked his grandmother's latest text to be sure that was the case. She knew he was here and was apparently pleased with his initiative to personally take care of the problem, which in her mind was Evangeline Christmas. If his grandmother only knew what he was up to.

"Here it is." He held up the phone, intent on getting out of there as soon as possible. "Your description was on the order form."

Theia had once described Evangeline as smart, beautiful, and exactly his type. And while he'd seen evidence the owner of Holiday House was a bright woman and admittedly attractive with her lush, dark hair and hazel eyes, his best friend didn't know him as well as she thought if she believed Evangeline Christmas was his type.

As the woman in question squinted at the screen as though trying to find the aforementioned description, he brought up the signature app and then held out the pen and phone. "If you'll just sign here."

Santa *ho*, *ho*, *ho*-ed and let in a gust of cold air and

three older women. The one who looked like Sophia Loren, with her dark, shoulder-length hair, seemed familiar. As soon as she said, "*Madonna Mia*, what has happened here, Evie?" he knew why.

It was Theia's grandmother-in-law-to-be, Rosa DiRossi, and the two women with her must be part of the infamous Widows Club. And if this morning's run of bad luck continued, Kitty Gallagher, who just happened to be Rosa DiRossi's best friend and a member of the same club, would be walking through the door any moment now, no doubt with Theia in tow. Because these days his best friend couldn't get enough of her new family. If only she knew...

"Just a little mishap," Evangeline said with a smile, and he saw why Theia called her beautiful. "Nothing to be concerned about. We'll have it cleaned up in no time. Help yourself to some gingerbread cookies while you browse."

At her *we'll* have it cleaned up, he looked around the shop and, seeing no one else about, looked down at her. "I'll be on my way."

"No. You owe me."

He supposed she had a point but he couldn't afford to dally, so he bent down, picked up the red and white roses, crammed them into the vase, then straightened to hand it to her. "There you go."

"You can't be serious? I have to soak up all the water and—"

"Evie, the candles, they look nice, but we can't see. And this one here"—Rosa DiRossi nodded at her friend—"nearly set her coat sleeve on fire."

Caine gave Evangeline a *told you so* smile, which she completely ignored because she seemed to be thinking about something else. Something that put a determined look in her eyes. "My fuses blew, and I'm embarrassed to admit it, but I don't have a clue how to change them. But I've found just the man for the job." With a smug smile, she patted his arm.

If the circuit box was in the basement of a house this age, she couldn't pay him enough to go down there and flip her breakers. He had people who did those sorts of things. "Sorry, I—"

"You look familiar. Do I know you?" Rosa DiRossi asked him.

"I don't believe I've had the pleasure." He tapped the brim of his ball cap as though to say goodbye, lowering it further over his eyes. "Now, I—" He took a step toward the door and caught a glimpse of Kitty Gallagher and Theia across the street. He needed to find another way out. Bollocks.

"Fine, then. Get me a torch and I'll go have a look," he said to Evangeline as he moved toward the back of the store and out of Theia's line of sight.

"Ha ha. Holiday House might be old, but it was hardly built in the Dark Ages, so sorry, we don't have any *torches* lying around."

"I meant a flashlight. You must have one—"

"I knew it! I knew you were somehow connected to Wicklow Developments."

"How do you figure that?"

"*Torch.* You're Irish!"

"So what if I am? We're in Massachusetts. You

can't throw a stone without hitting an Irishman or -woman."

"Really. So why would a man disguise his accent if he didn't have something to hide?"

"Because this man doesna have an accent unless he's bedeviled by a woman, is why. So if you're done with your inquisition, hand over your bloody flashlight, and I'll go down and take care of your breakers for you."

"Thank you, and you've just proved to me that you have nothing to do with Wicklow Developments and that ogre of a CEO Caine Elliot." She stopped at the sales counter to retrieve a flashlight.

"And how exactly did I do that?" he asked as he accepted the flashlight, not in the least surprised that she'd referred to him as an ogre.

"Because you're helping me even though you don't want to, that's why. Caine Elliot is a coldhearted, vengeful billionaire who wouldn't lift a finger to help anyone but himself."

Now, that he did take offense to. He'd gone out of his way to protect her from his grandmother's wrath. Emily Green Elliot, his grandmother, would do whatever was necessary to get what she wanted. She didn't care at what cost or who she hurt. She was a cutthroat businesswoman and had become more so after the doctor's diagnosis. Neither age nor cancer had softened her. She was as formidable and as rigid as the day Caine's mother had left him with her.

At the sound of Santa *ho*, *ho*, *ho*-ing, Caine said, "Which way to the basement?"

Evangeline had barely finished pointing him in the

right direction when he strode toward the back of the house. Not a moment too soon, he thought, upon hearing Theia's voice in the shop.

As he made his way to the kitchen, the flashlight's beam landed on the door to the basement. He got a little squirrely just looking at it, knowing what was probably down there. He hated dark, old, rat-infested houses with a passion.

He moved the light to the right. All he had to do was take ten steps and he'd be out the door. He'd hire an electrician to fix the woman's bloody breakers, save himself the trouble. He'd already gone to enough trouble on her account.

Bollocks. He was no longer a scrawny twelve-year-old trying to befriend the boys in town by acting brave. He was thirty-seven, for feck's sake, long past time for him to have gotten over his fear of rats. Besides, what if it wasn't a bunch of blown fuses after all? What if this was his grandmother's doing? As Caine had discovered over the years, anger was a powerful motivator, a tool to combat fear.

His anger had been doing a fine job combating his fear up until he found himself standing in an unfinished basement with rough-hewn walls and a dirt floor that made it difficult to see droppings. Good. He'd convince himself there wasn't— The thought broke off when a pair of beady red eyes peered at him through the beam of light. Cocky bastard didn't even move when Caine took a fierce step toward him. Fecking brilliant. Another of his pals joined him.

At the ring of Caine's phone, the rats skittered away.

He glanced at the screen. It was his uncle. Caine would call him back once the job was done. He'd buy him a pint for saving his pride. He'd been seconds away from turning tail and running back up the crooked, wooden staircase. It didn't matter that no one would know. Caine would.

He let the call go to voice mail, moving the light over the walls. The beam landed on a rusted circuit box. With his eyes focused on the spot, he walked across the basement floor, refusing to look anywhere else but straight ahead. Ignoring the tremor in his hand, he opened the cover and spotted the problem right away. He flipped the four breakers. *Success*, he thought at the sound of cheering from above.

No one had messed with the fuses, not even the rats. But time had, time and a lack of capital to invest in upkeep. Wicklow Developments was doing Ms. Christmas a favor. She'd tied herself to a sinking ship. He, out of anyone, understood loyalty to family, but there were times when you had to think of yourself. For Evangeline Christmas that time was now, and it was also long past time he was gone from this place, but something kept him down there.

It was Emily. He didn't trust his grandmother. She didn't make idle threats. He reached up and pulled the string dangling from the bare lightbulb. And there, on the opposite wall, was a heart drawn in red with the words *EC and AP together forever* in the center.

It didn't make sense to him. Had his grandmother had this done, and if so, why? There'd been nothing in Evangeline's background check to make him see this as a threat. To him it made more sense that this was something a young Evangeline had done when she'd visited her great-aunt during summer holidays.

Caine pulled the string, pitching the basement into complete darkness—except for the two pairs of disembodied red dots coming toward him. Feck it. He turned and ran up the stairs, his size and heavy boots ensuring he wasn't quiet about it. As he reached the landing, he heard Theia and Evangeline talking about the messenger, Theia in a decidedly suspicious tone of voice. They also sounded like they were coming his way.

Pulling his hat lower and his scarf up, he sprinted across the kitchen to the back door, grateful to find it unlocked. It wasn't until he was halfway down the lane that the door being unlocked struck him as odd, especially as he'd seen the number of dead bolts on both the front and back doors. But he didn't have time to think about it because his uncle and his car weren't at their meeting place.

His cell phone rang at the same time a door opened. He glanced at the screen. It was Theia. Shutting off the ringer, he ducked behind a hedge. A bitter wind rustled the crumpled leaves at his feet, and he huddled in his jacket as he scrolled to his uncle's text.

Give me a ring when you need me, boyo. I'm having an Irish breakfast at Jolly Rogers.

"I'll ring you all right," Caine muttered as another text came in. This one was from Theia.

A messenger? Really? You have some explaining
to do, my friend.

After sending his uncle a text to come get him, Caine
pulled off the fake black beard with a wince. Next time
he'd go with cheap and easy to remove. It felt like he'd
gotten a close shave. He probably could use one. He'd
been up close to thirty-six hours.

Peering through the hedge to ensure Theia wasn't at
the back door or looking through the kitchen window of
Holiday House, he stood to toss the beard in a garbage
can at the side of the shed the hedge backed against. At
a guttural yell, he stopped midstride.

"Mangy mutt! I'll shoot you next time I see you
around my garbage."

Caine looked about, trying to figure out how the man
had spotted him. Then something pinged off the tin can.
A dog whined, and what looked like an underweight
and uncared-for golden retriever came into view, trip-
ping over its paws as it scrambled backward.

"Easy now. Come here. That's a boy. You're a
friendly one, aren't you?" he said when the dog licked
his hand, pushing against his legs. Caine crouched
beside him, giving him a scratch behind the ears as he
checked for a collar. "Looks like you're on your own
and not having an easy time of it, are you, mate?"

Caine remembered well what it was like to live a hard-
scrabble life, as did his uncle. But while Caine's fortunes
had improved at the age of twelve, Seamus had spent
most of the past twenty-five years on and off the street.

"You could use a hand up too, I'm thinking," Caine

said to the dog, glancing back at Holiday House. "This just might be your lucky day. I think I can solve your problem and hers. Although she'd never admit to having one." An unfair assumption on his part. She had no idea her back door had been unlocked and wouldn't suspect anything nefarious because she'd now assume he was the one who had unlocked it.

Both he and the dog looked up when a black Mercedes drove up the lane, mowing down two garbage cans along its way. Caine's gaze shot to Holiday House, and he released a relieved breath when the back door didn't open in response to the noise. Had Theia appeared, his uncle would have rolled over faster than Caine's new canine friend.

Seamus got out of the car to check the bumper for scratches, using his jacket to buff one out. "I swear those cans came out of nowhere." His uncle turned, smiling at the dog. "Now, who is this fine fellow? Oh, but you are a lovely boy, aren't you?" He patted the dog. "He reminds me of your Max. He was a grand dog." His uncle teared up, as he tended to whenever he talked about the past. "She should have let you take him. A boy who'd lost his family should've been allowed to keep his dog."

"It was a long time ago, so let's concentrate on the problem at hand. We have to get Ms. Christmas to adopt Max."

His uncle gave him a watery smile.

Caine sighed. "You cry more than any woman I've ever known. It was a slip of the tongue. Dry your eyes and let's get the job done. Ms. Christmas needs a watchdog, and this dog needs a home."

"You barely gave me enough time to break my fast, so I have a take-away bag in the car. How be I get some sausages? We'll toss them into the lass's kitchen, shut Max in, then run."

"If we do that, we won't know if she keeps him." Though she seemed the type who would. "If she doesn't, she needs an alarm system." Which he knew she couldn't afford, and it wasn't something someone could donate to her without drawing suspicion. "And we can't leave the dog wandering the streets."

"Aye, I see what you're saying." His uncle tapped his white-whiskered chin. He hadn't been pleased when Caine had dragged him out of his warm bed last night. Seamus wasn't a fan of flying, even if it was his nephew at the controls. But Caine didn't have a choice. He had to bring him. It had taken him four days to teach his uncle to use a smartphone and three days for his uncle to finally understand how the television and appliances worked. Seamus was as lost in Caine's world as Caine himself had once been.

His uncle also found trouble faster than a two-year-old.

"I've got a plan. I just need a few things." Seamus walked off, leaving Caine with the dog.

And perhaps because his uncle had lived on the streets, he was very good at scavenging for what he needed, because ten minutes later he returned with some rope, tape, paper, and a pen. In the time he'd been gone, Theia hadn't texted Caine again or opened the back door of Holiday House, so he figured they were good.

His uncle had Caine tie the rope loosely around the dog's neck while Seamus wrote on the paper. *My name is Max, and I need a home. I like yours.* Then he taped the note to the rope.

Caine scrubbed his hand over his face, thinking he'd need to come up with another way to deal with both Max's and Evangeline's problems.

"All right, come on now, boy." Seamus pulled a sausage from the takeout bag, then dangled it in front of the dog's nose.

"Uncle, I'll stay here in case she opens the door before you get away."

Seamus nodded as he led the dog across the frozen ground to the back of Holiday House, breaking off a piece of sausage to reward Max once they reached the top of the steps. With the dog busy wolfing down the meat, Seamus tied the other end of the rope to the railing. "Okay, now, do your best to look pathetic," his uncle told the dog while pounding on the door. A minute later, he pressed his ear to it. "Someone's coming." He gave Max another bite of sausage, then ran down the steps to hide beneath the stoop.

Caine decided it was a good thing he'd left Seamus to execute the plan. Even though his uncle was five-seven with the build of a fifteen-year-old boy, he was barely able to squeeze beneath it.

Caine ducked behind the hedge at the side of the shed when the door opened to reveal Evangeline. "You poor thing. You must be freezing." She looked around, luckily not down, then went to untie the rope. "Come on, Max. Let's get you warm."

His grandmother would say there's a sucker born every day.

Chapter Three

♥

Colleen Gallagher stood in the grand hall oversee-ing the arrival of Greystone Manor's Christmas tree. The majestic twenty-five-foot fir was well suited to the hall's soaring timbered ceilings, magnificent stone fire-place, and elegant staircase with its red velvet runner and brass railings.

The manor had been built in the early nineteenth century to resemble a castle, complete with the requisite turrets, stained-glass windows, and extensive gardens. Twenty years before, Colleen had taken advantage of the fairy-tale beauty of the family home to turn it into a hotel. She'd liked to stay busy, and they'd needed the income—upkeep on an estate Greystone's size and age was costly.

Colleen returned her attention to her great-grandsons, who were struggling to get the tree through the oak doors. If they weren't more careful, it would soon re-semble a Charlie Brown Christmas tree only bigger.

"Mind where you're…" she began before remem-bering it would do her no good. Colleen was a ghost, you see. Silently overseeing was about all she could do, which she found annoying.

She liked to be in on the action, especially Christmas action. Her great-grandchildren used to say she had FOMO—fear of missing out, in case you're wondering. She'd had no idea what it meant at the time they'd said it either, but lately she'd come to think they were right.

Still, while she missed out on a lot, she was here. And for that she was eternally grateful, because three years before, on All Saints Day, only yards from where she now stood, her heart had given out. Truth be told, it had been beating for a hundred and four years, so it hadn't come as a complete surprise.

What did shock her though? She'd seen the light, heard the chorus of heavenly angels sing, and still managed to miss out on her ride to the great beyond. As her great-granddaughter Theia liked to say, Colleen was gone but hadn't left the building. And she had no intention of leaving until she secured the manor's future and that of her great-grandchildren. She wanted them settled with their one true love just as Colleen once was.

Oh, but she and her Patrick had had a grand love affair. They'd been happily wed for fifty years before her husband's heart gave out. Patrick had been seventy-eight at the time, working as a superior court judge right up until the day he died.

It was the ideal profession for the man. Though she'd been less than thrilled over the years when he judged her tendency for sticking her nose in other people's business and managing the state of affairs to go the way she wanted.

Those very things she'd done that had turned Patrick's hair gray before its time were the reason she may have dragged her feet when the golden light beckoned. She'd been afraid Saint Peter would slam the pearly gates in her face and send her straight to hell. Which was why, along with protecting the manor and matching her great-grandchildren with their loves, she needed to right the wrongs of the past.

She shivered a little at the thought her work here was almost done. She had only one great-granddaughter left to see settled, she'd righted the majority of wrongs from her past (at least the ones she remembered), and the manor... The manor was in grave danger from its greatest threat to date, Caine Elliot.

She was afraid she'd met her match, and not only because the lad was canny and rich, but because she couldn't put her finger on his motivation. If she wanted to win the battle, she had to know her opponent. He wanted to do more than tear down her beloved manor to build condos—of that she was certain.

The tall silver-haired man in the bespoke black suit directing the lads to lower the tree into the stand beside the fireplace was Jasper, her once–right hand man and confidant. In the past, he would have known exactly what Caine Elliot was up to, but things had changed over the last year. Jasper had fallen in love with the woman in the elegant white blouse and black pants who crossed to his side. Her white-blond hair framing her classically beautiful face, Kitty offered Jasper a winsome smile that clearly captivated the man.

Truth be told, Jasper had been in love with Kitty for

as long as Colleen could remember. But Kitty had been married to Colleen's son Ronan, so in love she'd had eyes for no one else. It wasn't until years after Ronan's death that the pair's relationship had changed. Colleen believed it was her death, and not her son's, that eventually brought them together. Still, she couldn't believe Jasper had let love cloud his mind and judgment so completely. He had to know something about Caine.

Kitty complimented her grandsons on their choice of Christmas tree, suggesting that they move it a tad to the left to ensure the roaring fire they kept going this time of year didn't dry it out.

Jasper frowned. "What's wrong? You don't sound like yourself."

"I can't hide anything from you, can I?" Kitty smiled faintly, then lifted a narrow shoulder. "It's Evie. I feel horrible the town council voted against her. She's done so much for the town, and she's worked so hard to turn Holiday House around. I suppose it's a blessing that her father and Noelle are no longer with us. It feels like the end of an era."

Colleen waited for Kitty to say more, or at the very least for Jasper to. But all he did was gently kiss the top of her daughter-in-law's head and say, "The pastry chef has made shortbread for tomorrow's high tea. Let's go and have a sample. It'll help lift your spirits."

"Lift her spirits? You need to do more than lift each other's spirits by drinking tea and eating cookies. You have to be ready." Frustrated with the pair, Colleen looked at the black cat sitting at her feet. "Simon, I need your help." He was the only one who could see and hear her. Although her great-great-grandchildren also saw and heard her before aging out of the ability. Eight seemed to be the cutoff. "As Jasper doesn't appear capable of seeing it for himself, we must alert him to the danger. Now that Caine has secured the office tower development, it's only a matter of time before he makes his next move on the manor."

Some people might think it odd she was asking a cat for help, but they didn't know Simon. He was far from your average cat. Over the past year, she'd become convinced he was actually the family's patriarch, William Gallagher. He had a lord-of-the-manor air about him.

Simon had arrived a week before Colleen died. They'd gotten off to a rocky start. Truth be told, she was a dog person, but he'd won her over.

Meow. He raised his white-whiskered brows and turned his head toward the grand staircase.

She was getting much better at understanding catspeak, but she had no idea what he meant. Which she told him. He gave a chest-expanding sigh and then nudged his head at the grand staircase as though urging her to follow.

"You're getting testy in your old age," she said, hurrying toward the grand staircase after him. She didn't know how old he was, but she'd noticed tips of silver peeking through his sleek black coat of late. Apparently, he took umbrage at her remark, sprinting ahead of her.

Being that it was the Monday after Thanksgiving, the manor was quiet, so the ding of the elevators opening on the second floor and the rattle of a housekeeping cart seemed overly loud.

"You're lucky I didn't run you over, cat," a young woman said to Simon from behind the housekeeping cart. Her voice held the musical lilt of the old country and the disgruntled tone of someone whose life wasn't going according to plan.

The redheaded girl with creamy skin was Colleen's twenty-year-old great-granddaughter, Clio. She'd arrived at the manor a month before full of anger and attitude, looking for her father, Daniel, who had conveniently left town. He'd also left it up to them to break the news that he'd seen the light after his near-death experience this past summer and he was turning himself in to the Greek government for stealing artifacts he'd uncovered in a dig. He wanted to start over with a clean slate.

Which was all well and good, but Daniel had also failed to fulfill his promise to cover Clio's school expenses, and the child couldn't afford to continue her studies. Her plans to become an archaeologist like Daniel were now on hold. Her current plan seemed to be to make the rest of the Gallaghers pay for being related to her father.

"Perhaps she'll get in the holiday spirit once the manor is fully decorated, Simon," Colleen said with more hope than conviction in her voice.

She got a doubtful *meow* in response before Simon raced off toward the spiral staircase that led to the third floor, where the family suites were housed in the tower. He bounded up the wrought-iron stairs to park himself in front of the door to her old suite. Her great-granddaughter Theia resided there but would be moving out in a few short weeks. Theia and Marco DiRossi were getting married at the manor on Christmas Eve. Colleen was beyond thrilled. To her mind, there was nothing more romantic than a Christmas wedding.

"Now, don't get maudlin," she said, thinking that was why Simon brought her here. Theia was his favorite. "It's not like she'll be far." The couple were moving into one of the winterized cottages on the estate.

Simon lifted his chin at the door as though she'd missed the point. She cocked her head, frowning at the sound of a man's muffled voice coming through the closed door. It was deep and had the same musical quality as Clio's. Colleen's eyes went wide. Caine Elliot. He must have used the secret passageway to get to Theia undetected.

Her great-granddaughter had worked for Caine until last summer, when she'd learned she was a Gallagher. And despite his intention to steal the estate out from under them, they remained the best of friends.

Because Theia was a lot like her, Colleen believed her great-granddaughter was simply keeping Caine close to learn what he was up to. She scowled at the sound of their laughter. Theia was a far better actress than Colleen if that were the case.

"Be on alert, Simon. I may have need of Jasper."

Colleen walked through the door and into her old suite, fit to be tied when she saw the handsome blue-eyed devil sitting as though he owned the place on a wingback chair near the roaring fire with a crystal tumbler of whiskey in his hand.

"I don't know what to make of you, Theia, I surely

don't," she said to her great-granddaughter, who was sitting on the end of the four-poster bed sharing a drink with the man, though hers appeared to be water.

"Wicklow Developments was well represented, T. My attendance for today's vote wasn't necessary. Besides, I had a pressing matter in Boston that required my attention."

"I don't believe you. The reason you weren't there was because you knew exactly how the vote would go, and you didn't want to see what the council's decision to take her home and business would do to Evie."

"If I weren't confident the council would decide in our favor, I would have been there. But since I was, my time was better served elsewhere." He swirled the whiskey in his glass. "How did Ms. Christmas handle the decision?"

"I knew it. I knew that's why you wanted to stop by. Admit it. You feel bad that you're to blame for Evie losing everything."

"I'll admit nothing of the sort. I haven't seen you in a couple months and thought, since I had some time to spare, I'd drive out to visit my best friend. And may I remind you that it was Ms. Christmas who brought up the parking bylaw to the council."

"I know you're right. And I'm glad to see you. I've missed you. But Evie's worked so hard—"

"To scuttle the deal for Wicklow Developments? Yes, I'm well aware of that. And you seem to forget that less than a year ago you saw the benefits of relocating our East Coast division to Harmony Harbor from Boston the same as I did."

"I know, but it's different now."

"Of course it is. Because you broke one of the most important business principles. You've allowed your emotions to cloud your judgment. Other than you forming a friendship with Ms. Christmas, nothing has changed."

"Okay, let's say that's true. What would it hurt to talk to your architects and find a way to create the extra parking that doesn't involve bulldozing Holiday House to the ground? The house and business have been in Evie's family for a century. One hundred years, Caine."

Colleen smiled. Her great-granddaughter hadn't gone back to the dark side after all.

"I'm well aware of the sentimental attachment Ms. Christmas has to Holiday House. But seriously, I'm doing the woman a favor. From firsthand experience, I can tell you that the house is ready to fall down around her ears."

"Trust me, I'm well aware you have firsthand experience. I figured out you were the messenger. Which you know from my texts that you chose to ignore. But what I'd really like to know is what you were doing there in the first place?"

"I was trying to save the woman from herself. Evangeline Christmas is even more hardheaded than you. She doesn't know when to quit or when to cut her losses, as evidenced by her unwillingness to even look at the offer I made."

"You were pretending to be a messenger, Caine. Why couldn't you just make the offer in person? You might have been able to convince her to take it if you had."

He looked at her over the glass. "If you believe that, I have a lovely piece of property on Rikers Island to sell you. Come on, T, you know the woman would just as soon shoot me as have a reasonable conversation with me."

Colleen would be tempted to do the same, but she found it interesting that he'd been making Evie an offer when, from what she'd gleaned from the staff, there'd been little doubt in anyone's mind which way the council would vote. "So you have a heart after all, laddie. And not just where Theia is concerned."

She settled herself on the bed beside her great-granddaughter. This conversation might prove fruitful after all.

"Can you blame her?" Theia held up her hand when he looked like he might protest. "I know it's not personal for you, but it is for Evie. And it's become personal for me too, Caine. Unlike you, I can't keep my emotions out of it. Evie's a good friend. I hate to see her hurt."

"Then you should advise her to accept the council's decision. And if you can get her to accept the offer I made in October, and tried to make again Friday, I will honor it. But she has until the end of the week to accept."

"You're worried what Emily will do if Evie tries to have the council's decision overturned, aren't you?"

"I am." He took a deep swallow of his whiskey before saying to Theia, "It's the reason I was at Holiday House Friday. As you know, Evangeline has delayed the project for months and cost us a good deal of money, but that isn't the worst of it. A woman who's one holiday away from going broke took us on and nearly won. She's made us look weak, and our competitors smell blood. A punishable offense in my grandmother's eyes."

"Emily threatened Evie?"

He nodded. "I went there to protect her."

"Max, the stray dog with fleas that ended up on her back porch. That was you?"

"Yes, but I didn't know he had fleas at the time. The back door was unlocked. Someone had been in there before me. The dog is cheaper than an alarm system and more effective."

"And the black Mercedes that's parked outside Holiday House twenty-four-seven?"

He sighed. "My uncle Seamus. He doesn't take direction well. He was supposed to remain vigilant but not draw attention."

Theia laughed.

"What's he done?"

"He's been flirting with Evie and her customers when he comes in to chat and to sample whatever she's offering for the day."

"Brilliant. So she knows he works for me and is keeping an eye on her."

"Not at all. She thinks he's a lonely old man who loves the holidays. So honestly, I'm a little surprised to hear he's related to you, Mr. Scrooge."

"I seem to remember you playing the Grinch to my Scrooge, so don't cast stones just because your new best friend is Harmony Harbor's Christmas elf."

"You're still my bestest friend, and don't you forget it. I just wish I wasn't in the middle of two people I care about. You know, if you'd just spend some time with Evie—"

He put his glass on the side table and went to stand. "And that's my cue to leave."

"Oh, come on, what could it hurt? You need to go out with a normal woman, not your usual A-list models and celebutantes."

"I like my celebutantes," he said with a grin, clearly teasing her.

Colleen sometimes forgot how close the two were. Until that moment, she'd also forgotten they owed Caine a debt of gratitude. He'd come to the family's aid last summer. Though they wouldn't have needed his help had his grandmother not hired an enemy of the Gallaghers in her bid to wrest control of the manor from them. Honestly, she didn't understand what drove Caine.

"You're a lost cause," Theia said as she placed her glass on the nightstand and stood up.

Caine pulled his ringing phone from his pocket, glanced at the screen, tapped it, then put it back in his pocket.

"Emily?" Theia asked.

He made a noncommittal sound as he lifted his jacket from the back of the desk chair.

"She must be thrilled the office tower is a done deal so she can focus all her energy on stealing Greystone Manor from the Gallaghers." Theia crossed her arms, clearly as unhappy as Colleen about the prospect, which was a relief.

"Theia"—he put a hand on her shoulder—"I'd stop her if I could."

"You're CEO of Wicklow Developments, Caine. If you really wanted to stop her, you could."

"You don't understand. I—"

"No. I don't understand. I don't understand how you can do this to my family. You say you love me. You say you're my best friend, but—"

"Dammit, Theia. Don't make this a test of my loyalty to you. I love you, but she's my grandmother."

"So that's what this is about? Friendship isn't a strong enough bond? I'd have to be a member of your family to warrant your loyalty."

"You are my family."

"Oh, I know that's what you always say, but clearly that's not the case. I guess it's really true that blood is thicker than water." Theia swiped at her eyes.

Colleen could tell her great-granddaughter's tears bothered him. He opened his mouth, then turned away, shoving his fingers though his hair, clearly struggling with something. Moments later he said, "The Gallaghers don't deserve blind loyalty from you or anyone else. My grandmother isn't the villain in this story."

"I don't know how you can—"

"I can say it because I do know the story. When I say you're my family, I mean it, T. I'm a Gallagher. I'm your cousin."

Theia laughed. "Yeah. Right. As if I believe that."

"Whether you believe me or not, it's the truth."

With her mouth hanging open, Colleen looked from the lad to Theia, who lowered herself onto the edge of the bed to stare up at him. "What? How? I don't understand."

"My grandmother and Ronan Gallagher had a child

together, my father. He was Ronan Gallagher's illegitimate son."

"But why—"

"I can't do this now, Theia. I have to go," he said, his phone ringing incessantly in his pocket. He pulled it out, glanced at the screen, and frowned.

"Caine, look at me. This is important. I need to know what happened. I need to know why Emily is hell-bent on bringing *our* family down. And why doesn't any of the family know about this?"

"Of course they know. Maybe not all of them, but I guarantee Ronan and Colleen did. Kitty too. I've tried to tell you, they're not as perfect as you think they are. They have skeletons in their closets."

"I don't believe you. They wouldn't deny their own blood. They must not have known about your father or you."

"They knew."

"Unlike you and your grandmother, I need proof before I condemn someone, and I know exactly where to find it." She went to Colleen's desk.

As shocked as Colleen was to learn Caine was a Gallagher and another wrong she had to right, even if it wasn't of her own making, she was stunned when Theia removed the brown leather-bound book from the hidden compartment in the desk.

It was Colleen's memoir, *The Secret Keeper of Harmony Harbor*. A book that contained the secrets of Colleen's family and friends. Secrets that in the wrong hands could serve as weapons.

"Is that what I think it is?" Caine asked, looking

intrigued, which would have stopped Colleen's heart if it hadn't stopped already.

"Have you lost your mind, Theia? Put my book back and put it back now!" Colleen yelled in hopes her great-granddaughter would hear her.

There was something special about Colleen's old room. It sometimes served as a conduit to the other side. If she put all her energy into it, she could sometimes make herself heard. Theia had heard her months before.

"If you think it's Colleen's memoir, then you'd be . . . Caine, what's wrong?" Theia asked as the lad let out a groan while looking at the screen of his pinging phone.

"What's wrong? I'll tell you what's wrong. Evangeline Christmas has chained herself to the bulldozer on Wicklow Developments' property to protest the council's decision. The press has been alerted."

"Emily?"

"What do you think?" he said, heading for the door.

"I'm coming with you." Theia ran to the closet to grab her coat.

"Wait! The book. Theia, you need to put the book away!" Panicked, Colleen hurried after Theia to yell in her ear, but the girl appeared to be in a panic of her own and didn't stop at the sound of Colleen's shouted words. Rushing from the room with her coat in hand, Theia shut the door behind her.

Colleen hurried to the door and stuck her head straight through it. "Simon, get Jasper! Theia left my memoir out."

They both turned their heads at the elevator's *ding*, the door sliding open to reveal Clio and the housekeeping cart.

Chapter Four

♥

Evie sat shivering in the dark, chained to a yellow bulldozer on the fenced-in lot beside hers. The smell of diesel and a hint of charred wood from the fire filled her nostrils. Beneath her jeans-clad bottom, the earth was as cold and as hard as the bulldozer at her back. Adding insult to injury, thick, wet snowflakes began to fall.

"What was I thinking?" Evie muttered to herself, feeling almost as bad as she did when they'd announced the results of the vote.

She'd lost by an overwhelming majority. The petition signed by three hundred people, great weekend sales, and her impassioned speech weren't enough to turn the vote in her favor.

The council members who'd voted against her had assured her it was one of the toughest decisions they'd ever made, but the town needed the jobs and revenue that the office tower would bring. While she hadn't been impressed with Caine Elliot's business degrees, money, and success, the council members clearly were.

And she couldn't fault them for putting the needs of Harmony Harbor above hers.

From the shadows, a lilting male voice responded to her question. "I imagine you're not thinking so much as reacting out of a desperate need to save your shop."

It was a voice she'd grown accustomed to the past few days. She gave Seamus O'Leary a weak smile as he stepped from the shadows. "You're right, and desperation has clearly wreaked havoc on my cognitive abilities, because this has to be the worst idea I've ever had."

"Well, now, don't judge yourself too harshly just yet, lass."

"I've been out here for an hour, and all I have to show for my effort is a frozen butt and bone chill."

"There's potential in your idea if you play it right," Seamus said as he crouched in front of her with a steaming take-out cup in his hand.

There was something about him that reminded her of an older version of Jimmy Stewart in his role as George Bailey. She'd been thinking about good old George a lot lately. But despite the deep creases beneath Seamus's monk-style gray bangs and the lines etched into the corners of his pale blue eyes, the man's youthful energy and fun-loving manner made him seem younger than his careworn face suggested.

He offered her the cup with a smile, and she inhaled deeply, wrapping her mittened hands gratefully around it. "Hot chocolate," she hummed, taking a sip. "Thank you. It's just what I needed."

"Good. Now, let's give your plan some thought."

She wrinkled her nose. "I didn't really have a plan. All I kept thinking was they're going to bulldoze my home and business to the ground, and then I looked over here while I was cursing Caine Elliot and spotted this." She lightly clunked the back of her head against the bulldozer. "I remembered seeing people chaining themselves to trees to stop them from being cut down, so I thought, 'I'll chain myself to the bulldozer.' But money is no issue to the ogre. He'll just buy another one. What I should have done is chain myself to Holiday House."

"I don't know. This makes more of a statement, I think. Or it will once we draw a crowd."

"A crowd? I thought a few friends with signs would be enough." She'd sent out the text, but they had yet to show up. Maybe they'd thought she was joking. "I really didn't think this through," she said, imagining how pathetic she looked, shivering in the falling snow.

She'd had enough sympathy today to last a lifetime. The aftermath of the vote had been worse than hearing that she'd lost. She'd had to stand there and hold it together while everyone came over to offer their sympathy and ask what she was going to do next. Holiday House had been her nest, her refuge after New York. She'd felt like she'd come home. She felt safe.

"I appreciate your support, but I don't think this is going to work, Seamus." She handed him the cup and then dug in her pocket for the key to the lock. It wasn't there. Her other hand was chained to the bulldozer, so she used her mouth to take off her mitten to once again dig in her pocket. Empty but for some fluff. "I've lost the key."

"No matter. We'll get someone to cut off the chains, but not before you get some publicity out of this. You're friends with the reporter at the *Gazette*, aye?"

She nodded, not surprised he knew she and Poppy Harte were friends. Seamus had been a permanent fixture at Holiday House for the past few days. She'd liked having him around once she realized he was harmless. *Lonely* had been the conclusion she'd drawn about him. And now it made perfect sense why he was trying to help her—other than being a kind man, of course—Holiday House had become a refuge for him too.

And maybe because she began to think of what Holiday House meant to someone other than herself, a tiny spark of determination ignited inside her.

As though he saw it, Seamus said, "That's a girl. Now, before we put the word out, you need to come up with a plan to keep Caine in town long enough to change his mind about your shop. It won't be easy—I can tell you that. He's a bit of a Scrooge, my nephew is."

"Um, excuse me. Did you just say Caine Elliot is here, in Harmony Harbor, and that he's your nephew?"

He pulled a face. "I let that slip, did I?"

"Ah, yeah, you did. Why didn't you tell me when I was, ah—"

"Ranting about him the other day and calling him names just now?" He grinned. "Don't give it another thought, lass. I knew where your anger was coming from. But you're wrong about him, you know. He's a brilliant lad, the best. Kind, generous to a fault. He'd give you the shirt off his back if you but asked."

"Unfortunately, that's not the man I know. But why

haven't you said anything before this? You weren't spying on me for him, were you?" Her chest pinched at the thought.

"Not the way you're thinking, but that's all I can say. I never reported back to him about your business or what you were up to with the petition. And you might want to remember who it was that got you the last names on your petition."

"You were a wonderful help this entire weekend. But I don't understand why you were helping me when your nephew is putting me out of business. It's a little like you're working against him, which doesn't make sense either because you clearly love him."

"Aye, I do. And I owe him much, lass. Because of me he…" Seamus turned his head as if to listen to the cars driving along Main Street, their lights cutting across the empty lots. Then he returned his gaze to hers. His eyes were shiny, as though he'd blinked tears away. "I'm not working against him and never will. I'm trying to save him. I'm trying to save his immortal soul, and I see you and your shop as a way to do so."

"Save his soul? That sounds ominous and a lot to ask of me and Holiday House. Other than people's hopes and dreams, he hasn't, uh, actually killed someone, has he?"

"Saints alive, no. He'd never be a part of something like that. He's a good man. I know you've seen another side of him, the high-powered businessman, and he is that. I've seen it too. He can be ruthless, hard-hearted even, but it's not who he really is. Emily—his granny— she's made him that way. All the lad thinks about now is making more coin. He's forgotten what's important in life: love, family, and friendship. If we can force him to stay in Harmony Harbor, we can remind him of what matters most in life. Maybe then the boy I remember will return. If he does, I guarantee my nephew will move heaven and earth to save your shop—and the manor," he murmured as an aside.

Seamus seemed as anxious to save his nephew as she was to save Holiday House, and while she wouldn't share with him that she didn't believe Caine Elliot could be redeemed, she didn't have anything to lose. She had to try something. And it would be nice to have a partner. Her friends were wonderful, but they were all involved with someone and had supportive family close by, so she'd sometimes felt alone in her fight against Wicklow Developments.

"Okay. We have a goal. Now we need a plan to keep your nephew in town long enough to change him from Scrooge at the beginning of *A Christmas Carol* into Scrooge at the end of the book."

Seamus chuckled. "It's a good analogy, lass. But he's not easily fooled, so we won't be able to haunt him into changing his ways."

"No, but there's nothing better than the holidays to remind people of the importance of love, family, friends, and community. And I don't want to toot my horn, but I am something of an expert on the holidays."

"That you are, lass. That you are."

Evie smiled, thinking it was amazing what a little hope could do. She barely felt the cold through her jeans. "So, any suggestions as to how we can keep him around long enough for the magic of the holidays to do its work?"

"I might have an idea there. When he was a boy, not a day would go by that he wasn't betting on something with someone. He was a canny lad, and not often did he lose. Which is probably why he loved it so much." His grin faded. "He used his money for good back then, putting food on the family's table. Buying small treats for his mam and da, never once for himself."

"He sounds like he was a sweet boy. Are his mother and father still alive?"

Seamus looked away, shaking his head. "No. He's lived with his granny since he was twelve. I've just reunited with him myself. Hadn't seen him since he was a lad."

He looked so sad that she reached out to touch his hand. "Don't worry. We'll make this work. I promise."

"Aye, we will. And we'd best get on with it before the two of us freeze to death. It's cold enough to freeze the balls off a brass monkey." He made a face. "My apologies, lass."

"I'm actually quite familiar with the phrase. It's one of Charlie Angel's favorites. He owns the Salty Dog." With her unchained hand she pointed to the local pub on the corner across from the harbor.

"Now that you mention it, I'm pretty sure that's where I picked it up. I shared a pint with Charlie and his friends after learning of the council's decision. They're as unhappy with the outcome as a lot of the shop owners on Main Street. You're well liked, lass—though I can't say I'm surprised. My nephew is another story.

They sounded like they wanted nothing more than to keelhaul the lad."

"Trust me, they're more bark than bite. They're a bunch of old softies, really. They're the first to arrive at Holiday House when I put up the angel tree." She angled her head. "Seamus, I might have thought of a way to show your nephew the error of his ways."

"You're not thinking of letting Charlie and his friends have a go at him, are you? Because while he might wear expensive suits, drink fine wine, and listen to classical music, the lad is a brawler. He's six-four of sharply honed muscles."

Had Evie taken a mouthful of hot chocolate just then, she would have choked on it. The man Seamus described had been the man she'd cast in the starring role of her mildly erotic fantasy when she'd heard Caine's voice for the first time.

"Um, no. No one is having a go at him." Including her, especially her. "We'll have your nephew pick three angels from the tree, and he'll have to fulfill the wishes. We'll have him pick one at a time, and he can't pick another one until his assignment is deemed a success by the person who made the wish. The wishes will serve as his Ghost of Christmas Past, Christmas Present, and Christmas Future. I'll need your help with the first one."

"Aye, and I'll gladly give it to you. But, lass, I can tell you're getting excited about this, and I don't want to burst your bubble, seeing as it's been burst plenty this week. I'm just not sure how we'll get him to agree."

"But it was your idea."

"I did say he liked to bet, but the angel-tree wishes

were your idea—a good one, I might add. It's just that I'm not sure how to go about getting him to agree to what you're suggesting. He can be a tad stubborn. Has a few issues with control. Oh, who am I trying to kid? You might as well hear it now so you know what we're up against. Caine is a law unto himself. Everyone does his bidding, and in the end, he always gets what he wants. So I'm having a hard time figuring out what we can offer to entice him…"

His eyes narrowed, and because they appeared to be narrowed at her, she said, "Oh no, I draw the line at that. I will do anything to keep Holiday House from being mowed to the ground, other than, well"—her cheeks warmed, and she cleared the embarrassment from her throat—"sleeping with your nephew."

Seamus hooted with laughter.

Okay, so obviously not what he'd been thinking. "You know I'm just teasing, right? I thought I'd break the tension by giving you something to laugh about. So now that we got that out of the way—"

"I meant no offense, lass. You're as lovely as a pitcher of warm milk on a bitter day in December."

The hot chocolate curdled in her stomach.

"But my nephew wouldn't know what do with someone as sweet as you. He needs a woman who will go toe-to-toe with him, a woman as stubborn as he is, a woman who can stand up to Emily and show him the light. I've been keeping my eye out, but I haven't found a suitable candidate—not that he's looking for a wife. Or even a long-term relationship. So I think it's best if we narrow our focus and leave love off the table."

"Agreed." She looked past him. "No need to alert the press. Here comes Poppy."

He glanced over his shoulder. "And she's not alone. See, it's just like I told you: The people in this town love you." He turned back to her with a grin. "I've figured out how to get my nephew to take you up on your bet. Now to get him down here." He took out his phone, gave her a look, then began peeling off her hat, scarf, and mittens.

"What are you doing?"

"Making you look truly pathetic, lass. If you could manage some tears, that would be grand."

Chapter Five

♥

Stop pretending you're busy on your phone and answer my question," Theia said to Caine as she drove her compact car through the gates of Greystone Manor, the wipers slapping at the snow building up on the windshield.

"I'm not pretending. At the moment, I'm trying to avert a minor crisis. Some of us don't have the luxury of unplugging. But instead of glaring at me, perhaps you should focus on the road. I highly doubt we'd survive a crash in your charming car," Caine said, his knees practically to his chest.

"Has anyone ever told you you're a snob?"

"Yes. You. Repeatedly. It's the one thing I don't miss about you."

"Well, there're several things I don't miss about you, one being your inability to call your grandmother on her crap. Not to mention that, in the almost three years we've known each other, you conveniently forgot to tell me you're a Gallagher."

"I didn't mention it because, as far as I'm concerned, I'm not."

"You're as much a Gallagher as me. You have to tell them. Fine," she said when he gave her a look. "But give them a chance, for me if not for yourself. I'll keep my mouth shut. I won't say anything to them if you promise to at least try to get to know them. You'll see that I'm right. You'll see that Emily has poisoned you against them. She's lying, Caine. She has to be."

"You know me better than that, T. I've substantiated some of what she's told me. But for you, and for the sake of keeping the peace at your wedding, I'll keep an open mind." The last place he wanted to be on Christmas Eve was Greystone Manor surrounded by the Gallagher family.

"So you'll back off trying to gain control of the manor?"

He didn't want to do this right now. He had enough to do dealing with Evangeline Christmas. "I had hoped that, with today's vote going in our favor, we would finally be able to move forward with the office tower, which I would then use to distract my grandmother with make-work projects while I hammered out an offer that would be acceptable to both—"

"You can't be serious! Caine, there's nothing you can offer the Gallaghers that would make them agree to sell."

"Everyone has a price. You know that as well as I do. You also know that they don't have the money to repair the flood damage in the tunnels." The Gallaghers had had a streak of bad luck of epic proportions last summer. Not only did they have to deal with the havoc one of his grandmother's minions had wrought, but a category-three hurricane had hit Harmony Harbor in August, causing extensive damage to the manor.

"They don't have the money because the man your grandmother hired made sure that the one person who would have happily bailed them out financially can no longer afford to."

"Yes. That was unfortunate. But as you know, none of what he did was under Emily's directive. I looked into it myself."

"Oh, please, Emily was no doubt cheering him on."

"I wouldn't be surprised if that were the case given her feelings for the Gallaghers. And while I don't approve of or condone her tactics, no crime was committed on her part or that of Wicklow Developments."

"Stop making excuses for her. The woman is a manipulative tyrant who doesn't care who she hurts as long as she gets what she wants."

"I know you think I let loyalty blind me to my grandmother's faults, but I don't. Despite what you think, I do call her on her crap. But she's eighty and dying, T."

"And that's supposed to excuse her threats against Evie? Come on, Caine."

"I may have overreacted Friday. I've been in the air more than I've been on the ground lately, and I was knackered. I still am. And, as proved by my uncle's text of moments ago, Ms. Christmas is alive and well and stirring up trouble. Again."

His frustration at the owner of Holiday House leaked into his voice. He should have kept his concerns to himself and dealt with the matter quietly and privately. Theia may be his best friend, but she was no longer in his employ and her loyalties were clearly torn. The last thing he or the company needed was for her to repeat his concerns to Ms. Christmas. The woman would no doubt take full advantage of the opportunity to paint them as evil villains and gain public sympathy. Exactly what she was doing right now with her publicity stunt. Honestly, he wanted to throttle Evangeline Christmas.

"Sorry. You can't tell me in one breath that you're concerned what Emily might do if Evie manages to block the development again and then pretend you might have overreacted because you're tired. You look like crap, by the way."

"Thank you. I wish I could say the same about you, but you look great, T. You look happy. You are happy, aren't you? DiRossi is good to you?"

"Yes." She bit her bottom lip as though trying to contain a smile but was unable to. She glanced at him, her eyes sparkling. "I didn't think it was possible to be this happy, Caine. Although I could do without all the wedding crap. If it weren't for Rosa, we'd elope. You're still going to be my man of honor, right?"

"Of course, and I've just come up with the perfect wedding gift for you. A Mercedes SUV. What color would you prefer—pearl black or midnight?"

"My car is perfectly fine, thank you very much. Besides, we're asking guests to donate to the Greystone Manor Repair Fund in lieu of gifts." She grinned at him. "Feel free to donate the cost of a loaded Mercedes SUV."

"Right, because you know how much I love to throw away money." He didn't want to, but he had to be honest with her. "T, you've worked with me long enough to know that I eventually get what I want. You also know that the amount of money required to make the manor architecturally sound, let alone get it up to code, is exorbitant. Not to mention the health risks. Do you have any idea how dangerous black mold is? And if you don't think there's mold in the tunnels, and in a dozen other places I can think of, I'll pay for an expert to check."

"What is it with you and old homes? And I know it's not just Greystone. You've been like this since I've known you."

"I don't just have an MA in finance and in global business, you know. Emily insisted I learn all aspects of the company. I spent my teen years working for contractors after school and weekends and have first-hand experience with the dangers of historic homes." Although all the evidence he'd needed to support his theory was provided the summer he turned twelve.

Traffic slowed to a crawl in front of the town hall with its copper-domed clock tower. From where the car idled on top of a hill overlooking the harbor, Caine could see all of Main Street. The lights from the family-owned boutiques, art galleries, pubs, and gift shops twinkled in the heavy falling snow.

The town had a seafaring history he admired. The twisty, narrow streets of Harmony Harbor were lined with Cape Cods, Colonials, and Victorians that had once been owned by sea captains and merchants. William Gallagher, who'd founded the town in the early seventeenth century, had captained a fleet of merchant ships. He was also reputed to have been a pirate.

But while Caine admired the maritime history, he thought it was about time the town embraced the twenty-first century as well. His glass-and-steel office tower would be the first step in doing so. And despite concerns that it would ruin the coastal charm of Harmony Harbor, Caine was positive that once the tower was built and the town began to feel the economic benefits, they would come to view the tower, built to reflect the blue of the sky and ocean, in a more positive light.

The sound of sirens drew his attention. Theia moved to the right side of the road as a fire truck turned onto Main Street, followed by an ambulance. In a swirl of red and white lights, they passed Theia's car.

"Any idea where they're headed?" he asked Theia, who was waving at a dark-haired firefighter with a lovesick smile on her face. Caine gave his head a disbelieving shake. The woman was a former navy fighter pilot who had once been as unromantic as him. Now look at her.

"If I were a betting person, I'd say your property."

There went his hope of keeping it quiet. Given the time difference, at least he'd have a few hours to do damage control before word reached his grandmother in Ireland. But as another thought came to him, his worries about keeping it quiet were replaced with a whole other worry. "Why would they send out emergency crews?" Before Theia had a chance to answer, he called his uncle. "Seamus isn't picking up."

"He probably can't hear his phone." She pulled her car to the side of the road. "It looks like half of Harmony Harbor showed up. And, um, they don't appear happy with Wicklow Developments if they're chanting what I think they are." She grimaced. "You should probably stay in the car while I see what's going on."

"Yeah, like that's going to happen." His anger served to make the already difficult job of getting out of the car even more difficult and frustrating. "Your bloody car was built for leprechauns."

"Do you need a hand?" Theia offered sweetly, coming around the hood to hold the door open for him.

"No, I do not..." He made an aggravated sound when she walked away with one of those lovesick smiles spreading across her face, completely forgetting about him and her offer to help as a familiar-looking firefighter approached. Marco DiRossi was wearing a stupid smile on his face too.

Apparently the car wanted to get rid of Caine as badly as the people of Harmony Harbor, because on his final pull on the strap as he levered himself out, he was ejected from the vehicle with such force that he landed on his knees on the sidewalk.

"You okay, Caine?" Marco asked from where he stood with his arm around Theia, who was looking at Caine as though she'd just remembered he was there.

"Never been better, mate." He got to his feet and slammed the car door. If it weren't for his audience, he'd kick it. "Everything okay over there?"

"It depends on how you define okay and in reference to whom. If you're asking about Evie, she's okay. A little cold and wet, but otherwise good. And I'm sure all the support she's receiving is giving her the warm-and-fuzzies," Marco said.

"The warm-and-fuzzies? Really?" Caine said, unable to keep the irritation from his voice, especially now that he heard the crowd chanting that he was the one who should be in chains.

"What can I say? I have a ten-year-old niece. As to you"—Marco jerked his thumb at the crowd—"you and Wicklow Developments are taking a beating in the court of public opinion."

"Yeah, I figured that one out on my own, thanks. But it's a very small and biased court, as it appears to be made up entirely of Ms. Christmas's friends and fellow business owners." Caine joined the couple as they walked toward the Evangeline Christmas show.

"Crowd is growing." Marco nodded at a group of people crossing the road.

"Yes, ambulances and fire trucks have a tendency to draw one, especially in small towns. Why exactly are you here?"

Theia gave Caine a look.

"What? It's a legitimate question. Ms. Christmas is obviously trying to turn the public against Wicklow Developments, and HHFD is ensuring she draws a crowd."

"We were responding to a call of a female in distress, who turned out to be Evie. Paramedics checked her over, and now we're just waiting for someone to convince her to give up her protest so we can cut the chain." At a whirr of sirens and more flashing lights, Marco said, "Looks like HHPD is coming to manage the crowd."

"I'll convince her to stop this—" Caine began as a redheaded woman, followed by a cameraman, broke from a group of people near the temporary fencing to head his way. "It's him. It's Caine Elliot. The CEO of Wicklow Developments," the reporter said as she hurried over to shove a microphone in his face at the same time the cameraman's light burned his retinas.

"Mr. Elliot, Evangeline Christmas believes that Wicklow Developments—"

"Everyone knows what Ms. Christmas believes. It's not new news. We've heard her feelings about the development for a year. But the time for debating is over. The office tower won by an overwhelming majority because the people of Harmony Harbor are looking to the future. This is a difficult time for Ms. Christmas. She's obviously distraught, and the last thing she needs is to have you people exploiting her breakdown."

"Caine," Theia muttered from behind him.

"Now, if you'll excuse me, I'd like to check on her."

"How could you do that, Caine? You made Evie sound like she's having a nervous breakdown," Theia said, hurrying after him.

"How else do you explain her chaining herself to a bulldozer in the middle of a snowstorm when there's absolutely no chance of changing the outcome? If she wanted to make a statement that had even a slightest chance of making a difference, she'd have been better off chaining herself to Holiday House. It's easy enough to rent another bulldozer."

"If you say that to her…" Whatever else Theia had been about to say was drowned out by the boos of the crowd as Marco helped clear the way for them.

The disapproval of Ms. Christmas's supporters, no

matter how virulent, didn't bother Caine. What did bother him was seeing the owner of Holiday House shivering in the cold.

"Of all the lamebrained schemes," he muttered as he went around Marco to push through the temporary fence. As Caine strode across the frozen ground littered with bricks and charred wood, he realized he'd been wrong. Evangeline chaining herself to the bright yellow bulldozer wasn't as ridiculous as he'd first thought. The contrast between the heavy piece of equipment and the delicate woman chained to it twigged his protective instincts. And obviously not just his, based on the expressions of the faces in the crowd.

Ms. Christmas's eyes rounded as he strode toward her. "It's you. The messenger. You're the messenger," she said through chattering teeth.

"Yes, and you're an idiot," he said loud enough that his remark drew censure from the crowd and from his uncle, who walked over to join him.

"That's no way to speak to Evie, lad. He didn't mean it, lass."

"I bloody well did," Caine said as he took off his wool coat, then crouched in front of her to tuck it around her. "You've had your fifteen minutes of fame. And other than pneumonia, your little stunt isn't going to get you anything." Her hair was plastered to her head, snowflakes melting on her face. "Give me the key to the chains."

"Don't you listen to him, Evie. What you're doing here matters."

Caine came to his feet and scowled down at his

uncle. "What do you think you're doing? You're on my payroll, not hers."

Seamus dragged him out of earshot. "Have a heart. The poor thing has lost everything because of you, lad. Surely you can do something for her."

"I tried, and she told me what to do with my offer. And let's remember who brought the bylaw to the council's attention in the first place, shall we? If she'd left well enough alone, she wouldn't have lost the building." Although, given its condition, it probably would have caved in during the construction phase of the office tower. Something he'd keep to himself because she'd used that same argument this summer to get the vote delayed in order to allow a company that specialized in heritage homes to render an opinion similar to Caine's, that construction would cause Holiday House irreparable damage. But they hadn't because Evangeline couldn't afford a company that actually knew what they were doing. "If you think you can get her to take the offer, the money will be in her bank account tomorrow morning."

"She won't take it," his uncle said.

Caine's scowl deepened as he rubbed his arms against the cold. His black suit jacket was no doubt ruined. "How do you know she won't?"

"Because I already asked. She sees it as a handout."

"Of all the..." He stalked back to the woman, noting the stubborn tilt of her chin as he did. The crowd, who'd been quiet while he spoke to his uncle in an effort no doubt to hear the conversation, started cheering the woman on.

"Don't give up, Evie! You're our hero! Stay strong!"

"You'll be a dead hero if you don't give this up. Take the offer I made to you last month, and I'll increase it by fifty thousand dollars." He held up the phone and set the alarm. "You have ten minutes to decide. No longer." He figured that was the amount of time she had before she became hypothermic.

Something changed in her hazel eyes, and for a moment he thought she'd agree, but then her damn chin went up again. "No. I don't want your money. I want to make you a bet."

"A bet? You want to bet me? With what? You don't have anything I want." He couldn't tell if she'd jerked from the cold or his words. It might be the truth, but it didn't assuage his guilt for saying it aloud.

Her eyes glinted with emotion, and he was relieved to see it was anger and not hurt. He felt like cheering her on and then thought how ridiculous that was when he was her opponent.

"Nephew, a word." It was the first time Caine remembered Seamus addressing him in a disapproving tone of voice, including when he was a boy.

"You're wrong, Mr. Elliot. I have something you need."

"And what would that be?"

"The approval and support of the citizens of Harmony Harbor. If you win our bet, I will do everything in my power to change the hearts and minds of the people who object to the office tower. As you can see, I have a lot of support in this town. You don't."

She had a point. And while they'd won the bid

and could now move forward with the project, he had time and money to recoup. They couldn't afford further delays. Delays that even a few disgruntled people could cause during the construction phase.

"All right, I'm listening."

Chapter Six

♥

There was a nervous flutter in the pit of Evie's stomach when she uttered what could very well be the most important words of her life. As soon as they were out of her mouth, her heart sank. She was terrified she'd made a mistake.

No matter what Seamus said, Caine Elliot wouldn't accept her bet. And she'd just thrown his mea culpa in his face. His offer had been generous before, and it was twice as generous now. Even so, if she accepted, she'd walk away with nothing once she paid off the bank and paid back her mother. That wasn't quite true; she'd walk away with something—a whole lot of guilt that she'd lost Holiday House. But as slim as her chances were of winning a bet with Caine Elliot, she'd have a chance, and that was all she could hope for right now.

She stared up at the man towering over her, thinking, *Holy heck he's gorgeous and really, really big and maybe just a little terrifying with that fierce expression on his face.* Her gaze took in the way his muscles strained against the confines of his expensive black suit jacket. She huddled deeper beneath his heavy coat, inhaling his warm, spicy scent. He even smelled incredible, which was totally unfair.

The man who was responsible for destroying her hopes and dreams should not look like every woman's fantasy come to life—least of all hers. He should look like Mr. Potter from *It's a Wonderful Life* or Ebenezer Scrooge. Yes, that's exactly what he should look like.

"Hello, Ms. Christmas. Are you in there?" He crouched in front of her.

Forget the face, body, and his incredible smell—she could listen to his smooth-as-silk voice and killer accent all night.

He clicked his fingers, pulling her from her enthralled daze. She blinked. "Did you just snap your fingers at me?" Her chattering teeth took away from the who-do-you-think-you-are attitude she'd been going for.

And right then she forgot how good he looked and smelled and sounded or that he'd fixed her circuit breakers on Friday or that he'd given her the coat off his very broad back. He was a high-powered gazillionaire who didn't care who he hurt, and he'd called her an idiot. An idiot!

It didn't matter that she kind of agreed with him. You didn't say things like that to people.

"It was either that or shake you. I'm waiting for your proposition, Ms. Christmas. And while you apparently don't have anything pressing requiring your attention, I do." He stood up, once again towering over her, an aloof expression on his face.

Who did he think he...? As what he'd said and not

how he said it penetrated her frozen brain, she goggled at him. "Did you say you're waiting for my proposition?" She glanced at Seamus, who was nodding at her, making a *hurry up* gesture with his hands. Hands that were covered in her pink mittens.

"Yes. And it's the second time I've done so." The high-powered CEO of Wicklow Developments held up his phone and gave the screen an impatient tap. "Time is running out, Ms. Christmas."

Oh no. She huddled deeper beneath his coat. She didn't do well under pressure. She was really good at coaching other people to deal with their phobias and fears but didn't do a very good job when it came to her own. Except saving Holiday House wasn't just about her, she reasoned, trying to take herself out of the equation. Saving Holiday House was like—he tapped his screen—like saving Scrooge.

"There's a tree at Holiday House," she began, picturing him in his underwear. Okay, totally not helpful, she thought when she felt more hot and bothered than confident. She quickly redressed him in her mind.

"That's not really a surprise, is it? You are a Christmas store."

"Yes, but it's a special tree. An angel—"

He made a *hurry this along* gesture with his hand.

"It's an angel tree. People, mostly children, write their wishes on a paper angel and then customers pick one off the tree and fulfill the wish."

"Ticktock, Ms. Christmas."

"I'm talking about angels and children's wishes and all you can say is *ticktock*?"

"Would you prefer I simply said no? Because if you walked into my office at Wicklow Developments and were presenting a business proposal to me, I would have shown you to the door by now."

And it was at that exact moment that Evie knew, if she could get him to agree to the bet, she'd win, because Caine Elliot truly was Scrooge.

"All you have to do to win the bet, Mr. Elliot, is fulfill three wishes from the angel tree before Christmas Eve. If you do, I will do as I promised and help you win over the hearts and minds of your many detractors here in Harmony Harbor."

"And if you win?"

She smiled, and his eyes narrowed. "If I win, you don't build your office tower in Harmony Harbor."

"All right, let's see if I understand this." He then repeated everything she had just said, almost verbatim. "Is that correct?"

"Yes," she said, feeling hopeful for the first time in a week.

He smashed her hope with a single, blunt "No."

"Lad, come here for a sec, would you?" Seamus didn't wait for Caine to respond, tugging him by the arm out of earshot. She didn't need to be able to hear him to know Seamus was doing his best to convince his nephew to take the bet.

Evie glanced at the crowd from under her lashes and wondered how she'd face her friends and customers after tonight. They probably thought she'd lost her mind. Her mother certainly would, especially if she found out Evie had refused Caine's latest offer.

At that moment, the man in question threw up his hands as though admitting defeat and walked back to her. Evie's heart began to race. From behind him, Seamus gave her a grin and a thumbs-up. She thought she might faint from relief.

And maybe because she'd closed her eyes and rested her head against the bulldozer, Caine actually thought she'd fainted because he yelled while coming to kneel at her side, "Get the bloody paramedics over here now."

"I'm fine," Evie said, hugging his coat tight.

"You are stubborn, contrary, impulsive, and foolish, but the one thing you are not, Ms. Christmas, is fine. Now give me the key."

"I can't. I lost it."

He held back a sigh and called for a pair of bolt cutters, then said to her, "Give me my coat so I can get a look at the chain."

"Not until you tell me we have a bet."

"You do realize that I could take my coat from you if I wanted to?"

"Yes, but you won't."

"Why's that?"

"Because while you are arrogant, controlling, bullheaded, and cynical, you are also a gentleman, Mr. Elliot."

The corner of his mouth twitched. "Is that so?"

"It is." She withdrew her chained hand from under his coat. "Do we have a bet?" she asked, the metal links rattling as she offered him her hand.

* * *

"Yes. We have a bet, Ms. Christmas," he said, enfolding her hand in his. His was cold, hers was colder. The tips of her fingers were turning blue. He didn't know who he was angrier at, himself or her. "There were easier ways to get my attention, you know. Like a phone."

"Would that have worked?" she asked as he clasped her hand with both of his, lowering his mouth to warm her fingers with his breath.

"No." He lifted his gaze to hers as he continued to blow on her hand.

She smiled at his admission. He tried to think of something to make her stop, but that would mean putting the look back in her eyes that he'd seen when he'd first arrived. So he glanced over his shoulder to break a connection he didn't want to acknowledge or feel.

It would only make it worse when he won her silly bet. And he would win. After all, how hard could it be to fulfill three wishes from an angel tree? He'd have his assistant at his Boston office do the shopping. A mother of three, she'd know better than him what the children wanted.

His hope was to have his angel-tree assignment over and done with before his grandmother caught wind of what was going on. She wouldn't be suspicious if he was in Harmony Harbor for a day or two. She'd basically told him to drop everything in order to focus on Greystone Manor.

Oh, what a tangled web we weave, he thought when Marco and Liam Gallagher walked their way. Liam was a firefighter as well as Marco's best friend.

Liam nodded at him, then knelt beside Evangeline.

"How are you doing, Evie? Paramedics had another call. We're both certified, Elliot," he said to Caine, answering the question he'd been about to ask. He'd also answered another one.

Liam knew who he was, knew he was the CEO of the company who for the past few years had been making a play for Greystone Manor. If not for last summer, when Caine had put up the ransom money for Liam's wife and children, the other man's reception might have been chillier. Caine's friendship with the woman walking over to join them probably helped too.

"Are we all good here?" Theia asked.

"Wonderful," Ms. Christmas said, and despite her lips turning blue, she gave Theia a smile that suggested the owner of Holiday House believed she would win their bet handily.

Which made Caine wonder if maybe, just maybe, he should have done his due diligence the same as he would have for any deal. He brushed the thought aside. Evangeline owned a Christmas store. She wasn't some Fortune 500 executive with years of negotiating experience or a master manipulator like his grandmother. He had nothing to worry about, nothing at all.

"Really? Well, that's, ah, awesome." Theia gave him a *go, you* look, which was better than the looks she'd been giving him over the last couple of hours.

"Yes, Mr. Elliot and I have a bet," Evangeline said, and then proceeded to share with them exactly what their deal entailed while Marco attempted to break the chain with the bolt cutters.

Caine should have had her sign a confidentiality

agreement, he thought when the two men and Theia started to laugh.

"I'm sure it won't be as easy as it sounds," he said, feeling a little sorry for Evangeline.

Liam, Marco, and Theia laughed harder, and Ms. Christmas didn't look like the three of them making fun of her idea to save Holiday House was bothering her in the least. In fact, if he wasn't mistaken, she was holding back her own laughter.

He turned to look at his uncle, who was rocking back and forth on his boots, hands in his pockets, whistling "Santa Claus Is Comin' to Town" while keeping his gaze averted from Caine.

"Obviously I'm missing something. Would one of you care to enlighten me?" He motioned for Marco to hand him the bolt cutters after the firefighter's second failed attempt.

"Evie's angel tree is famous for bringing the true meaning of the holidays to both giver and receiver," Liam told him.

Other than sounding a bit twee, Caine didn't understand why they'd been laughing. Unless they'd guessed at his feelings toward the holidays. "Well, then, it looks like I'll get in the holiday spirit early. The stores must be decorated by now, right? Carols playing on the sound systems," he said as he opened the bolt cutters to fit them around the chain. At Evangeline's nervous glance, he added, "Don't worry. I have plenty of experience."

"Uh, Caine, you do know that the wishes on the angel tree aren't something money can buy, right?" Theia asked.

"What?" His grip on the cutters slipped, and Evangeline gave a panicked *yip* as the blade slid toward her hand. "Sorry." He corrected his grip and snapped the thick chain in half. Then, handing the bolt cutters back to Marco, he reached out to help Evangeline to her feet. "Now, perhaps someone would care to explain this to me: What exactly is an angel-tree wish?"

"Babe, why don't you tell Caine about the angel wish you have to fulfill?" Marco suggested with a grin.

"I, um, got Marco's grandmother. Rosa DiRossi," Theia said.

"And..." Caine motioned for her to continue.

"I have to help her bake her Christmas cookies this year."

Okay, that didn't sound so bad. Except. "You don't bake," he said to Theia.

"She will after her weekend baking sessions with Rosa."

"You have to do this for more than one day?" Caine said.

"She'll be baking right up until the twenty-third, won't you, babe?" Marco grinned as he slid an arm around Theia's shoulder. "They have to make two hundred and fifty dozen. Rosa's big on tradition. She has a dozen kinds of cookies she makes every year, and she has a lot of people on her Christmas list."

"What's your angel-tree wish?" Caine asked Marco, thinking it was just Theia's bad luck she got a difficult one.

"One per family. Theia took care of ours this year. Liam got one though. Tell him about Mrs. Whittaker's wish, bro."

Liam sighed. "I have to decorate Mrs. Whittaker's house with her."

Since Caine figured that would take a couple of hours at most, he considered offering to take Mrs. Whittaker's wish as one of his, until Marco said, "Yeah, Mrs. Whittaker is big into crafts. She has a list as long as my arm of decorations she and Liam are going to make, doesn't she, bro?"

Caine looked at Evangeline, who avoided his gaze. She waved to the thinning crowd. They'd begun to disperse moments after he'd cut the chain. "Thanks for all the support, guys," she called to her fans, and then handed him his coat. "Thank you. I think I'll just go in now and warm up. I'll see you tomorrow."

"You will indeed. Ms. Christmas," he called as she turned to walk away with Theia. "You should probably know that I have yet to lose a bet."

"You've never made one with me, Mr. Elliot."

Chapter Seven

♥

Colleen had waited all night for Theia to return to her room, but she'd arrived home only twenty minutes ago. And while she didn't begrudge her great-granddaughter spending time with her fiancé…

"You're as bad as Jasper," Colleen said as Theia now frantically searched the tower room for Colleen's memoir. "Love hijacked your good sense. You left the book in plain sight, and Clio's a nosy one, not to mention a bookworm who loves old things. She couldn't resist taking a peek while she cleaned the room."

And a peek was all it took to pique the child's interest. The calculating smile that had come over Clio's face when she was only a few pages into *The Secret Keeper of Harmony Harbor* made Colleen nervous. "It could have been far worse though. Caine could have been the one to abscond with my book, and then we'd be in a right mess," Colleen said to Theia, who didn't give any indication she could hear her.

Colleen lay down beside her on the floor as Theia searched under the bed for the book. "You'll not find it there," she yelled in her great-granddaughter's ear. "Clio's got the book in her room."

Theia jerked, banging her head on the bedframe. "Really? You couldn't do your woo-woo thing when I was upright and away from hard objects? Your timing sucks, GG," she said, rubbing the back of her head.

"Ah, T, there's no one here but me?"

Colleen and Theia yelped in unison, both hitting their heads on the bedframe, only Colleen's passed through it. She turned her head to see Caine coming out of the closet to crouch near the bed.

"You knowing how to move unseen about the manor worries me, my boy. It makes me wonder what else you know about our secret passageways and hidey-holes," Colleen murmured as the lad helped a grumbling Theia from under the bed. "My, but you're a handsome devil though. You take after your grandfather, my son Ronan, you know. His eyes were the same vivid blue as yours, and in his youth his hair was the same raven's-wing black."

She moved closer to study him, this man who was one of hers. "Your intelligence shines from your eyes. You're smart like him. Too smart for your own good at times, I'd wager. He was the same. Charming when you want to be, no doubt. Just like Ronan. That boy of mine turned the ladies' heads, let me tell you. He caused Patrick and me many a sleepless night wondering if he'd ever settle down. He loved Kitty but chafed at the idea of being tied down. I'm sorry your grandmother got caught up in all that, my boy. Sorry I found out about your da too late. He'd been long since gone when I learned of his existence. The private investigator I hired said it was like you'd ceased to exist after his death. He'd surmised that you had died too."

"Where is it? And don't pretend you don't know what I'm talking about," Theia said to Caine as she brushed the dust from her white shirt and blue jeans.

"It's not the lad. It's Clio. She was too busy snooping about to get her housekeeping duties done," Colleen said, at the moment wishing Theia would let it go. The less Caine knew about Colleen's missing memoir the better.

"What I'd really like to know is who you were talking to. Who's…? Wait a sec. GG stands for great-grandmother, doesn't it?" He started to laugh. "You can't be serious. You were talking to Colleen Gallagher? Your dead great-grandmother."

"I know who she is, and she's also your great-grandmother. I wouldn't be surprised if that's what she was trying to tell me."

"No, lass." Colleen leaned into Theia to once again yell in her ear. "Clio. I was saying Clio, not Caine."

Theia rubbed her ear. "Okay, I hear you."

"Sit down, T. Sit down right now," Caine said, looking worried. "I'm not fooling around. This could be serious."

"No *coulds* about it. It's big-time serious. Colleen's memoir is missing, and there are things in *The Secret Keeper of Harmony Harbor* that could be dangerous if they got out."

"Now you've gone and done it. He'll be after it for sure," Colleen groused.

"I don't care about the book. I care about you. How long have you been hearing voices?" He lightly pushed Theia onto the bed and then sat beside her.

"I'm not losing my mind, Caine. I don't hear her all the time. Just once in a while, and only in this room."

"You know how crazy that sounds, right?"

"Of course I do, but you know me. I'm not given to crazy. The twins, my nephews, they can both see her and hear her."

"Then you should all be checked out. Immediately. This isn't something to be made light of. Old homes are nothing more than mold's petri dish."

Colleen frowned at the lad, wondering what he was so worked up about.

"Have you been dizzy, having headaches? This is important," he said when Theia stared at him. "If you won't do anything about it, I will." He pulled out his phone and punched in a number.

"Caine, what are you—" Theia began.

He held up a finger. "Caine Elliot here. I want a crew at Greystone Manor today. No, next week isn't good enough. I want a team here within the hour. Cost doesn't matter. Good. I want a full report before the end of the week. This week, yes. Black mold. All right. Thanks."

"I don't understand. What are you doing?" Theia asked.

But right then it made a sad sort of sense to Colleen. Killian, Caine's father and her grandson, had died of complications from lung disease. According to the medical records the private investigator had found, the true culprit in Killian's death was long-term exposure to black mold.

"I'm having a crew come in to check air quality and to inspect the manor from top to bottom for mold. And I'm taking you to the clinic. They can do a simple blood test. It shouldn't take longer than—"

"Okay. I'm not exactly sure what's going on with you, but I'm not sick. I've never felt better. And you can't just have a bunch of people come in here looking for mold. It's a hotel, Caine. You can't... Wait a minute. Is this part of a plan to bankrupt the manor so you can swoop in and get it on the cheap?"

"No, and I'm shocked and a little hurt you would suggest such a thing. I'm just trying to keep you safe. Please, let me do this."

"It's not up to me. It's up to Kitty, Jasper, and Sophie, the manager."

"Fine. I'll take care of it."

"How?"

"Don't worry about it. I'll handle it."

"Right, because you have someone on the inside to do your bidding. You didn't think I knew that, did you? You forget who you're dealing with. I figured out Jasper was your informant last summer."

If Colleen's heart were still beating, it would have stopped. Jasper had turned against her? Against them? She felt faint and walked to the bed to sit down. Her mind not working as it should, she sat on Caine and went through him to the mattress.

He shuddered and looked around. She moved to sit beside him. Caine frowned and patted where she sat.

The furrow in his brow deepening, he stood up, turning to the bed with his hands on his hips.

"You sense me here, don't you, laddie?" She would have taken some pleasure in that had she not suffered a blow to end all blows.

"Why are you looking at the bed like that?" Theia asked.

"I . . ." He lifted his hand to shove his fingers through his dark hair. "No reason. Now are you going to tell me why you summoned me to the manor this morning?"

"The book." Theia got up and walked to the desk. "Colleen's memoir was right here when we left last night. I showed it to you, remember? *The Secret Keeper of Harmony Harbor*. It's a brown, leather-bound book."

"Are you sure it's missing?"

"Yes, I'm sure. I've searched everywhere. And don't freak out on me again, but I'm pretty sure Colleen was trying to tell me you have it."

Colleen was too heartbroken by Jasper's defection to get up once more to yell Clio's name in Theia's ear.

"I wish I did have it, but I don't. If you'd stop and think about it for a minute, you'd remember that I was headed for the door when you went for your coat, and I was halfway down the stairs when you closed the door behind you."

Theia clutched her bottom lip between her teeth while looking up at the ceiling. "You're right. It happened just like you said." She cocked her head. "Hey, why didn't you freak out this time when I said Colleen was trying to tell me you have the book?"

"Because he might not hear me, but he knows I'm

here. Don't you, lad? Now the question is, will you share that with your best friend?"

"You told me not to freak out."

Theia raised her eyebrows at him.

"All right. I felt something odd when I was sitting on the bed. Like a presence. And the temperature dropped about ten degrees. You felt it too, didn't you?"

Despite being disheartened about Jasper and the part Caine had played in his defection, Colleen was pleased the lad hadn't lied to Theia. In her book, it spoke well of him, especially because men typically had a more difficult time believing in something they couldn't see or at the very least admitting to it.

"I honestly didn't notice. I guess I'm just so used to it now."

He looked back at the bed. "Does she visit you often?"

"I'm not sure she ever leaves. Why don't we ask her?"

"Okay, you've had your fun now. I'll just—"

"GG, say hello to your great-grandson. Maybe make one of the books fall off the shelf to let us know you're here."

"I'm sorry, lass. I'm not up to doing any parlor tricks today," Colleen said from where she lay on the bed. Yet when she saw Caine glance around the room, she was afraid it might hurt his feelings if she didn't acknowledge him in some way, so she stretched out a hand to the nightstand and, focusing all her energy into the tips of her fingers, she knocked over a glass of water.

"Interesting. But I'm still having the manor inspected for mold," he said, pulling his phone from his pocket. He glanced at the screen. "Since you've already figured out that Jasper's my mole at the manor, perhaps you'd like to figure out who is working for my grandmother in Harmony Harbor."

Theia looked from his phone to his face. "Emily heard about Evangeline's protest last night?"

"Oh, it's even better than that. She's heard about my bet with Ms. Christmas."

Theia's phone *ping*ed, and she glanced at her screen. "Okay, so your grandmother might have found out about that the old-fashioned way. The story has been picked up on the wire."

"You have got to be kidding me."

"Sorry. I wish I were, for your sake at least. It'll be great publicity for Evie. They're playing it up as a feel-good story leading into the holiday season. A Christmas Angel takes on Scrooge. Poppy says the *Gazette* has nine-to-one odds in the angel's favor."

"Trust me, Evangeline Christmas is no angel. The woman played me like a Stradivarius," Caine said as he turned to walk away.

"Where are you going?" Theia called after him.

He popped his head out of the closet. "To prove to an angel that the devil always wins. You might want to let Jasper know to expect the mold-inspection team before noon."

"He always has to get the last word in," Theia said, staring at the now-empty closet. Then she turned toward the bed. "Don't worry, GG. Jasper's still on our side. When I confronted him last summer, he asked if I'd heard the phrase *Keep your friends close and your enemies closer*."

Praise the Lord and the Holy Ghost, Colleen thought from where she lay, still recovering from her shock.

"But I have to be honest. It's hard to think of Caine as the enemy," Theia continued, coming to sit beside Colleen. "He's my best friend, and I love him. I know, with what Wicklow Developments has gotten up to in the past, that it might be difficult for you to see, but he's a good man. One of the best men I've ever known. You have to help me figure out what to do, GG. I won't let him hurt the family or take the manor, but I can't lose him either."

Colleen sat up, putting her hand on Theia's back. "We won't. He's mine as much as he is yours, Theia. We don't turn our back on family no matter what. But right now there's something more pressing we need to do. We have to get my book back. Clio, lass. Clio has my book," she shouted the last in Theia's ear, crossing her fingers as she did.

"Okay. I've got it. Clio has the book." She groaned. "Oh no, *Clio* has the book. If she's anything like her father, we're in trouble."

Chapter Eight

♥

Evie hung Caine's angel on the artificial Christmas tree. She'd gotten a little carried away with the glitter. She couldn't help herself. As her sparkling red sweater could attest, she had a thing for glitter. At first she'd thought the extra sparkle on the angel's wings would catch his eye, but now she was afraid he'd reject it on account it was a little girlie.

"We'd best batten down the hatches, lass. We have a nor'easter by the name of Caine coming this way," Seamus said from where he sat on the stool behind the sales counter, staring at his cell phone with a worried expression on his face.

"He heard about the story in the *Gazette*, didn't he?" Evie knew Poppy had been trying to help, and to sell a few newspapers, of course, but Evie imagined a man of Caine's stature wouldn't appreciate being cast as Scrooge in the local news. Then again, it might have been the part in the article about the odds being against him that he objected to. He seemed the competitive sort.

"I doubt he'd have a problem with the story if it were

just in the *Gazette.* But it's gone a little farther afield than that, I'm afraid. The Wicked Witch of Wicklow County has heard about it."

That wasn't good, Evie thought as she moved the angel a little higher to ensure it would be directly in Caine's line of sight. She'd heard more than she'd wanted to about his grandmother this morning. Seamus had shared his thoughts on Emily Green Elliot while helping Evie to come up with the perfect angel assignment for Caine.

An assignment that would put the CEO of Wicklow Developments in touch with his Christmas past. A past that had sounded difficult and painful. Perhaps even more painful than Seamus had told her. She had a feeling he'd held something back about Caine's past. In the end, she and Seamus had settled on the Murphy family.

Thirteen-year-old Jamie Murphy had lost the father he'd adored eight months before and was struggling with his grief. It didn't help that they were also struggling financially. But his mother, who was working three jobs, thought only of her son. She believed he needed a male role model. Evie believed they needed a Christmas miracle, and Seamus thought his nephew was it.

Evie hoped he was right. She used to be good at reading people. It was part of her training. She didn't end up with a PhD in psychology without learning a thing or two about what made people tick. But these days she had a harder time trusting her instincts. It was because of her ex, Aaron Peters. He'd hidden his dark side from her as easily as a chameleon changed its color.

Her fingers trembled as she moved Caine's angel an

inch to the right, and she lowered her hand, hating that the mere thought of Aaron still had the power to upset her. It had been more than a year since she'd left him and New York.

Her phone vibrated on the sales counter, the theme song from *The Grinch* jarring and shrill in comparison to the playlist of classical Christmas music she'd downloaded earlier this morning. She'd been trying to think of ways to put Caine at ease (before she sent him off to deal with the ghosts of his past) when she remembered Seamus commenting on his nephew's love of fine wine and the classics.

She went with the music since offering him a glass of wine at ten in the morning would no doubt be frowned upon. Though she'd probably want a drink after talking to her mother. Because if the Wicked Witch of Wicklow County had heard the news, there was little doubt the New York Grinch had too.

"Are you planning on taking the call, lass? I'll turn it off if you're not."

"My mother doesn't give up easily, and it's only a five-hour drive—although she'd make it in under four, so yes, I think I'd better get it."

"Here"—he smiled and got up to pat the stool— "we'll trade places."

He cocked his head, no doubt at the sound Evie also heard coming from the kitchen. Max was at it again, snuffling and scratching as if his favorite squeaky toy were on the other side of the basement door.

"Sounds like Max is up to no good," Seamus said. "I'll go take a look."

"Would you mind taking a look in the basement?"

"Aye, I'll check what he's about."

"Thanks, Seamus," she said as she picked up her phone, not surprised her mother had yet to disconnect. Lenore was nothing if not stubborn. "Hey, Mom. Isn't your spin class on Tuesday mornings? Is everything okay?" It had never occurred to her to worry about her mom before now. But her mother's days were carefully scheduled, every minute accounted for and color-coded in her planner. Nothing kept Lenore from her morning exercise classes. Even an audit.

"No. Everything is not okay. I was at my spin class, and instead of biking in the Andes, Alundra made us watch the guest spot he taped for *Coffee with Claire*. Imagine my surprise when, on the morning news, I see a photo of my daughter chained to a bulldozer to protest her Christmas store being made into a parking lot!"

"Mom, I can—" She was almost glad her mother interrupted her because Evie didn't want to admit she was ultimately to blame for the council's decision.

"And instead of calling her mother to discuss how much her compensation should be, she makes a ridiculous bet with the CEO of Wicklow Developments rather than take his more-than-generous offer. An offer that was at least five times the compensation she would have received from the town council!"

Instead of asking how on earth the press had learned of the offer, Evie said, "I'm sorry. I didn't—"

"Apologies will not heal my broken hand, Evangeline."

"You broke your hand?"

"Yes. I was so shocked I forgot that I was strapped into my pedals and fell off the bike. I'm at the hospital waiting for an X-ray."

"Mom, I really am sorry. Is it, um, your left hand or your right?" *Please be her left. Please be her left.*

"My right. I don't know what I'm going to do. I'll go insane if I can't—"

"Dictation," Evie blurted. "You can get one of those voice-activated programs. I'm sure you'll love it." She'd hate it.

"I've contacted Dean and Dan," she said, referring to her partners at the accounting firm. "They told me—"

"To use your left hand? That would be great for you, Mom. Great for your brain. There's all kinds of studies—"

"To take time off to heal."

Nooooo! "Oh my gosh, Mom, that's nuts. You'll be bored out of your mind. Are you sure there isn't something else going on? They're not trying to push you out of the company, are they? Ageism is an issue, you know."

"Don't be ridiculous, Evangeline. I *am* the company. But I think Alundra is right. This was preordained. I broke my hand so that I could take the time off to get you out of this mess. I'll be there tomorrow."

"No. It's fine, Mom. I've got everything under—" She stared at her phone. Her mother had hung up. Evie hit Redial and got kicked to voice mail. After the fifth time it happened, she decided to text instead of calling.

Mom, I don't think you've thought this through. It's really important that you get in a good healing place—I'm sure Alundra can help with that—and rest. You need lots of rest. Because while I don't want to bring up the age thing again (just FYI, as much as I love Uncle Dean and Uncle Dan, you did officially become a senior citizen last month so the probability they're trying to oust you is HIGH) but as ~~you~~ we get older ~~you~~ we don't heal as fast…

The bubble appeared on the screen, and before Evie could complete her text, she received one from her mom.

Hello. I am Alundra. Lenore asks that you pick her up at South Station in Boston at 5 p.m. tomorrow and DON'T BE LATE. She also says to remove EVERYTHING from her bedroom as the witch costume you have stored in the closet nearly gave her a heart attack last time and she can't afford to fall and break anything else as you have already caused her to BREAK HER HAND.

Evie stared at the text. Her mother coming to Harmony Harbor wasn't preordained; it was foredoomed. How was she supposed to deal with Caine Elliot *and* her mother?

The bubble appeared again.

Please, please let Alundra have misunderstood Lenore, Evie prayed.

Sorry for the caps. She made me do it. I think
it is the pain.

Then you don't know her very well, Evie wanted to
write. But instead she typed:

You know, she really likes you, Alundra, and
I think she'd heal faster if she was in familiar
surroundings, like her apartment. So if you
could maybe check on her once a day and
pick up what she needs, I'll pay you. An hour a
day should be good. For maybe a week.

She thought about her nearly empty bank account
and maxed-out credit cards.

Actually, three days should be fine.

Crossing her fingers, she hit Send.

"No, no, no," she cried when one of those audio
things appeared. She fake-sobbed when she stood up
the phone and Lenore's voice came through loud and
clear. "Stop trying to pawn your mother off on someone else."

Followed by a second audio message. "You can't
afford Alundra. He makes more in a day than you do
in a year."

And George Bailey thought he had it tough when
Mr. Potter tried to send him up the river. As though
mocking her, Santa *ho, ho, ho*-ed, her door opening
and closing. It kept opening and closing. And while it

did, Evie was reminded of the verse on the needlepoint pillow on her bed.

It's always darkest before the dawn.

All these lovely customers were her light. Her gift for having to put up with Lenore for who knew how long. She'd need a lot more customers than the ten who'd crowded into her store and were headed her way to shine through the dark cloud that was her mother.

At the determined strides and equally determined expressions on the faces of the women walking her way, Evie glanced at their hands as she came to her feet. Other than their purses, none of them appeared to be returning anything. She sagged with relief against the sales counter.

"Hi, ladies. What can I do for you today?" She didn't recognize any of them, which was a little surprising since she knew so many people in town.

"I'm here to put a wish on the angel tree," one woman said. Hands went up. "Me too. Same."

The rest of the women were drowned out by Santa *ho*, *ho*, *ho*-ing as the door opened and closed and kept opening and closing as more women flocked to the angel tree in hopes that Caine Elliot would make their dreams come true.

Evie wondered how much darker her life had to become before she got some light.

* * *

"All right, Gran. Let's try this one more time. Do you or do you not want me to secure Greystone Manor for you by the end of the year?" Caine rested the back of his head against the tan leather driver's seat where he was parked outside O'Malley's Hardware on Main Street. He'd received an urgent text from his uncle for rat traps while he'd been on FaceTime with Emily. Caine had hoped to finish up his conversation with his grandmother by now.

"Of course I do, but I don't see what that has to do with your ridiculous wager with that Christmas woman. A foolish name for a foolish woman," she muttered before continuing. "You should have freed her from the chains and then immediately bulldozed her silly shop to the ground."

"I'm surprised you didn't suggest I leave her chained while bulldozing her silly shop to the ground, Gran. You've gone soft in your old age."

"There were witnesses. If there weren't, it would have been a different story."

He hid his smile at her dry sense of humor. As strained as their relationship had become, he still felt a familiar twinge of affection for the older woman on the screen—affection and concern. She'd swiped her favorite peach lipstick on her thin lips, a color she'd been wearing for as long as Caine could remember.

Even now, despite her being unwell, it complemented her pale complexion. But he knew the lipstick and brown eyeshadow and the effort she'd made to tame her thick white hair were an attempt to hide the ravages of her illness from him.

Still, he couldn't let his sympathy for her distract him. Her amusement didn't fool him. He had to spin this in such a way that she'd leave Evangeline alone and back off the manor until he figured out what to do. The last thing he wanted was Emily sitting in her mausoleum concocting schemes of her own. He didn't put it past his cousin Alec McCleary to lend her a helping hand.

A distant cousin on the Green side of the family, Alec was the head of Wicklow Developments' legal department. Before Emily's health had begun to deteriorate, the man had been a mild irritant at best. That was no longer the case.

"Ms. Christmas has a month to vacate the property, and as you know, the woman is adept at stirring up trouble in a short amount of time. So this seemed a good way to keep her busy and focused on something other than bringing us down in a more direct way," Caine said.

Sort of what he was trying to do with his grandmother. He made a mental note to consider a wager that would intrigue Emily. A wager that did not involve Wicklow Developments as the prize. He'd gamble anything but his stake in the company.

"And while I'm being painted in the media as a modern-day Scrooge, everyone in the business world sees this for what it is—an act of kindness. Charity, if you will." He smiled when his grandmother unconsciously nodded. There were benefits to talking to her on FaceTime.

"As to what the wager has to do with the manor?" he continued. "We've wasted too much time and money using intermediaries in the past. As you and I both know, to get things done right, you have to do them yourself. Which will be easier for me to do now that I'm operating in the open. From what I've learned about the angel wishes so far, there's little doubt I'll be spending time with the locals. And what better way to manage things to our advantage?"

"All right. We'll play it your way for now. You have a week—"

"Give me two, Gran. Remember, I'm not only trying to win the bet with Ms. Christmas."

"*Trying* is unacceptable, my boy. You will win the bet and give me the manor, or you will no longer be CEO of Wicklow Developments." As she tapped the phone, she turned her head. "Did you get that, Alec?"

"Gran, it's not—" She'd disconnected. He wished he could pretend that she'd had a memory blip and mixed him up with his cousin, but he knew better. She was as shrewd and conniving as ever. But the question was: Had she really been talking to his cousin, or had she been playing Caine? Either way, the stakes had been raised.

He got out of the car and slammed the door.

"Are you having a bad day, my friend?" asked an elderly man who was holding open the door to the hardware store for two older women. The man wore a Santa hat and a flashing red bow tie that matched his suspenders. With tufts of white hair at his ears and his diminutive stature, he looked more like an elf than Santa Claus. Though he had the *ho, ho, ho* down and seemed the jolly sort with a twinkle in his eyes and a wide smile.

"I've had better, thanks," Caine said as he entered

the store. With its warm, honey-colored wood floors, shelves, and walls and a potbellied stove sitting in the middle of the store, he felt like he'd walked back in time. A time when people looked out for their neighbors and knew one another's kids by name, which meant the older man probably had a fairly good idea who he was.

"I imagine you have." The man nodded with a mischievous grin. "Why don't you tell old Santa your troubles and see if I can't grant you an early Christmas wish or two?"

"I'm hoping you can help me with one at least. I need rat traps."

"I can indeed help you out with that. But if the traps are for who I think they are, you'll need to do better. They've had a problem with rats at Holiday House for as long as I can remember."

On one hand, Caine was glad to hear his grand-mother wasn't responsible, while on the other hand, Santa looked like he had a few years on him, so if Holiday House had a rat problem as long as *he* could remember, Caine should probably forget the traps and call in the experts.

"Evie thinks she has mouse in the house. I didn't have the heart to tell her she had a bigger problem than that. I guess it doesn't really matter now though. Unless she beats you." The older man winked.

"So you do know who I am."

"Not much goes on in Harmony Harbor that I don't know about." He offered his hand. "Tommy O'Malley. And I'll be honest with you, I'm rooting for Evie. I'll do whatever I can to help her win your bet. She's got a heart of gold and does more for this town than anyone I know."

Afraid Mr. O'Malley was going to list all of Evangeline's accomplishments, Caine said, "She seems like a nice woman. Now, about those traps…"

"Regular traps won't do you any good. Noelle, Evie's great-aunt, she got rid of the beta rats. What you're dealing with now is the alphas. They're cunning buggers and about yea big." He spread his hands.

"Bigger. I've seen two of the cunning buggers, and I don't wish to further our acquaintance."

"Oh, but I hear home in your voice, lad. And it is a lovely sound."

"I heard it in yours when you were talking to the ladies." He nodded at the two women who were perusing the shelves of Christmas lights toward the back of the store.

"At my age, you'll use whatever you can to charm the ladies," he said with a chuckle, then walked to the long wooden sales counter and picked up the phone. "Mrs. Crenshaw, the lady who lives behind the store, she has just what you need." He held up a gnarled finger as he waited for someone to pick up the other end. "Lettie, do you still have that cat trapped in your shed?"

A muffled voice responded and Mr. O'Malley nodded. "I've got someone who's going to take it off your hands. I'll send him over to you now. You'll know him when you see him. City boy. Slick clothes and a handsome face. Too young for you." He listened, then laughed and disconnected. "Might be safer if you get the cat for yourself. I'll let you out the back door and point you in the right direction. Just in case you still have some beta rats, I'll get you a couple of those electronic rat traps."

Two hundred dollars later, Caine met Mr. O'Malley in the back alley. The older man walked with him to the shed. "You ready?" he asked before opening the door.

Caine looked around. "Is there a reason why Mrs. Crenshaw keeps her cat locked in the shed?" he asked, thinking it was a question he should have thought to ask earlier.

"He's not hers. He's a stray. He keeps getting in her garbage and making a mess of things."

Learning the animal was a stray gave him pause. This would make the second stray he'd taken in in less than a week. Remembering that it wasn't him but Ms. Christmas who would be taking in the cat, he smiled. It seemed only fair after the problems she'd caused him— and continued to cause him—that she suffered a little.

"We call him Bruiser," Mr. O'Malley told him while sliding open the rusted green door. And out walked the ugliest cat Caine had ever seen. He had a pug face and half a right ear. Patches of his ginger fur were missing, and he had a crooked tail.

"What do you think?" Mr. O'Malley asked.

"That he'll terrify the rats," Caine said as he ran his eyes over the cat. "Do you have any animal supplies? I have a feeling I'll need something to take care of fleas."

After parting with another two hundred dollars for cat supplies, Caine found a parking spot just up from

Holiday House. Once he got his bag of traps and another bag of animal supplies out of the car, he picked up the crate that Bruiser unhappily sat in. "Sorry, mate, but until you've had a bath, I'm not carrying you."

Holding the crate and a bag in one hand, Caine tucked the other bag under his chin to open the door to Holiday House.

"Rat!" someone cried, and several women began to shriek.

"I don't think there's cause to call me names," Caine said, thinking the women were referring to him until he spotted an actual rat tearing through the store with Max tearing after it. *Feck!* Caine let the door go, effectively trapping the rat in the store with fifteen terrified and screaming women and one hyperactive golden retriever.

Chapter Nine

♥

Evie's relief upon seeing Caine arrive at the front door of her shop made her weak from her head to her toes. *My hero*, she thought from her wobbly perch on the stool behind the sales counter. She didn't have the heart to berate herself. How could she? Their gorgeous white knight was about to save them from a rat the size of a cat and her shop from Max, who'd just taken out a table and one of her customers.

"It's okay. Look, Caine is…" she began to call out in an attempt to calm the screaming women and draw their attention to the man opening the front door. *Wait. What's he doing?* "Open the door!" she yelled as he let it swing closed, blocking the rat's escape route, which the rat proved by bouncing off the glass.

Caine jumped back from the door.

"Seriously? You're six foot four and built like a line-backer and you're afraid of a rat?" she shouted, waving her hands to get his attention. "Open the door!" Even if he did, she didn't know if it would matter since the rat was now headed her way. "Seamus, open the back door!" she cried, praying the man wasn't a scaredy-cat like his nephew and standing on her kitchen table.

She looked down at herself. Okay, so she wasn't one to talk. For all she knew, Caine had seized on the rat situation as the perfect opportunity to chase her and her customers away for good.

"It's okay, ladies. I've got this," Evie shouted, wincing as a shriek was followed by the sound of shattering glass. She grabbed on to the sales counter for balance as she began her awkward descent off the stool. As though cheering for Evie when her feet touched the wood-planked floor, Santa *ho*, *ho*, *ho*-ed. She turned her head in time to see the door open and what appeared to be a cat, a sumo cat with half an ear and patches of missing fur, stalk into the store.

Several women didn't appear to like the look of the cat any better than the rat and screamed.

"Go get him, Bruiser," a familiar voice said.

She didn't find his accent quite so fascinating now, she thought as their gazes locked across the shop. He grimaced, holding open the door for the four women running terrified onto the sidewalk. Two of whom forgot their terror when they recognized the man holding the door and pressed their angels on him. Evie figured they didn't realize he'd been the one to trap them inside with the rat.

Another crash and what sounded like a dozen screams drew her back to the disaster at hand. Max and the rat had brought down the angel tree. Apropos, she thought. When they veered to the right, heading for a table of ceramic nativity sets, Evie had had enough.

She strode from behind the counter and shouted, "Max, sit. Stay!"

When he did exactly what he was told, she wished she'd thought of it sooner. But as a flash of ginger darted past her, she realized him obediently staying put had nothing to do with her. Max had spotted the fat cat. So had the rat.

Seamus appeared with a broom in his hand, his hair plastered to his flushed and sweaty face. "Sorry, lass. I didn't mean to let them out of the basement."

"There's more than him?" Her voice went up a panicked octave as she pointed at the rat trying to burrow its way under the stairs to escape the cat.

"Aye. I got the other one." His gaze followed her finger, and he reared back. "What the bloody hell is that?"

"My hero," Evie said when Bruiser pounced on the rat.

"I don't think I've ever seen a cat as ugly as that one."

"Heroes don't always have a pretty face. In my experience, it's often the villain who does," she said, casting a pointed glance at the man sidestepping broken cranberry glass to walk toward them.

Caine gave her a look. "I'm hardly the villain in the piece, Ms. Christmas."

She raised her eyebrows.

"A good businessman does not a villain make, a point you'll no doubt stubbornly argue with your usual *tasteful* remarks, so I'll just say I'm not the villain in *this* piece." He held up two bags and an animal crate. "I was coming to your rescue. And may I point out that I brought Bruiser." He watched the cat walking away with the rat and shuddered. "Uncle, perhaps you could intervene."

"Boyo, I think it's time we talked about a raise." Seamus smiled at the ladies who were huddled in a corner of the store. "I'll have this taken care of in no time at all, and you can get back to your shopping." He glanced at Evie. "Perhaps some refreshments are in order, lass. I'll take mine with an added pick-me-up, if you know what I mean."

"That's a great idea, Seamus. I should have thought of it." But right then she was preoccupied with the state of Holiday House. "How could a rat and a dog do this much damage in less than five minutes?" she asked no one in particular.

"Why don't you get the refreshments, and I'll get started cleaning up out here?" Caine offered, handing her the bags and the crate.

"Thank you. That's kind of you to offer. Max, come here, boy," she called to the dog, who remained sitting by the stairs, before she glanced at her now loaded-down hands. "Why are you giving me the crate? Bruiser is your cat."

Caine laughed, and she couldn't help but notice the funny things that deep rumble was doing to her stomach. But she had no problem ignoring the butterflies when he opened his mouth and said, "No, he's not. He's yours."

"No way. I can't. Someone pawned"—she lowered her voice as her dog came to her side—"Max off on me. I can't take in another animal. Especially now."

"You're right. I didn't think about what you'd do

with them when you lose Holiday—" He grimaced, then said, "I better get started out here."

"That's not it at all. I have no intention of losing our bet, Mr. Elliot. And if my mother weren't moving in with me for a couple of weeks, I'd take Bruiser." The poor thing looked like he could use some love.

"Lenore is moving in with you? Nothing's the matter, is it?"

Her mouth dropped at the familiarity in his voice. "Oh my gosh, I should have known. You've been talking to her, haven't you?"

"We've spoken, yes," he said, looking uncomfortable.

"About me? Her foolish daughter who doesn't have a lick of business sense? You're just like her with your logical, mathematical intelligence. Well, let me tell you, Mr. Elliot, I have more intrapersonal intelligence than you and my mother combined."

"I'm sure you do. But perhaps you should get your emotions in check and go use your superlative intrapersonal skills on your customers before you lose them."

"You are just like her," she huffed, barely stopping herself from stomping her foot. "Being emotional is not a sign of weakness, Mr. Elliot. Nor is owning a business that celebrates the holidays year-round a sign of no business sense or a person with a Pollyanna approach to life."

"I never said—"

"No, but I'm sure you've thought it." Catching his eyes shift up to the right, she stabbed her finger at him. "You have! And don't bother denying it. You just gave yourself away."

As though seeking patience, he drew in a deep breath through his nostrils. A habit her mother had once been noted for when *dealing* with Evie and her father.

"Take care of the refreshments, and I'll take care of cleanup and your customers, who appear to be waiting for me, not you." Caine put his hands on her shoulders, turning her toward the kitchen.

She glanced over her shoulder. The women had righted the angel tree and were clutching their paper angels while looking their way. *Caine's way*, she corrected. And tried not to resent their easy defection. Did no one remember that he was the man trying to put her out of business? She supposed she couldn't blame them. He was ridiculously handsome and ridiculously rich. But it wasn't his face or his bank account that caused a tiny softening of her anger toward him. He'd brought her a cat and rat traps and a flea bath, she thought, as she glanced in the bags.

She put the bags on the kitchen counter, steeling herself to look at the basement door. She needn't have worried. Bruiser had made himself at home in front of the door. She sighed, knowing she couldn't get rid of him now. Nor Max, who lay beneath the kitchen table eyeing the cat with trepidation. It was clear who would rule the roost at Holiday House.

Evie pulled out her phone and called Truly Scrumptious. "Mackenzie, I have an emergency."

"I heard." She dropped her voice to a whisper. "Four of your customers ran in here half-hysterical. They're having coffee and cupcakes to relieve their trauma, or relive it as the case may be. Once they're finished, I'll ask them to do me a favor and bring your order to you. Then it's up to you to keep them there, girlfriend. Although if Caine Elliot is there, you shouldn't have a problem. It's a good thing he got there in time. They said your shop would have been trashed if he hadn't arrived when he did."

Evie took her phone from her ear and stared at it. She had to be joking. "You're joking?"

"About what?"

"Nothing." It would take too long to explain, and she'd probably sound ungrateful when she got to the part about Bruiser and the rat traps and Caine tidying up her store—she tilted her head at the sexy rumble of laughter coming from her shop—and entertaining her customers. "Your plan is perfect. Thanks so much, Mackenzie."

"No problem. I have an adorable hero cupcake I'll send for Caine. Tell him thanks for looking out for our girl."

"Handsome men get away with murder," Evie muttered as she pulled a pot from the cupboard.

"You can't be talking about Mr. Ugly over there, so I imagine it's my nephew putting the puss on your face," Seamus said as he closed the back door. "I can set your mind at ease on one count. He gets away with plenty, especially with the ladies, but murder isn't one of them. And while he has no problem omitting the truth, he'll tell it to you if you ask him straight out. But be careful if you do—he's blunt." Seamus came to stand beside her, turning on the tap to wash his hands. As the women's laughter floated into the kitchen, he chuckled. "Caine has a way, he does. I'll wager you each and every one of those women buy something before they leave."

"I'd take your bet, but it wouldn't be fair. They only came in to put a wish on the angel tree. But even if they had planned to shop, it would be a little hard for a man who doesn't like Christmas to sell them anything. Customers pick up on your passion and enthusiasm, you know. They can tell when someone is faking it."

"Evangeline, could you give me a hand up here? I'm not sure how to ring a sale through," Caine said from where he stood at the entrance to the kitchen.

Seamus lightly elbowed her in the ribs, his eyes glinting with suppressed laughter. "You go ahead, lass. I'll take care of the hot chocolate."

* * *

Caine should have volunteered to mop the floor after closing instead of giving Bruiser a bath.

"I'm warning you, don't come in here, Evangeline. The animal is either rabid or possessed," Caine said through the closed bathroom door on the second floor.

"Or terrified. I heard you yelling at him from downstairs, Caine. If we weren't closed, you would have terrified the customers too."

He reached up from where he sat on the floor by the door and turned the knob. "Does he look bloody terrified to you?"

Evangeline peeked her head around the door. "Um, no, but he doesn't look possessed or rabid either," she said of the cat, who sat on the windowsill yawning. Then Evangeline's gaze dropped to Caine, and her eyes went wide. "What happened to you?"

"He did," Caine said, dabbing at the red and raised scratches on his arm.

"You're bleeding, and you're soaking wet."

"I got soaked trying to bathe him in the tub, and when that didn't work, I held him under the shower. Which is when he shredded my shirt and arm."

She knelt beside him and took the cloth from his hand to dab at his cheek. They'd spent almost the entire day together putting the store to rights. At times they'd been as close as they were now, but this felt different. Intimate somehow.

"I have some antibiotic ointment in the first aid kit," she said, leaning past him to open the cupboard under the sink, and he couldn't help but notice her shapely backside in her black slacks.

It wasn't the first time he'd noticed. The woman had a lovely figure. Though she didn't flaunt it like so many women he knew. It was a nice change.

She turned with a first aid kit in her hands, and he jerked his gaze back to the cat, who meowed. Bruiser locked eyes with him as though warning him off. "I wouldn't want to run into you in a dark alley, mate. You have a face only a mother could love."

"I don't know. He's mangy and flea-bitten and a little surly, but there's something sweet about him." She glanced from the cat back to Caine, a touch of color pinking her cheeks as she took the cloth and began cleaning his forearm. She was gentle, and he liked the way she felt against him. She smelled good too, like oranges and cloves.

"Here." She handed him the cloth and pushed to her feet. He probably smelled like the bottom of a garbage bin, thanks to the cat. "Take off your shirt and clean up. I'm going to get you something to wear."

"Thanks a lot," he muttered at Bruiser. Then it hit him that he did indeed owe the cat his thanks, because the last thing Caine should be doing is regretting the loss of Evangeline's hands on him, the loss of her body's warm weight leaning against him.

Caine stood up and took off his shirt, dropping it on the closed lid of the toilet seat. "Okay, Bruiser. You either have your flea bath or you go back to the old lady's shed. Take your pick." Caine gingerly reached for the cat, who took a swipe at him, but it wasn't as aggressive as the last time. He took that as a good sign and got ahold of him. "No scratching or biting. Let's get this done."

"Oh, look at you. Aren't you a good boy," Evangeline said, coming to his side to pet the cat.

"Thank you. I'm very good at doing what I'm told." He lowered himself to the side of the tub while holding the cat over the water.

"Ha. You know I was talking to Bruiser."

"And apparently he does too. Keep up your crooning and we'll get this done." Feeling the weight of her gaze, he glanced at her. "What?"

She lifted a shoulder as she knelt beside him. "You're not what I expected, that's all."

He could say the same of her, but it wouldn't be true.

She was exactly what he'd expected: sweet, compassionate, kind, and loyal without being a total pushover. What he hadn't expected was how much she would appeal to him. She wasn't his type.

"What were you expecting? Big head, overlong hair, greenish cast to my skin, voracious appetite, freakishly strong?"

She took a moment to answer, and he glanced at her while he gently scooped warm water onto the cat. Her eyes were on his chest. As she raised her gaze to his, her face flushed, and she cleared her throat. "I didn't say you looked like an ogre. I said you acted like one."

"And now?"

"I've discovered when you're not in high-powered-businessman mode, you're actually a very nice man. Theia always said you were kind and thoughtful, generous to a fault, and so does your uncle. But I didn't see how that could be true. You are though."

"Be sure to keep it to yourself. You'll ruin my reputation."

"We wouldn't want that." She smiled and returned her attention to the cat, gently kneading the shampoo into his mangy coat.

Caine tried to picture his last date leaning over a tub crooning sweet nothings as she washed a flea-bitten cat. She wouldn't be alone in her horror. None of the women he'd dated in the past ten years would take in a stray cat and a stray dog. The closest they'd get to helping out was donating money, but only if it came with a photo op.

"Caine, can you rinse him off while I hold him?"

He shook off the unsettling feeling that came from comparing the women he'd dated to Evangeline.

"Of course," he said, and she glanced at him. The words had come out sharper than he'd intended. Or had they? Maybe his subconscious knew what he didn't want to admit. That he'd let Evangeline get a little too close and he needed to put some distance between them. No doubt their bet would accomplish that.

Once Bruiser was thoroughly rinsed, Caine stood up and grabbed a towel off the rack, handing it to Evangeline. She placed it over her knees and then lifted the dripping cat from the water. Bruiser couldn't have looked more pathetic had he tried. But he didn't look pathetic when Evangeline wrapped him in the fluffy white towel and cradled him against her chest.

Lucky bastard, Caine thought, and briefly closed his eyes. It was past time for him to leave. He turned to wash his hands. Glancing in the mirror over the sink, he caught Evangeline eyeing his back. There was interest and a touch of heat in her hazel eyes, and his own desire flared to life in response. His hand tightened around the tap as he warred with what was right and what was wrong and what he wanted. It had been a long time since he'd damned the consequences and given in to his desires. But no matter how strong his desire, the consequences would be dire.

Caine shook the water from his hands, then dried them on a hand towel by the sink. "I'd best be going. I have calls to make. We can do the angel wish to-morrow." A fair number of the paper angels had been damaged when the tree fell, and Evangeline hadn't had a chance to replace them. "Will you be all right tonight? My uncle can stay with you if you'd like." Seamus had gone to have a couple pints at the pub.

"If he's planning to stay at the Salty Dog until closing, he's welcome to stay here. But I'm fine. I have Max and Bruiser."

Caine reached out to help her up. She stood, resting a palm on his chest as she adjusted the cat in her arms. She jerked her hand back as though shocked she'd touched his bare skin. He understood her reaction. He felt the imprint of her palm on his chest. He wanted to take her hand and press it there again.

Without meeting his gaze, she pointed at the door-knob. "There's a sweater for you."

It was a red sweater with the words *Get Lit* above a gaudy Christmas tree. "The tree lights up," she mur-mured, glancing at him with a self-conscious grin.

"Thanks. What do I owe you?"

"Nothing. Not everything has a price tag attached to it, Caine. I appreciated your help. That's all."

Her reaction was stronger than he would have ex-pected given what he'd said. She was reacting to more than his question. She was reacting to her reaction to him, to his reaction to her. To the sexual tension swirl-ing around them in the small, confined space.

"You're right. I'm sorry." He picked up the sweater and discovered a small bag underneath. It was from the local bakery. He held it up. "What's this?"

"Just a cupcake. Mackenzie made it for you."

Chapter Ten

♥

The next day Evie heard Caine's voice through the vent of the guestroom she was cleaning out for her mother. She frowned, thinking he was early to pick his first angel wish until she looked at the pumpkin alarm clock on the nightstand. He was right on time. She doubted he was ever late or that he'd ever made a single misstep in his life.

"He's perfect, and I'm perfectly inept," she said to Bruiser, who was soaking up the sun shining onto the bedspread.

Her mother would arrive in less than four hours, and Evie had barely boxed a quarter of the decorations. The guest bedroom served as an overflow room for stock from the Halloween room, since it was Evie's second-favorite holiday and she tended to buy too much. At least she didn't have to close up shop to get her mother. Seamus had offered.

She didn't know what she'd do without the older man. He was a godsend. Who'd been provided courtesy of the devil, she reminded herself. At least that was how she used to think of Caine. Ogre, devil, they were one and the same. Devilishly handsome and devilishly charming more like, she thought, remembering her reaction to him last night.

She lowered herself onto the end of the bed, a box of purple, orange, and black feather boas and witches' hats on her lap, and allowed herself a mini vacay from the reality of her life or what her life would become at six tonight, when her mother arrived.

Lenore wouldn't give Evie a moment's peace. She'd have no time to fantasize about a man she had absolutely no business fantasizing over. But, oh my gosh, how could she not? As his deep voice came through the vent, she flashed back to last night, when she'd heard him swearing at Bruiser in what she'd assumed was Gaelic. His voice all gravelly and commanding.

"If you were a Betty instead of a Bruiser, you would have rolled over and showed your belly. I certainly would have," Evie murmured as images of a shirtless Caine flitted through her mind. From somewhere below, she heard him answer his phone. His rolling baritone managed to make what sounded like a tense conversation deliciously sexy.

Who had she been trying to kid yesterday? His accent turned her on as much as the sight of his broad back with its sculpted muscles and skin the color of liquid honey. She was surprised she'd managed to keep from smoothing her hands over all that taut muscle and warm skin when she'd accidently placed a palm on his chest. Only to jerk it away when a low hum of appreciation began in her throat.

Somehow the part of her that kept her out of trouble managed to push past the heavy, pulsing desire she'd felt for the man, saving her from making a complete fool of herself. Caine Elliot wanted only one thing from her—to wipe Holiday House off the map of Harmony Harbor.

It didn't matter that he'd brought her Bruiser and bought her rat traps, flea baths, cat food, and squeaky toys. It didn't matter that his uncle (at Caine's directive, she assumed) was helping her at the store or that Caine had agreed to a bet when all he had to do was charm the people of Harmony Harbor to have them fall in line just like he'd charmed her.

It didn't matter that she thought she'd seen another side of him yesterday: a kinder, gentler side. Caine Elliot used charm, money, and his big, logical mathematician brain to get exactly what he wanted. She was lucky. She'd seen the look in his eyes when he'd read the look in hers. He might as well have put up his hands and told her to back off. She'd misread the heat. She wasn't his type.

"And he's not mine," she told Bruiser, and came to her feet.

"Who's not yours?"

She looked over to see Caine leaning against the doorframe, hands in the pockets of his leather bomber jacket, a half smile on his face. She wondered how long he'd been standing there, at the same time thanking God that she hadn't been confiding her feelings for him and his body to Bruiser. At least the feelings she'd had for him and his body yesterday. She didn't have them today. Uh-uh, no way.

Ignoring the traitorous flutter in the pit of her stomach when he walked into the room, she lifted her chin at the closet. "The skeleton. He was my aunt Noelle's."

"Ah, I see." He nodded at Bruiser as he walked to the bed. "He seems to be enjoying your conversation."

"He was until you walked in. He's pretending to sleep. You traumatized him yesterday."

"I can tell," he said when he lightly scratched behind Bruiser's half-bitten ear and the cat purred loudly. "Evangeline?"

She tore her gaze from his big hand and his long, blunt-tipped fingers. "What?"

"It looked like I'd lost you for a minute."

"Lots on my mind." She stood up and put the box on the bed.

"So I gathered. Do you need a hand? Seamus says you have to clean out the room before your mother arrives."

"Yes. She's not a fan of the holidays. Any holiday. She says they're a bunch of sentimental claptrap and a waste of time and money. I'm sure you agree."

He shrugged. "I don't have an opinion on them either way. Seamus is another story. He loves them. Thanks for letting him stay, by the way. He enjoyed sleeping in the St. Paddy's room."

All she'd done was move a few display tables and pull down the Murphy bed. "I'm happy to have him. He's been a great help. He offered to pick up my mother in Boston at five. Is that a problem for you?"

"Not all. I figure for the next couple of days I'll be busy fulfilling my angel-wish assignments, so it's best if he's busy. It keeps him out of trouble."

"Wonderful. It'll be good to have the extra help during the holiday season. All four weeks of it," she added as she began emptying the closet of Halloween costumes.

He reached past her to grab an armful. "It's not going to take me four weeks to fulfill three holiday wishes, Evangeline."

"I have a feeling it will," she said as she walked from the bedroom to the stairs in the hall that led to the attic. The other bedrooms were crammed with their particular holiday paraphernalia, and Evie didn't want to traumatize any children who might happen upon the costumes.

"And would that feeling have anything to do with you curating my wishes?" Caine asked as he followed behind her.

She gave a noncommittal *hmm* to his question, then said, "Thanks, but you can just leave the costumes here. I'll take them to my room later." She wouldn't be able to go into the second-floor bathroom without thinking of him, so she didn't want him anywhere near her bedroom. She didn't need to start imagining him there. Her bedroom was her sanctuary.

"It won't take as long with me helping."

She stopped halfway up the narrow staircase and turned, coming almost face-to-face with him as he stood two steps below her. "Here." She held out her arms. "Just pile them on."

His gaze dropped to the costumes in her arms, and the corner of his mouth twitched as he lifted his eyes to hers. "Is the sexy maid's uniform popular?"

She wondered if he'd intended for her to imagine herself playing sexy maid to his sexy billionaire self, because that's exactly what happened. Such was the problem of a vivid imagination. Sometimes it could be used against her. Like now.

"Not as popular as the sexy nurse. It's probably in the closet," she said when he appeared to be searching their piles for it.

"I can't see it being more popular than the sexy maid. I'll have to check it out." He nodded at the stairs. "Let's go."

"Has anyone ever told you you're a very bossy man?" she said as she headed the rest of the way up the stairs, fully intending to stop him at the entrance to her room.

"Yes. Several people. A good number who actually think it's a positive attribute, not a character flaw like you appear to."

"The ones who approve, would they be women in sexy maid uniforms, by chance?"

His warm, rich laughter rolled over her, and she found herself smiling. Reluctantly, of course. She turned to him at the entrance to her room. "I can take it from here."

Instead of piling the costumes on top of hers, he nudged her back. Not forcefully but just enough that she knew to argue with him would be a lesson in futility. She made an irritated sound in her throat, uttering *Fine* with enough attitude that he knew she wasn't happy about him invading her space.

"Do you want to tell me why you're so intent on

seeing my bedroom?" she asked as she walked to the closet, surreptitiously checking to be sure she hadn't left anything embarrassing out.

"I was just lending a hand, but the fact you obviously didn't want me up here made me curious. I thought maybe you were hiding a man in your room."

"You did not, and even if you did, what would it matter to you?"

"You're right, I didn't. My uncle would have told me," he said, looking around her room.

She followed his gaze, seeing the space through his eyes: the framed photos of her with her dad at a Christmas craft fair when she was twelve; her graduation photo with her parents, her dad wearing her cap with his usual playful grin, her mother clearly unamused; a picture at her twenty-seventh birthday, laughing and surrounded by her girlfriends. Friends that had slowly disappeared from her life as she allowed Aaron to isolate her. She turned off thoughts of the man she'd run from. This was her safe place.

Her decorating style was warm and cozy. She loved the shades of blue and cream, touches of fur and heavy wool, the twinkling lights she'd strung from one end of the room to the other. The way the ceiling slanted over her bed, which was covered in pillows and a fur throw. The low cream-colored bookshelf beside the big comfy chair with an even bigger ottoman was decorated with Christmas ornaments, a small ceramic Christmas tree sitting on top of it.

Caine's expression tensed as his eyes seemed to search every corner of her room.

"Okay, you've seen enough. It's obvious you have a problem with my room, but that's not a surprise since you have a problem with my entire house. So, bye-bye." She walked to the door and motioned for him to leave. "You're going the wrong way," she said when he strode to the opposite end of her room. "What do you think you're doing?" she cried as he pulled the plug on her twinkle lights.

"What I'm doing"—he waved the cord at her—"is saving you from burning down Holiday House with you in it. This is a death trap up here. Start packing your things. You're not staying here another night."

She opened her mouth, but nothing came out. Instead she stabbed her finger at him, hoping to convey how ticked off she was while she waited for her temper to unfreeze her brain or her tongue or both. "You, you—"

"Sputter and stutter and point your finger at me all you want. It won't change the outcome. Look at the outlets and tell me you don't see what I do, Evangeline. See here, where it's black?" He rose to his feet and moved to the other end of the bookshelf to push the chair out of the way. Swearing under his breath, he held up another cord. "Do you have a death wish, woman? The bloody thing is frayed. Obviously rats are not your only problem. You have mice." He pulled out his phone. "You're not sleeping here until I have your electrical looked at."

How was she supposed to argue with him? She might hate what he saw and hate what he said, but she didn't have a death wish. Still, she couldn't give in. "I'm not letting you kick me out of my room. You're already trying to—"

He held up his finger. "Caine Elliot here. I need an electrician—on second thought, send me a team to check the electrical at Holiday House on Main Street. Yes, one and the same." He turned his back to her. "I don't want it burning to the ground before I tear it down. Yes, I realize it's crazy. So is the woman I'm dealing with." Shoving his phone in his pocket, he turned to her. "Until the house has been given the okay by the electricians, you plug in the bare minimum of small appliances and lights. Do you understand?"

Panicked tears prickled the backs of her eyes at the thought of being left in the dark. She couldn't sleep without her twinkle lights. Afraid she might not be able to hold back tears, she lowered her eyes and heard Caine draw a deep inward breath.

"I'm sorry." He stepped closer, lifting his hand to gently stroke her hair. "I overreacted. But it's not safe, Evangeline. I'm not trying to scare you to get out of the bet or to make you walk away from Holiday House before your month is up."

She nodded, curling her hands into fists, clenching her teeth in an effort to regain control. And she had to regain it fast or she might give in to the temptation to take two steps closer and lean on Caine. She hadn't had anyone to lean on in a long time. She didn't like burdening her friends with her problems. Yet oddly, since Caine was the one who had created her biggest problems, she felt like he was the one person she could unburden herself to. She didn't understand why she felt that way, nor did she like it. The only reason she could think to explain the feeling was because he was rich and powerful and had shoulders that looked like they could take on the weight of the world.

"I know you have a lot to deal with and that your mother coming is an added stress you didn't need. So I have a suggestion that might help."

"What is it?" She raised her gaze but looked beyond him. Not ready to look into those piercing blue eyes just yet.

"You stay in the guest bedroom until the electrical is taken care of. That way you don't have to clean everything out. I'll put Lenore up at Greystone Manor." He raised his hand. "Before you tell me you're not a charity case or start looking for an ulterior motive, I'm not doing this out of the goodness of my heart. I'd like your mother's opinion on the day-to-day operations of the manor."

"You want my mother to spy on the Gallaghers?"

"No. I want her opinion as to whether or not the manor is self-sustaining."

His offer was incredible. The best offer she'd had in weeks, months, years, but she couldn't accept it. "An opinion you'll use to what? Lower your offer for the estate? Use to convince the Gallaghers the manor isn't worth saving? Just like you've tried to convince me to give up on Holiday House."

He studied her for a long moment before answering. "I'm a businessman, Evangeline. I don't make my decisions based on emotion. I deal in facts. But I do require that the facts are based on the truth and that those facts haven't been colored by emotions—mine or anyone else's. If your mother's analysis of the situation agrees with mine, then I'll move forward as I had intended. If it turns out the manor's future is not as bleak as the one I envision, then I will reevaluate my options."

"So it's possible my mother's opinion could save the manor?"

"The probability of that happening is the same as you winning the Powerball."

"But there is a chance?"

"Yes. Now let's get out of this death trap. And, Evangeline, this conversation never happened."

* * *

Whoever said food was the way to a man's heart had it wrong. It was tears. Or the hint of tears, because Evangeline hadn't cried. Caine inhaled a noisy breath. Why was he talking about his heart? She hadn't gotten into his heart; she'd gotten in his head. And clearly, he'd lost his mind. How else could he explain telling her, a woman who was compassionate and kind and good friends with half the Gallaghers, including Theia, that there was a chance (no matter how slight) that he'd reconsider his plans for the manor?

He had, of course, been having doubts about how they were going about acquiring the manor, but not once had he considered abandoning the takeover all together. He still hadn't. And the reason he hadn't was because of his grandmother. The resort deal he was days away from closing in the Canadian Rockies, the office tower on Main Street, the developments in Portugal—those were the projects Caine believed in and was passionate about. Acquiring the manor had been all about satisfying his grandmother's need for revenge.

But now it seemed there was something else at stake.

As if his grandmother knew he'd be torn between his loyalty to her and his loyalty to Theia, she was holding everything he held dear over his head. If he didn't bend to her wishes, she'd strip him of everything he'd worked so hard to achieve. The company was his life.

Just like Holiday House seemed to be Evangeline's, he thought as he unplugged the last of the artificial Christmas trees. He stood up to see her looking around the shop with a disheartened expression on her face. It bothered him, which didn't make sense since he'd no doubt put that same expression on her face at least a hundred times over the past year. He wondered if he'd made her cry too.

Feck. He had to get away from the woman and this house and get back to his real life. The one where he knew exactly what he was doing and didn't second-guess his decisions.

"All right. Don't plug anything else in, and you should be good until the electricians arrive." He brushed glitter off his knees, turning over his hands to see they sparkled too. "The stuff multiplies," he said when Evangeline came over. "It's like glittergeddon in here."

Her lips tipped up—and he was glad to see her smile. "It won't hurt you. It's pretty," she said.

She looked pretty with the touch of glitter on her face and in her hair. "I'm a man, Evangeline. I don't do pretty."

"I know that, but it's not like you have a phobia or anything, right? I'm sure you've bought a card decorated with glitter before."

"Is this going somewhere? Because you seem a little too interested in my thoughts about glitter."

"No. It's just that some of the angels on the tree have been decorated with glitter, and I wouldn't want that to impact your decision. What if the perfect wish for you was on an angel decorated with glitter. It would be a shame if you lost—"

"One of them is yours, isn't it?" he said as he walked over to the tree decorated in paper angels.

"It's possible. Okay. One of them is mine," she admitted when he raised an eyebrow.

He nodded, keeping an eye on her as he reached for a powder-blue angel with wings that sparkled. Bingo, he thought when her eyes flicked to him. The blue angel was hers, which meant it would probably be the most difficult wish to fulfill. He reached for the white angel beside it, and Evangeline's face fell.

Bollocks. She'd had a crappy day, indirectly because of him, an even crappier week, indirectly because of him, and a crappy year, for which he took credit, although unintentionally because he hadn't set out to hurt her. Like he'd told her, he didn't let emotions factor into his business decisions. It was nothing personal.

He picked the powder-blue angel with the sparkly wings off the tree and was rewarded with a smile that took Evangeline from cute to beautiful. He turned the angel over to read the wish, then lifted his gaze to the woman with sparkles on her face and in her hair. She was a devil disguised as an angel. And if he needed further evidence that he should never allow emotions to factor into his decisions, this was it.

Chapter Eleven

♥

Colleen trudged after Clio and the housekeeping cart. *The Secret Keeper of Harmony Harbor* was still missing, and Theia's search of Clio's room had proved as unfruitful as her own. Colleen was beginning to wonder if she'd imagined the whole thing. Maybe Clio hadn't slipped the leather-bound book under the towels on the housekeeping cart after all.

But her memoir hadn't vanished into thin air, and Colleen was positive she hadn't been having an out-of-body experience. Except, in a way she was, wasn't she, she thought with a chuckle. Then she shook her head at herself for finding humor in the situation. The consequences could be dire should her book fall into the wrong hands.

Her inner chatter was brought to an abrupt halt when she walked into Clio. Something had caused her great-granddaughter to stop on her way to the elevators. Colleen looked around the grand hall (or lobby, as the younger generation referred to it) but didn't see any reason for the calculating expression that had come over her great-granddaughter's face. Until Colleen heard a familiar deep voice that made her think of rolling green hills and Guinness.

As though the sounds of home called to her, Clio parked the housekeeping cart beside the elevator and set off in search of the man behind the voice.

"He'll draw you in as easily as his voice has, lass, but you keep your eyes in your head and your hands to yourself." Born with a winsome charm and a sweet face, Clio was as big a flirt as her father. "Caine Elliot is your cousin. Cousin," she yelled near the girl's ear as she followed her to the bar, where Caine spoke with Jasper, but her warning had no effect on the child.

Whatever the two men were talking about was serious, Colleen surmised from the tense expressions on their faces. They turned as Clio approached.

"Miss Clio, is there something I can do for you?" Jasper asked in a resigned tone. Clio hadn't been making Jasper's life easy these past weeks.

If only he knew how difficult the child could make their lives. *Ignorance is bliss*, she thought, while also reminding herself there was a possibility, no matter how slight, that the child didn't have the book. Or if she did, she'd gotten bored and put it aside. Colleen scoffed at the idea of anyone getting bored reading her memoirs.

"The front wheel on my cart is wobbling." The girl pointed to where she'd parked it at the elevator. "I'll have myself a coffee while you fix it." Bold as brass, she moved to the coffee urn on the bar.

Jasper looked down his long nose at Clio, drawing in a frustrated breath that caused his chest to expand beneath his black suit jacket. He nodded at Caine. "The team can continue their work in the tunnels, Mr. Elliot. But I'll need more time to address your request about Ms. Johnson."

It was a good thing Colleen knew what Jasper was about or their conversation would have done more than give her pause. Though she wondered who Ms. Johnson was and vowed to find out.

"As always, it's been a pleasure doing business with you, Jasper," Caine said with a touch of a smile before turning his steely gaze upon Clio.

"You're not pleased with how she disrespected Jasper, are you, my boy? Good, because neither am I, and I can't do anything about it. If you ask me, the whole family is cutting the child too much slack on account of Daniel."

"If you worked for me, that move would have cost you your job. You owe Jasper an apology."

"Good thing I don't work for you, then, isn't it?" Clio looked at him as she added a tablespoon of sugar to her coffee. "I shouldn't have to work for them. I'm one of the owners of this fine establishment, you know?"

"Ah, I see." Caine nodded. "You're Daniel's daughter. Clio."

"I am, and I know who you are, Mr. Elliot. My father worked for you, and now he's in jail." She took a sip of coffee, made a face, and set the cup on the bar. Then she gave Caine a smile. And not a nice one at that. "From where I'm standing, that means you owe me."

"You silly child. Can you not see he isn't a man to trifle with?" Colleen said.

"Your father is in prison because, for once in his life, he's trying to do the right thing. He's owned up to his crimes. He didn't report ancient artifacts from a dig in Greece and tried to sell them on the black market."

"I know what he did. But I shouldn't have to suffer for it. You were supposed to help him."

"I did. I hired him an excellent attorney, who ensured that your father will be out of jail in three months and will only serve a hundred hours of community service instead of the four hundred hours the prosecutor wanted. As to his time in my employ, Daniel was paid for his services. How he chose to use that money is on him, not me." He pulled his vibrating phone from the pocket of his leather jacket and glanced at the screen. "Now, if you'll excuse me, I have things to attend to."

"No. Wait. I have something. Something you'll want."

Colleen pressed a hand to her chest, praying Clio wasn't about to offer Caine her memoir.

"If you plan to offer me your share of the estate, you're wasting both our time, Clio. Your sisters have made it clear—"

"I don't have sisters."

"Really? Because from what I've heard, Theia, Daphne, and Penelope consider you their sister. And from where I'm standing, you could use them right about now. Talk to Theia. She—"

"I don't care about any of them. They're not my family. I just want what is owed to me."

"Be careful. You're beginning to sound like your father, and look where that got him."

Caine went to move away, and Clio grabbed his arm. He looked down at her fingers clutching the black leather and raised an eyebrow.

She dropped her hand, the look in her eyes suggesting she had seen the other side of Caine. "I have the book. Colleen's memoir, *The Secret Keeper of Harmony Harbor.*" When he didn't immediately respond, she said, "I'll sell it to you."

Colleen didn't know when she'd ever been more disappointed in one of her great-grandchildren. "Caine's right. You're just like your father, taking what isn't yours for ill-gotten gains."

"How much?" Caine asked, stealing what little hope Colleen had that he'd tell the child to give the book to the family. Then Colleen remembered that he was family too. Only he had an ax to grind. She supposed in Clio's mind, she did too.

"A million dollars," the child demanded.

Caine laughed and turned to walk away.

"A hundred thousand, and I won't go lower than that. I know what you were willing to pay for the shares in the estate. I know what it's worth to you."

"I'd have to authenticate the book before I gave you the money. I need proof it's real."

"I was unable to locate the problem..." Jasper looked from Clio to Caine. "Am I interrupting something?"

"Not at all. It was nice to meet you, Clio. I'm sure I'll see you again, Jasper."

* * *

As he headed for his car in the manor's parking lot, Caine returned his uncle's call. He noted Theia wasn't back from her fitting for her wedding dress, which was good. He didn't relish the idea of running into her right now. Not with Colleen's memoir within his grasp. Theia would know something was up and not give in until he told her. There was a time when he could have shared this with her, but not anymore.

"Uncle Seamus, what's the emergency this time?" Caine had to raise his voice to make himself heard over the bitter, salt-tinged breeze coming off the ocean. Tiny pellets of ice water stung his cheeks, and the wind whipped his hair from his face. "Hang on a minute," he said, unable to hear anything but a muffled voice on the other end. Caine beeped the lock on his fob and opened the car door, sliding inside.

"Okay. What's going on?" He frowned at the silence. Seamus must have hung up.

Caine wasn't worried the emergency was something serious, like a fire at Holiday House. The electrician had called him with his findings last night, and he and his team of three were back at the house today. They'd be finished with the job tonight. Caine refused to pay for a complete electrical overhaul on a building that would be bulldozed to the ground in a matter of weeks.

He had a feeling his uncle's emergency had to do with Evangeline's mother. Seamus had been calling to complain about Lenore from the moment he'd picked her up at the train station. As Caine had learned earlier today, Lenore wasn't an easy woman, but he did admire her work ethic. Since he hadn't cleared access to the

manor's books, she'd insisted Caine pick her up at the
manor this morning and deliver her to Holiday House
at eight a.m. sharp, which he'd done.

He'd dropped her off at the front door and then
headed for the hotel he owned in Bridgeport, only to
turn around on the highway when he received a call
from Jasper, demanding he return to the manor to deal
with an issue with the mold-inspection crew.

It turned out to be a more productive meeting than he
had hoped for thanks to Clio Gallagher. He'd bide his
time, let her sweat a bit, and reach out to her in a day
or two. She knew he was her best bet. But he wouldn't
be paying a hundred thousand dollars for Colleen Gallagher's memoir. And once he read it, he'd give it to
Theia as an early wedding gift.

Now, with everything resolved in Harmony Harbor,
Caine could return to the suite he was working out of
in Bridgeport. His staff had begun the onerous job of
packing up the offices in Boston to move into the rented
space nearby. Hardly the ideal solution to the problem
created by Evangeline's delay tactics.

If it hadn't been for her, they would have been
packing for their move to Harmony Harbor. Caine had
received an offer for his building in Boston early last
year, an offer that had been too good to refuse. He
would have had he known just how difficult Evangeline
would make his life.

Now she was doing it again. His appointment with
his wish family was at seven this evening. As soon as
Evangeline had relayed the information to him yesterday, he'd left Holiday House for his hotel. He didn't

wait for the electrician or for Seamus to return from the train station. He'd been too furious to stick around.

He'd been played, and he resented it. He resented Evangeline digging into his past. Just as he resented the part his uncle had played. Evangeline wouldn't have found the information from simply Googling him. His grandmother had buried his past as easily as she'd cut ties with his family.

Caine's phone rang, and he pressed the dashboard screen. "Okay, Uncle, what's the problem now?"

"It's not your uncle. It's me, Evangeline."

It surprised him to hear her voice coming through the speakers. A sweet voice that wrapped around him, reminding him of the moments he'd spent with her in the attic yesterday and the bathroom the night before. *Warm* and *soft* were the words that came to mind to describe her in those brief intimate moments they had shared. At the flicker of need and want he felt building inside him, he replaced *warm* and *soft* with *cold* and *hard*. Words that better described the stubborn woman he'd dealt with on an almost weekly basis this past year.

"I told you I'd be there at seven, and I will, Evangeline," he said as he drove under the manor's stone arch.

"There's a problem. The principal called. Jamie was in a fight at school, and she's threatening to expel him for the rest of the school year. I need you to come with me to talk to her."

"And why would I do that? My angel assignment is to find the boy a mentor, not to become one."

"I know, but these are extenuating circumstances. Please, Caine, you out of anyone know what—"

"Don't try to use my past against me, Evangeline. It won't work. The boy lost his father; I lost mine. So what? It happens all the time. If the principal believes he should be expelled, then he probably should. You're not doing the kid any favors by coddling him."

"He's acting out because he's angry and he's in pain. In an instant his world was turned upside down, Caine. He lost the father he adored, the house he grew up in, and his mother is working three jobs to keep a roof over their heads and food on the table."

His grip on the steering wheel tightened, his finger hovering over the button to end the call, to stop the words that recalled a past almost identical to his own. "I'll write the mother a check for fifty thousand. That should be enough to take care of their rent and expenses until they get back on their feet. The boy can work. He's old enough to help out his mother." It would be money well spent. Each week of delay to the office tower development cost more than that. "Now, I have a conference call I can't miss, but I'll stop by this evening to pick my second angel-wish assignment."

"Are you really so hard-hearted that Jamie's plight doesn't affect you?"

"Did you miss the part where I said I'd write the family a check?"

"Money can't solve everything! You can't just buy people off and get what you want."

And there was the woman he was used to dealing with. She'd said the last through gritted teeth. He was sure of it. She'd wear them down to the gum if her angel assignments took him longer than a few days. "In my experience, money does solve everything. It certainly would have solved some of your problems, wouldn't you agree?"

"No, I wouldn't. But what—"

"So you're telling me that having enough money to offset your less-than-stellar sales this past summer wouldn't have been helpful? You can't tell me that Lenore hasn't exacted a pound of flesh over the loan you had to ask for and will probably continue to do so."

It sounded like she'd had to stifle a snort of agreement before she ground out, "My sales were fine. It was damage from the hurricane that caused my cash shortfall."

"Because you were unable to afford insurance that included coverage for—"

"This isn't about me! This is about you. And just FYI, you cannot buy your way out of our bet. Jamie's mom didn't ask that her rent and bills be paid. She asked for a mentor for her son. Someone who will fill the role of an uncle or big brother."

"All right. I'll find him a mentor." Surely there was someone in this town who would take the boy under his wing. "What time is the meeting with the principal?"

"In twenty minutes." She gave him the address of the school. "Please don't be late. The principal is a stickler," she said. Then, after a brief pause, "Thank you. I know how busy you must be, and I appreciate you taking the time to come with me."

"You're welcome. I'll see you at the school." He turned the steering wheel toward town instead of the highway, deciding to head directly to the school. He'd sit in the parking lot and get some work done while he waited for Evangeline to arrive. He plugged the address into his GPS and turned onto Main Street.

Outside the hardware store, Mr. O'Malley adjusted the wreath in his window. The older man looked up and, upon seeing Caine driving by, flagged him down.

He slowed to a crawl and lowered his window. "Hello, Mr. O'Malley. What can I do for you?" Caine glanced in the rearview mirror. Seeing several cars coming up behind him, he pulled to the side of the road.

"Nothing. Just wanted to congratulate you on a job well done yesterday, son," Mr. O'Malley called out when the last car had gone by.

"I can't take credit. It was all Bruiser's doing. So thanks for that."

"Anything for Evie."

Caine cast the older man a speculative glance. He seemed spry and certainly had his wits about him, and while he'd been kind and helpful, he was clearly no pushover. "Mr. O'Malley, do you have children of your own?"

"I do. I have two boys and five grandsons. Why do you ask?"

He'd found his perfect candidate. And if Mr. O'Malley wasn't up for the job, maybe one of his sons or grandsons would be. "I was wondering if you'd be interested in mentoring a thirteen-year-old boy? Becoming a surrogate grandfather, if you will. It wouldn't be more than a few afternoons a week. He could help you around the store."

"The lad in question, he wouldn't happen to be young Jamie, your first angel assignment, would he?"

Bollocks. "Let me guess. Everyone in town knows about Jamie, and Evangeline has warned all of you not to help me." He'd badly underestimated the woman.

"No. Small town. Jamie's mother works weekends at the flower shop with my son's girlfriend. As to helping you, the ones supporting Evie won't; the ones supporting you will. But I'm a good judge of character, and I think you're just what the boy needs in his life."

"That's just it, Mr. O'Malley. I'm only here for a short time."

"I can't tell you how often I've heard that. Give us some time—we'll grow on you." He doffed his Santa hat at an older woman and held open the door to his shop, giving Caine a wink as he followed the woman inside and saying, "Top of the morning to you, my lady. May I say you're looking particularly lovely today."

"Best-laid plans," Caine muttered, about to pull away from the sidewalk when he was flagged down by Theia. She was with her grandmother-in-law-to-be, Rosa DiRossi.

The curse of small towns, he thought as he lowered the passenger-side window. Theia stuck her head inside, and Rosa joined her.

"Hello, ladies. How did the fitting go?" He still couldn't believe Theia was going through with a traditional wedding.

She lifted a shoulder. "Good."

"Good? She looked beautiful. Now, when are you coming for your fitting?"

He looked from Rosa to Theia. "I agreed to be your man of honor. I didn't agree to wear a dress."

Rosa reached in to swat his arm. "*Stupido*. You don't wear a dress. You wear a tux. Like Marco and his groomsmen. They rent them from Merci Beaucoup."

"Okay. I'll stop by later and make an appointment," he said, despite owning three tuxes of his own. "When are Marco and his groomsmen going for their fitting?" He might get lucky and find a mentor in the group.

"This weekend," Theia said, then added, "But if you're thinking of tagging along just to hit one of them up to be Jamie's mentor, forget about it."

"Is there one person in this bloody town who doesn't know my business?"

The two women looked at each other and grinned. "No."

From across the road, he heard Mr. O'Malley calling his name. He turned to see the older man waving at him and pointing to a dark-haired woman shivering on the sidewalk. She wore some kind of uniform, and whatever Mr. O'Malley said to her had the woman turning Caine's way, a hand pressed to her mouth. Then, without any concern for her own safety, she ran across the street to his car. He knew without anyone telling him who the woman was. He'd seen the mark grief and hopelessness left on a woman's face, a mother's face, before. And now he saw a desperate hope shining in the woman's eyes, and that hope was directed at him.

"Caine, lower the driver-side window. It's Jamie's mother. Mrs. Murphy," Theia said before pulling her head from the passenger-side window to smile and greet the woman.

Like bloody hell he'd open the window. He wasn't

being dragged into this family's drama. Evangeline Christmas was not using her psych degree and her angel wish to make him confront his past.

With his hands wrapped around the steering wheel, he stared straight ahead. "I have to go."

Theia stuck her head back inside. "If you don't lower your window right now, you and I are done. Because the man I know and love would not turn his back on that woman and her son."

Chapter Twelve

♥

The clock loudly ticked down the seconds on the wall behind the principal as Evie sat perched on a chair across from the woman. Principal Wright was a study in gray today. Her steel-colored blazer matched her hair, glasses, and demeanor.

"I'm sure Mr. Elliot will be here any minute." The need-to-please tone in Evie's voice made her cringe. She didn't know how Principal Wright did it, but she made her feel like a teenager who'd been caught smoking in the girls' washroom every single time she was called to the woman's office. Which happened on an almost-twice-weekly basis as the principal was hands-down the biggest proponent of Evie's after-school program.

Within weeks of moving to Harmony Harbor, Evie had begun volunteering at the community center. As much as she loved Holiday House, she'd missed her job at the hospital. At least aspects of her job.

After what had happened with Aaron, she saw a monster in the eyes of every patient on the psychiatric ward. During her first week back to work, something as simple as a loud noise or a patient's abrupt movement triggered a memory and a panic attack. She didn't blame the hospital administrator for suggesting she take a leave of absence. She wasn't doing her patients or herself any good. The first place that had come to mind when Evie had thought of healing was Holiday House, and she'd known she wouldn't leave once she got here.

The families she counseled at the community center didn't trigger her PTSD. She found the work emotionally fulfilling and satisfying. It helped fill the void. But more importantly, the programs she'd introduced were making a difference for families in Harmony Harbor. Evie had met Jamie through her after-school program.

Principal Wright had recommended that Mrs. Murphy sign him up for the program after his first schoolyard fight. The principal was responsible for at least half the participants in the program. Which was why Evie ended up in her office so often; the only students Principal Wright sent to her were the ones she'd labeled problem children. One day Evie vowed to work up the courage to tell the stern-faced woman that the children were simply living up to her expectations.

At the sound of Principal Wright impatiently clicking her pen, Evie silently cursed Caine for putting her in the woman's bad book. It was not a pleasant place to be. Not to mention putting her in the position of having to lie to defend him. She didn't know why she'd trusted him to be here. "Mr. Elliot had a conference call he couldn't reschedule, but he promised to be here as soon as he can."

Evie forced a smile and pushed her glasses up her

nose with her forefinger. She didn't need them to see. She'd had laser surgery a month before moving to Harmony Harbor. But weirdly, the glasses made her feel more professional and in control. A little more like the woman she was before Aaron. She used to put them on whenever she spoke to Caine on the phone.

"Mr. Elliot is not the only one with a busy schedule, Ms. Christmas. If he isn't here within—" The woman pursed her lips at the decisive knock on her office door. "Come in."

"Sorry I'm late, Principal Wright," Caine said, shutting the door behind him. He glanced at Evie, did a double take, then said, "Evangeline."

He reached across the desk to shake the principal's hand before taking a seat beside Evie. Or tried to, she thought, pressing her lips together when he stood to remove his coat. She doubted it would help. The man was too big for the chair. Still, he managed to get himself situated after several tries. But no matter how awkward he looked with his knees practically to his chest, he took control of the room without trying.

Evie could feel the subtle shift in Principal Wright. The older woman's rigid posture softened ever so slightly, her features no longer pinched as she reacted to the power and confidence the man exuded.

Or perhaps, like Evie, Principal Wright was reacting to the man and not the aura of power and confidence. Because there was no denying Caine Elliot was a sight to behold with his wind-tousled ebony hair curling at the collar of the pristine white shirt he wore beneath his expensive black suit, a touch of scruff shadowing his strong jaw, and those brilliant blue eyes alert and assessing.

Caine smiled as he withdrew a pen from inside his jacket. "Are there any papers you need me to sign? Jamie's mother said she'd call ahead to ask that I be added as his secondary emergency contact as well as granting permission for you to share information about his grades and such. I'm assuming you've heard from her?" He clicked his pen.

Evie's jaw dropped as it became clear why Caine had been five minutes late for their meeting.

And from the way Principal Wright's narrowed gaze moved from Caine to Evie, the older woman believed they'd tag-teamed her. This was not going to end well for any of them, most especially Jamie.

What were you thinking bringing a shark into a pool of guppies? she inwardly berated herself.

Principal Wright planted her hands on the desk—she had incredibly big hands for a woman of average height, Evie thought inanely as her nerves got the better of her. The principal's chair scraped across the floor like nails on a chalkboard when she rose to her feet. Now looking down her nose at them, the older woman appeared taller than usual and Evie resisted the urge to peek under the desk to see if she was standing on the tips of her toes.

"I'll need to have my assistant verify your claims, Mr. Elliot. But even if Mrs. Murphy has authorized you to become a guardian of a sort to Jamie, it has no bearing on my decision as to whether or not the boy will be expelled." She walked around her desk and headed for the door. "I am well aware of who you are, Mr. Elliot. And I highly doubt your schedule will allow you to make Jamie a priority, as you have already proven today." With that, she opened the door, then firmly closed it behind her.

Caine stood and stretched. "I wonder if she'd notice if I traded chairs with her," he said, and walked around the desk.

"What do you think you're doing?" Evie cried when he sat in the principal's chair. "Get out of there right now!"

"I'm used to being on this side of the negotiating table. I have to say I prefer it." He angled his head to study her as he swiveled back and forth in the chair as though he didn't have a care in the world. "This is the first time I've seen you wear glasses. They give you a certain gravitas." A slow smile spread across his face. "You don't need them, do you?"

Heat crawled up her cheeks not only because she was embarrassed he saw through her so easily, but because he obviously didn't take this seriously. "I don't know why I asked you to come. You've made it worse by being late and then coming in here acting like you own the world. You don't care that your arrogant disregard of other people's feelings may cost Jamie his year. Now get out of her chair before Principal Wright sees you and throws us out."

His expression hardened, a glint of fire in those cool blue eyes. She would have sworn he was furious with her if not for the smile that curved his lips seconds later. But at the next words out of his mouth, she realized she should have looked closer at his smile.

"It'll be at least another five minutes before she comes back. It's a negotiating tactic. She's trying to regain control of the situation. I've dealt with her type before." He rose from the chair. "She knows she intimidates you. She's hoping you'll be able to keep me in line." He placed his palms on the desk as the principal had done moments before and leaned toward her. "Don't make the same mistake, Evangeline."

"I don't know what you're talking about." She leaned back in the chair.

His eyes moved over her, and he gave his head a slight shake. Then he straightened and came around the desk, taking the chair beside her. "Why do you let her intimidate you? Do you believe Jamie deserves to be expelled?"

She was glad he asked her a second question because she didn't want to answer the first. She wasn't sure she knew the answer herself. "Of course I don't think he should be expelled. I wouldn't be here defending him if I did. Principal Wright believes that the only way to get through to Jamie is to show him the error of his ways and make him suffer the consequences. But all expelling him from school will do is guarantee the small improvements we've seen these last few months will be wiped out. It will only serve to deepen his pain and anger, not weaken their hold on him."

"So tell her that, and if she doesn't listen, tell her you'll go before the board." He pulled out his phone, typed something with his thumbs faster than she'd seen anyone type before, and then she heard the *ping* of an e-mail coming from her purse. "It's the contact information for each member of the board."

"I can't do that, Caine." Before she had a chance to react, he took her glasses. "Give me those." She reached for them, but he raised his right hand to block hers while he held her glasses to his eyes and then lowered them to look at her.

"You don't need fake glasses to appear older and wiser and in control of the situation, or whatever it was you were going for. Don't you see? You intimidate her. She hears what the parents of the kids in your program are saying. You've made a difference with their children. They love you and so do the kids. But aside from that, you have a doctorate in psychology, Evangeline. You know what you're talking about."

She stared at him, taken aback by what sounded like praise and admiration. She let his words sink in, and just for a minute, she let herself believe they were true. It was a nice feeling to have someone as confident in her abilities as Caine seemed to be. But if he knew about Aaron, he would doubt her as much as the hospital administrator, as much as her mother, as much as she herself did.

"Thank you." She reached for her glasses, relieved when he let them go. "But I highly doubt I intimidate Principal Wright. She's been principal here for twenty-five years and is well respected."

"So are you." He linked his fingers and stretched his arms over his head, glancing at her as he did. "You do know she's using you as a de facto guidance counselor to replace the one who quit last year?"

"No," she said, shocked that he'd even suggest such a thing. Yet at the same time wondering how on earth he'd learned so much in such a short time.

"Yes. You're helping her to stay under budget, and no one is complaining because you're doing more for their kids than the counselor ever did."

The door to the office opened, and Caine subtly moved the cuff of his jacket to show Evie his Rolex. He tapped the face. "I was off by twenty-five seconds," he whispered, then offered Principal Wright a smile. "Everything in order?" he asked as he withdrew his pen from the inside of his jacket and clicked it several annoying times.

Evie looked from the pen to him. At first she'd thought he and Principal Wright shared an irritating quirk, but now she had a sneaking suspicion Caine knew about the principal's habit and this was another of his tactics. When he caught Evie looking at him and winked, she knew she was right.

"If you mean did we receive Mrs. Murphy's request? We did." Principal Wright went to take her seat, glanced at her desk, then raised her gaze to Caine.

Evie looked at him too. For whatever reason, he'd wanted the principal to know he'd sat at her desk and had left some small sign to ensure that she did. And for some reason, Evie found that incredibly hot, even though she should probably find it more alarming than sexy.

"Why don't we just put all the cards on the table, Principal Wright? I'm a busy man and you're a busy woman, and I can tell you like games about as much as I do. So, have you made a decision on Jamie's expulsion?"

"Yes. I have."

"Without speaking to Ms. Christmas? Wasn't that the reason you wanted to meet with her today? To get her take on the situation? Which, as you well know, she's remarkably qualified to give, not only because of the amount of time she spends with Jamie but because of her credentials."

With each word out of Caine's mouth, Evie sank lower in the chair. If he didn't soon shut up, she'd slide off and onto the floor. She must have lost her mind to think this was a good idea. It was her mother's fault. When Lenore wasn't ordering Seamus around this morning, she was following Evie, pointing out everything that was wrong with Holiday House.

So when the school called, Evie's confidence was at a new low, and she couldn't face the thought of dealing with Principal Wright on her own. Thinking about it now, the fact Caine was the first person she thought of should have her reevaluating her sanity. The man was her enemy, the bogeyman in her dreams, yet she was acting as if he were her knight in shining armor, her champion.

He was so not her champion in black Armani, she thought when Principal Wright turned her steely gaze on Evie and said, "By all means, Dr. Christmas, please share your expert opinion on the matter with me."

Not once had the principal ever called her *Dr. Christmas* or asked for Evie's opinion in their meetings these past ten months, so Evie knew this was for Caine's benefit alone. Just like she was positive the woman would make Evie feel as qualified as an undergrad offering an opinion to the head of the department, slaying what little confidence she had left with an eviscerating rebuttal. But just as Evie considered caving, she felt the weight of Caine's gaze and glanced at him. He smiled and minutely nudged his head in the principal's direction.

Evie looked down at the papers on her lap. They were her notes on Jamie. She stood and offered them to the principal, surprised when she took them, as she'd never done so before. "As you can see, Principal Wright, there's been a noted improvement in Jamie's ability to manage his anger, his willingness to open up and to interact with the other children in the program. His mother and his teachers have all noticed a marked improvement in his behavior, as mentioned in their weekly feedback. If Jamie is expelled, my concern is that all of our efforts will have been for naught, and he'll become more difficult to reach. There's also the question as to whether he will lose his year and be held back, which in my opinion would be the worst-case scenario."

The principal looked up from the reports to raise a quelling eyebrow. "Is that so?"

Evie felt the weight of Caine's gaze, offering his silent support, she suspected. It was pathetic she needed it. There should be no question in Principal Wright's mind that holding Jamie back would be a mistake. He might be having difficulty with some of his peers, but he'd grown up with these kids, and several of them had stuck by him even when he made it difficult for them to do so. He was also big for his age, and smart.

"It is, and I'm sure you'll find that Jamie's teachers agree with me."

Principal Wright pushed the papers aside, and Evie's

shoulders sagged. Challenging the woman had been the wrong tactic. She shouldn't have let Caine's confidence in her go to her head.

"I'm afraid I disagree. And while I don't have a doctorate in psychology, I have been principal here for twenty-five years. I even taught two of the teachers whose opinion you seem to value more than mine. But while you might question my judgment, I'm confident in my decision to expel Jamie."

"I'm not. Not at all. And I'm going to send a written request to the superintendent of the board to look into the matter," Evie said, shocking not only herself but Principal Wright.

"Pardon me?"

As though he didn't hear the principal, Caine smiled at Evie and said, "You could always ask your friend the mayor to speak to him."

"If you think you're going to blackmail me into changing my mind, you have another think coming. And while you might be friends with the mayor, Ms. Christmas, I have been a friend of the superintendent for years. And I can tell you that he's never sided with a complainant against me in twenty-five years."

She was sunk, and she'd brought Jamie down with her. "I'm sorry, Principal Wright. I shouldn't have threatened to contact the—"

"Evangeline, would you mind if I had a word with Principal Wright? Alone," Caine added when she nodded but didn't move.

"Oh. Okay." She stood to gather her things and then said to Principal Wright, "I'll need my files."

Caine stood and walked to the door, holding it open for her. "I'll bring them with me when I leave."

"Don't say anything to make it worse," Evie murmured as she brushed past him, but he probably didn't hear her because he was already closing the door behind her.

She took a seat outside the principal's office, trying to hear what was going on inside. Caine seemed to be doing most of the talking. She hoped he'd figured out a way to get Principal Wright to relent on the expulsion. Evie had been going to suggest a five-day suspension as a compromise before Caine had high-handedly kicked her out of the meeting. A meeting she'd been invited to. She'd barely had time to contemplate next steps when the office door opened.

"Once you've completed your list and have an amount, e-mail it to me and I'll have it taken care of," Caine said, offering his hand.

"It was a pleasure doing business with you, Mr. Elliot." Principal Wright shook his hand. "I'll have Jamie brought to my office, and you can take him with you. I expect a letter of apology to both myself and the student when Jamie returns to school tomorrow morning, along with a list of tasks he will perform over the next month that both benefit the school and meet with my approval."

"Agreed."

"I don't believe this. You bribed her!" Evie whisper-yelled when the principal closed the door.

Caine shrugged as he put on a wool coat that probably cost more than her entire inventory combined. "You either want the boy expelled or you don't."

"Of course I don't want Jamie expelled, but I don't want you to pay—"

"The sooner you accept that you don't get anywhere in this world without money, the better off you'll be, Evangeline."

Chapter Thirteen

♥

Evangeline turned her nose up at what Caine felt was the best advice he could give the woman. He didn't understand why she was mad at him. She'd gotten what she wanted: The boy was getting a second chance. Principal Wright got what she wanted: repairs and upgrades to the school that she never had the budget for. And Caine had gotten what he wanted: his grandmother's name on the library.

Which he hoped would go a ways in assuaging Emily's need for revenge, as the library had been dedicated to Colleen Gallagher twenty years before. He'd needed to give his grandmother something. There'd been an uptick in her texts this morning. He'd be able to hold her off for only so long.

"All right, then. I'll see you around seven to pick up my second angel assignment," Caine said, adjusting the collar of his coat before heading for the door.

Evangeline latched on to his arm. "Hold it. Where do you think you're going? You're not done with your first angel assignment."

"Where I'm going is to try to run a billion-dollar corporation out of a hotel suite."

"If you're running it out of a hotel room, then it shouldn't be too difficult to run it out of Holiday House."

"And why would I do that?"

"Because until Jamie...You remember him, don't you? Your first angel assignment? The one you haven't completed yet."

"I haven't completed it? I've more than completed my assignment. I didn't just find the boy a mentor; I became his mentor. I had to give so much personal and private information that I'm surprised Principal Wright didn't ask for my blood before I signed the papers. I'll be updated regularly on the boy's academic performance until he's eighteen."

She didn't bat an eye. Between the black-framed glasses and the knot she'd twisted in her dark hair, she looked like an uptight professor. And why that made him want to back her against the wall and kiss her until her glasses fogged and her long, silky locks escaped from the knot to fall about her shoulders, he didn't have a clue.

"Eighteen," he repeated. His voice held the heat of the image he was having a difficult time erasing, coming out more sensuous rasp than angry snap.

"So, that's how you think it works? Hand over some cash and sign a few papers and the deal is done?" She stepped into his space and inched up on her toes. "That may be how it's done in your world, Mr. Elliot. But it's not how it's done in mine."

Wrapping his hands around her biceps to lift her off her feet, bringing them eye-to-eye, nose-to-nose, mouth-to-mouth, he said, "Be careful, Ms. Christmas. You know what they say about playing with fire."

"Are you the fire?" Her voice was soft and sexy, and she sounded interested, which was exactly the opposite of what he'd intended. He'd wanted to scare her away. The heat between them was dangerous. This was dangerous, he thought as he bent his head to kiss her.

"Evie, is everything okay?"

At the sound of a young male voice that cracked on the last word, Caine immediately let Evangeline go, reaching out to steady her when she stumbled. The flush on her cheeks deepened, and hazel eyes that only seconds ago had gazed up at him as if he were a present she wanted to unwrap now looked at him like she wanted to give him back and demand twice the amount she'd paid.

Caine wasn't angry at her or at himself, though he knew he should be. He was angry at the boy who'd interrupted him before he'd gotten one small taste of Evangeline.

She turned away from him to go to the boy. "Yes. Everything's okay, Jamie."

Caine had known the kid was going to cause him no end of trouble from the second his mother slid into the passenger seat of his car and cried her heart out on his shoulder while Theia and Rosa DiRossi looked on. Still, until his very moment, he'd had no idea how bad it might get.

The boy was tall for his age, lanky and lean, just like

Caine had been at thirteen. But it was the emotion in his eyes, the grief he couldn't hide behind the defiant tilt of his chin, and the angry fists balled at his sides that reminded Caine most of the boy he used to be. A boy who'd spent the first month in his grandmother's house muffling his cries in his pillow, grieving for his father, his mother, his uncle, and his dog.

Caine wanted to cross the small space, grab the boy by his narrow shoulders, and shake him. He'd lost his father, and for that he had Caine's sympathy. But the boy had no bloody idea how good he had it. He had a mother who loved him, who was working her fingers to the bone to keep a roof over his head and food in his belly. And he had Evangeline and half the town doing what they could to help. Caine didn't know who he was angrier at, Evangeline or the boy for making him remember.

"Are you okay, Jamie?" she asked, gently brushing back a lock of dark hair to reveal a shiner.

Caine noted the boy's cut and swollen upper lip when he curled it in response to Evie's question. The kid pushed her hand away, not roughly or Caine would have intervened. Jamie had brushed it aside like a boy who no longer wanted to be touched or coddled in case those who offered the kindness were taken away from him too.

Evangeline had been right. The worst thing for Jamie would have been being expelled. He would have taken it as proof that he didn't deserve any of this, that the familiar and good could be taken from him in the blink of an eye. That if he broke the rules and acted out, they'd toss him away. The hurt was on his terms then. They hadn't abandoned him if he pushed them away first. He'd build another wall inside himself, strong enough to keep the pain from touching the soft parts of him that he didn't want.

"Don't coddle him, Evangeline. He's fine." Caine nudged her aside to offer Jamie his hand. "Caine Elliot. Your mother and Evangeline have decided you need a mentor, and I'm it." Once again the boy curled his upper lip without allowing the pain to show on his face.

"You may want to come up with another way to show your contempt," Caine suggested. He'd once been the master of the contemptuous sneer. He curled his own upper lip and touched it. "At least until the cut heals. And so you know, I'm about as happy with the arrangement as you are. Now, if you've got your things, we'll be on our way. You're sprung for the rest of the day. But by the time I'm done with you, you'll be wishing you kissed the boy instead of punching him."

The boy and the woman stared at him. Evangeline recovered first. "Jamie, wait here a moment. Caine, I'd like to speak with you. Alone."

"No. The time for talk is over. Unless you don't want me to mentor him? I didn't think so," he said when she looked from him to the boy and nibbled on her pouty bottom lip. "Come with me, Jamie. We'll meet you at Holiday House, Evangeline."

"If you don't mind, I could use a ride. I walked here."

"What do you mean you walked? It's got to be at least a twenty-minute walk from Holiday House, and the temperature is dipping well below balmy."

"Thank you for the weather report. I'm well aware how cold it is, as I'm the one who had to walk the twenty-five minutes to get here. Because I'm the one who had to sell my car to keep my business afloat."

"I suppose you're going to blame me for that too, aren't you?" Caine said, taking a step to close the distance between them.

The boy moved in front of Evangeline and lifted his chin, puffing up his scrawny chest.

Caine smiled. "There may be hope for you after all."

*　*　*

Three hours later, Caine stood on Evangeline's back porch with his uncle. "There's no hope for the boy. He's a surly, argumentative pain in the arse."

"Aye, he reminds me of you." Seamus's smile didn't reach his eyes. His uncle had spent part of the morning trying to win over the boy while spending the other half looking like he was about to cry.

"Don't get maudlin on me, Uncle. The past is in the past. I think you'll agree I turned out all right."

"If you're talking about living the life of Riley, I'll give you that. But you're missing all that's real and good, boyo. The parts that will bring you true joy. Like a woman, a family."

"I have you, Emily—" He held up his hand. "Don't say anything against the woman who raised me. I have Theia too. As for women, I make out well often."

"Aye, and making out is all you do. You need someone who loves you enough to stick by you through the good times and bad. Mark my words, the women you *date* would be out the door should your star start to fall."

"No chance of that happening. Besides, I'm happy with the status quo," he said, even though his uncle's prediction hit a little too close to home. His grandmother's threat had taken up residence in the back of Caine's mind. He'd texted her the news about the library being named after her. She'd yet to respond, which was unusual. He pulled his phone from his pocket and sent a text to her nurse. He'd hired the woman when Emily had refused to move in with him.

Her nurse, Mrs. Jordan, responded right away, as he'd paid her to do, though he would have preferred anything to the text he received.

Everything is fine, sir. She's just having a visit with her nephew. Alec McCleary.

"Is everything okay, lad?"

Obviously Caine's ability to keep his emotions from showing had slipped. "It's fine. I'm just trying to figure out how I'm supposed to stay on top of Jamie when I have a company to run."

"I suppose you wouldn't appreciate me repeating Evie's words back to you, then?"

"That parents all over the world do it every day? No. I wouldn't. Even though you just did in that sly way of yours."

"You can't blame the lass. She doesn't know what you're up against with the Wicked Witch. Oh, go on with your castigating looks. I can say what I please about her. She has to be wicked to expect her grandson to seek revenge on his father's family, threatening to steal the company away from you if you don't do her bidding. Your da was a good man, one of my best friends, and I tell you straight, Caine, he wouldn't want you to do this."

"So you've been telling me since you listened in on my conversation with her."

"Someone has to protect you from selling your soul to the devil on her account."

Caine's phone *ping*ed several times with incoming text messages. He glanced at the screen. They were all from his grandmother. Alec must have left. At least Caine hoped he had and wasn't reading the texts over her shoulder—or worse, dictating them to her.

She was pleased the library was being renamed after her. She only wished she had the honor of ripping Colleen Gallagher's plaque from the library wall herself. She immediately followed that text with one demanding an update on his strategy to wrest the manor from the Gallaghers. Followed by a threat.

"Give me that phone, and I'll give her a piece of my mind. You can't let her get away with this, lad. You can't let her force you to turn on your own family. I've been here long enough to have heard talk of the Gallaghers. And what I've heard leads me to believe that whatever she told you and Killian to turn you against them is a lie."

Theia had said as much to Caine over the past year, so it wasn't as if he hadn't had some doubts of his own. "I'll know the truth soon enough, or at least a portion of it." He told Seamus about Colleen Gallagher's memoir and Clio's offer. "But in the end, I'm doing them a favor, just like I'm doing Evangeline a favor. Neither the manor nor Holiday House are worth saving. They're not only money pits—they're death traps."

"You know it wasn't the house that killed your da, don't you? It was his weak lungs."

"He was dirt poor—that's what killed him, Uncle. Too poor to get the medical attention he needed. Too poor to fix the house, to put nourishing food in his belly, to allow him to take time off work."

"We were poor, and we didn't die. We were happy too. Don't let the bad times color all your memories. There were plenty of good ones. Your mam and da—"

Caine raised his hand. "I can't do this now. I have to get through to the boy. Get him to see that he's standing in his own way. He's also standing in mine. I need him to write the letter and a list of actionable steps to get back in the principal's and his classmates' good graces."

His uncle gave him a disappointed look.

"Just because I'm looking out for myself doesn't mean Jamie doesn't benefit. I'll honor my word and keep him on the straight and narrow. I've also taken care of their rent for the next two years and made a deal with Rosa DiRossi to provide them with meals three times a week."

"I think you're missing the point, but I canna say I'm surprised. Let me help with the boy. It'll be like helping you. I should have been there for you, Caine. Not drowning my sorrows in a bottle of Jameson when

we lost Killian. You needed me, and so did my sister. If
I had been a better man, she wouldn't have—"

"Don't. Don't go there, Uncle," Caine said, then
opened the back door to the kitchen.

The sight of Jamie on the floor with the dog, his face
buried in Max's fur, threw Caine back into a past he'd
blocked for the last twenty-five years. He saw himself
walking into the living room on Christmas morning. He
and his mother had found a tree someone had tossed and
brought it home, using whatever they could find in the
house to decorate. They'd glued some glittery pieces
from an old party dress of his mam's to his uncle's and
his da's work socks, using them for stockings.

He'd known there'd not be much under the tree, so
the big wrapped box had taken him by surprise. He'd
tried to hold back tears when he'd gotten his first look
at Max, but lost the battle when the dog licked his face
and snuggled against him all warm and soft. His uncle
and da hadn't given him the gears about his tears, but
they'd teased his mother when she joined him on the
floor and did the same. But soon they were laughing,
the four of them on the floor playing with the dog.

Seamus was right. They'd been happy once. All of them
together, a ragtag bunch, living in a run-down house.

But no sooner had he had the thought than the image
of him with his dog on Christmas morning morphed
to him sitting on a faded linoleum floor with his tear-
streaked face buried in his dog's fur on the day his
father died. Nothing—not money, not his mother, not
his uncle—had offered him the level of comfort that
Max had that day.

Chapter Fourteen

♥

If you'll sit at that kitchen table now and stop giving me such a bloody hard time about writing your apology to Principal Wright, you can have the dog."

Evie stopped at the entrance to her kitchen to stare at Caine, who stood beside the kitchen table, his attention now captured by his phone. There was no way he'd said what she thought he had. She must have misheard him. No one in their right mind would give away someone else's pet.

"You'll give me Max?" Jamie's face lit up, and she blinked at the transformation from surly man-child to excited boy.

She didn't want to burst his bubble, but someone needed to correct his assumption, and obviously it had to be her because Caine was typing in that annoying speed-of-light way he had.

"I think what Caine meant was…" She trailed off. The idea that he'd bribed Jamie to get him to do what Jamie should be doing anyway because it kept him from being expelled was as outrageous as the idea that Caine would give her dog away.

"I will. Just get up to the table and do your assignment," Caine said to Jamie, and then went back to working his phone without so much as a glance her way. It was as if she hadn't said a word. No, it was as though he didn't care that she did.

She walked over and took his phone.

He looked from his empty hand to her. "What do you think you're doing? I'm in the middle of keeping a deal from going off the rails."

"There's a more important deal right in this kitchen that is about to go off a cliff, so your other deal can wait. Jamie, I expect you to have your letter of apology to Principal Wright and your class completed by the time I've finished speaking to Caine."

Jamie's eyes went wide. "But, Evie, I haven't even started it."

"And who's fault is that, Jamie?" His mentor's, she answered for him in her head. "But don't worry—you'll have plenty of time. My conversation with Caine will not be a short one." She nudged her head toward the hall in a *follow me* gesture to the man standing staring at her with his hands on his hips.

"Well, *Caine* has quite a bit to say to the person awaiting his response. So will you give me back my phone before you blow my deal?"

"No," she said, and walked out of the kitchen. She considered having their conversation in the store, but a glance in that direction ruled it out. Seamus was regaling a group of entranced older women with tales of Christmas in Ireland while her mother stood behind the sales counter with an expression on her face much like Caine's as she squinted at the screen of Evie's computer, probably looking at the profit line.

Evie opened the door to the storage room and motioned for Caine to follow. When he stood on the other side, looking at her with an eyebrow raised, she reached out and pulled him inside.

"Tell me you did not just try to bribe Jamie with my dog," she said as she closed the door.

He plucked the phone from her hand. "Two seconds and you'll have my undivided attention." He didn't wait for her response but did follow through with his promise, seconds later pocketing his phone.

Refusing to have their conversation interrupted again, she closed what little distance there was between them in the four-by-four-foot room and stuck her hand in his pocket. She realized her mistake as soon as the tips of her fingers grazed his hip through the fine fabric and her chest brushed against his.

His hand closed over hers, trapping it inside his pocket and against his body. "Are you looking for anything in particular, Evangeline?"

"You know what I'm looking for," she said, and made the mistake of lifting her gaze to his. There was something more than amusement in his eyes. It had been the same when they were outside the principal's office. When his strong fingers had closed around her arms to draw her lips within an inch of his.

She'd wanted him to kiss her then as much as she did now, and it annoyed her to no end that a man who pressed every one of her buttons, a man who was her total opposite in every way, lit her body up like a

Christmas tree. It was absolutely ridiculous. How could she, a woman who owned a Christmas store, be in lust with Scrooge? The question had barely entered her mind when she knew the answer. It had nothing to do with his devastatingly gorgeous face or body. The part of her that was drawn to the man was the part of her that made her good at her job.

She was drawn to the emotionally wounded. She empathized with them, wanted to help them, to make a difference in their lives. To guide them from the darkness to the light. But it was also her fatal flaw, because sometimes her empathy led her from the light and into the darkness—like it had with Aaron. Fingers of fear crawled up her spine at the memory.

Caine must have read the emotion on her face because he immediately released her hand. She pulled it from his pocket and stepped back. He took out his phone and, holding it up, turned it off.

He looked like he was about to ask her what had just happened, and she crossed her arms. She didn't want to talk about it. She also wouldn't let him distract her. "Did you honestly just give my dog away without asking me?"

"Well, technically, it wasn't your dog. I'm the one who found him, and I'm the one who gave him to…" He scrunched up his right eye while rubbing his hand along his jaw.

"Please, by all means, finish what you were going to say."

"All right, when I heard you and Theia coming toward the kitchen last Friday morning—"

"The morning you pretended to be a messenger, you mean?"

"And braved your rat-infested cellar to turn your lights back on? Yes, that'd be the morning I'm referring to."

She gave a full-body shiver. "Can you please not mention them again?"

"It'd be my pleasure to refrain from doing so. Though your rodent infestation was one of the reasons I left Max on your porch. And before you say anything, I didn't know he had fleas."

"He did indeed have fleas. And I'm the one who got rid of said fleas and took him into my heart and home."

"You've had him for less than a week, Evangeline. I'm sure your heart will survive."

"Are you laughing at me?"

"Not out loud, I'm not," he said, doing a horrible job of fighting back a grin. Then his expression became serious. "You've got Bruiser. You don't need Max. But Jamie does."

"You had a dog named Max when you were Jamie's age, didn't you?" She couldn't help herself. She wanted to know what made this man tick. What had hurt him so badly that he did his best to keep people away.

"Yes, I did, as you very well know. My uncle shared information that wasn't his to share." He shoved his hands in his pockets. "And you thought to use it against me."

"No. *For* you, Caine. Seamus loves you. He's worried about you."

"He has no cause to worry. I made peace with my past a long time ago."

"He doesn't think you have. He thinks you've just locked all your memories—the good and the bad—away."

* * *

Caine sat at the kitchen table reviewing the list Jamie had just finished for Principal Wright and glanced at his watch. It was almost time for dinner and for Evangeline to close the shop, and she hadn't invited them to stay. She probably meant for him to take Jamie home. His mother cleaned several of the shops on Main Street after hours, so she wouldn't be home until late that evening, which meant Evangeline probably expected Caine to stay with the boy until his mother returned. He wasn't quite ready to spend the entire evening with Jamie on his own. At least here Evangeline popped in and out, as did his uncle and Lenore..

When Evangeline walked into the kitchen moments later carrying a floral arrangement, Caine decided to take matters into his own hands. "So I was thinking, to thank you for giving Max to Jamie, we'd treat you to dinner. Your mother and my uncle too, of course. Do you have a preference?"

Instead of answering, Evangeline added fresh water to the vase. When the silence dragged on, he got a little anxious that she was trying to come up with a way to turn his offer down. He caught Jamie giving Evangeline a sidelong glance. The boy probably felt the same as Caine about spending time on their own.

Caine got up from the table and walked to the sink.

"You probably didn't hear me with the tap running, but I asked what your preference for dinner would be?"

Given her silence, he'd decided to make it more difficult for her to turn them away.

She glanced at Jamie and then up at him as she turned off the water. "I don't recall inviting you to stay to dinner," she said for his ears alone.

Caine turned on the water and lowered his voice. "You're still mad at me for giving Max away, aren't you?"

"This has nothing to do with you giving away my dog. I just think it's a good idea for you and Jamie to spend some time alone together."

"I don't, and neither does he. So can we stay?" He didn't care that he was practically begging.

"Fine. But if you're staying for dinner, you and Jamie have to make it."

"This is payback for Max, isn't it?"

"No, because you were right. Max will be good for Jamie. I also think Jamie will be good for Max." At a hissing sound coming from under the table, then a yelp from Max, she added, "And Bruiser will no doubt be happy to have the house to himself."

"It sounds like I should be rewarded for giving Max to the lad, not punished."

"I'm not punishing you, Caine. Learning to cook simple and nutritious meals is part of our after-school program. A lot of the kids in the program are from single-parent families, so we want them to be able to cook a meal for themselves if they have to. And they often do."

He was just about to make a case for Jamie deserving a break when Evangeline leaned back to look past him. "You and Caine are making dinner tonight, Jamie. Why don't you make the recipe we tried last week?"

Caine didn't cook, and he wasn't about to start now. He'd place an order with Theia's grandmother-in-law-to-be, Rosa DiRossi. As if she'd read his mind, Evangeline glanced at Jamie as she walked out of the kitchen with the flowers in her arms. "Don't let Caine order from DiRossi's."

"If you don't tell, I won't," Caine said once she was out of earshot.

"But that'd be a lie," Jamie said.

"Technically it wouldn't. But I was just joking," he said, cursing the woman in his head. "So, what is it we're making?"

Jamie closed his books to put them in his backpack. "Spaghetti and meat sauce and a salad."

"Evangeline said simple. That doesn't sound simple."

"It's not that hard." He came over and handed Caine a recipe.

"Okay. I'll read off the ingredients, and you get them out of the refrigerator and cupboard." If they were lucky, Evangeline wouldn't have everything they needed. Hopefully, it would be too late to go to the market, and they'd order in. By the time Caine got to the last ingredient on the recipe, he realized the woman had a well-stocked and organized kitchen.

Now that he knew there was no escape, Caine did what he always did. He rolled up his sleeves and got to it.

An hour later, he sat at the head of the table with

Jamie and his uncle on his right, Lenore on to his left, and Evangeline across from him. He glanced at Jamie, who was intently watching Evangeline as she lifted a forkful of spaghetti to her mouth. The boy was being obvious about his desire to know what she thought of their meal. Caine was trying to be less so.

She looked up as she chewed, then swallowed. "Wow. I'm impressed. This is really good."

Jamie gave him a fist bump, and they grinned at each other. So much for him not being obvious, Caine thought, when Evangeline smiled at him, her eyes shining with amusement.

"Evangeline is right, Jamie. This is very good," Lenore said, her colorful glass earrings swinging when she nodded. They seemed an incongruous choice for her. To his mind, Evangeline's mother was highly competent, intelligent, somewhat rigid, and uncompromising, not someone given to whimsy, as the pretty earrings suggested.

"Yes. Well done, lad. I don't know when I've tasted better, and that's a high compliment indeed, as my nephew likes the finer things in life," Seamus said, ruffling Jamie's hair.

"I did help, you know," Caine said drily.

"He did. He decided instead of using a jar of spaghetti sauce, we should make our own. He burned the onions and garlic twice. Then he added sugar instead of salt to the tomato sauce. What?" Jamie said when Caine gave him a look.

"You're a regular card," he said when the kid laughed.

And as he sat there in the small kitchen with its

cracked linoleum and peeling wallpaper, listening to his uncle regale Jamie and the two women with a tall tale about his days on the Black Sea, Caine was reminded of meals he'd shared with his family in happier times. He'd missed it, missed this, he realized, soaking up the warmth and the laughter as he glanced around the table, trying to understand the pull of a simple home-cooked meal in a room in dire need of repair.

His eyes were drawn to Evangeline, who was smiling at something Jamie said, and he wondered if Seamus was right. Maybe the hunger that drove Caine wasn't for more property and more money. Maybe the only thing that would fill the empty place inside him was home and family.

Chapter Fifteen

♥

Four days later, Evie knew she was in trouble when she asked Caine to pass the peas and nearly said *honey*. The endearment was right on the tip of her tongue. And the way his blue eyes held hers, he knew it too.

"So, Jamie, how was your day?" Evie asked, smiling her thanks at Caine as he sent the bowl of peas to her via her mother. Their *family* dinners had become a thing. Although it had only happened a couple days in a row, so Evie wasn't sure it even qualified as a thing.

But the warm and fuzzy feelings she was having for the man at the end of the table were definitely becoming one, and that was a problem. A big one.

His brow furrowed as he poked at the whipped potatoes and gravy with his fork, and she wondered if he thought so too. When the silence dragged on, Caine glanced at Jamie, the furrows deepening on his brow. He'd missed the teenager's sullen shrug. Evie hadn't.

"Evie asked you a question, Jamie." He lifted his fork, indicating he expected the boy to answer.

"It was okay, I guess."

She didn't need Caine to wave his fork at her. She knew the routine. It had played out before. Caine might be Jamie's mentor, but she was also a member of their team. It had seemed a foregone conclusion on both their parts that she would be. She didn't mind, really. She was thrilled that Caine's first angel-wish assignment had, for the most part, been a success. Well, she was thrilled for them—her, not so much. At least her warm-and-fuzzies would be taken care of if she lost their bet.

"How's the coat drive going?" she asked. It was one of the items she'd suggested Jamie include on his list for Principal Wright.

The teenager smirked. "I don't know. How is the coat drive going, Caine?"

"Nice. Throw me under the bus." He pointed his fork at her. "Look, she's getting her puss on."

"Really? You know how I feel—" It was an Irish expression for a sulky face and one she'd tried to cure him of.

"Her puss on," Jamie repeated with a grin. "What about duck face?" And that was it, game on. Laughing, the two of them tried to outdo each other.

"Her father used to call it her Mother Teresa face."

Seamus reached over and patted Evie's hand. "I think it's a lovely face."

"You would. You're just like her father, encouraging her in everything she does. Today your uncle told Evangeline she should be putting herself out there as the expert on all things Christmas."

"And so she should. There's nothing she doesn't

know about the holidays. Tell them what you told the customer when she was upset you had *X-mas* on one of your signs. She thought Evie was trying to take *Christ* out of Christmas. Imagine," Seamus said.

"No one is interested in—" Evie began.

Seamus interrupted her. "She told the woman that in the Greek alphabet, the letter X is the first letter of the word for Christ or Christos. Isn't that something? Tell them what the first artificial Christmas tree was made of. Come on, tell them."

"Goose feathers. They dyed them green. The Germans developed artificial trees in the nineteenth century because of concerns over deforestation," Evie said.

"Cool. Tell us something else," Jamie said.

"Well, in Germany they believe that the pure of heart can hear animals talking on Christmas Eve."

"And I bet you didn't know this," Seamus said. "In Iceland, they don't just have one Saint Nick. The children are visited by thirteen Yule lads. The holiday begins thirteen days before Christmas, and each day one of the lads creeps into the house to fill the shoes left by the tree, leaving sweets and gifts if they're good, a rotten potato if they're not. Seems to me an Irish lad must have given them the idea to use a potato instead of coal."

"My uncle is right, Evie. You should be promoting yourself as an expert whenever you have a chance. And I might just have one for you. Jamie, are you thinking what I am?"

"Ah, yeah. Principal Wright wasn't a fan of T-shirt Scrabble. Instead of tiles with letters, we all wear T-shirts with a letter and play the game on the gymnasium floor," Jamie explained for Seamus's and Lenore's benefit, then grinned when Evie gave Caine a *told you so* look. When he'd suggested Jamie add the game to his list for building school spirit, Evie had advised against it.

"She was a fan. It's the other teachers who weren't. They wanted something more *Christmassy*." Caine rolled his eyes.

"To which you no doubt replied *Bah humbug*," Evie said.

"Ha. No. I said 'not a problem.' But as it turned out, it was. Jamie and I've been racking our brains trying to figure out what to replace it with. Now, thanks to you, we have the perfect substitution. Christmas trivia."

"If you think that's good, you should hear her other idea. Tell them, lass," Seamus encouraged.

She glanced at her mother, who huffed a put-upon breath and was about to wave Seamus off when Caine said, "We want to hear your idea, Evie. I'm sure your mother does too. Don't you, Lenore?"

"Yes. Of course. Do tell us your idea, Evangeline," her mother said with a pointed look at her roast beef, which Evie had cut into bite-size pieces for her due to her broken right hand.

Jamie and Caine had graduated from simple meals to elaborate in a very short time. Evie supposed she shouldn't be surprised given that once Caine set his mind to something, the man gave it his all. And now she was going to embarrass herself by sharing her idea.

"It's nothing really."

"It's a brilliant idea," Seamus said, giving her mother

his own version of a puss face when she looked up at the ceiling as if asking for patience.

"It's just a game. Like Monopoly but based on *A Christmas Carol*. I called it Scrooged." She shrugged and picked up her fork. She wasn't about to share with him that he'd been the inspiration for the game. Though he might have some idea if he ever saw the outline.

"Uncle Seamus is right. It's a great idea. Do you have anything on paper?" Caine asked.

She choked on the peas she'd just put in her mouth.

"Anything? She's got the entire game mapped out. I tell you, the girl is a genius."

Caine had his phone out and was focused on the screen. "There is a game based on the movie *A Christmas Story*, but I'm not seeing anything based on *A Christmas Carol*. I'll dig around some more. If you want me to, I might know someone who would be interested."

Lenore lowered the fork she held awkwardly in her left hand. "Really? You think there'd be interest in a board game based on Christmas?"

"My mother refuses to believe that the holidays are a multi-billion-dollar industry."

"I'm obviously aware that holiday transactions represent thirty percent of retailers' annual sales. Sadly, that hasn't worked to your benefit, Evangeline." Her mother picked up her napkin to dab at her mouth. "But if Caine believes your game holds merit, perhaps your luck is changing. At least you'll have something to fall back on when Holiday House is gone."

Absolute silence followed her mother's remark. Even
Max and Bruiser, who'd been eating at their bowls,
stopped to look at the humans.

Jamie's fork clattered to his plate and he pushed
back from the table. "Maybe Caine won't have such an
easy time completing his next assignment now that he's
done with me."

"Jamie, come on. I told you—" Caine bowed his
head when the teenager stormed from the kitchen.

"Are you happy now? You've hurt both your daughter and Jamie with your unthinking remark," Seamus
said to her mother.

"I didn't intend to hurt anyone. I was just stating a
fact. I actually thought I was being…supportive."

"Aye, you would. You might be book smart, woman,
but you don't have a clue what really matters." Seamus
tossed his napkin on his plate as he got up from the
table. "I'll see to the lad."

"Well, I never!" her mother said, her eyes following
Seamus from the kitchen. Then she picked up her fork,
only to put it back down. "I'm afraid I've lost my appetite. But it wasn't on account of the meal. It was very
good. Thank you, Caine. Evangeline." She nodded,
then, holding her head high, left the kitchen.

"That went well," Caine said, scrubbing his hands
over his face.

"You told him you were picking another wish, didn't
you? That's why he was upset earlier." It had been only
a matter of time. She'd known that, but to hear the
words aloud made it real. The past few days had been
nothing more than a brief reprieve, a pleasant interlude.

A dangerous interlude, she thought, as her heart sank. She could only imagine how Jamie felt.

"What would have you me do? He knew I wouldn't be able to spend my afternoons and evenings with him forever." Caine seemed to be saying the words as much for her benefit as for his. The past few days had blurred the lines between them, and not just for her and Jamie, but for Caine too.

"Of course he did. What did you expect? Until you came into his life, he felt like he was alone and no one understood how he felt. Now he doesn't. You've been good for him. He enjoys spending time with you." *So do I*, she thought, chewing on her bottom lip. She couldn't believe she'd let herself fall in like with Caine Elliot.

"This is your fault, you know. Making me care about him, about…" He rubbed his palm along his jaw. "I'm not abandoning him, Evangeline."

She didn't miss that he'd called her *Evangeline* instead of *Evie*. His way of putting some distance between them, she imagined. It wouldn't be difficult for him to do, to distance himself from all of them, all of this. He'd had years of practice. No doubt he'd be happy for his life to return to normal.

"It's important that he understands…" At that moment the consequences of her wish hit her, and she covered her face with her hands. "I didn't think about Jamie. I didn't think what this could do to him. All I thought about was Holiday House and winning the bet." She lowered her hands. "What have I done? You've become important to him, Caine. Someone he's come to depend on. If he loses you—"

"Stop it." He got up from the table and came around to crouch in front of her. "He's not going to lose me."

And when Caine took her hand in his, a completely crazy thought came over her that it was his way of telling her that she wouldn't lose him either. If that wasn't a sign she'd lost her mind, she didn't know what was.

"I'll be in town for another week at least, and once…" He gave her hand a light squeeze and stood up. "Whatever happens, I'll see Jamie a couple times a month. And I'll call or FaceTime him every day until he tells me not to. Seamus has agreed to take him under his wing when I'm not around."

"But your uncle will be leaving when you do."

He picked up her plate and cutlery. "He hasn't said anything, but I have a feeling he wants to make his home in Harmony Harbor. He's happy here."

She studied him as she got up to help clear the table. "That doesn't seem fair to you. You've just got him back. I'm sure if you told him you—"

"I'll be fine, Evangeline," he said as he placed the plates and cutlery into the sink.

"*Fine* is a relative term. And just because you're *used* to being alone, it isn't the same thing as being happy with it." She set the glasses and napkins on the counter.

He glanced at her while he turned on the water to rinse the dishes. "Instead of wasting your time trying to analyze me, Dr. Christmas, you might want to give some thought to my second angel-wish assignment."

Chapter Sixteen

♥

Hours after what appeared to be her last *family* dinner with Caine and Jamie, Evie gathered with the other members of Harmony Harbor's book club at Books and Beans for their holiday gift exchange. Julia Gallagher, the adorable, dark-haired owner of the bookstore and coffee shop, was also a romance writer and had started the book club a few years before. They met once a month to discuss their current read, to drink wine, and to share life's up and downs.

Since Evie had joined the group last year, she felt like all she'd shared were her downs, and just this once she'd like to share an up. Which might have been the reason she told her friends about Caine's offer to shop her board game around.

"Yay, Evie! Wow, this is amazing!" Several of the women sitting in a circle of chairs in the middle of the bookstore jumped up to cheer. Evie laughed when a heavily pregnant Julia did an imitation of the Elaine dance from *Seinfeld*, and Cherry, the manager of the Salty Dog, encouraged her to twerk instead, getting up from her own chair to demonstrate. A former exotic dancer, Cherry had big blond hair and a curvy body.

"Are you crazy, Cherry? Sit down. Julia, you too. I promised Aidan you wouldn't overdo it tonight," Shay Gallagher said, referring to Julia's husband. Shay reminded Evie of the actress Angelina Jolie. Like Julia, Shay was also pregnant.

Theia stood up and put a hand behind her ear. "I'm waiting. Who would like to apologize first? I told you Caine was an amazing guy, didn't I?"

"I already apologized," Mackenzie said. "Any man who'll face down rats for a woman is a hero in my book."

"Well, he didn't actually face them down. He bought a cat and rat traps. Bruiser and Seamus did most of the facing down." Evie thought it only fair that her cat and Seamus got the credit they were due.

"But he did face them down. The day he went into your basement to turn the lights on for you, Evie. His uncle Seamus told me," Cherry said. "Seamus comes into the Salty Dog all the time. He's just the sweetest. I think he has a crush on—"

"Are you going somewhere with this, Cherry?"

"You're such a buzz kill," Cherry said to Shay before continuing. "So anyway, Seamus says that it was like a *huge* deal Caine went down in your basement, Evie. Which I hear is ten kinds of creepy, by the way. When Caine was young, some boys locked him down in the basement of the local haunted house, and he was bitten by a rat. His family didn't have a clue where he was because they'd just moved to the town and were frantic when he didn't show up for dinner. It sounded like they had to move around a lot. I got the impression they didn't have much money. Crazy how that works, isn't it? The guy is loaded now. Okay. Gosh, Shay," she said when her boss and best friend gestured for her to get on with it. "Anyway, after Caine's dad threatened them, one of the kids finally confessed."

Theia looked like she might cry, and Evie understood how she felt.

"I feel bad for him too, but come on, you guys. Evie's weeks away from losing Holiday House because of him. Not to mention everything he's put us through trying to wrest the estate away from the family," Sophie Gallagher, the manager of the manor, said. With her long, curly dark hair, luminous dark eyes, and olive skin, Sophie looked like a younger version of her grandmother, Rosa DiRossi.

"Look, I understand how you feel, but you have to trust me on this, Sophie. While Caine wants to buy the estate and build high-end condos on the ocean, any of the shady things that went on were his grandmother's fault. Honestly, if it weren't for Emily, I doubt Caine would even be interested in the manor."

Rosa patted Theia's knee. "I like him. He's a handsome boy and a good friend to our family. Remember last summer, *bella*," she said to Sophie. "Theia called him to say you and the *bambinos* were in trouble, and just like that"—she snapped her fingers—"he flew here with a bag full of ransom money."

"As far as Mrs. Murphy's concerned, the man walks on water. She says it's *Caine this* and *Caine that* in their house. Jamie adores him," Julia said, then sent Evie a look that had too much twinkle in it for her liking. "Is he as wonderful as Mrs. Murphy says, Evie? His car's been parked outside Holiday House every day this week, so I imagine you would know better than anyone who the real Caine Elliot is."

"You can't seriously think Evie would be entertaining the man who is..." Sophie stared at her. "Wow, it's true. You're dating Caine Elliot."

"No!" From the way the women blinked and shared sidelong glances, Evie's forceful denial made her look guilty in their eyes, but she couldn't help it. Harmony Harbor was a small town, where everyone not only knew your name but they had you on speed dial. If she didn't nip this in the bud, Caine would hear about it before their book club meeting was over.

Worse than that, the Widows Club (aka the matchmakers of Harmony Harbor) were always looking for a project, and she didn't want their latest to become her. Two members of the book club, Rosa DiRossi and Kitty Gallagher, were founding members of the Widows Club.

"Jamie didn't know Caine, but he does know me, so I thought it would be easier on both of them if they hung out at my place." She wondered if Rosa and Kitty bought the excuse and glanced at them from under her lashes only to see them share a look...and a nod. "No. No way," Evie blurted without thinking. Once again drawing the attention of the entire book club.

"One no I believe. Your excuse sounded believable too. But you blew it on the third." Sophie threw up her hands. "What are you thinking, Evie?"

"The no's were for them." She moved her finger from Rosa to Kitty.

The two older women looked at each other, then pointed at themselves. "Us?"

"Yes. And you can cut the innocent act. I saw the way you looked at each other. You nodded."

Beside Rosa, Theia pumped her fist in the air. "Yes!" Noting she now had the group's attention, Theia scratched her neck. "Sorry. I know what's it like to be caught in the crosshairs of Harmony Harbor's matchmakers, but Caine is like family to me, and I want him to be happy." She looked at Evie. "I think you could make him happy. And despite what some of you think, he'd make Evie happy too."

Cherry raised her hand. "If Evie's not interested, I am. I'm on the market again, and Caine Elliot checks all my boxes. A couple of them twice. Face, body, and money if you're wondering."

Evie forced a smile that became harder to keep in place when several members of the book club offered up the names of other single women in town who would be more than happy to take Caine Elliot off the market. Someone—she thought it might have been Mackenzie—hinted that Mrs. Murphy was interested too. And it sounded like Mrs. Murphy got the sympathy vote and went to the top of the matchmakers' list. While Evie was now at the bottom. Exactly where she wanted to be, she told herself, despite the unhappy weight in her stomach calling her a liar.

And as she listened to her friends wax poetic about Caine's positive attributes, the weight got heavier because deep down Evie knew that Caine was so much more than his money, incredible blue eyes, chiseled good looks, and Thor-like body and voice. He was smart and kind and generous and loyal, and as much as she didn't want him to tear down Holiday House and build his glass-and-steel eyesore, she didn't want him to leave Harmony Harbor. She wanted him to stay in her life, and she wanted him to stay in Jamie's. And that was the scariest thing she'd admitted to herself in a long time. Evie Christmas didn't just like Scrooge. She was falling for him.

Arianna Gallagher, a stunning blonde who shared the job as mayor with her husband, called for quiet. "Look, I know how much fun matchmaking is, and I'm as big a fan of happily-ever-afters as the rest of you. But we can't lose perspective here. Despite Evie's best efforts and ours, we lost the first round to Wicklow Developments. So, unless Evie wins her bet with Caine, the office tower will be built on Main Street. And I'm afraid, if he does win, he will redouble his efforts to gain control of the manor."

She cast Evie an apologetic glance. "Please don't be offended, but losing Greystone would be a devasting blow to Harmony Harbor. One, if I'm honest, I'm not sure we could recover from. For the past few years, Sophie and her team have focused on reclaiming Greystone's title of premiere wedding destination on the East Coast, and it's paid off big-time for all of us."

"But Caine has already completed his first assignment with a gold star from the sounds of it." Sophie sent another apologetic glance Evie's way (admittedly, they were getting harder to swallow). "So unless his next two wishes are harder for him to fulfill, we need a backup plan."

"Agreed," Arianna said. "What's his next angel assignment, Evie?"

With everyone turning their expectant gazes her way, the last thing Evie wanted to admit was that she didn't have a clue what Caine's next angel assignment was. For almost a year, she'd been in there fighting the good fight. Time and time again, she'd come up with a winning strategy to hold off Wicklow Developments. But the blow of losing everything, and losing it because of bringing up that stupid bylaw, had hit her hard. Maybe harder than she'd been willing to admit up until now. Because she should have a plan. A few months back, she would've had a plan. She would've had her entire game plan laid out.

She opened her mouth, praying that she'd have an epiphany at the last minute. "I . . ." She sighed. "I've got nothing." As the faces around her fell, she added, "But don't worry. I can stall Caine until I come up with one." That was an idea she was totally on board with.

"No. This is crazy," Julia said. "You can't do all this on your own. With the parade this weekend, you're going to be—"

Evie gaped at Julia. "It can't be. Please tell me the parade isn't this weekend. How can it be this weekend?" Evie looked around the circle, praying it was some kind of joke. But it couldn't be because these were her friends and they wouldn't joke about something this important.

"I told you we should've mentioned it to her,

Mackenzie," Julia said. "I'm so sorry, Evie. We should've said something when we noticed you hadn't put up your lights yet, but then we thought you might be trying to save on expenses."

"No. I just...I don't have an excuse. I completely forgot about it." She was as big a screwup as her mother thought she was. "But don't worry. I won't let you guys down. Holiday House will be lit up in time for the parade." She'd get it done if it killed her. And right then she thought it might. With her electrical issues, she couldn't use regular lights. "Sorry. Just give me a minute." She pulled out her phone to text Mr. O'Malley, asking if he had solar lights and if she could stop in after the meeting to grab them if he did. There was one piece of good news, she thought, when he responded right away in the affirmative.

A shrill whistle brought her head up. While she'd been texting Mr. O'Malley, the book club members had been brainstorming ideas for Caine's next angel assignment. Apparently too loudly for Theia's liking because she was the one who whistled.

"I know Caine better than you guys do." Theia smiled at Evie. "Although I think you've come to know him pretty well too. And in the end, it might just be Evie who saves the day. But since so many of you seem to have become cynical about the power of love, I have the perfect angel assignment for Caine. He has to help bring the spirit of Christmas to Greystone Manor." She made a *ta-da* gesture with her hands.

"Are you insane?" Sophie said. "That's like letting kids loose in a candy store."

"A fox in the henhouse," someone else said.

"No. Theia's right, it's perfect," Evie said.

"You better explain it to me because I don't see it," Sophie said, her arms crossed.

"Okay. Think of *A Christmas Carol*. Caine is Scrooge, and the angel wishes take the place of the ghosts in the book. We're using the angel wishes to show him his Christmas past, present, and future," Evie explained.

Julia nodded. "And by the time he finishes his last wish, like Scrooge, he'll be a changed man. A changed man who wouldn't have the heart to put Evie on the street or steal the manor out from under the Gallaghers." Julia clapped her hands. "I love it. It is perfect."

Evie glanced around the circle, gauging everyone else's reactions. They seemed cautiously optimistic.

Kitty smiled at Evie. "I say we give it a try. I'm sure we can figure out how to put Mr. Elliot in the Christmas spirit."

"Great. If you're okay with it, Kitty, on the angel I'll write 'help Kitty Gallagher bring Christmas to the manor.'"

The Gallagher matriarch nodded. "We'll have a family meeting first thing tomorrow morning to brainstorm ideas."

"All right," Sophie agreed. "Yes. You can come too, *Nonna*. Actually, you're all welcome. The more the merrier. Maybe you can hold Caine off until tomorrow night so we can have everything set, Evie."

"Sure."

"And while the rest of you are playing the Ghosts of

Christmas Past, Present, and Future, I'm going to dig into Wicklow Developments and the Elliots. Because there's more to this than we know," Shay said. Shay was a private investigator with an excellent reputation.

"What do you mean?" Julia asked.

"The way the Elliots have been coming after the manor is personal." She angled her head, her eyes narrowed on Theia. "You know something, don't you?"

"I know you're right, and that's all I can say."

"Am I wasting my time looking into it?"

Theia nodded. "Yes. The truth will come out. And trust me, Caine might be my best friend, but I won't let Wicklow Developments gain control of the manor."

"If you need me, say the word."

Theia grinned. "Your husband already gave me the word where you're concerned, and it was a very overprotective *no*. He's offered his services instead."

Since Shay's husband was a former FBI agent, Evie thought Theia would be well covered. But it worried her that there was more going on than she knew.

And after a raucous white elephant gift exchange, Evie cornered Theia in line at the coffee bar. "Cute unicorn snow tube," she said, referring to the gift Theia received when Julia and Cherry moved into hearing distance behind the coffee bar. She'd wait until she got Theia on her own to question her.

"I'll have to hide it from my sister. Your umbrella is pretty cute too," she said, nodding at the "Raining Men" bubble dome umbrella Evie had managed to hang on to. Probably because, other than Cherry and Rosa, everyone else had a man of their own.

"It is. And I can put it to good use tonight." Evie said as sleet *ping*ed against the window, which was decorated in colorful Christmas lights, smiling when Julia leaned across the counter to hug her.

"I love my mermaid-tail throw blanket. It is awesome. Now, what would you like—a tipsy s'more cocktail or a non-tipsy cocktail?"

Cherry made prayer hands. "Please have a tipsy cocktail. I don't want to drink alone. I think we're the only thirtysomethings in this room who are single and aren't pregnant or nursing."

Great. Just the reminder she wanted after listening to everyone's holiday plans earlier—their romantic and sometimes sexy plans. If things continued the way they were, Evie would spend the holidays alone packing. "Make it a triple tipsy," Evie said, then glanced at Theia, who was avoiding her gaze.

"Are you kidding me? You're pregnant too?" she whispered to the other woman.

"Yeah. But don't tell Rosa. Or Caine. He'll be worse than Marco."

"I won't. And congrats. I'm happy for you. Even though it might not have sounded that way," she said, feeling bad for how she'd reacted.

"Trust me. I get it. I've been where you are. The only single in a crowd of women who are singing the praises of love and commitment." She made a face. "Sorry. Blame it on hormones."

"No. It's fine. I'm better off being single this time of year anyway. I don't have to obsess about what to buy for someone. Plus, it's a little-known fact, but the two weeks leading up to Christmas have the highest breakup rate of the year."

"Well, aren't you just a font of Christmas cheer?" Theia laughed and then handed Evie her tipsy s'more while ordering herself a virgin hot chocolate. "By the way, if you're wondering, the best Christmas wedding gift you could give me is to give Caine a chance. I saw your face when Cherry was telling us what happened to him when he was a kid, so don't pretend you haven't got feelings for him. You care about him. I know you do, Evie. And he is so worth caring about." She gave her a watery smile and swiped at her eyes. "Stupid hormones."

Evie followed Theia to one of the tables. "I do care about him. Which is absolutely insane, because the man is going to bulldoze Holiday House to the ground. I mean, if I lose the bet he is."

"Take a look at half the women in here. At least the ones married to Gallaghers. You know the story about Julia and Aidan. Look at Shay and Michael. He was an FBI agent investigating her uncle. Even me and Marco. I was working for Wicklow Developments. Love does conquer all, or at least it can get you over some pretty big hurdles."

"Love? Oh my gosh, we're not in a relationship or anything. Caine's not interested in me that way." Although she had the feeling he wasn't immune to her either.

"But you are interested in him, aren't you? Attracted to him?" When Evie hesitated, Theia said, "Come on, we're friends. You can be honest with me."

"Okay. I admit it. I'm attracted to him. Not that I think anything will come of it, but"—she glanced around—"do I need to be concerned about anything? You said something about the truth coming out. You'd tell me if Caine wasn't who I think he was, wouldn't you? Like if he was...I don't know, dangerous?"

"I'll tell you exactly what I tell Caine—you're as much my friend as he is. And he isn't dangerous, not to you, Evie. If you matter to Caine Elliot, he will protect you with his life."

Chapter Seventeen

♥

At the low purr of an engine and the headlights' beam shining in her eyes, Evie raised the hand holding a string of Christmas lights to shield her eyes. Her heart thumped an excited beat when she recognized the car and the man behind the wheel.

She tried to pretend it was because one of her favorite Christmas songs had come on the radio, but as much as she wished it were true, Mariah Carey's "All I Want for Christmas Is You" didn't cause the excited pitter-patter. The honor went to the man currently unfolding his big body from behind the wheel of his luxury automobile with all the grace of a lethal jungle cat. Theia was wrong. Caine Elliot was as dangerous to Evie as the erratic beat of her heart proved.

At the slam of his car door, she jumped a little, and the ladder upon which she stood wobbled. She jumped again when he practically roared, "What the hell do you think you're doing?"

The pitter-patter in her chest was no longer caused by

the heat of attraction but by the heat of temper. "What does it look like I'm doing?"

"Being an idiot," he muttered as he prowled toward her.

"You did not just call me an idiot!"

"Yes, I did. No one but an idiot would be out in the dark putting up lights in weather cold enough to freeze—"

"Feel free to finish. I've spent enough time with your uncle to have heard the phrase, and I can tell you freezing the brass balls off a monkey is much less offensive than being called an idiot." She turned away from him to swag the string of lights above the door, only to let out a startled yelp when his big hands clamped on either side of her waist and he hauled her off the ladder. "What do you think you're doing?" she asked when he set her on her feet.

"The same thing I've been doing since the first day I met you, Evangeline. Saving you from yourself."

"Oh, that's rich. I'm putting up Christmas lights, Caine. I'm also wearing a winter jacket and gloves." She wiggled her fingers at him. "And I was perfectly safe on the ladder until you arrived."

"What part of me telling you to be careful and not to overload your electrical because they've done a temporary fix did you not understand? Because this"—he waved his hand at the lights she'd decorated the exterior of the store with—"looks like overload times ten."

"And it's because you don't like the holiday and have probably never decorated a house with Christmas lights that (a) you'd think this constitutes overload or going overboard and (b) you don't know that these are solar lights."

"They are?"

"Yes, they are. Are you happy now, Mr. Scrooge? Can I finish putting up the lights now? Because as you so eloquently put it, it's cold out."

"Yes, I am happy that you actually listened to me." He took a step back to look up at the house. "But unless it's necessary for Holiday House to be seen from the International Space Station, you don't need any more lights."

"That's your opinion. But this weekend is the Parade of Lights, and since I'm the only Christmas store in town, people expect me to do it up big." And thank goodness they'd mentioned it at book club tonight, or she'd have let everyone down.

"So this is a competition, then? There's a prize?"

"And if it were a competition and there were a prize involved?" she asked, amused by the transformation that had come over him.

"You'd lose." He glanced at her. "No offense intended. You obviously haven't had the funds or the time to do it up right."

"Caine, it's not a competition, and there's no prize." She looked up at Holiday House again, this time seeing it through his eyes and that of the town's. "But you're right. It's a good thing there isn't because I would lose." And that made her a little sad. If Caine won their bet, this would be the last time the parade would go by Holiday House.

"Get inside. I'll finish up for you."

Since she was feeling a tiny bit depressed and a whole lot cold, she took him up on his offer. He bent down and picked up her radio, handing it to her. "Let me guess, you don't like Christmas carols," she said.

"I don't like that Christmas carol." He took his phone from his pocket and pressed Play. "But I do like this." It was Handel's *Messiah*.

The man had good taste, not only in music but in clothes. "You're not really dressed for this, you know. Didn't you say you had to go back to Bridgeport to work after you dropped off Jamie?"

He wouldn't meet her eyes. "Evangeline, go inside while I take care of your lights. Your teeth are chattering."

"Something happened. What's wrong?"

"Nothing really." He averted his gaze to look toward the harbor. "Jamie called his mom to tell her I had to go out of town on business and Seamus would be filling in for me. She was upset. They both were."

Her stomach gave a nervous clench. Jamie's mom was still at the top of the matchmakers' list.

"What happened? Did they change your mind?"

"Of course not. I have a business to run."

"Then why did you come here and not go to Bridgeport as you'd planned?"

His gaze moved over her face. "Because I heard there was an idiotic woman putting up Christmas lights in the freezing rain after imbibing something called a tipsy s'more cocktail."

"Theia. I should have known." Her cheeks warmed as she thought back to their conversation. "What else did she say?"

"That I'm an idiot if I don't see what's right in front of me." He reached out to tuck a piece of her hair beneath her hat. "But she's wrong. I do see what's right in front of me."

"What?"

He smiled and tweaked her hair. "You. But I'd be an idiot if I acted on my attraction to you, and you'd be an even bigger one to want me to."

She studied his face under the glow from the outside light, the tension around his eyes and mouth. "I don't believe you. I don't think that's why you're here at all. I think you used what Theia told you as an excuse to come here."

"Is that so? Then why do you think I'm here, Evie?" He moved closer, close enough that she could feel his heat.

"Because you're a good man, and you feel bad for disappointing Jamie and his mother. It was hard for you. It brought back memories—"

"Don't." He moved in to her, nudging her back against the door. "You're afraid. You're turning the tables on me, analyzing me because you don't want to analyze yourself. Why don't you believe that I want you?" He bent his head, his warm lips grazing her cheek. "Because I do, Evie. I want you."

Her heartbeat quickened, and her knees weakened. "You can't keep using sex and money to mask your pain."

He smiled. "Is that what I've been doing, Dr. Christmas? And here I thought I was having sex and making money because of how much I liked doing both."

"You know what I mean," she said, flustered by the heat in his gaze and her own desire.

"And I know what you want. What we both want. Are you going to let me kiss you, Evie?"

"It won't stop at a kiss."

"It will if you want it to." He leaned around her to open the door with one hand while wrapping his other around her to keep her from falling. "Say the word and I leave."

She fisted her hand in his coat. "Stay," she said, and kissed him.

* * *

Evie lay beside Caine on the queen-sized bed in the guest bedroom. She'd been right; they hadn't stopped at just a kiss. She'd never understood the words *basking in the afterglow* until now. If she weren't a woman who was intrigued and entranced by the man beside her, a woman who after making love with Caine didn't want it to end with one night, she would have continued floating on a cloud of ecstasy for the next several hours without rocking the boat.

But she was a woman who wanted to shine a light on the places inside him that he'd rather hide. And between frantically kissing and tearing off each other's clothes as they made their way upstairs, she'd gotten him to tell her about the day he'd been trapped in the basement with the rat. In the telling of that story, she'd learned about his own Max. The dog his parents had bought him in hopes it would help him deal with the loneliness of moving to yet another town.

"Now that I've told you my deep, dark secret, are you going to tell me yours?" he asked, rolling on top of her but using his elbows to keep his full weight off her.

"Your grandmother refusing to let you bring your dog when you moved in with her was heartbreaking, but it's not your deep, dark secret, Caine."

"And how do you know that?" He nuzzled her neck until he made her squirm. Then he lifted his head to look down at her, his eyes a glittering, gleaming blue beneath long, dark lashes that unfairly curled at the tips.

He was beautiful, a dark and tortured angel if she wasn't mistaken. Which should scare her, she knew, and she prayed that she could trust Theia and the part of herself that said the darkness inside him would never harm her. But it had—and it would continue—hurting *him* unless he brought it out into the open.

Aaron had used her empathy, her need to help and to try to heal, against her. Caine didn't want her help or her sympathy. He wanted to lose himself inside her, in pleasure, but she wanted more...from a man who had the power to steal her dreams. She didn't hold out hope that whatever he felt for her right now would result in him changing his mind about the office tower. He'd told her repeatedly that he didn't allow emotions to factor into his business decisions, and she believed him.

She lifted her hand to stroke his beard-stubbled face. "I know it's not your deep, dark secret because it's how I once made my living."

He lowered his head and kissed her, long and deep, his hand stroking her side.

Breaking that kiss was perhaps the most difficult thing she'd done in quite some time, but she did. "Please, Caine."

"I must have lost my touch if you'd rather talk than make love."

His frustration thickened his accent, and for a second she almost relented. But she knew he was vulnerable now, and as much as she didn't like to use that against him, she would. It was for his own good. Tomorrow his walls would be up again.

"Tell me, and then we'll make love for the rest of the night."

"Until the sun comes up?"

"Or when we hear Seamus come in, whichever comes first."

"He won't be coming back before the sun comes up. He's found a place more comfortable than your St. Paddy's Day room to lay his head."

"You can't distract me, you know."

"I should know better. You've been driving me mad for the better part of a year."

"And yet here we are. Here you are. Ready to tell me your deep, dark secret."

"It's not that deep or dark," he said as he rolled off her to lie by her side. His voice was flat, and he raised his arm to cover his eyes.

She turned on her side to wrap an arm around him, tucking herself close.

He lifted his forearm to look down at her. "You're a snuggler, aren't you?"

She couldn't tell if he thought that was a good thing

or a bad thing, and she lifted a shoulder. "My dad's nickname for me was Snugglebug."

"A week ago that would have surprised me. Not anymore."

"Did your mom have a nickname for you?" she asked to nudge him in the direction she wanted the conversation to go. Both Seamus and Caine spoke about his father's death, but they didn't speak of his mother's.

"Perhaps you shouldn't have given up your job poking into people's minds. I have a feeling you were very good at it."

"What happened, Caine?"

"After my father died, things went downhill. It hadn't been good for months, but Uncle Seamus took my da's death hard and disappeared into the bottle. He rarely came around. There was no one else. No family or friends to speak of. We'd gotten kicked out of our last place and had only been in town for less than a year. As you obviously know, I was a lot like Jamie. Acting out, getting in fights. I didn't have someone like you standing up for me, and I got kicked out of school. My mother had had enough of me. Looking back, I can't say I blame her."

"Don't do that. Don't lie to me. Not while you're lying in my arms."

"You're right. I did blame her. She sold me. Sold me for fifty thousand pounds to my grandmother and then left and never looked back. I never heard from her again, not a word."

Evie tightened her arm around his waist, pressing her lips to his chest as she fought back tears. "I'm sorry," she murmured on a hoarse whisper. "I'm so sorry."

He lowered his arm from his eyes to wrap it around her and stroke her hair. "Don't cry for me. It was a long time ago, Evie."

"Don't try to pretend it didn't hurt then or it doesn't still. The pain doesn't go away just because you want it to or you demand that it does. You have to acknowledge it." She lifted her face from his chest. "And then you have to find a way to forgive your mother so you can move on."

"I thought I had. About six months after she left me with my grandmother, I made up a story in my head about why she'd had to leave me. I had to do something or I knew it would eat at me forever. Over time the story took root, and I began to believe it. Then, a couple weeks ago, my uncle came back into my life and brought it all back. But being around Jamie these past few days, and then watching him with his mother tonight...If someone in Mrs. Murphy's family had offered her fifty thousand dollars for Jamie, she wouldn't have taken it."

"Does she know that you've paid her rent for two years and Rosa DiRossi will be making her meals?"

"Bloody small towns," he said without heat.

She reached up to curve her hand around his neck, drawing his mouth to hers. "You are a good man, Caine Elliot," she murmured against his lips.

"I'm still the same man I've always been, Evie. Tonight doesn't change that, you know."

"I know. I'm still the same woman I was last week."

"I might argue that a bit." He rolled to his side and brought her close. "You're much softer and sweeter in bed. Maybe I should keep you here." As though he sensed that she wanted to ask more about his mother, he said, "Let it go for now. I just want to hold you." He glanced around the room. "But seeing as how I've told you my secret, it's only fair you do the same." He lifted his chin at the battery-operated twinkle lights she'd decorated the room with. "Are you afraid of the dark, Evie?"

"Yes." And she left it at that because they'd had enough of the dark for one night.

"If I promise to stay by your side the whole night through and chase your nightmares away, can I turn off the lights?"

Chapter Eighteen

♥

Caine felt like he'd been hit by a truck that had taken its time running over him. Not how he typically felt after spending the night making love with a beautiful woman. It certainly wasn't the outcome he'd been hoping for when he'd left the Murphy house last night.

As much as he didn't want to admit it, he'd been seeking comfort from his past, from the emotions stirred up by being with Jamie and his mother. Emotions that Caine didn't want to face or acknowledge. Clearly, he hadn't been thinking straight. Because the last person a man who wanted to bury his emotions should be with was Dr. Evangeline Christmas. The woman who'd set him on the road down memory lane in the first place.

He glanced at her curled into his side. Took in the way her silky, dark mane spread over his chest and wrapped around his bicep to ensnare him. Took note of the sweet innocence of her profile, long lashes puddling on her smooth, creamy skin, delicate pink lips softly parted, warm, womanly curves that had offered both comfort and wanton pleasure. They were a lie, a deception. She wasn't sweetly innocent; she was dangerous.

She'd poked and prodded and hadn't let up. She'd dug things out of his head and his heart and made him remember. For what? She hadn't erased his pain; she'd made it worse. He'd thought he was free of his past, but she'd exposed the truth, found its hiding place, opened the door and . . . let it out.

"So maybe you're a miracle worker after all, Evie Christmas," he whispered, trailing the tips of his fingers along the dip of her waist and the curve of her hip, wishing he'd met her in New York when she was Dr. Evangeline Christmas and not the owner of Holiday House.

Nothing good would come of this. The odds were stacked against them. Caine only gambled when they were in his favor. He had too much to lose. So did Evie, only she didn't know just how much. With Emily dealing from the bottom of the deck, the game was too dangerous to play. Despite the pleasure, and there had been hours of pleasure interspersed with the pain, he wouldn't put his future or Evie at risk. Last night, he'd done what he hadn't done in years: He'd acted on his emotions. His wants, his needs.

He lifted his arm to glance at his watch, surprised to discover it was seven thirty. He was usually up by five. But he understood the draw of remaining in bed with the woman snuggled against his side. Looking down at her, he wanted nothing more than to remain in her bed for the rest of the day.

At the unexpected thought, he felt the same clutch

of worry in his chest that he'd experienced when he'd told her he'd spend the night and chase away her nightmares. If he wasn't careful, he would become her nightmare. In some sense, he supposed he already was, or had been.

But this time it would be worse. Emily would ensure that it was. The tightness in his chest increased at the knowledge that this would be the last time he held Evie in his arms. The last time he'd kiss her, he thought as he lowered his head, unable to resist one more touch of his mouth to hers.

She smiled against his lips and stretched, wrapping an arm around his neck and pressing a shapely leg between his thighs.

"You don't make it easy for a man to leave your bed, Evie." *Especially when he knows it's forever.*

"I don't want you to leave," she murmured, kissing him back.

He nipped her bottom lip, drawing away with a smile he had to force. "I promised Jamie I'd drop him off at school. And you have a shop to run."

She reached up to comb her fingers gently through his hair, her eyes searching his face. "Are you okay? You look tired."

He leaned back, lightly swatting her behind so she wouldn't take offense or read more into his need to get away from her searching eyes and gentle touch. "Says the insatiable woman who wore me out. Though you, Ms. Christmas, look none the worse for wear. You're glowing."

Her cheeks flushed. "Well, I—" She broke off, her

eyes going wide when her mother's voice came from down the hall. "Evangeline, have you lost your mind? What on earth were you thinking buying all of those lights?"

Caine cursed and dove back into bed, meeting Evie under the covers they'd pulled over their heads. "Get out there and send her away."

"I'm naked!"

"So am I, and she's your mother. She's seen you naked before." At the sight of Evie pressing her lips together and the crinkles at the corners of her watery eyes, he whispered, "It's not funny. I'm warning you, Evie, don't you dare"—he bowed his head when she cracked up—"laugh."

"I'm sorry," she said between hoots of laughter.

"Evangeline, what in the world is the matter with...?" Her mother whipped back the covers. "Oh, I...This is a surprise. Hello, Caine."

"Good morning, Lenore," Caine said, which made Evie laugh all the harder. He was just glad he'd grabbed the covers when her mother pulled them back. They weren't completely indecent.

"What's going—" His uncle walked into the room, and his mouth fell open. It didn't take him long to recover, as the smile now lighting up his face proved. "This...you two together"—Seamus moved his hand back and forth—"I can't tell you how happy you've made me."

Caine frowned when his uncle lifted his hand to wipe away...a tear? Was he crying, or did he have something in his eye?

"You'll have to excuse me for getting emotional. It's just that I didn't expect this. Not in a million years."

"You and me both," Lenore said, pursing her red-painted lips as she glanced down at them, her dark-penciled, judgmental eyebrows disappearing beneath a helmet of wavy silver hair.

Caine cleared his throat, not sure what to say that wouldn't offend Evie or her mother. "Perhaps you could let us get dressed first."

"I will. But this is important. It's best said in the moment."

"Uncle, I don't know what kind of moment you think this is, but I'm willing to wager it's not—"

"Ho, and how's that wager working out for you, nephew? You didn't count on Evie, did you? She beat you at your own game, she did. I didn't think you were his type, lass, but I canna tell you how glad I am to be proved wrong. Now"—Seamus walked over to sit on the end of the bed—"have you settled on a date yet?"

"A date for—"

His rheumy eyes focused on Evie, who appeared to be frozen to the bed, Seamus went on as though Caine hadn't spoken. "I don't want to put any pressure on you, and it's not like I'll be going to meet my Maker anytime soon. Though I admit I'm a little too fond of Jameson and greasy spoons for my own good." He winked at Evie's mother. "But we're working on that, aren't we, love?"

Evie stared at her mother. "You and Seamus?" Then she stared at Seamus. "You and my mother?"

"Perhaps this conversation would be better off had

downstairs," Caine suggested, leaving out the two most important points, *in clothes* and *without him*. When none of them moved, Caine held the covers to his waist and swung his legs off the mattress. "I have to get Jamie to school."

His uncle patted the bed. "Righto. We'll discuss the date for your wedding later. And like I said, I plan on being around for a while. But I would like to spend some time with your children before I meet my Maker, so perhaps you can keep that in mind."

It was too bad his uncle hadn't saved the last until Caine had gotten both his feet on the floor. As it was, his uncle mentioning them having children after they'd spent the better part of the night having sex, albeit safe sex, caused Caine to jump from the bed without ensuring his foot wasn't tangled in the sheet, and he fell on the floor.

"I'm fine," he muttered when Evie's cry was joined by her mother's and his uncle's. He glanced over his shoulder to send them a look that would shut them up. Couldn't they see he was embarrassed? It was sheer luck that he wasn't lying on a heap on the floor with his bare arse in the air. But as he looked over his shoulder, he discovered luck didn't have anything to do with it. He'd pulled the covers down around him. All of the covers.

Her face in the pillow, Evie said, "I can hear you laughing."

"They're gone." With her whole body flushed, he couldn't resist one last pat to her rosy behind before tossing the blankets over her. "Too bad we hadn't thought to flash your mother when she first walked in. We could have gotten rid of them sooner."

"And saved your uncle from jumping to conclusions. Who's going to break the news we're not getting married and there are no babies in our future? You or me?"

She lifted her head from the pillow to look at him, and it took him a moment to answer. Because right then he saw what his uncle had. Hope. A future. "You. I don't have time to argue with him."

"Right. Because you're busy buying up the world while I'm just the owner of a little Christmas store."

"Not the world." He leaned across the bed to kiss her. It would be the last time, he promised himself. "Just a resort in the Rockies. And you're far more than just an owner of a Christmas shop."

"And you are more than a billionaire businessman."

"You're the only person I know who makes having money sound like a bad thing."

"It is when it becomes the entire focus of your life." She sat up in bed, her hair a dark cloud around her earnest, heart-shaped face. "You know what drives you, don't you, Caine?"

"Can we not do this? I have to grab a shower." He turned to gather up his clothes, closing his eyes at the sound of her moving off the bed. Sighing when her arms went around his waist from behind. "I don't know why I thought you'd let this go."

She rested her soft cheek against his back. "All the money in the world won't protect you from being hurt again."

"If you think my ambition has something to do with my mother abandoning me, you're wrong."

"I'm not wrong. Your past drives you, and you know it does. But contrary to what you think, I don't believe money is the root of all evil. It's everything we attach to it that causes the problem."

"Well, thank you for the—"

She ducked around him and reached up on her toes to kiss the underside of his jaw. "I'll stop. Thank you for opening up to me last night. I know it wasn't easy for you. I hope you know I won't betray your confidence. If you ever want to talk—"

He had to shut her up before he did something stupid like throw all caution to the wind and tell her that he wanted her in his life. Not like the women who'd come before her. He wanted...He couldn't have what he wanted, and she deserved better. He dipped his head to kiss her, and because he vowed it was the last kiss he would share with this woman, he made sure it was one she would never forget.

A kiss she'd remember when some other lucky bastard took her to bed, took her to wed, gave her children...He tore his mouth from hers. Instead of torturing her, he was torturing himself.

"Caine, what—"

He needed to remind her who he was. What was at stake. "I'll be by tonight to pick another angel wish off the tree." When she looked like she might argue, he said, "I went above and beyond for my first assignment, Evie. About four years and twenty-five thousand dollars beyond by my calculation."

The remark had the desired effect; her delicate jaw hardened. She'd be as pleased with his next shot.

"You'll want to think long and hard on this next wish, or I'll have our wager won before the week is out."

He regretted having to hurt her as much as he regretted putting an end to their brief affair. He didn't have to tell her. She was a smart woman, and her face as he walked out of the bedroom had said it all.

As he left Holiday House, his phone in his coat pocket signaled an incoming text. He waited until he was behind the wheel to check the screen. Some of his regret over ending things with Evie lessened the moment he opened his grandmother's text.

Emily had raised the stakes. She'd sent a photo of him on the front step of Holiday House with Evie last night, and one of him leaving only seconds ago. He looked around.

Her message was clear: She knew he'd spent the night with Evie. The threat wasn't as overt but just as obvious. In order to protect Evie, he had to give Emily something. He had to make a move on Greystone Manor.

Today.

Chapter Nineteen

♥

Colleen stood overseeing the decorating of the grand staircase for this weekend's Christmas parade. The banisters were being wrapped with red garland and decorated with white satin bows. It was a change from previous years, and Colleen wasn't sure she was a fan. But she did approve of the white ceramic containers of red poinsettias that were being placed on the steps leading to the second floor.

The Harmony Harbor holiday parade was a decades-old tradition, one in which the Gallaghers had taken part for almost that long. After the loss of her great-granddaughter and her mother, and Colleen's son Ronan but a week later from a broken heart, they'd forgone their hosting responsibilities for several years.

It took her great-grandson's wife, Sophie, manager of the manor, to reinstate the tradition. It was a good thing that she had. It went a ways to helping them heal.

A cold breeze blew across the lobby to ruffle the white satin bows, and Colleen turned to see what had caused the draft. It was Caine. And the lad didn't look happy as he strode across the entryway. He looked like a man on a mission.

"Now, that's a worry," she said to Simon, who was batting at the bows. "Stop playing and have a look at the lad. He's wearing a face of thunder, and I for one would like to know the cause."

Simon meowed, sounding like he was agreeing with her. No, not agreeing with her, she thought, when he nudged his head at the stairs at the same time she heard the rattle of the housekeeping cart on the second level. He was warning her. "You are a smart one; that you are. It's just too bad you aren't smart enough to tell Jasper that Clio has my book."

She'd been hoping Theia might mention to Jasper that the book was missing and suggest that Clio was the thief. But she should have known Theia wouldn't want to admit the book had been stolen on her watch. She was, after all, the one who'd stolen it from Jasper and Kitty. Albeit for a good cause.

If Colleen's memoir hadn't helped to right the wrongs of the past over the last few years, she would have regretted writing *The Secret Keeper of Harmony Harbor* and putting the people she loved at risk. But the book had helped several people, including Jasper. It had kept him out of prison. So Colleen couldn't regret this new mess they found themselves in thanks to Clio and Caine. All she could hope to do was find a way to somehow minimize the damage.

"Caine," Jasper hailed her great-grandson, "I'd like a word."

"Oh my, this doesn't bode well, Simon. Look at

Jasper's face." She glanced at Caine. "What have you done, laddie?" An odd question, she supposed, given everything he'd done these past few years.

"I don't have time for this, Jasper," Caine said, his hands in his coat pockets.

"Too bad. You'll make it for me. You played me for a fool, and I don't take kindly to it. Your concern for Theia and the family seemed genuine, so I agreed to allow the inspection team in."

"My concern was genuine—is genuine, as are the dangers. I didn't make up the results. As the report clearly outlined, you have a serious issue with mold that needs to be dealt with."

"But you didn't give us a chance to do that, did you? I just got off the phone with the health department, who faxed me the very same report I had in my hand. A report you had assured me was for our eyes alone."

"It would have been had you given any indication that you were going to address the issues in the report."

"No. This was your plan from the beginning. I'm sorry to say that you fooled me. It doesn't happen often, but you did. It won't happen again. You're not welcome here. See yourself out before I do it for you."

Colleen pressed a hand to her chest at a hurt that felt all too real. She understood why Jasper wanted Caine gone. She was angry with him herself. But he was family, and you stand by family no matter what. "I hope you have a plan, my boy," she murmured to Jasper. "I surely do, because I've never been more worried about the manor than I am now."

"I was never welcome here. Don't pretend that I was.

But one of your guests, Lenore Johnson, Evie's mother, asked that I pick up her laptop for her. So unless you want—"

Jasper lifted his chin at the stairs, granting his silent permission, before he said, "And it goes without saying that Ms. Johnson will not be given access to our books."

"Your loss. She might have actually been able to save this place." He turned away from Jasper to stride toward the stairs.

"He's played you again, my boy. There's only one reason he's here and one reason alone." And there was nothing Colleen could do about it. She'd never felt so helpless. Still, with Simon leading the way, she raced up the stairs. She didn't have far to go before her worst fears were confirmed. Caine was talking to her great-granddaughter. Clio looked around and then nodded, digging around in her cart. She pulled the brown leather-bound book from under the towels, handing the Colleen's memoir to Caine.

No wonder Colleen hadn't been able to find it. Clio kept the book with her at all times.

Caine pulled out his phone and, as he leafed through the pages, checked something on the screen. Colleen moved to his side to peek at his phone. He had a photo of her handwriting, comparing it to that of her memoir. Ensuring its authenticity, she imagined.

"All right, but I won't agree to your price. Fifteen thousand and not a penny more," Caine said.

Clio took back the book. "No way."

"No one will give you more than what I've offered,

Clio. And if they do, I'll tell Theia and Jasper you have the book and you planned to sell it to me." He swiped the screen of his phone several times before holding it up. He'd taken a picture of Clio removing the book from the housekeeping cart.

"He's a canny lad, Simon. Scarily so. What's worse, he'll stop at nothing to get what he wants."

After shedding some tears and calling Caine several uncomplimentary names, Clio accepted his deal. "Don't waste your brains pulling stunts like this or you'll find yourself in serious trouble. Finish school. They've got a good archaeology program in Boston. You're a smart girl. Apply for a scholarship."

"If you'd given me what you promised, I wouldn't need a scholarship."

"You asked—I didn't promise. If I had, I wouldn't be where I am today." He tucked the book beneath his coat and headed for the stairs.

Colleen followed Caine. "I can't let him out of here with that book, Simon. We have to do something." She noticed the way he held his coat. "Something that will make him lose his grip on my memoir. We could trip him. No, not at the top of the stairs!" she cried when Simon darted in front of him. "I don't want him dead. I just want the book."

"Don't cross my path, cat. I've had enough bad luck for one day," Caine said as he hurried down the grand staircase.

Two steps from the bottom, Colleen decided it was safe for her to try. She made a run for Caine, grabbing at his coat as she sailed by. The lad didn't so much as wobble. The poinsettia wasn't so lucky, falling down the two steps to crash on the slate floor.

"Don't blame me," Caine said as Jasper strode toward him. "Just a friendly piece of advice, but you might want to put that cat on a leash. He nearly tripped me at the top of the stairs. You can't afford to be sued."

"If you'd fallen from there, I don't think we would have worried about you suing."

"It's not me you have to worry about it. It never has been," Caine said, leaving Jasper to frown after him.

Simon dashed after Caine, intent on his prey.

"What are you and Simon up to now, madam?" Colleen heard Jasper murmur.

"If you knew, you'd have a heart attack," she called back to him as she raced after Caine. She was fast, but not as fast as Simon or Caine. Her great-grandson obviously wanted out of there and wanted out quick. "Hurry, Simon. He's getting away!" Colleen cried when Caine reached the entryway.

Simon shot through Caine's legs and then ducked to the right. Caine stumbled, and Colleen held her breath. He grabbed the door at the last minute, saving himself from falling.

Colleen raced after him. Unable to stop as the door closed behind him, she prepared herself to be bounced back into the entryway. Instead she went through the four-inch-thick slab of centuries-old oak and tumbled down the stone steps and onto the front path.

For a moment she sat there stunned. Before last summer, she'd never been able to set so much as a toe out of the manor. If she tried, she'd bounce off what felt like an electrical force field. It was a shocking feeling, to say the least. Yet here she was, sitting outside.

Caine. She still had a chance to stop him. At the sound of a car door slamming, she jumped to her feet, rushing to the end of the pathway. A sleek black car started up.

"No!" she cried as the car backed out of its spot, and she ran across the parking lot. If not for Caine having to slow for another car, Colleen wouldn't have caught up with him. But he did, and she threw herself into the car, landing face-first in the back seat. She rolled over, pressing a hand to her chest. Had she been alive, she wouldn't have survived the excitement, let alone her run across the parking lot.

She pushed herself upright. He was speaking to someone, a woman. An older woman from the sounds of it. One who was having a difficult time breathing, if Colleen wasn't mistaken.

"Don't be so stubborn, Mrs. Jordan," he said over the older woman's muttered protests, "if she doesn't stick the oxygen tubes in her nostrils within the next two seconds, I order you to do it. Don't listen to her if she threatens to fire you. I'll just hire you back. You don't have to worry if she bites you. She's had her rabies shot."

There was a gasp and then a raspy snort of laughter. "I've got it. Go and make me a cuppa," the older woman said, a hint of amusement still in her voice, which led Colleen to believe she'd been the one who laughed.

"Your time in America has made you cocky. Don't forget who runs the show, my boy."

It was clear now that this was not only the woman who laughed, but she was Emily Green Elliot. The woman Colleen's son Ronan had an affair with when he fled to Ireland all those years before. A fit of wedding jitters and old jealousy had caused Ronan and Kitty to break off their engagement, sending Colleen's son to Ireland to heal his hurt pride and explore the country of his parents' birth.

"I haven't forgotten. But you seem to have forgotten who's been running the day-to-day operations of the company for the better part of three years. And if you'd bother to read the latest projections, doing a bloody good job of it," Caine said.

"I don't care about that right now, and well you know it. What I do care about is your lack of progress on the manor. But I found you out, didn't I? Playing house with that Christmas woman."

That was news to Colleen. And apparently news Emily Green Elliot wasn't pleased about. Colleen couldn't say she was pleased with how the other woman spoke about Evie either.

"You didn't have to resort to spying on me, Gran. All you had to do was ask. Who do you have working for you in Harmony Harbor?"

The lad was worried. Colleen could see it in the way his jaw clenched and unclenched and by the white-knuckled grip he had on the steering wheel.

"It's of no concern of yours."

"You're wrong. It's very much my concern. You leave Evie out of this."

"Oh now, you may be a canny lad, but you've just

made a big mistake. You've shown her you care about Evie. You've given her something to use against you, and she seems the type who would," Colleen murmured, not liking that she recognized the tactic because she may have used it herself a time or two. She wasn't a saint, after all.

"Give me what I want and I will," the older woman said on a wheeze.

"That's what I'm doing. I—"

"No, what you've been doing is wasting time on this ridiculous bet you made with the Christmas woman."

"That ridiculous bet is what has allowed me to remain in Harmony Harbor without drawing too much suspicion. I'm also gaining goodwill and support from the town, which will work in our favor once we get the shovels in the ground. I don't want any further delays or protests."

"There are more expedient ways to deal with protestors. If you had let me handle the Christmas woman as I wanted to in the beginning, we wouldn't be having this problem now."

"We're not the Irish mob, Gran."

"It doesn't mean we can't borrow from their playbook."

"If you want me to remain as CEO of Wicklow Developments, it most certainly does."

"You'd do well not to threaten me, boyo. I could take everything away from you with a stroke of my pen."

"And give it to Alec? Yes. I've heard the threat before, and I'm growing tired of it."

He wasn't as blasé as he pretended. Colleen was sure his grandmother knew it too.

"Then do something about it. I want the ownership papers for the Gallagher estate in my hands before I die."

"And you'll have them. But you need to back off and stop threatening Evangeline. You're distracting me from getting the job done."

Colleen bowed her head. He kept walking into Emily's trap. Colleen understood why. Whether he knew it or not, he had strong feelings for Evie. Something Colleen wasn't above exploiting herself. But for the lad's own good. He was one of hers. He belonged in Harmony Harbor, and she'd do whatever she had to do to keep him here. Evie might just be the key.

"From what I can see, you're no further ahead."

"Check your e-mail. The health department should be arriving at the manor any moment now to shut them down. I've alerted the local newspaper, of course. We'll also be offering their guests accommodations at our hotel in Bridgeport."

Colleen gasped. They were in bigger danger than she'd ever imagined.

"It's a start. The disruption should put them one step closer to bankruptcy, with the added bonus of ruining their Christmas festivities. Has the bank manager agreed to sell you their loan?"

"No. So I've made an offer for the Savings and Loan. But Mr. Bradford isn't interested in selling just yet."

"Then you'd best make him interested."

"You underestimate me. And you underestimate the benefit of my presence in town under the guise of fulfilling angel wishes. People talk, and I'm here to listen. So is Uncle Seamus, who spends his evenings at the local pub."

"You'd best not let him know how you mean to use the information he gives you. He's a sentimental fool, just like my son was. It's a good thing I beat that out of you, my boy."

"Bejaysus, I'd like to reach through that screen and beat you for what you've done to my great-grandson. If it's the last thing I do, I will stop you once and for all, Emily Green Elliot. Your reign of terror over my family ends now," Colleen said.

There was a muffled noise, and then another voice came over the line. "Mr. Elliot, I think it best that your grandmother have her tea and rest. Perhaps you can call back in an hour?"

"I will, and I'll get in touch with her doctor to have him stop by. The oxygen doesn't seem to be helping as it should."

"I noticed that as well and called the doctor myself, sir. He'll stop in after her evening meal."

"Thanks, Mrs. Jordan. I should have known you'd be on top of it. I probably haven't said it enough, but I appreciate everything you're doing for my grandmother. I don't know what we'd do without you."

"That's kind of you to say, sir. And the pay raise was much appreciated."

"A pay raise? What bloody for?" came the querulous voice in the background. "It seems you're a sentimental fool after all."

"Lucky for you that I am or I would have saved my money and put you in a home instead of hiring private nurses. Now, behave yourself or I'll tell Mrs. Jordan where to find the arsenic."

"Sir!" the nurse cried, while his grandmother's snort of laughter turned into a coughing fit.

Colleen could see the concern on Caine's face. Whatever she might think of Emily Green Elliot, it was clear the boy loved the older woman, and as the teasing indicated, they were close. But there was a strain in their relationship too. He didn't like how his grandmother conducted business. Yet it looked like he was willing to do whatever he had to in order to grant her final wish.

Or was it merely a ploy? Colleen wondered, thinking back to his obvious concern about Evie. It sounded like Emily had made a threat against the girl just prior to Caine pulling the stunt with the health department. She hadn't seen an ulterior motive when he'd initially called in the air-quality team. He'd been genuinely concerned about Theia's health.

Colleen sat back in the seat to ponder her options. She hadn't thought to wonder where they were going until she looked out the passenger-side window. "Oh my," she cried, pressing her hands to her chest. It had been years since she'd seen her beloved hometown. And to think, caught up in the machinations of Emily Green, she'd almost missed it. She pressed her face to the window to get a better look at the familiar shops along Main Street.

Oh, what a beautiful sight. They were decorated for the holidays. She checked the faces of the people hustling along the snow-dusted sidewalks, searching for someone familiar.

"Mr. O'Malley," she cried, smiling at his familiar holiday getup as he welcomed a couple into his shop. He caught sight of Caine and waved. The smile on the lad's face was genuine. Just like the one he offered to the owners of Truly Scrumptious and In Bloom.

Whether he knew it or not, he was becoming one of them. He could pretend with his grandmother all he wanted that he had an ulterior motive for agreeing to Evie's bet, but Colleen didn't believe him. There was goodness in the lad. He just needed...the love of a good woman to put him on the road to redemption.

To Colleen's mind, there was no one better suited for the job than Evie Christmas. And given Caine's defense of the girl during his conversation with his grandmother, there was already some interest on his part. All that was left for Colleen to do was work her matchmaking magic.

She smiled when Caine parked just up the street from Holiday House. "And it looks like the Fates are on my side."

Chapter Twenty

♥

Colleen got out of Caine's car to stand with the small crowd that had gathered on the sidewalk. There was quite a commotion in front of Evie's store, as an army of workers appeared to be decorating the outside of Holiday House.

"Won't be but a few minutes more, folks," a man with a thick Irish accent informed the crowd with a winsome grin. Colleen suspected he was Caine's uncle. Seamus, the one who was spending his evenings at the pub. She didn't mean to be judgmental, but his red nose gave him away. Although there was a brisk breeze, so it was possible Jack Frost had been nipping at his nose.

"How's it going, Uncle?" Caine asked as he came to stand by the older man to look up at the house.

His uncle patted him on the back. "You're a sly one, you are, and you know your girl well. You would have thought you'd given her diamonds and free rein with your American Express card when she came out here and saw what you've done."

Caine didn't fool Colleen with his nonchalant shrug. She'd seen the pleased look on his face before he replaced it with one of indifference for his uncle's benefit. She smiled. It seemed the couple didn't need any matchmaking help from her. They were already well on their way to their happy-ever-after. Then Colleen remembered the voice in the car, and her smile fell.

Emily Green Elliot would not be happy to learn her grandson had fallen in love with Evie. Colleen didn't doubt the woman she'd heard on the phone would do whatever she had to do to put a stop to it. And she wouldn't care who got hurt in the process.

This job was too big for Colleen alone, especially in her ghostly state. Somehow, she had to get Caine to stay at the manor. Preferably in her tower room. With that in mind, she followed him into Holiday House.

The shop smelled like gingerbread and brought back memories of Christmases past. Colleen used to love to visit Holiday House. It was one of her favorite shops in Harmony Harbor. She couldn't believe the town council had played a part in having the old place torn down. The council and the man who Evie was practically gobbling up with her eyes. The lass was smitten, of that Colleen was certain. She glanced at Caine. Over the moon in a yellow balloon, she thought.

Evie smiled at the woman she'd been serving and then walked over to Caine. "I don't know what to say," Evie began. Then, looking like she might cry, she threw her arms around him. "No one has ever done anything like this for me. I can't tell you how much it means to me." She leaned back to look at him. "Especially when I know how you feel about the holidays. Thank you."

His reserve melted in the face of Evie's pleasure, and a smile creased his handsome face. Until the front door opened, and he stepped away, his mask sliding back into place. "You're welcome. But you're making too much of it. I told you I'd put up the lights for you. I simply paid someone to do it for me."

Evie looked like he'd slapped her, but she quickly recovered. "Of course, what was I thinking? After all, it's not like we're in a relationship or anything. We just slept together. No biggie."

"Dammit, Evie." He looked around the shop and took her by the hand, tugging her to a private corner by the fire.

Colleen supposed she should give them some privacy after Evie's surprising revelation, but it wasn't as if they'd know she was there. And she wanted to find out exactly what she was up against.

"I'm sorry," Caine apologized. "I shouldn't have said that."

"No, you shouldn't have. But I know why you did. Intimacy scares you."

"I should've known you'd try to analyze this to death." He put his hands on her shoulders. "You don't scare me, Evie. Intimacy doesn't scare me, and in no way did I mean to diminish our night together. It's just that..." He dropped his hands to his sides and stepped back. "It's complicated."

"You're right, it is. And I'm okay with complicated.

But obviously, you're not." She smiled at a woman who called her over. "I'll be right with you."

"You're busy. I'll pick an angel off the tree and get out of your way."

"No," she said, looking frantic. "You can't."

"Why not?"

"Because." She looked around. "Because someone wanted to put up an angel wish and they're not here yet."

"When do you expect them?"

"Tonight. Around seven o'clock. Maybe eight. You can come back tomorrow."

"No. I want to get it over with now. Tell them they can put their angel on the tree in time for my last wish."

That's it, Colleen thought, looking beyond Caine and Evie to see the angel tree. *That's how I'll put my plan into action.* Now all she needed was someone to help her write out the wish, because that was one skill she'd yet to master. She looked around the store while Caine and Evie argued, ruling out the baby boy in the buggy.

But the little blond girl who was sitting playing with a teddy bear appeared to be the perfect age. Colleen crouched beside the table in an effort not to scare the child away. "Hello, little one."

The child's brown eyes rounded. "I wasn't taking him. I just wanted to play with him."

"I don't blame you. He's a very nice Santa bear."

"Are you a ghost?" the little girl asked, nibbling on her bottom lip.

"No. I'm a Christmas angel, and I need your help. Is your mommy here with you?"

"Yes. She's buying my grandma's Christmas present." She pointed out a woman at the cash register. "What do you need me to do?"

"Let's go to the angel tree, and I'll tell you. But we have to hurry because we want that big man over there to get our very special angel wish. And if he does, you can tell him the Christmas angel says you were a wonderful helper and he should buy you the bear."

Any hesitation on the child's part vanished after that, and she did an excellent job dictating what her mother was to write on the angel.

"Who did you say told you to write the note, darling?"

"Her." She pointed at Colleen. "The little old lady. She's a Christmas angel."

"Darling, she's not old. She's a beautiful angel."

"Why, thank you," Colleen said, thinking her wrinkles must be invisible in her ghostly state. And wasn't that a marvelous thing. "I didn't realize you could see me or I would have—"

From directly behind her, a voice said, "I need a new angel for my tree. What do you think of this one?"

Colleen turned to see a woman holding up an angel for her friend and sighed. The little girl's mother hadn't been talking about her after all.

"I'm supposed to give the angel to that man." The child took the paper angel from her mother and walked over to Caine, who was waiting impatiently for Evie to get off the phone.

The little girl tugged on his arm. "This is your angel wish."

"Is that so?" He smiled at the child and took the pink

paper angel from her, turning it over to read the wish.
His smile fell. "You put her up to this, didn't you?" he
said to Evie, who'd just ended her call.

The child's mother stepped forward. "My daughter
dictated the angel wish to me. Is there a problem?"
she asked, resting a protective hand on the shoulder of
Colleen's little helper.

"No problem at all," Evie said as she crouched in
front of the little girl. "It's the perfect angel wish. Did
you think of it all by yourself?"

The child shook her head. "No. The Christmas angel
did. Her name is GG." The little girl looked up at Caine.
"She said you'd buy me Santa Bear."

* * *

Caine stood at the kitchen sink, running the water before
filling his glass. He could use a shot of whiskey, but
a search of Evie's cupboards proved futile. He glanced
at Bruiser. The cat was acting weird. Weird in that
he wasn't comatose in a puddle of sunshine. He stood
staring at something behind Caine.

Feck it. Caine turned around. There was nothing
there. Well, there hadn't been until Theia walked into
the kitchen. "I should have known she'd call you. How
long have the two of you been planning this? Don't
even try to deny you had something to do with that
angel wish." He turned back to the sink.

"I didn't. Actually, that's not completely true," Theia
admitted.

"I knew it," Caine said, relieved that he'd been right

and his best friend and Evie had cooked this up because he didn't want to consider the other option.

"Don't get ahead of yourself. I had nothing to do with the wish the little girl gave you. It's just that it's uncannily similar to what I suggested."

Caine pointed his empty glass at her. "Aha, there it is. Admit it. You were talking to Evie about it on the phone seconds before the little girl handed me the angel. Somehow Evie got the message to the child's mother."

"Good try, but no. Last night at book club, when Evie was stressing about coming up with a second angel assignment for you, I suggested that you help bring the holiday spirit to the manor."

"And why the bloody hell would you suggest that?" He waved his hand. "Never mind. I know the answer already. You want me to lose."

She scrunched up her nose. "Yes and no."

"You can't have it both ways."

"I know the office tower's important to you, and you've put a lot of time and money into it, so no, I wouldn't want you to give up on that. But I don't want Evie to lose either. And she's got so much more to lose than you do, Caine."

"I know she does." He set the glass on the sink. The situation was untenable, and he'd made it ten times worse. He never should have gotten close to Evie.

"You have to tell her, Caine. You owe her the truth."

He turned to frown at Theia. "The truth about what?"

"About who you really are. It's important she hears it from you. I made the mistake of not telling Marco, and I nearly lost him. I don't want you to risk that with Evie. You guys—"

"Theia, I don't know what Evie's told you, but there's no *us*. It was only the one night. I was upset, and she had one too many...Ouch. What was that for?" he said, rubbing the arm she'd punched.

"You slept with Evie?!"

"Uh. Yes. What were you talking about if not that?"

"The lights! You had her house decorated for the parade. I've been around you long enough to know that you don't do things like that for women who don't mean something to you. And you've spent more time with her than half the women you've dated combined."

"Of course she means something to me, T. But we're not like you and Marco. We—"

"How do you know if you don't give it a chance?"

Caine looked up to see Evie hovering at the entrance to the kitchen, and he glared at Theia. There was no way Evie had missed some of their conversation, which was evident when her eyes met his. "Sorry. I didn't mean to interrupt. I was just wondering if you were okay. You seemed upset."

Which was no doubt why she'd called Theia to come. "It's me who should apologize. I'm sorry I overreacted, Evie. I thought you and Theia had conspired to come up with a wish that...I couldn't possibly complete."

"I'm sure Theia already told you this, but the Gallaghers were the reason I suggested you wait until tomorrow to pick your wish. They wanted some time to think about what they would have you do. They were in a meeting discussing it when I called Theia."

"The pick-a-wish meeting was postponed. We had an emergency come up, which I'm sure you know about, Caine. Since you're the one who orchestrated it."

And the timing couldn't be more perfect, he thought. "It's not like I was going behind anyone's back. No doubt you've seen the results of the manor's air-quality tests. I had an obligation to alert the authorities. It was obvious no one at Greystone was going to do anything about the problem."

"Of course they were. Just not as fast or to the degree you wanted them to. Which, by the way, was over-the-flipping-top. Because you have a problem. Seriously, you should talk to Evie about it."

"I don't have a problem, T. I—"

"He does, Evie. He has a phobia about old houses. He thinks they're death traps of one kind or another. Don't tell me he hasn't tried to convince you that Holiday House is going to fall down around you."

"Now that you mention it…" Evie began, looking at him like she wanted to get him on a couch and probe his mind while taking notes.

It'd be a cold day in hell before he'd let anyone dig around in his head. "I didn't say Holiday House was going to fall down around you. I said it was going to burn up with you in it. So did the electrician, if you remember. Just like the team of professionals said the manor had black mold."

"I read the report, and nowhere did it recommend closing the manor until the mold was dealt with, which the health department just did by slapping a notice on the door of the manor," Theia said.

"Oh no, that's terrible. So they won't be hosting the open house after the parade tomorrow?" Evie asked.

"I don't think so. In fact, thanks to Scrooge here, it looks like there'll be no Christmas at the manor."

"Apart from the bit about it being my fault, I have to agree. So"—he handed Evie the pink paper angel—"I'll pick another angel off the tree."

"Oh no, you don't." Theia took the paper angel from Evie and pressed it to his chest. "You're not getting off the hook that easy."

"Really? You think they'll want me there after this? Jasper already kicked me out of the manor and told me not to show my face again."

Theia blinked. "He did?"

"Yes. He did." Caine had known all along that Jasper's loyalties lay with the Gallaghers. But he'd enjoyed his battle of wits with the older man. He'd come to admire Jasper and appreciated the unlikely friendship that had developed out of their unholy alliance. So while he wasn't completely surprised, he'd been hurt by the disdain he'd seen in the older man's eyes.

"Too bad. He doesn't get a say. If he has a problem with you being there, he can take it up with me. You're my best friend, and you're..." She glanced at him and then at Evie, but instead of outing him like he thought she might, Theia said, "Colleen obviously wants you there, so he'll just have to suck it up."

"Um, the only Colleen I know is Colleen Gallagher, and she, uh, died years ago, Theia," Evie said.

"Oh, she knows she died," Caine said. "She just doesn't think Colleen made it to the other side."

"I don't understand..." Evie's eyes went wide, and Caine grinned when she began looking at Theia like she'd been looking at him only moments before.

"Yes, she thinks the Gallagher matriarch is a ghost who haunts the tower room. Perhaps you should talk to her about it, Evie. It's becoming a bit of a problem."

"Don't pretend you didn't feel something in the room. You admitted as much." Theia smoothed out the paper angel that Caine had crumpled. "How do you explain this, then? The little girl said the Christmas angel was named GG. That's what all the great-grandchildren called Colleen," she explained to Evie. "And who other than Colleen would want you to do this? She knows who you are. She wants to..." She trailed off.

"What do you mean, she knows who he is?" Evie asked.

He could tell by Theia's face that she didn't want to lie to Evie, but she would, for him. "Just that she knows he's the CEO of—"

Caine interrupted Theia. She'd spent the past year lying because of him, and he wouldn't make her do it again. Besides, she was right. He needed to be the one to tell Evie. He didn't want her to hear it from someone else. Not because he thought they had a future together but because he'd already hurt her once today by downplaying their night together. "Evie, I'm a Gallagher. I'm Theia's cousin."

She blinked. "Oh, I, uh, wasn't expecting that. Now that you mention it, I can see the resemblance. You have the Gallagher-blue eyes. But I don't understand. If they're your family, why are you trying to destroy them?"

"I'm not trying to destroy them. I—"

"His grandmother is, and she's using him to do her evil bidding. She's brainwashed him into believing the Gallaghers deserve to lose everything, and she won't be happy until they do. Maybe he'll listen to you, Evie. Because he won't listen to me. His grandmother is a sociopath, and she needs to be stopped before she hurts somebody. Before she hurts him," Theia said, then burst into tears.

Stunned by her emotional display, it took a moment for Caine to react. Shaking off his shock, he walked to Theia and took her in his arms. "T, you're getting worked up over nothing. Emily won't hurt me. She can't. Please stop crying. You're going to make yourself sick." He patted her back, looking to Evie for help.

"It's okay. It's just the baby. She—" Evie pressed a hand to her mouth, casting an apologetic glance at Theia. "I'm so sorry. I didn't mean to tell him, but he's obviously worried about—"

"A *baby*. You're having a baby?" He held Theia away from him, his gaze moving from her tear-filled eyes to her flat stomach before jerking back to her face when the reality of the situation hit him. "You're having a baby and you've been living in a mold-infested manor!" he practically roared. He pulled out his phone.

"What are you doing?"

"I'm calling Marco, and we're moving you out of the manor today. Now. This very minute."

"Good. That's a great idea," Theia said, wiping her face on her sleeve.

"And don't try to...Wait a minute. What did you just say?"

"I said it's a great idea."

"It is?" he said, thinking his best friend was losing her mind, and he blamed it entirely on Marco and the mold.

"Yes, it is. Because now you can stay in the tower room while you complete your second angel assignment."

Chapter Twenty-One

♥

Evie sat at the kitchen table watching Caine prowl from one end of the room to the other like an angry lion trapped by his feelings for his best friend. It amused her that, for a smart man, he couldn't see that Theia was playing on his emotions and his concern for her.

His vulnerability surprised Evie. Though she supposed it shouldn't. She'd seen hints of his softer side. A man couldn't be as thoughtful or as generous as Caine without having one. It's just that he was exceptionally good at convincing people otherwise. The better to keep them at arm's length, she thought.

But his worry over Theia was real. Evie had known they were best friends, but she hadn't seen them interact much before today. She was envious of their friendship. It was a rare gift to find someone who you knew with complete certainty would stand by you no matter what. It was just one more side of Caine that Evie could have done without seeing.

She was halfway in love with him. Something she hadn't truly realized until she stood outside watching the men put up the Christmas lights. Yet it wasn't until Caine dismissed their night together as if it had been nothing more than a one-night stand that she'd understood how quickly she'd gone from crushing to caring to falling. She wasn't all the way there, so it wasn't too late to save herself from potential heartbreak. She'd have enough to deal with if she lost Holiday House. She didn't need to lose Caine too.

"Would you explain to the crazy pregnant woman that I can't fulfill the second angel assignment at the manor, so there's no reason to stay there? And while you're at it, can you explain to her that her hormones are messing with her mind and there's no such thing as ghosts?" Caine said to Evie.

"Please don't talk about the crazy pregnant woman as if she isn't here." Theia waved her spoon. She was sitting with her feet up on a chair, eating candy-cane ice cream. "And second..." She frowned. "Does anyone else hear scratching and meowing?"

Evie looked for Bruiser on his favorite braided rug by the window, but he wasn't there. "Where's Bruiser?"

"After staring at that spot on the floor for about fifteen minutes, he took off." Caine pointed at a patch of faded tile near the refrigerator, then walked to the back door. He opened it and looked down. "I don't bloody believe it."

"Whose cat is that? And why did you just let it in my house?" Evie asked, staring at the black cat who padded across her kitchen to the exact spot Caine had just pointed at. The cat sat down.

"You see! She's here. Standing right there," Theia said.

"It's Simon. From the manor," Caine explained to

Evie. "And I couldn't very well leave him outside. His paws appear to be frozen."

Theia took off her jacket and went to wrap it around Simon. "The story goes that he arrived at the manor just days before Colleen died and was with her when she did. He went and got help for her, didn't you, Simon? And now you're here to bring her home. She must have hopped a ride with you," Theia told Caine.

"You do know how crazy you sound, don't you?" Caine said, though he didn't sound as convinced of that as he was before.

"GG, if you want Caine to fulfill your angel wish, give us a sign," Theia said.

Simon meowed.

"Sorry, that doesn't count…" Caine trailed off as the pink angel that he'd left on the counter floated to his feet. "The wood around the windows are rotting. It's the draft that made it fly."

"Well, that settles that. You're off to the manor to perform your second angel assignment," Theia said cheerfully.

Caine crossed his arms and looked at Evie. "There's no sense in asking you for help, is there? There's no way the Gallaghers will let me win this assignment."

"I don't think that's true. But obviously I have more faith in you—and in them—than you do. However the angel wish came about, it's meant for your benefit, Caine. Just like Jamie was."

"You know that makes you sound as crazy as Theia, right? Because that sounds like you want me to win my second angel assignment."

"I absolutely do." She smiled. "And since you're always telling me that money can solve any problem, prove it. Get the health department to rescind their order so that you can bring Christmas back to the manor."

* * *

Colleen smiled as she followed Caine into her tower room after arriving back from her trip to town and to the Bridgeport Hotel. "You could have knocked me over with a feather when I found out my great-grandson owned our biggest competitor, Simon. Honestly, what the Elliots wouldn't do to get their revenge. Well, that's all in the past—of that I'm certain. The family will win Caine over in no time at all. Though it might take longer for the lad to gain Jasper's trust. He wasn't exactly welcoming, now, was he? I think he may have hurt Caine's feelings. Sophie wasn't much better. I suppose I can't blame them for being less than friendly after he got the manor closed down. Thank goodness Evie got Caine to make the call to the health department. Though it sounded like he had to grease a few palms to get them to rescind the order. I guess he proved to Evie that money comes in handy after all."

She glanced over her shoulder at Simon, who was following her. "Did you see what I did? The two of them are head over heels and don't even know it." Colleen smiled as she flopped down on the couch. "I haven't had that much fun in years. Wasn't it grand to be out and about, Simon?"

He lifted a whiskered brow as he stretched out on the

back of the couch. "Not so grand for you, I suppose. But your paws seem to be none the worst for your frostbite. I hope you know I appreciated you coming after me. I must have given you a fright."

From where she lay, Colleen watched her great-grandson bang about. "He's not thrilled the ladies in his life have put him in this position, is he? It'll be for the best, laddie," she called out to Caine, testing to see if he could hear her. He showed no sign that he had, and Colleen wasn't surprised. Gadding about had cost her her strength. "It's a good thing the family won't be needing my help this evening. I—" She sat up. "Simon, I think there's someone in my closet."

She looked to see if Caine had noticed, but the lad had his phone pressed between his ear and shoulder, allowing him to talk while at the same time unpacking his bag, from which he pulled Colleen's memoir. He left her book on the end of the bed while continuing to settle into the room. With a shaving kit in hand, he walked into the en-suite bathroom. As he did, a redhead popped out of the closet. Clio. The girl tiptoed to the bed to retrieve the book, but just as she reached for it, Caine said, "Give me a second, and I'll grab the information for you."

At the sound of him returning to the bedroom, Clio dove under the bed.

*　*　*

"Thank God," Caine said when he opened the tower room door to see Evie standing there. She wore a red ski jacket and a knitted hat and held a take-out bag in her mittened hands. He pulled her inside. "I've never been so glad to see someone in my life."

"Are you talking about me or your burger and fries?" She held up the bag.

"Both." He grinned, then kissed her because he really was glad to see her. He felt like he was in the enemy camp, and it was good to see a friendly face. How she'd ended up being the first person he thought of when he was sitting alone and feeling sorry for himself, he didn't know.

"You do realize that the manor has a dining room and the food is very good, don't you? I'm pretty sure you can get room service too."

"I don't trust them not to poison me," he said, only half-joking. "Jasper and Sophie aren't exactly thrilled that I'm here."

"You didn't tell them you're Colleen's long-lost great-grandson, did you?" she said as she took off her hat and coat.

"No, I didn't. And give me those." He put the bag of food on the dresser and motioned for her hat and coat. "I think the room is haunted."

"Maybe you have—"

He held up a finger. "Don't mention the R-word."

"I was going to say the M-word, but I'm sure Simon would have taken care of either problem." She nodded at the cat stretched out on the back of the couch as she pulled off her boots and smiled. "I hope you're prepared to share. I'm starved."

She wore a pair of faded jeans and a red sweater

that made her look soft and womanly, and suddenly he wasn't hungry for food anymore. He'd been going to suggest they eat on the bed, but he no longer thought that was a good idea. "I might be able to spare some fries," he said, picking up the bag from the dresser.

"You should grab a towel so we don't get crumbs on the bedspread," she suggested as she crawled onto the middle of the bed.

"Right." He leaned across to hand her the bag and then walked into the bathroom, thinking a cold shower might be in order. His stomach growled, reminding him he was indeed starved.

Both his desire and appetite vanished when he returned to the room to discover Evie propped against the pillows reading *The Secret Keeper of Harmony Harbor*. Her wide eyes moved to him. "Um, have you read this? The title is not a lie. Colleen knew everyone's secrets."

"I haven't had a chance. I planned to read it tonight," he said, unable to keep the irritation from his voice.

"I'm sorry." She closed the book and put it on the nightstand. "I shouldn't have picked it up. It was just sitting there, so I assumed—"

"No. I'm sorry. I shouldn't have snapped at you. It's just that I'm not looking forward to learning what happened to my grandmother at the hands of the Gallaghers. It was pretty awful from what she's told me."

"Maybe it would help if we read it together. That way you'd have someone to talk to about it. Sometimes it helps to get another person's perspective. Someone who's not emotionally involved." She kept her eyes on the towel as she helped him spread it and then set about laying out the food. "Just a thought," she said.

"A good one. If you're willing to hang around for a bit, I'd like you here when I read the book." He hadn't realized how apprehensive he'd been about reading the memoir until the weight lifted off his shoulders at Evie's offer. He joined her on the bed, smiling at the double order. "You didn't intend to make me share after all. You're a keeper, Evie Christmas."

"You're easy to please," she said, looking flustered.

"Far from it." Their eyes met and held, and he was the first to break contact. If he didn't, he was afraid he'd tell her he meant what he'd said. And not for the first time, he wished he could keep her in his life. Instead he took a bite of his burger.

She smiled at what must have been his expression of surprised delight. "Amazing, aren't they? Jolly Rogers makes the best burgers. Fries are fantastic too."

"I've heard they also make a brilliant Irish breakfast. Uncle Seamus has hit every pub and restaurant in town." He frowned as she dipped her golden French fry in a container of something white. "What are you dipping your fries in?"

"Mayo."

"No accounting for—"

She popped the fry in his mouth.

"I take back what I was about to say. You have excellent taste."

They spent the rest of the meal talking about her day, about how her mother had surprisingly become quite the saleswoman and how Evie thought it was all thanks to his uncle's influence. "And what are they up to this evening?"

"When I left, they were arguing over which movie to watch."

"Are you okay with all the time they're spending together? If you aren't, I can talk—"

"No. Seamus is good for my mom. And I think she's good for him. Did you notice he's not going to the pub as much?"

"I did. And I agree, although they're complete opposites, they seem to be good for each other."

"There's a reason opposites attract, I guess," she said, then became overly interested in the pattern on the red-and-gold comforter.

It wasn't hard to understand why. Like Seamus and Lenore, he and Evie were each other's opposites. He opened his mouth, thinking they needed to talk about it, about them and why there couldn't be a them. He'd messed things up earlier today and didn't like how he'd left things.

But apparently Evie didn't want to talk about it because she began cleaning up the wrappers and containers. "You'd better wash your hands before you pick up the book. You don't want to get grease on the pages."

"Right." He gathered up the towel and went to the bathroom to shake it off in the tub before doing as she suggested.

She did the same, then rejoined him on the bed. "You can tell me if this is none of my business, but I have heard a little about this book. You don't live in

Harmony Harbor long before someone brings it up. I heard it was missing, yet..." She made an open-palm gesture to the leather-bound book now in his hands.

"Yeah, and from what I've heard, it would probably be best if it had stayed missing. I wouldn't want to think what would happen if my grandmother got ahold of it. Promise you'll keep this between you and me?" It was a stupid question really. He trusted her implicitly. He probably shouldn't, but he did. And it was odd, because he didn't trust easily.

"Of course. I've told you before that I'd never betray your confidence, and I won't."

"It's not that I doubt you. It's just, if word got out the book had been found, there might be people willing to do whatever they had to do to keep their secrets hidden. Theia had the book. I don't know how she got it, and I don't really care. But as soon as I've read what I need to, I'll return it to her to do with what she will. I trust her to do what's right, and I think Colleen would too."

"I think your great-grandmother would trust you to do what's right with her memoir too, Caine."

"I'm not so sure about that, but I appreciate that you think so. Now, when you were looking through it earlier, did you get an idea how she set it up? Was it alphabetically, by year, or—"

"By year."

"Let's open it in the middle and go from there. My dad would have been fifty-nine last month so that would mean she should have written about him and Emily somewhere around 1959 and 1960." He flipped through, trying to look at dates without focusing on the stories of anyone who wasn't an Emily or Killian. "There's nothing. Absolutely nothing about them from 1959 to 1970."

His phone vibrated on the bedside table with incoming texts. He glanced at the screen, groaning when they kept coming, and he tossed it on the bed. The phone slid off, falling onto the floor.

Evie put a hand on his arm. "Everything okay?"

"My grandmother found out about my latest angel assignment. She's less than pleased I'm staying at the manor. Though I'm sure, in the next few minutes, she'll figure out a way to use it to her advantage. Don't worry about it," he said when a frown furrowed Evie's brow. He leaned over to grab his phone off the floor, only it wasn't there. "I'll deal with it tomorrow. She should be in bed by now anyhow. It's almost one in the morning her time."

Evie opened her mouth. Then, seeming to think better of it, she took the book from him. "Here, let me look," she offered, and then, whether she did so to comfort him because she sensed he was upset or it was unintentional, she snuggled against him.

Distracted, he stopped patting the floor for this phone and put his arm around her shoulders, resting his chin on her head. "I'm glad you're here."

"I am too." She tipped her head back and kissed the underside of his chin. "And now I'm going to say something that may have you wishing I weren't."

"About this morning, Evie. I—"

"Not about us or what happened last night. It's about what you've grown up hearing about the Gallaghers. I never met Colleen, and admittedly I haven't lived here all that long, but from what I've seen and heard, if the Gallaghers had known about your dad, they wouldn't have turned Emily away. They would have brought them into the fold. That's what they do. With everyone. They've even done it with me. And it's not just them. It's this community. They're good people—"

"You did read some of the stories in here, didn't you?" He tapped the book. "Because as much as I tried not to—"

"Everyone has skeletons in their closet. Everyone has done things they're not proud of. None of us is perfect. Not you, not me."

"I don't know. I think you're pretty perfect."

"Sure you do. What was it you called me, a shrew? Or was it a harpy?"

"That wasn't me. It was my evil twin." He grinned down at her, and the way she was smiling up at him, the way she felt in his arms, made him forget all about the book and his need for answers. "Evie, I—" He broke off at a knock on the door.

"Mr. Elliot, it's Kitty Gallagher. I was wondering if you could spare us some time to talk about your duties." The older woman's voice came through the door.

Evie elbowed him when he didn't answer. "Duties?" he whispered to Evie, then loud enough for Kitty to hear him, "Certainly. Just give me a minute. I'll be right with you."

"Take your time. We're meeting at the bar."

"Do not even think about leaving," he said to Evie when she scooted off the bed. "You're coming with me to this meeting. I need your protection."

Chapter Twenty-Two

♥

"You're a six-foot-four gazillionaire. I hardly think you need my protection from Kitty Gallagher," Evie said to Caine as they got in the elevator.

But she did feel protective of him. It was obvious that the world as he knew it was becoming unglued. He was completely out of his element. Family and holidays were an enigma to him. And because of her, he was wading into the middle of both. And if Emily Green Elliot was a sociopath—*antisocial personality disorder* was the term Evie would use—like Theia believed, the older woman would know how to use the Gallagher family to her best advantage.

Though these days, thanks to Hollywood, people were often inaccurately labeled a sociopath or psychopath. Evie prayed that was the case with Caine's grandmother.

"I'm not a gazillionaire, and it's not Kitty I need protection from. It's Jasper and Sophie."

Evie went up on her toes to wrap her arms around his neck. "I won't let anyone be mean to you. And I promise not to let them give you a job that makes you uncomfortable," she said, then kissed him, because that was as close as he was going to get to comfort sex. They were in an elevator, after all.

No, it's not because you're in an elevator! It's because you're not having sex with him anymore!

"Evie," Caine said as he broke the kiss, sounding all gravelly and sexy. "I appreciate you trying to comfort me...That is what you were trying to do, isn't it?"

"Yes. Comfort. I was trying to comfort you," she said, thinking she would be a gazillionaire if she could bottle this feeling. She gave her head a small shake to get rid of the warm-and-fuzzies as the elevator *ding*ed and the door went to open onto the lobby.

Caine leaned across her to press a button, and it closed again.

"What are you doing?"

"I need a minute. Your comforting worked a little too well."

She followed his gaze to the front of his jeans. "Oh, I see," she said, and pressed her lips together to keep from laughing.

"You have an odd sense of humor, woman."

* * *

Colleen looked at her memoir on the nightstand. "Caine and Evie have left the book in plain sight. Are they mad? Do they not know the danger they've put everyone in?"

Spotting a hand coming out from under the bed,

Colleen flung herself across the mattress to grab the book off the nightstand, but her hand went through both. "I need your help, Simon. The trip downtown wore me out. I have no energy left to make my hands work as they should."

Simon jumped onto the bed and went to the nightstand. He tried to fit his mouth around the book, but it was too thick. At the sound of Clio cursing as she pulled herself from under the bed, he tugged on the book with both paws. It fell between the bed and nightstand.

"It's not ideal, but perhaps she'll think Caine took the book with him," Colleen said as her great-granddaughter stood, brushing off her dusty sweatshirt and jeans.

Simon gave a pessimistic meow.

"Leave me with some hope because right now I need something to hang on to. I fear she heard what Caine said, Simon. And if she did, and uses it to her advantage, we are in big trouble. Pretend you're asleep. Guard the spot. If you have to take a swipe at her to do so, go right ahead."

Beside the bed, Clio said, "I know you're here, GG. And I know it was you who tried to spook me from under the bed. My da told me all about your tricks. So you don't scare me. Neither do you, cat. Now move away or I'll move you. I heard the book fall. I'm not deaf like my *cousin*," she said, and shoved Simon out of the way.

"No, don't do it," Colleen warned when he went to take a swipe at the girl. "I don't trust her not to toss you off the bed. She has a temper, and she blames all of us for the trouble her father got into. If only she could see she's headed down the same path."

Clio's arm disappeared up to her shoulder as she dug between the bed and nightstand. A triumphant smile spread across her face when she straightened, holding the book aloft. "Now let's see what Caine's grandmother is willing to pay for the book. I'd wager a lot more than the pittance her grandson foisted on me. No one cheats me and gets away with it," she said as she pulled a phone from her back pocket. It had to be her own. Caine had retrieved his from the floor before heading out the door.

Colleen had watched Clio snatch up the cell phone when Caine first dropped it, getting a good long look. Once she'd gotten the information she needed, she'd pushed it in front of the nightstand. Colleen had prayed Caine would see Clio when he'd bent to retrieve it, but he'd been anxious about his meeting with the family.

"Cheat you?" Colleen said when Clio sat on the side of the bed. "You stole my memoir, and you're doing so again, preparing to sell it to the one who means to bring us down. But you don't care as long as you get what you feel you deserve. One day soon, like your father did, you'll discover the happiness money buys is fleeting. It's the love of family and friends that brings you true joy. In some ways, you're like Caine. Only he's closer to learning that truth than you. Which is why you're about to make a deal with the devil. May God help us all."

Noting the way Clio straightened her spine and pulled in a deep breath through her nostrils, Colleen said, "You *should* be nervous, child. What you're about to do can't be undone." But Colleen's warnings fell on

deaf ears as Clio began typing on the phone. "Stop!"
she yelled beside the girl's ear, but again it did her no
good. She'd picked a bad day to take a trip to town.

When there was no immediate response to Clio's
text, hope rose inside Colleen. Caine had said his grandmother should be in bed. If they were lucky, she would
be, and Clio would miss her opportunity. Because once
Caine returned to his room and saw the book was missing, he'd put two and two together and know who the
culprit was. Clio would see the other side of her cousin
then—of that Colleen was certain. And she was glad of
it. Someone had to take the girl in hand.

The cell phone rang in Clio's hand. They were
doomed. Unless…Colleen dove at Clio's arm in an
attempt to grab the phone from her hand. It didn't work,
and she ended up sailing off the bed. From the floor, she
watched as Simon pounced, succeeding where Colleen
had failed. He batted the phone from Clio's hand and
then jumped down to push the ringing phone under
the bed. Cursing, Clio went after him. Colleen heard
a throaty meow, followed by an *Ow*, and then Clio
pushed herself out from under the bed.

"Hello. Hello," she said into the phone. "Clio. My
name is Clio Gallagher. Please, don't hang up. I have
something you want. It's a book, written by my great-
grandmother Colleen. It's called *The Secret Keeper of
Harmony Harbor*. I heard Caine. He doesn't want you
to have it." Clio paused to listen to the woman on the
other end of the phone. Colleen pressed her head close
to Clio's, but the only thing she could make out was
that the voice was Emily's.

"He was looking for anything written about you and his father. He sounded upset that there wasn't anything. The woman with him…" She nodded. "Yes. I think that's her name. He called her Evie. He sounded… They seemed close. Like they were together, you know. Um, boyfriend and girlfriend? I can't remember what she said exactly, but it sounded like she thinks you lied to him." Clio made a face and pulled the phone from her ear.

"Are you hearing it now, child? Are you sensing you may have gone too far? It's not too late. Hang up. Hang up now."

"I think this was a bad idea. I'm sorry to have… How much?"

There'd be no turning back for Clio now.

"Just a sec. I'll get a piece of paper." Clio jumped up and ran to Colleen's desk. Finding a pen and a pad of paper, she took a seat. "I'm ready. What do you want me to look for in the book? Mr. Bradford. The owner of the Savings and Loan. Okay, got it." Colleen lowered herself to the floor beside the desk as the child scribbled Bradford's name on the pad of paper.

Emily was going after the bank, and she was going to use what Colleen had written in the book against Bradford. He'd sell. He wouldn't want his wife to learn about his affair or the child he'd fathered. Colleen remembered his wife well. She'd divorce Bradford and take him for everything. And now Emily would have the opportunity to do the same to them. Unless Colleen figured out a way to stop Clio from sharing the information. "Anything about you and your son and Caine. Okay. I'll have it for you tomorrow. No, I won't mention it to anyone."

Clio disconnected and then went to the bed to retrieve Colleen's leather-bound book. Returning with it to the desk, Clio grabbed the pen and pad of paper. Then she looked around the room as though ensuring she hadn't left any evidence of her visit behind before heading back to the closet with her head bowed.

"You'll not say anything to me, will you? Is it beginning to sink in what you've done? You're not a stupid girl. You know well and good what she'll do with the information on Bradford. But in case she doesn't, Simon, we need to…Holy mother of God, we might be saved," Colleen said at the beep of the door lock disengaging. She jumped to her feet, her gaze shooting to the closet.

Clio had already used the hidden door to the passageway to disappear from view. It wouldn't matter though. As soon as Caine discovered the book was missing, he'd know who'd taken it. The door opened. It wasn't Caine. It was Jasper, and he wasn't alone. Sophie was with him. She was carrying a box, and Jasper was hauling in a tree.

Jasper was the next best thing to Caine, but Colleen knew her once-trusted confidant would ignore any attempt she and Simon made to engage him with Sophie in the room. Jasper would worry that Sophie would think he was losing his mind. As far as Colleen knew, he'd never let on to anyone that he sensed her presence, not even Kitty.

"We'll just have to bide our time until Sophie leaves," Colleen told Simon.

"I don't understand why Kitty insisted we decorate

the tower room for the CEO of a company who will use any means to wrest the estate from the family," Sophie grumbled while setting the box on the end of the bed. "The man doesn't even like Christmas from what I've heard."

"You know Kitty. She'll do whatever she can to ensure that Evie wins her bet with Mr. Elliot."

"I think it's more than that. She wasn't acting like herself. I caught her staring at Caine a couple times, like she knew him. Then she asked him if he had any musical talent, which seemed odd because the choir is women only. But what stood out the most was when he mentioned his grandmother. Do you know her, Jasper? Because I could have sworn Kitty did, and she looked like someone had walked over her grave."

"Kitty's guessed that Caine is one of ours, Simon. Learning his grandmother is Emily Green will have confirmed it. Now to see what she does with the information. If I know Kitty—and I've known her for more than sixty years—she'll do right by the boy. She'll tell Caine what she did and ask his forgiveness. I'd be surprised if he didn't give it to her. Maybe then she'll be able to forgive herself. Sadly, that won't be the end of it though. Even if Kitty were to apologize to Emily and to beg her forgiveness, Caine's grandmother won't give it to her—of that I'm certain. Our only hope is for Caine to stop Clio before she gives his grandmother the ammunition she needs to seek the ultimate revenge."

* * *

"See, I told you Kitty was a lovely woman, and you had nothing to worry about," Evie said as Caine took out his card to unlock the tower room door after their meeting at the bar.

"Easy for you to say. She didn't have a list of Christmas activities as long as her arm that she expected you to take part in."

"Other than playing Santa Claus tomorrow after the parade, they weren't that bad," Evie said, doing her best to hide the amusement in her voice.

"Well, don't count on my uncle helping out at Holiday House tomorrow, because he's the one who will be putting on the red suit, not me." His voice trailed off as he opened the door to the suite.

Evie squeezed by him to walk into the room, turning in a circle to take it all in. "This is gorgeous. It looks—"

"Like someone's idea of a practical joke." Caine surveyed the room with his hands on his hips. "And they like glitter almost as much as you do."

She laughed because she could tell that he was putting on a show for her, but then his eyes went to the canopy bed dripping in gold garland, and the semi-amused expression left his face. "Colleen's memoir is gone," he said, and strode to the nightstand, moving it to search behind and beside it. When he came up empty, he went down on his hands and knees to look under the bed. Then he walked around the bed to the other nightstand to do the same.

While he'd been searching near the bed, Evie had searched the desk and sitting area. "It's not here, Caine.

Do you think whoever took it was the same person who decorated your room?"

"I do. Jasper." He pointed at the footprint left in the ashes beside the stone fireplace. He crouched to examine it and then looked up at Evie, the dancing flames of the fire casting his handsome face in shadows and light. "Seems a shame to let all his hard work go to waste." He nodded at the bottle of wine and the plate of grapes, assorted cheeses, and crackers on the end table beside the leather wingback chair. "You want to spend the night with me? At least one of us will enjoy sleeping in Santa's bedroom."

"You're not concerned that Jasper has your great-grandmother's book?"

He shook his head as he came to his feet. "From everything I've learned, there was no one more loyal to Colleen than Jasper. I'm actually more worried that you're going to say no. I'll understand if you do though. I know I messed things up this morning."

"What's changed between then and now?"

He shrugged. "You know who I am. I don't have to hide anything from you." He tucked her hair behind her ear. "And maybe I'm tired of doing what I think I should instead of what I want to."

She understood what he meant. She'd been prepared to say no for exactly that reason. She should say no. There was no doubt in her mind that Caine had the power to hurt her in myriad ways. But the more time she spent with him, the more layers were peeled away, revealing a man she thought might be worth the risk.

She smiled and pointed up at the ball of mistletoe hanging from the light over their heads. "I think that's a sign I'm supposed to stay."

"Huh. I've never been fond of mistletoe before, but suddenly I've had a change of heart."

Chapter Twenty-Three

♥

"You're awfully smiley today," Evie's mother said from where she stood behind the sales counter awkwardly counting the cash thanks to the cast on her right hand.

"Come on, Mom. Even you have to admit our sales were fantastic today."

"Well, it didn't hurt that Santa Claus was giving you free advertising during the parade." Her mother's red-painted lips twitched as Evie fought a smile of her own.

"Or that his elves were." Evie laughed, thinking of the three of them up on the float. Caine as Santa Claus, and Seamus and Jamie as his elves. When Caine wasn't *ho ho ho*-ing while promoting his favorite Christmas store, his elves were. "Seamus gave a pretty special shout-out to the lovely Lenore. Is there anything you'd like to share with your daughter?"

"Don't be ridiculous. The man hasn't held a steady job in decades. He doesn't own a home or have a bank account. Though he does have an extremely wealthy nephew, who seems to be as fond of his uncle as his uncle is of him."

Evie ignored the part about his wealthy nephew and said, "Seamus is also one of the sweetest, kindest men I've ever met. And the customers adore him."

"Because he's charming and has the gift of gab, just like your father. But I've already spent twenty-five years of my life with a man who went from one get-rich-quick scheme to the next. I'm not spending the next twenty with another one. But what about you? Is there anything you'd like to share with your mother? I noticed you didn't sleep in your bed last night."

"You know, you were never as nosy about or as nice to my other boyfriends as you are to Caine. I wonder why that is, Mom. It wouldn't have anything to do with his bank account, would it?" She hoped her mother didn't notice she'd basically admitted they were in a relationship.

"I've always told you it's as easy to fall in love with a wealthy man as it is a poor one. But it has nothing to do with his bank account. I admire Caine. He's smart and ambitious and doesn't let anything stand in the way of what he wants. He's a good man. Your father would have liked him."

"I think he would have too." Evie rested her elbows on the sales counter to look to where the holiday lights glowed warm and bright in the dark night. "But because of him, I'm going to lose Holiday House. How do I reconcile that with my feelings for him?"

"I don't know why, but you've made something more of Holiday House than what it is. It's a house. It's a business. But it's not a home, and it's certainly not who you are. And for the love of God, don't let it stand in the way of you being happy with Caine."

"You think he's going to win our bet, don't you?"

"As I said, he doesn't let anything stand in the way of what he wants, and he wants that office tower. So yes, he'll win the bet, and you'll move on from here." She put the cash in the bank bag and then bent down to put it in the safe. Once she'd closed the door and spun the combination lock, she straightened. "Now, I'm going to change for the holiday party at the manor, and I suggest you do the same. Your Christmas-tree sweater is as blinding as your Christmas-tree hat is ugly."

"Aw, thanks, Mom. I'll just mop the floor, and then we can go."

Lenore sighed. "At least take off the hat and comb your hair. I'm sure Caine would appreciate it."

Since this was the closest they'd come to having a proper mother-daughter chat in a long time, Evie didn't intend to let her mother's remark about her hat and sweater bother her. Honestly, she didn't think anything could bring her down today. She'd been walking on air since she woke up beside Caine this morning. They were a thing, a really good thing, she thought as she wheeled the bucket of soapy water to the front of the shop. A text *ping*ed on her phone, and she took it out of the back pocket of her jeans.

You better hurry up, Evie. The lad's been bitten once, peed on twice, and had his beard pulled three times, but it's the way the grown-up lassies are looking at him that has me concerned.

LOL I'm sure he can handle the grown-up lassies,
Seamus. I should be there in twenty minutes.

And the lovely Lenore?

Will be there with bells on.

He sent an emoji of a leprechaun dancing a jig.

"Evangeline, I need you." Her mother's voice came
from the kitchen.

"I thought you went upstairs." Evie put the mop in
the bucket and rested the pole against the wall. "What is
it?" She walked into the kitchen, but no one was there.
Not even Bruiser, which was odd.

She was about to walk back in the shop when her
mother called her again. Evie followed the sound of
her voice. She wasn't in the kitchen. She was in the
basement. "What are you doing down there? Come
up here."

"Evangeline, I need you."

There was something off about her mother's voice.
She sounded desperate, and no matter how much Evie
didn't want to go down the stairs, she had no choice.
She called for Bruiser as she opened the basement door,
shivering at the drawn-out creak. "Come here, kitty,
kitty, kitty."

"Evangeline!"

"I'm coming. What's wrong?" she said, trying the
light switch several times with no luck. She turned on
the flashlight on her phone and inched her way down
the stairs. "What are you doing down here? Mom,

where are—" She began when she reached the bottom step. A dark shadow rushed toward her, and she opened her mouth to scream, whirling around to run back up the stairs, but a gloved hand clamped over her mouth and the person dragged her off the step and deeper into the dark. Her heart pounded, and the room spun, the phone falling from her hand.

The man clamped an arm around her chest and then pressed cold steel against her throat. "This is a message from Emily. Stay away from her grandson or the next time it will be Aaron who delivers her message. Do you remember Aaron?" The man pressed the blade deeper into her throat. Fear made her gag. "Nod your head if you remember him."

She managed a tiny nod.

"Emily knows where he is. She'll make sure no one interrupts him next time. She'll offer you to him on a silver platter should you so much as breathe a word of this." He lowered the blade and pushed her hard. She stumbled and fell on the damp dirt floor, hitting her head on the corner of the furnace. "Stay away from Caine if you know what's good for you."

She curled into a ball on the floor, shrinking away from her attacker, whimpering when his boots came close. There was a *click*, a bright flash, and then the sound of heavy footfalls on the stairs.

The door closed, and she was left in complete darkness. She sobbed, struggling to her hands and knees. "Mom," she whispered, but almost as soon as she did, she realized he'd used a recording of her mother's voice. Her mother wasn't down here.

Meow.

"Bruiser, where are you?" She patted the dirt floor, searching the dark with her hands. They landed on a cage.

Meow. His raspy tongue licked her fingers, and hot tears of relief tracked down her face. She found the latch and opened it. He purred, rubbing against her arm. She picked him up and held him close, feeling steadier with his heavy weight in her arms.

Her phone *ping*ed, and the screen lit up. She struggled to her feet and went to retrieve her phone. On the screen was a selfie of Caine with his two elves, telling her to hurry up. Telling her that if she was a good girl, he'd make all her wishes come true.

* * *

Colleen sat between young Jamie and Seamus in the back seat of Caine's car.

"You could have let us change out of our costumes, nephew. The poor lad's friends are having a good chuckle at his expense," Seamus said as Jamie sank lower on the seat.

"Evie's not answering her phone, and it's been more than an hour since she responded to your text." Caine glanced in the rearview mirror. "Jamie, if you'd take off your hat, no one will know you're in costume."

The lad lifted his hand to his hat.

"Yes, but I told you what Lenore said. Bruiser got caught in a trap in the basement, and Evie took a spill trying to rescue him. She's fine though, lad. No need to worry about her."

"Don't you listen to him," Colleen said. "You need to check on the girl. Thanks to Clio, your granny knows you and Evie are an item and that she's questioning the stories Emily's been telling you. And I very much wish you could hear me because we're in trouble, lad. Clio gave Emily the information she requested. It's only a matter of time before she uses it."

"That ship has sailed, Uncle. Something isn't right. Evie should have texted me."

"She didn't want to interrupt your Santa duties. You did a good job, lad. I'm proud of you. So is your stepgran—" Caine sent him a silencing stare in the rearview mirror. "So was Kitty. I have a feeling she would have declared your second angel assignment a smashing success and given you a gold star had you but asked."

"Of course she would have. She feels guilty he's spent thirty-seven years without his family in his life," Colleen said, annoyed that Kitty hadn't worked up the courage to tell Caine the truth. He needed to know because, in this case, Colleen believed the truth would set him free. Free him from Emily, who Colleen was positive had filled Caine's head with lies about his family. Once he knew the truth, she was hopeful he'd stand for the Gallaghers and the manor.

"Lad, why is Simon riding shotgun and not one of us? It doesn't seem fair we're stuck in the back seat. It's a little drafty back here."

"Odd. I have the heat on and the windows are closed." Caine raised an eyebrow in the rearview mirror as if looking directly at Colleen. Sometimes he reminded her of Jasper. Her old friend had sensed her presence from the beginning. Although it didn't seem to be helping her these days. Jasper hadn't picked up on one of the clues she and Simon had been leaving him that they had a dangerous traitor in their midst. He seemed to be getting his wires crossed, thinking they meant Caine.

"We're here now anyway. Jamie, you can wait in the car if you want or come in. I'll drive you home as soon as I check on Evie," Caine said.

The boy glanced out the window and slouched down. "I'll wait here."

Caine reached in his glove box and pulled out a wrapped present, tossing it back to the lad. "That's for helping me out today."

"Anything in there for your uncle?" Seamus asked.

"Sweet. This is awesome, Caine. Thanks." Jamie beamed at the man and then at the iPhone in his hand.

"You're welcome, and we'll talk about your screen time limits later. As to you, Uncle, we need to have a talk about your future before you get yours."

"That sounds ominous, lad."

"I'm sure it does. You were never one who liked to plan for the future. But I think it's about time you did. Now, if you don't mind, I'd like to check on Evie."

Seamus, Simon, and Colleen got out of the car to follow Santa Claus Caine to Holiday House. Several cars honked their horns, and he waved.

Seamus laughed. "This falls under an *I never*, lad."

"Tell me about it. Seems to be happening a lot in Harmony Harbor."

"Would one of those be 'I never thought I'd fall in love with the owner of Holiday House'?"

"I haven't said I am, Uncle." He rapped on the front door.

"You haven't said you aren't either. Here"—he nudged Caine aside—"I have a key." He unlocked the door, sending a bucket of water rolling across the floor as he pushed it open. "Looks like they didn't get the floor done."

"Who's there?" Evie called out, her voice shaky. Colleen caught a glimpse of her on the stairs.

"It's us, Evie. Caine and Seamus. We just came to check on you. Lenore said you fell?" Caine said as he walked into the store.

"I'm fine. I have a headache, that's all. Thanks for checking on me, but I'm not up to talking." She backed up on the stairs when Caine strode across the store. "I don't—"

Caine frowned. "What's wrong? You're not acting like yourself. I'll take you to the clinic."

"No. I said I'm okay. I just want to be left alone."

Caine looked to his uncle for help. "Why don't you let me have a look at your head, lass? It'll put my nephew's mind at ease. He's worried about you."

A snowball hit the window, and Evie blanched. "You have to leave. I can't do this anymore. Just go away. Go now."

"There's something very wrong here, Simon. Very wrong indeed. Evie's terrified. You'll stay here with her. She needs protection. We all do, I'm thinking, including my great-grandson."

Chapter Twenty-Four

♥

Caine looked at the sign on the ballroom door, CHRISTMAS CRAFTS WITH CAINE, and managed a smile for the woman beaming at him. He hadn't felt much like smiling since the night Evie had kicked him out of Holiday House. But four days had passed, and this morning he'd given himself a long-overdue kick in the arse. He'd wasted too much time worrying and wondering about the woman. He had to get her out of his head. It was ridiculous she'd managed to carve herself a place inside of him in so little time. No other woman had.

But Kitty had ensured that he hadn't spent the last few days moping about and feeling sorry for himself. Not that he would have, he assured himself despite a little voice in his head calling him a liar. Fine. He'd missed Evie. A lot. He scrubbed a hand over his face, worried his overly emotional and sensitive uncle might be rubbing off on him.

And thinking of his uncle, Caine made a mental note to text him. He'd tell him to stop updating him on Evie: how she looked, what she was doing, if she needed something, if she'd told him why she no longer wanted Caine in her life.

"The children are very excited about doing crafts with you this afternoon, Caine. My great-granddaughters and great-grandsons have all requested to be at your table. Your storytelling won them over."

Caine looked across the ballroom at the children of varying ages who sat at one of the four tables. He was glad to see Jamie sitting with them. He thought the kid might bail on him after Christmas Carols with Caine.

"Caine, over here!" a little girl with dark curly hair yelled. She had a deep and booming voice for a child.

"I'll be right with you, George," Caine called to the little girl, unable to resist her smile. The kid was a handful, an adorable handful but a handful nonetheless.

"If you can't tell, George is very fond of you. They all are, really."

"They're good kids." They were, fun, sweet, and polite. Mostly polite, he corrected, thinking of yesterday when George challenged her cousins to a burping contest.

He watched as Jasper delivered craft materials to the tables. They were lucky to have the older man and Kitty in their lives. The couple doted on the kids. He imagined the children's parents appreciated Kitty and Jasper even more than the kids did. And though he was loath to admit it, they were lucky to have the manor. There was something special about the place, and it wasn't just that they were surrounded by family.

His grandmother lived in a mausoleum on a hill, well away from the village. Isolated, just the way she liked it.

Once his memories of his life with his family had begun to fade, Caine had come to feel the same as Emily.

"So, what's on the agenda today?" he asked as Kitty walked with him into the ballroom. Like the rest of the manor, the massive room was decorated for the holidays. They'd gone with a winter wonderland theme, all white and sparkly. Evie would love it, he thought. He pushed the thought aside to smile at the children smiling at him.

"Santa and Rudolph puppets, followed by sugar cookies, hot chocolate, and a movie. George picked today's feature film, *Mickey's Christmas Carol,* starring Uncle Scrooge McDuck."

"Are you sure George picked the movie?"

Kitty twinkled up at him, looping her arm through his. "She might have had some gentle nudging in that direction."

* * *

Another day, another dollar was Evie's weary thought as she walked to the front door to turn the sign to OPEN and to flick Santa's button from Off to On. It was pretty pathetic that ten days before Christmas she couldn't work up even a little enthusiasm for the holiday. It was Emily's fault. The woman had ruined Christmas and Evie's relationship with Caine.

"No, you did that all by yourself. You let her win," she murmured as she walked back to the sales counter to open the safe.

She could hear her mom and Seamus arguing as they

came down the stairs. She was ruining their relationship too.

Her grace period was up. The wound on her head was healing. Her days of blaming the blow to her head for pulling away from Caine were over. She looked up at Santa's *ho, ho, ho*. She hadn't realized just how over her grace period was until the moment Theia walked into the store.

Caine's best friend stalked to the sales counter and stabbed her finger at Evie. "I trusted you. I trusted you not to hurt him. I thought you would be the best thing for him, and you turned out to be the worst. How could you? How could you turn your back on him?"

"It wasn't like that." It was exactly like that, and she knew enough about his past to understand that to Caine it would feel like she'd abandoned him. Her heart hurt at the knowledge. "It's not like we were in a real relationship."

"Yeah? Does that lie help you sleep at night?"

She barely slept at night, which was becoming more obvious every day that passed. She was surprised Theia hadn't noticed. Then again, Evie had hurt her friend. She no longer ranked as someone Theia Gallagher cared about.

"She doesn't sleep," Evie's mother said, coming to stand beside Theia. "Maybe you can get her to tell you what's wrong. She won't tell me. And don't let her pretend she doesn't care about Caine. She was in love with him."

"Stop giving her a hard time, Lenore." Seamus came around the counter to rub Evie's shoulder.

She didn't understand how he could defend her when she'd hurt his nephew, a man he loved like a son. It made her feel like crying every time he came to her defense.

"Maybe if you'd stop coddling her, we'd get to the bottom of this," her mother said. Lenore's sympathy had lasted less than forty-eight hours.

"I'm sorry. I have a headache," Evie said. Raising her hand to the taped piece of gauze on her forehead, she walked from behind the counter to the kitchen. Usually it was all she had to do to get them to leave her alone. But the tactic didn't work with Theia. Evie heard footsteps following close behind her. She turned on the tap at the kitchen sink, keeping her back to Theia.

"How did you hurt your head?"

Evie repeated the same story she'd told to half the town.

"Hard to believe Bruiser got trapped in a cage. How did the cage get down there anyway?"

No one had asked her that question before. "My aunt Noelle must have had it."

"Noelle was allergic to cats. Your father's entire family was," her mother said.

"What aren't you telling us, Evie?" Theia asked.

"Oh, now, come on. Don't the two of you be ganging up on her."

"Maybe if you'd come by the manor to see your nephew, you wouldn't be so quick to defend her, Seamus," Theia said.

"He told me I was to stay with Evie. Is he not well?"

"What's wrong with Caine?" She couldn't shut off

her feelings for him no matter how hard she tried. But one look into Theia's eyes told her she should have tried harder.

Caine's best friend narrowed her eyes. "You say that like you care. But if you cared, you would have taken his calls or answered his texts."

He'd stopped calling and texting two days ago. "Of course I care. But you know as well as I do that nothing could have come of this. It was better this way."

"So that's it? You're just giving up? Forfeiting the bet?"

"No. Why would you think that?"

"You haven't seemed too interested in his progress on his second angel assignment." She took her phone from her pocket and came to Evie's side. "The kids love him. This is at yesterday's breakfast with Santa. It was Caine's idea after hearing a few kids missed out when he'd cut out early after the parade to check on you. Do you remember that? He said you basically threw him out." She shrugged. "So, kinda hard to believe you when you say you care." She swiped the screen. "Look at this one. He took over the bedtime reading program from Julia. They're reading *A Christmas Carol*. Caine says Scrooge gets a bad rap."

The picture showed Caine with a half smile on his handsome face as he sat in the red velvet chair beside the fireplace in the manor's lobby with a group of children at his feet. Jamie was there with Max, who wore a pair of antlers.

"This is my favorite though. Christmas Crafts with Caine." She'd caught him mid-laugh. He was gluing

googly eyes on a piece of red construction paper while a
little girl with dark curly hair was sticking what looked
like white cotton balls on his face. At the head of the
small table, Jamie was laughing harder than Caine.

Evie didn't know what brought on the tears, seeing
the relationship he had with Jamie or seeing what she
was missing out on. If it weren't for her fear, she would
have been there. If it weren't for her fear, she wouldn't
be missing him; she'd be with him.

"It looks like he succeeded in bringing Christmas to
the manor," she said, her voice husky with emotion.

"He sure has. Kitty says he didn't just pass his second
angel assignment; he surpassed it. So he's two for two.
That's why I'm here, actually. It's time for his third and
final angel assignment." She pulled an eight-by-eleven
white paper angel from her jacket. "The Gallagher kids,
the little ones, made this. They wanted me to put it on
the tree for Caine to pick, but since you made it clear
he's not welcome here, I said I'd do it for him. And
guess what?" She held up the angel. "This is my pick.
And it's kind of perfect because it looks to me like you
could use some Christmas spirit around here."

As her meaning became clear, Evie put up her hands
and backed against the sink. "No. I can't. He can't be
here, Theia. Please. Pick another wish. Any wish but
that one."

"What the hell is going on? You've gone as white
as the snowman on your sweater. Evie, please tell me,"
Theia said, her voice gentle and full of concern.

Evie wanted hard-ass Theia back. She was easier to
resist. But her mother wasn't, she thought when she

took Evie by the arm and walked her to the table, pulling out a chair for her to sit. And when she didn't immediately do so, her mother lightly pressed on Evie's shoulders with her hands.

From the front of the store, Santa *ho, ho, ho*-ed. "I need to…" She went to stand up, and her mother pressed her back down. "Seamus."

"Aye, I'll see to the customers. And, Evie, you'll be answering their questions true. I see what I wasn't seeing before. You're scared. She got to you. The bloody Wicked Witch of Wicklow County got to you."

Theia's eyes went wide and shot from Seamus to Evie. "He's right, isn't he? Why didn't we see it before? Why didn't you tell us?"

"Who are you talking about?" her mother demanded of Theia.

"Caine's grandmother. What did she do, Evie? What did she threaten you with?"

"Evangeline Christmas, if someone is threatening you, I want their name, and I want it now."

"They're right." Evie caved to the fierceness in her mother's voice. "Seamus and Theia are right. It was Emily." As she told them what happened five nights ago, her mother slowly lowered herself onto the chair.

"Aaron Peters. Your old boyfriend. How did she know about him? And why would it matter to you if she sent him next time? I mean, it's horrible what she did, and we won't let her get away with having someone hurt or threaten you. I just don't understand how she was able to threaten you with Aaron."

"Because he hurt her—didn't he, Evie?" Theia said.

"No, that can't be true. Evie?"

"He terrorized me for three months before I left New York." And then Evie shared the nightmare she'd run away from more than a year ago. "We'd been dating for two years before I recognized the signs. The way he'd isolated me from my friends—from you too, Mom. How one week he'd be telling me how smart I was and how proud he was of me, and the next week I was clumsy, stupid, a hot mess, and he didn't know how I'd survive without him. Then he began manipulating situations to the point I didn't think I *could* survive without him.

"I started to think I was going crazy until I had a patient whose husband was gaslighting her." She buried her face in her hands and shook her head. "It took only two sessions for me to recognize the signs in her relationship, but it took me two years to recognize them in mine. Me, the one with the diplomas on her wall, didn't realize what was happening to her."

"And you've earned every one of those diplomas," her mother said. "You can't blame yourself for this. He was charming. You were in love with him, and I can see how things I've said over the past year have been hurtful. I've never doubted your abilities, Evie. I just couldn't understand how you were giving up a job you loved and were so well suited for...for a Christmas store."

"I didn't have a choice. I couldn't function at work." She rubbed a scratch on the table with her thumb, trying to erase it just like she'd tried to erase the residue of fear from the night she thought she was going to die. It never really went away. "Aaron didn't want to let me go. When I first broke it off with him, he pulled out all the stops. He'd drop off a latte from my favorite coffee shop, then lunch, flowers, books. He kept it up for a month, and when he realized it wasn't working, he changed tactics. I couldn't go anywhere without seeing him. He was stalking me. I'd see him outside my apartment in the middle of the night. I tried to get him to stop, to get help. He tried to make me think I was the one who needed it. Then one day he went too far. He grabbed me at work, yelled at me, and shook me. Security called the police. I pressed charges and got a restraining order."

"Evie, why didn't you tell me any of this?" her mom asked.

"At first because I felt so stupid."

"And you thought I'd say the same." Her mother nodded. "I'm sorry. I know I'm not an easy woman and I can be hard on you. I was hard on your father too. I think I was a little jealous of your bond and felt inadequate. And that inadequacy made me lash out, but that's no excuse. I hope you can forgive me. And I hope you know the reason Aaron was able to fool you is also the reason you're so good at your job. You're kind and empathetic, always looking for the best in people. Always willing to give of your time and yourself to help someone else. You are your father's daughter." She gave Evie a sad smile.

"Back then, especially that last night, I wish I had been more like you, Mom."

"What happened?" Theia asked.

"The laundry in my building was in the basement.

I was doing a load of wash when the lights went out. There was some light from a small window, but that only helped for a second because Aaron—I didn't know it was him at the time—pushed me from behind and my glasses fell off. I think the phrase *blind as a bat* was invented for me," she told Theia, attempting a smile. "Aaron broke my glasses, and when I went to scream, he gagged me. Then he tied me up, and that's when the real torture began."

Her mother started to cry, and Evie reached for her hand. "No. He didn't rape me, and one of my neighbors broke down the door before I suffered more than minor cuts and bruises. It was psychological torture, and I came here to recover. Holiday House became my safe place."

"And now Caine's grandmother has taken that from you." Her mother squeezed her hand. "She's not going to get away with this."

"No, she's not." Theia scrubbed her face. "Caine is going to lose his mind."

Evie's first reaction was to yell, to plead with her not to tell him, but she pushed that back and said, "I need to be the one to tell him. If he'll talk to me."

"I'm not sure he will, Evie. That's why I was so mad at you. Don't get me wrong. Now that I know what happened, I completely understand why you reacted the way you did."

"No, you don't. You can't because you'd never let fear stop you from doing the right thing."

"That's not true. But right now you're facing your fear. You're not letting Emily win. You're going to talk to Caine, and hopefully you can knock down the walls he's put up and get him to listen. Because, Evie, I can't lie. You shutting him out hurt him badly. You opened up an old wound."

They turned as Seamus walked into the kitchen. "It's the one my sister gave him. Me too. So, lass, I'll do what I can to help you. But right now we have a bigger problem. Emily's on her way to Harmony Harbor."

Chapter Twenty-Five

♥

It didn't matter how many blankets she was bundled up in, Caine would know the woman in the sleigh anywhere. "I don't have time for this, Evangeline," he said as he led the two Clydesdale horses to the front of the red wooden sleigh, the bells on their harnesses jingling. "I'm expecting paying customers any minute now."

It didn't seem to matter that his assignment as the manor's resident Christmas elf officially ended today. He'd been railroaded into taking on this last gig as a favor to Kitty after Jasper came down with a case of the sniffles. Caine was beginning to think he'd been set up. A common occurrence not only at the manor but in Harmony Harbor.

"I'm your paying customer. Kitty made the reservation for me."

And there it was, evidence that Kitty and Jasper were indeed conspiring against him as he'd suspected. No doubt they'd see it as helping, not conspiring. The couple seemed to have become his self-appointed guardians.

For some unknown reason, Kitty had taken to him immediately. Jasper had been another story, but over the past few day, there'd been a gradual softening in the older man. Today he'd acted downright grandfatherly when he'd delivered the news that Emily had made a reservation at the manor. She'd done so mere minutes after he'd called her, demanding to know how she'd threatened Evangeline. Something he'd learned from his uncle earlier that morning.

"Caine, I know you're upset with me."

"Upset? You think I'm upset with you?" he said, looking up from hitching the horses to the sleigh. It had been just under a hundred and twenty hours since he'd seen her face, but his gaze drank her in as though seeing her for the first time in years.

As much as he'd tried to deny it, he'd been desperate to see her, desperate for her to let him in. Anger at the evidence that she'd worked her way into his heart only to throw him away now sizzled beneath the words he spoke. "Upset doesn't begin to describe how I feel. How I felt when you cut me out of your life without an explanation." Brilliant. He sounded pathetic. They hadn't been together for years. They hadn't even been together a bloody month.

"I'm sorry. I should have taken your calls and re-sponded to your texts. I didn't mean to hurt you, Caine. I was scared."

He climbed into the sleigh, grabbed the reins, and shot her a hard look over his shoulder. "Do you think it makes me feel any better to know that you were afraid because my grandmother threatened you?"

She blinked in surprise.

"My uncle texted me that Theia had gotten through to you and that he'd known straightaway that it was my grandmother who'd put the fear in your eyes. Too bad you didn't trust me enough to take care of it. To protect you." Furious, he turned away from her and snapped the reins, the bells jingling as the horses trotted along the snow-covered path.

"It's not that I didn't trust you. I freaked out, Caine. It doesn't make me proud to admit that just the mention of Aaron, the memory of a night from more than a year ago, still had the power to terrify me."

"What are you talking about?" He shifted on the bench seat to look at her, and he saw what the haze of his anger had blinded him to. She was ashen, with dark shadows under her eyes.

She made a face. "Seamus didn't tell you what your grandmother threatened me with, did he?"

"No. Nor did he tell me how she went about it."

"She sent a man. I don't know who he was. It was too dark in the basement for me to make—"

"Stop. Not another bloody word. Not yet," he said as he tugged on the reins to bring the horses to a standstill on the trail leading into the woods. Then he stood and climbed over the board to sit beside Evie and take her into his arms. He buried his face in her neck, breathing in her now familiar scent of oranges and cloves. She smelled like the holidays and home. He'd missed holding her, missed her smile, missed her laughter, and he wanted to kill his grandmother for the haunted look she'd put in Evie's eyes.

He lifted his head. "You can tell me now."

"Are you sure? You—"

"Tell me. All of it." By the time she'd finished, he felt like putting his fist through the sleigh.

She reached up to cup the side of his face with her gloved hand. "I'm sorry I let her win. I'm sorry I wasn't brave enough—"

He covered her hand with his. "It's me who's sorry, Evie. I shouldn't have let you push me away. I made it about me, let myself get caught up in the hurt. Theia's right. Sometimes I'm blind to my grandmother's faults. I never would have thought she'd go that far. I talked to her the morning of the parade. She'd told me she'd had a change of heart and my stay at the manor under the guise of fulfilling the wish was a good idea. She even gave me a couple of suggestions how to use it to our advantage. I see now that she was playing me. She's on her way here. To Harmony Harbor."

"Seamus told us. He's worried."

"So am I. She's been too quiet the past few days. But I can't get anything out of anyone at Wicklow Developments. Her nurse hasn't seen or heard anything that was of use to me. And my cousin won't take my calls, which is another red flag."

"Because…?"

"It means he no longer sees me as a threat." He looked at her, her eyes filled with concern for him. "Don't worry about me. I can handle my grandmother and my cousin. But I'm not letting her get away with this, Evie. She will pay for terrorizing you, as will the man she hired to threaten you. So will Aaron Peters."

His prominent family may have gotten him off with six months in prison and community service for the assault, but there were other ways to make him pay.

"Aaron may not have served his full sentence, but his parents weren't able to make his record go away. He's paying for what he did. And while I'm all for you finding out who broke into my home and threatened me and passing the information on to the police, you can't press charges against your grandmother, Caine. She's dying, and I know it's not right that she doesn't have to face the consequences of her actions, but I don't want her to take her revenge out on you."

"You let me worry about that. Just know I won't let her hurt you again."

Evie leaned against him and looked up at the snow-draped trees forming an arch high above them. It was like being in an outdoor cathedral, a sweet silence broken every so often by the jingle of bells and the trill of birds. "As awful as these past few days have been, they made me realize I'd run away from my fear. I hadn't dealt with it. I'm dealing with it now. And I won't be doing it alone if my mom, Theia, and Seamus have their way."

"You can add my name to that list."

"On one condition." She reached under the blanket and pulled out a white paper angel that was about three times the size of the angels on the Holiday House tree. "You have to accept your final angel assignment," she said with a smile.

He took the paper angel from her and turned it over. "'Help Evie make Holiday House the best Christmas shop around.' Signed 'Caine's Christmas elves, George, Ella Rose, and Mia.'" He laughed and shook his head. "Did you know my name has become synonymous with Christmas at the manor? Yesterday it was Christmas Crafts with Caine. The day before that it was Christmas Carols with Caine."

"I saw a picture of you doing crafts with the kids. Imagine my surprise when you weren't mouthing *bah humbug* but laughing. You looked like you were having fun—so did Jamie."

"It would have been more fun with you there. I've missed you, Evie."

"I missed you too." She plucked the angel from his hands. "If you accept the challenge, we can make up for lost time."

"I accept, but I need you to make me a promise."

"Let me guess: classical carols instead of pop rock? Regular candy canes instead of cinnamon and chocolate?"

"I had no idea there was such a thing as cinnamon and chocolate candy canes."

"That's because you're a Christmas virgin."

"I'm beginning to think you'll turn out to be my favorite angel assignment, Evie. Which leads back to my promise. However this ends, me winning the bet or you, we won't let it come between us. We'll keep it strictly business. I know you hate everything about the office tower, but I do have the perfect space for Holiday House. And I won't charge you rent for a year."

"You know, that almost sounds like you think you're going to win the bet."

"Evie, I wrote the book on the secrets to succeeding in business. There isn't a company I can't turn around."

* * *

Two days later, Evie had had enough with Caine and his ideas for turning Holiday House into a success story. "Please, I'm begging you, pick another wish assignment." Evie plucked a green angel off the tree. "This doesn't look too hard." She turned it over. "Help Mrs. Whittaker decorate for Christmas. Wait a second. I thought Liam already got that wish." She put the angel on the sales counter, making a mental note to call Mrs. Whittaker. She wasn't allowed to double dip in the angel wishes pool.

Caine took the cinnamon and chocolate-filled candy cane from Evie's hand. "Stop eating the merchandise."

"I can't help it. You're stressing me out." She looked for reinforcements, skipping over her mother, who was gleefully discounting the entire table of Fitz and Floyd dinnerware as Caine had directed.

Evie spotted his uncle ducking behind the antique Christmas tree. "Seamus, look what Caine's doing. Please tell him he's ruining the look of the store. The singing cookie jars do not belong on the table at the front of the store, and neither do three boxes of Christmas candles. He's turning us into a mass market retailer."

Seamus peeked around the tree. "I got in the middle of your last spat, and it didn't end well for me."

"He won't take you off his payroll, Seamus. He was

just teasing. Now, come on, don't be afraid to tell him the truth. I'm right, aren't I?"

"Well, your candles have a lovely scent to them, and they haven't really been moving. I think we still have four cases in the storage room."

Her mother snorted a laugh.

"Thanks for that, Seamus. Remind me not to take your side next time Mom changes the channel in the middle of the Hallmark movie," Evie said.

"The lass is right, nephew. It's looking a little junky."

Her mother sniffed. "There's something not quite right about a man loving those sappy movies as much as you do, Seamus."

"There's nothing wrong with a man being in touch with his feelings. Besides, Evie and I love our Hallmark movies," Seamus said.

"And that's the problem. There's no room for—" Caine began.

"Sentimentality in business," Evie and Seamus said at almost the same time.

"Mock me all you want. We'll compare profit-and-loss statements at the end of the week."

"I can hardly wait," Evie said, and stuck the candy cane in her mouth.

Caine laughed, took the candy cane from her mouth, and kissed her. "You're right. Cinnamon-chocolate-filled candy canes are the best."

"It's a Christmas miracle," Seamus said. "They actually agree on something."

The four of them turned toward the door when Santa *ho, ho, ho*-ed. Jamie walked in with a gallon of paint in one hand, a bag in the other, and Max on his heels. Jamie held up the paint can. "Mr. O'Malley says this should do the trick."

"Okay, then. Let's get to it." Caine gave Evie a light swat on the butt. "And while we're off to paint the little shop of horrors, you can update your blog. I left some suggestions beside your laptop."

"I really appreciate the thought, but I know you have a thing about basements, Caine. You don't have to do this."

"For you, I'd wade through rat-infested waters."

"My hero," she choked out. Then, through the laughter she could no longer hold back, "You look like someone poured a bucket of spiders down your shirt."

"Holy Mary Mother of God, you have the oddest sense of humor of anyone I know," he said with a full-body shiver.

* * *

Much later, after Caine had given her several full-body shivers of her own, Evie snuggled against him on her bed in the attic, which the electricians had recently deemed safe.

"This is my favorite part of your angel-wish assignment," Evie said.

Caine laughed, kissing the tip of her nose. "Progress— something else we agree on." His cell phone vibrated on the nightstand. As he went to turn it off, he glanced at the screen. "I have to take it. It's Theia. Hey, T...What? She did what? Calm down, okay? I'll be right there. Tell everyone not to worry. She may own controlling interest, but I'm still CEO of the company." He disconnected and got out of bed.

Holding the covers to her chest, Evie sat up. "What is it?"

"My grandmother arrived at the manor and wasn't there two minutes before announcing that she now owned Bradford's Savings and Loan and the Gallaghers had until midnight on Christmas Eve to pay off the debt or she'd foreclose."

"Can you stop her?"

"Yes, I..." He looked up from fastening his jeans. "I can if she hasn't already put a plan in place to stop me."

"You think she has, don't you? The cousin who wouldn't take your calls—would he be involved?"

"He nodded. I have a feeling Alec is up to his ears in this. But they aren't the only ones who know how to play the game. I was trained by the master." He leaned across the bed to kiss her. "They can't shut me out of the company for long. And if worse comes to worst, I can personally cover Greystone's loan."

"You're not leaving without me," she said, scrambling off the bed. She wouldn't let him face this on his own. She knew what the company meant to him. And while he might not know it yet, the Gallaghers and the manor had worked their way into his heart, as his willingness to cover their debt proved.

She wondered if the man who didn't let emotions interfere with business even realized that he'd broken his own cardinal rule.

Chapter Twenty-Six

♥

Caine didn't know how he could want to throttle his grandmother and hug her at the same time. Emily stood dwarfed by the majestic fireplace at her back. She played to her audience of both Gallaghers and guests, refusing to go somewhere private as Caine had suggested upon his arrival. Beside him, Evie's hand brushed his. He linked his fingers with hers. Despite her obvious exhaustion, Emily noticed, and her peach-painted lips tightened.

She must have refreshed her makeup on the way here. She'd want the Gallaghers to see her for who she'd become: rich and powerful. It was why she'd worn her fur coat, with diamonds and rubies glistening on her fingers and at her throat.

"May I get you something to drink, madam? You've had a long flight," Jasper said.

"A long flight indeed. In a private plane with anything I want there for the asking."

"Gran, there's no need for that. Sit," Caine said, moving from Evie's side to guide his grandmother to the chair. "Where's your oxygen tank?" he whispered near her ear.

He should have known better than to ask, he thought, when her eyes sparked with fury. She wouldn't want to seem weak in front of the enemy.

She brushed him aside to look at the Gallaghers, who sat on the leather couch. Kitty perched on the edge with Jasper standing behind her. "I'm not the same young woman who you threw out of here nearly sixty years ago, when I came begging for help, now, am I? I'd had to beg, borrow, and steal to get here. Sick and alone, scared, cast aside by my own family, carrying the child of the young master of the manor. It's a tale as old as time. You looked upon me as if I were nothing." She lifted her chin. "I'm no longer nothing. It's your turn now, the high-and-mighty Gallaghers will be brought to their knees to beg and borrow."

Emily smiled, obviously pleased with the shocked gasps that ran through the crowd.

Pale, looking frantically from one family member to the other, Kitty clutched her pearls. "No. That's not true. No one threw you from the manor, Emily. You didn't come here. You sent a letter telling Ronan you were carrying his child. We'd just been married, and I…" Her voice caught on a sob, and Jasper gave her shoulder a comforting squeeze. "I didn't give Ronan the letter. I'm so sorry, Emily. So very sorry. I know that words can't make up for all you must have suffered and lost, but Ronan never knew you carried his son. I kept the secret from him until the night he was on this death-bed. To this day, I don't know if he heard me. I begged

his forgiveness, as I beg for yours." Tears rolled down
her cheeks, and one of her sons, the fire chief, took her
hand. It was obvious none of them had heard the story
before. "And yours, Caine."

"You'll not have it. From either of us," his grandmother spat out, then began to cough. Jasper hurried
away and returned with a glass of water and a cloth.
Caine didn't know what the cloth was for until he
noticed blood on Emily's hand.

His chest tightened on a spasm of panic. "Gran, you
need your rest."

"No. I need to make them pay."

"For what?" His uncle pushed past several people to
stand in front of his grandmother's chair. "You've done
far worse than what's been done to you. You sit here
on your red velvet throne, the high-and-mighty Emily
Green Elliot, lying through your teeth like you've been
lying to my nephew for twenty-five years. Your mother
didn't abandon you, Caine. She didn't have anyone to
turn to."

"Because you were a drunk, panhandling on the
streets," Emily said, gasping for breath by the end.

Somewhere in Caine's mind he knew he should
bodily carry his grandmother from the room, but he
was caught up in his uncle's tale. *Was that all it was
though?* he wondered.

"Aye, and that's my cross to bear, and I'll bear it
until the day I die. But I can no longer stay quiet, even if
it means my nephew will hate me for the role I played."
He lifted his gaze to Caine. "My sister left you with her
so she could get back on her feet. She took the fifty

thousand pounds, aye, but she thought it was a gift, not a payment. She came back for you, Caine. Your mother came back for you time and time again, but she'd not let her see you. The last time was too much for her. It was your fifteenth birthday. Weeks later your mother died of a broken heart."

"Don't listen to him!" Emily staggered to her feet. "You can't believe a word he s-s-ays..."

"Gran, please, calm down. Uncle, stop."

Kitty's son came over and crouched by Emily's chair. "You need to listen to your grandson."

"I'll not have him listening to her lies, to his lies. You're liars. You're all—"

"Gran." Caine caught her as she toppled over. "Help. Please, I need help."

"It's all right, son. The ambulance is on the way. Here, let me help you," the fire chief said.

* * *

Caine sat in the chair beside his grandmother's hospital bed, holding her hand. He'd been there for five hours, and so had Colleen. She'd joined him in the ambulance, unwilling to see him go off on his own. Both Seamus and Evie had tried to come with him, but he'd pushed them away.

Colleen couldn't imagine how her great-grandson felt after listening to his grandmother's lies. It had been hard for her to listen to them too. Kitty had told the truth. The only reason Colleen had learned about Emily and the baby was because she'd walked into her son's hospital room and overheard her daughter-in-law's confession about the letter. If Caine had continued reading Colleen's memoir up to the year 2009, he would have seen the truth in black and white. She understood why Emily didn't want him to get close to the Gallaghers. Her lies would have been exposed.

The machine attached to the older woman began to beep, and the red and green lines on the screen went flat. A nurse hurried in and then a doctor. There was nothing they could do for Emily. Once they'd detached her from the machines, they offered Caine their condolences and left him to say his goodbyes.

Colleen stood behind him with a hand on his shoulder. He didn't feel it, didn't sense her trying to offer him comfort. She didn't like that he'd chosen to say goodbye to his grandmother on his own. He didn't have to be alone. Evie, Seamus, Theia, and young Jamie would be here with him if he'd allowed them to be. Kitty and Jasper too.

As Colleen looked at the older woman on the bed, a perfect but faded image of Emily sat up. She turned to look back at herself lying on the hospital bed and gasped. Her gaze shot to Caine and then to Colleen.

"You. I know you." She looked back at her body again. "I'm dead. I died."

"You are. You did." Despite the pain this woman had caused her family, Colleen couldn't help but feel a touch of sympathy for her. She knew what she was going through. It would have been nice to have had someone to talk to when she'd died, a guide of sorts, she supposed. She could do that for Emily. "You'll be all right. There'll be a light, and you'll go to it. It's beautiful and warm. Don't dally or you'll be left behind like me."

"There'll be no light for me." Emily's gaze left Caine to return to Colleen. "Ronan showed me your picture all those years ago. He loved you and his father. He would have stayed with me if it weren't for you, his family, and the manor. Oh, but he loved Greystone. He talked about it all the time."

"Is that why you wanted to destroy the manor, because it took him away from you?"

Emily's gaze was considering, and then she lifted a shoulder as if there was no longer a reason to hide the truth. "I wanted to make you suffer like I had."

"But we never did what you accused us of doing. If you had come, we wouldn't have turned you away. And while I'm sure it gives you little comfort, it must be said: Kitty is a good person who did a bad thing, and I'm sorry for that, Emily. Sorrier than you'll ever know. My son, my family, we would have done right by you."

"Ronan's wife ruined my life. And aye, I lied, and what you heard tonight was not a tenth of what I told my son and grandson. I wouldn't lose them to the Gallaghers. You'd taken enough from me by then. I'd shamed my family with the pregnancy and they abandoned me. I had to marry a man who made my stomach turn to put a roof over my head and food in my belly. I'd convinced him the baby was his, but those damn Gallagher-blue eyes were our downfall, just as your son's had been mine. My husband kicked me out with nothing but the clothes on my back and a six-month-old baby.

"Again I found a man who was willing to put a roof over our heads and food in our belly, only this time without the benefit of a wedding ring. Like everyone else, he used me and threw me away. But him I made pay. And with the coin he tossed at my feet, I clawed and fought my way to the top. When I made it, I bought his land and his businesses out from under him. I ruined him, but I held true to our bargain and his wife never knew why."

"Did you tear his home and businesses down like you intended to tear down Greystone?" Colleen asked.

"No. And truth be told, it would have been difficult to do so. The manor is as beautiful as Ronan made it out to be. I would have liked a chance to see more of it. Unlike my grandson, I admire the architecture of the past."

"I don't understand."

"So Ronan never did tell you...I suppose I'm not surprised. He was afraid you'd laugh at him, and if you laughed at him, the historical society to which he aspired would do so too. He was a proud man, like this one." She nodded at Caine. "He looks like Ronan."

"He does. Did his father?"

Emily nodded. "Spitting image, but it's Caine who was most like Ronan." She smiled. "Although he didn't acquire his love of history or architecture. It wouldn't have bothered him to bulldoze the manor to the ground. Whereas Ronan's second biggest fear to besmirching his reputation was that the search for the pirate's treasure would destroy the manor."

"Pirate's treasure?" Colleen stared at the woman in surprise.

"Aye, Ronan believed William Gallagher buried the treasure in the tunnels and that the excavation would bring down the manor."

"So that's why you wanted to bulldoze Greystone? To find the treasure?" A treasure her son had never told her about, but she thought perhaps Daniel had. She remembered brushing it off as a foolish notion. But what if it wasn't? What if this had been the answer to their prayers all along? If there was any truth to this, she knew where to find it. In Ronan's journals and writings. It had been too painful to look at them when he died, and she'd locked them away in her desk. Somehow she had to get them, or better yet, have someone who could do something with the information unlock her desk drawer.

"Aye, and now it's lost to me like everything else in my life." She looked down at Caine, who sat with his elbows on his knees, his head in his hands. "I was going to lose him. He was going to abandon me just like his father did all those years before. I offered Killian the world, and he chose the O'Leary girl over me. She had nothing, just like Evangeline Christmas."

Emily brushed her fingers over Caine's dark hair. "He thought he had the best poker face, but I could always read him. I could see he was falling in love with her. Never before had he put anyone ahead of the company, but he did for her. And then there were all of you."

She lifted her gaze to Colleen. "I lashed out, and he'll pay dearly for it. He'll need you, all of you. And he'll need that uncle of his too. You don't know how much it galled me to spend good money getting him off the street and into a treatment center." She shook her head. "He still has no idea it was me who got him dried out. Imagine, someone puts you up in a private clinic for two years and you don't even ask who it was or why they'd do such a thing. Or how after twenty-five years of not seeing your nephew, he turns up out of the blue at the warehouse you've been hired to clean."

"Caine doesn't know any of this, does he?"

"No. He'd ask too many questions."

"Then why did you do it?"

"Because I didn't want Caine to be alone when I was gone, and Seamus was right—I owed him for taking the boy from his mother. I didn't intend to, you know. But I couldn't lose him. I couldn't face one more person I loved leaving me."

A warm glistening light appeared above the hospital bed, shining down on Emily's body. "I'm afraid," she said to Colleen. "I don't belong there. I've been selfish, cruel, and greedy."

"You have, and you've also suffered." Colleen looked down at Caine, who'd picked up his grandmother's phone to scroll through her contacts. "And for all your faults, he loved you."

"But will he forgive me?"

"Do you ask it of him?"

"I do. Please, if you can find a way to tell him, tell him I'm sorry for the hurt I've caused him. I love him. He needs to know I loved him."

"I'll do my best. Now go to the light, Emily. They're waiting for you."

Emily lifted her face, and her features began to fade,

sparkling in the golden light. "Killian. Oh, Killian," she whispered before disappearing from sight. Without the heavenly light, the stark room grew cold.

"It's time to go, Caine. Go to Evie. Go to Theia, your family. You're going to need them. I think we're all going to need one another."

Caine stood with the phone to his ear. "Aidan, it's Caine. I have the name of the man who broke into Evie's and threatened her. He's the head of security at the Bridgeport Hotel."

Chapter Twenty-Seven

♥

Evie paced behind the sales counter at Holiday House with her cell phone pressed to her ear. "Pick up, pick up," she said, blinking back tears. She shook her head when it went straight to voice mail again. "Why isn't he answering? The hospital said he left at five this morning. But Jasper checked, and it doesn't look like he's been back to the manor. You don't think he left Harmony Harbor, do you?"

"Of course not. I'm sure he just wants to be alone." Her mother handed a cup of coffee to Evie and one to Seamus." Evie felt like she might float away. It was her seventh cup of the morning. They'd been pacing the store since four a.m., when they'd given up trying to sleep. She'd met her mom and Seamus on their way down to the kitchen.

"Why did I listen to him, Seamus? I shouldn't have let him push me away," Evie said.

"I did the same, lass. He's not an easy man to sway once he's made up his mind."

Santa *ho*, *ho*, *ho*-ed, and their gazes shot to the door.

They barely managed to swallow their disappointed groans when Jamie walked in. "Is Caine here? I heard his grandma died, and I've been trying to call him and text him, but he's not responding." He held up his phone. "He always responds right away. Doesn't matter if he's on a conference call; he always takes my call."

"He just needs some time to himself. He'll be fine. We just have to give him some time," her mother said, and patted Jamie's shoulder. "Come with me to the kitchen. I'll get you a cup of hot cocoa. Would you like some toast?" she asked as they walked to the kitchen together.

"Lenore's right. The lad's a loner and likes his own company well enough. He just needs some time."

"My mom was like that when my dad died. I didn't understand it then. It felt like she was shutting me out," Evie said. Their relationship had changed after that; they'd become distant. She wouldn't let that happen to her and Caine. She didn't want to lose him.

"Aye, we all grieve in our own way, on our own timeline."

They turned once again when Santa *ho, ho, ho*-ed, and Evie was tempted to flip his switch and close up shop until Caine was found. This time it was Theia. Her gaze moved from Evie to Seamus, their disappointment reflected on her face. "What is wrong with him? Doesn't he know we're worrying ourselves sick?"

"Here. Come sit down." Evie patted the stool. Theia didn't look like she'd slept either.

"You sound like Marco and Rosa," she said, but she walked behind the counter, hugging Evie before sitting down. "They're both calling everyone they know, which means the entire town of Harmony Harbor is now on the lookout for Caine." She gave them a watery smile. "Won't he love that?"

All eyes went to Evie's ringing phone on the counter. She picked it up and checked the screen, giving her head a disappointed shake. Theia slumped on the stool, and Seamus rested his elbows on the counter, holding his head in his hands.

"Hi, Arianna," Evie said, trying not to let her disappointment leak into her voice.

"Hi, Evie. I know this must be a really difficult time for Caine, so I won't keep you, but I just wanted to call to say congratulations on winning the bet. Connor and I are so happy for you," she said, referring to her husband.

"But I haven't won the bet." Evie looked at Theia and Seamus and held up a hand in a *what the heck is going on* gesture.

Seamus and Theia straightened to stare at her.

"You must have. Hang on." She heard Arianna talking to someone in the background before she came back on the line. "The man introduced himself as Alec McCleary. Connor says he's head of Wicklow's legal department, and he called to say they regretted to inform us that they won't be building the office tower in Harmony Harbor. We're rescinding the demolition order on Holiday House this morning. You won, Evie!"

And Caine lost was her only thought. "That's wonderful news, Arianna. Thank you so much."

"I thought you'd be happier. I'm sorry—that's a terrible thing to say under the circumstances."

"No, it's fine. I understand. It's just that we're really worried about Caine. We can't find him. He just lost his grandmother, and no matter how we all felt about her, he loved her. And if what I think has happened did…"

"You're right. It must be awful for Caine. But I think I might be able to help with locating him. Let me make a few calls, and I'll get back to you."

"What's going on, lass? The Wicked Witch pulled something, didn't she?"

Theia took out her phone and got up from the stool, walking away as she put it to her ear. Evie assumed she was trying to get details of what was going on at the company since she'd worked for Wicklow Developments for several years.

Evie returned her attention to Seamus. "I think she did. Caine's cousin Alec McCleary just informed Arianna and Connor that they would no longer be building the office tower in Harmony Harbor."

"So you won, then. Holiday House is saved…" Seamus nodded as it sank in. "She removed him as CEO."

"It's much worse than that," Theia said as she got off her phone. "They've frozen all of Caine's assets and seized his home and his cars until they've done a forensic audit. Alec is claiming that Caine's been stealing from the company since he was named CEO. Emily leveled the charges five days ago."

Evie's phone *ping*ed with an incoming text. She glanced at the screen. "Caine is at the harbor. Someone spotted him on the wharf." Overcome with guilt for the part she'd played, she said, "You should go to him, Theia. You too, Seamus."

"No," Theia and Seamus said at almost the same time. "It's you he needs." Theia held up her hand when she went to protest. "Trust me. He needs you, Evie."

* * *

Evie spotted Caine standing on the wharf looking out to sea. The water was dark, the foam-topped waves angry as they slapped against the pilings. The dull gray day suited the man standing alone with his hands in the pockets of his black wool coat, his dark hair whipping in the icy winds.

He turned as though he sensed her there watching him. His face looked ravaged, his eyes haunted. He knew. His greatest fear had come true. He was penniless and powerless, and she couldn't love him more. The hard part would be getting him to believe her.

"Go away, Evie. I don't want or need your sympathy." The words were as angry as the sea, and they slapped at her.

But she wouldn't let him drive her away. "I don't blame you for being angry at me," she said as she walked toward him. "It's my fault Emily turned on you. If you hadn't agreed to my bet, if you hadn't gotten involved with me, you wouldn't have lost everything." She wrapped her arms around him from behind, pressing her cheek to his broad back. "But you still have me. I love you, Caine."

"Then you're a fool."

She drew her arms away and wanted to cry when his head bowed as though he'd taken a blow. Yet she knew that had been exactly the reaction he'd expected from her. He'd expected her to walk away. Instead she took him by the arm in an attempt to make him face her, but he wouldn't be forced, and he was too powerful for her to move. So she wiggled in between him and the railing.

He looked down at her. "You don't understand. I have nothing to offer you. She took everything and more."

"I know what your grandmother and cousin have done. Theia talked to someone at Wicklow Developments. But you're wrong. You have everything to offer. I didn't fall in love with you because you were rich or were the CEO of Wicklow Developments. If anything, those were the reasons I tried not to fall in love with you. But your money and title don't define you or make you who you are. Emily didn't make you who you are. You're smart, ambitious, and driven. Once you've moved past the shock and the anger, you'll get back on your feet, and you'll build something bigger and better than Wicklow Developments. Because it will be yours. Your goodness, your generosity, and kindness will shine through in whatever you do. Look at this as a gift, Caine. A fresh start."

He raised his hand to gently move her hair from her face. "Only you could look at this and see a new beginning."

He obviously didn't want her love. It hadn't escaped her notice that he hadn't said he loved her in return. Afraid he'd see the hurt in her eyes, and not wanting to make this about her, she looked down at her boots.

Caine's hand curved around the back of her head, and he drew her against his chest, then wrapped his arms around her. "I'm not discounting your love. That in itself is a gift, Evie. But I'll not have you throwing it away on me."

She lifted her head to look up at him. "I once thought you were the worst thing to happen to me, but you've turned out to be the best. So even if you don't feel the same about me, it's okay."

"It's not a question of me loving you, Evie. I knew I was in trouble the moment I willingly—albeit reluctantly—walked into your rat-infested basement and left a flea-ridden golden retriever at your back door to protect you. But that's not the same man I am now. I'm not joking when I say I have nothing, Evie. I'm penniless and homeless."

"No, you aren't the same man you were when you arrived in Harmony Harbor. You're a better version of you, Caine. And while I might have cost you all your material goods, I think I can take a little credit for you becoming the best you you can be."

His lips twitched. "You sound like an advert for the military, Evie."

"You can make fun of me all you want, but it's true. Something that isn't true though? You're not penniless, and you're not homeless. You're a Gallagher and part owner of Greystone Manor."

"They'll want nothing to do with me now. They're

losing the manor because of me. I haven't the money to pay off their loan."

"I have an idea." He was going to hate it, and no doubt the rest of his family would too, but Evie wasn't about to let the man she loved give up without a fight. "Have you ever seen the movie *It's a Wonderful Life*?"

Chapter Twenty-Eight

♥

Caine sat at his great-grandmother's desk in the study at Greystone Manor, staring at the numbers on the screen. He didn't know who he felt sorrier for, Evie or the Gallaghers. He sighed and corrected himself even though he hadn't said the words aloud, the family. His family. Evie had corrected him so often he was surprised he still slipped.

It had been a week since she'd presented him with her idea to save the manor that day on the wharf. The family had been about as happy as he had been about reenacting the scene from *It's a Wonderful Life*. It was the scene where everyone in Bedford Falls arrived at the Bailey house with their piggy banks and jars full of coins to save George and the savings and loan.

Only this time, it was the people of Harmony Harbor coming out to save Greystone Manor from foreclosure. He wondered if, like him, the family felt it came a little too close to fulfilling his grandmother's wishes that they get down on their knees to beg and borrow to save the manor.

"Mr. O'Malley got here just under the wire," Evie said, ushering the older man and his glass jar filled with nickels and dimes into the study. Caine's gaze moved from the older man in his Santa hat and light-up bow tie and suspenders to Evie. He wished some of Mr. O'Malley's good cheer would rub off on the woman Caine loved. Poor Evie was having a tough time keeping her optimistic spirit alive.

They'd agreed the cutoff for accepting donations would be eight p.m. on December twenty-third. It was thirty minutes to, and they were 300,000 dollars short. Or, judging from the size of Mr. O'Malley's jar, somewhere around 299,950 dollars short.

Still, Caine dutifully poured the silver coins onto the desk and counted them out, typing in *$50.05* beside Mr. O'Malley's name and phone number. Caine had insisted that every donation be recorded, whether the person wanted to remain anonymous or not. He'd known that in the end they'd fall short and the money would need to be returned.

He thanked Mr. O'Malley and wished him a Merry Christmas, assuring him there was still hope—more for Evie's benefit than for the older man's, whose wink as Evie led him from the study seemed to indicate he thought Caine had kissed the Blarney Stone.

"You know," his uncle said as he walked in to deposit a large envelope on the desk, "I've had three ladies tonight tell me I remind them of Clarence from *It's a Wonderful Life*."

"Then they should have their eyes checked," Lenore said, depositing another envelope on the desk. "You're

an older version of George Bailey. What's the actor's
name?"

"Jimmy Stewart." His uncle looked like he was wondering what he'd done to warrant the compliment. "And
you, love, are as pretty as a pitcher of warm milk."

Caine hid his smile behind his hand, amazed that his
uncle managed to amuse him with only ten minutes to
go before he had to tell Evie and his family that their
bid to save the manor had failed.

He glanced at the two envelopes, praying for all their
sakes that the checks would put them over the top. "It's
not enough, is it?" Lenore said, turning the screen as
Caine added the names and amounts, a hundred dollars
each, to the electronic ledger.

"You had no luck getting your cousin to relent?"
Lenore asked him.

"None. If anything, the call made matters worse,"
Caine admitted.

"He had it on speaker, and Evie happened to be
there. She shared what she thought of Alec McCleary,"
Seamus said.

"She gets that from me." Lenore smiled, then glanced
at his uncle. "I think it's time to put our plan into
action."

"Aye. I agree, love."

"What plan are you talking about?" Evie asked as
she walked into the study. She came around the desk to
lean over Caine's shoulder and peer at the balance on
the screen.

She made a small disappointed sound, and he reached
around to take her hand, bringing it to his lips. He

turned her hand over to kiss her palm. "It was a brilliant idea. It just wasn't meant to be."

"Lenore has a brilliant plan too, and while it might not save the manor, it will ensure that McCleary doesn't try to cook the books. If he does, Lenore will uncover his subterfuge. Won't you, love?"

"I have yet to have anyone fool me, but I've always enjoyed a challenge. So with your permission, Caine, Seamus and I would like to go to Ireland to oversee the audit."

"I appreciate the offer, and there's no one else I'd want overseeing the audit other than you, Lenore, but I highly doubt Alec will let you in the door."

"I believe Seamus has taken care of that," Lenore said, casting his uncle an admiring smile.

"I have indeed. And while I may have spent a fair amount of time with my face in a bottle, so have plenty of politicians. I'm also charming, with a gift of gab and have, for a man who spent most of his life living in low places, friends in high places who were willing to put the squeeze on Alec McCleary."

"Thank you, Uncle, and thank you, Lenore. I couldn't ask for two better people in my corner. I just wish I could pay you—or at the very least pay for your flight, but I'm afraid even that's beyond me."

As though sensing how difficult that was for him to admit, Evie wrapped her arms around his neck and pressed her cheek to his. "It's as important to learn to receive as it is to give."

"My daughter's right. And in a way, you'll be paying me more than what a couple of plane tickets and my time are worth. Now that you'll be working at Holiday House with Evie, I'm sure she'll be able to pay back my loan in no time at all."

"Thank you for your confidence in me, Lenore." He tipped his head back to look at Evie. "Did you forget to tell me something?"

She made a face. "It's always good to have a backup plan, right? So if we didn't raise enough money to save the manor, I thought you could move in with me and help at the store." She shrugged. "Good idea?"

"That depends. Am I going to be CEO of the LLC I've set up for you or manager of Holiday House? And we'll need to talk about my compensation package."

"Mom, you need to use your wizard brain to get Caine back his money, and you need to do that as quickly as possible," Evie said.

Caine laughed, but he sobered quickly when the Gallaghers entered the study en masse. "I'll go and—" Evie began.

Caine put out a hand to stop her. "No. You belong here too."

"Caine's right, Evie. We couldn't have done any of this without you." Kitty gave him a tremulous smile. "And you wouldn't be here without Evie, and for that she will always have our gratitude. I know I speak for all of us when I say that you've made our family complete, Caine.

"I just wish your grandfather'd had a chance to meet you. Ronan would have been so proud of the man you are. I see him in you." Jasper handed her a hankie, and she sniffed and dabbed at her eyes. "And he would have tried as hard as you have this week to save the manor, but it can't be saved, can it, Caine?"

"I'm sorry, and I know some of you have yet to forgive me for my part in this." He looked to the back of the study, where several of his Gallagher cousins stood with their arms crossed. "Trust me, I know how you feel."

"Do you blame me for this, Caine?" Kitty asked.

"No, of course not. How could I?"

"Then you can't blame yourself. And neither will any other member of this family. Because a case could easily be made that I'm the reason for all of this. We are in this together, and we will still be a family once the manor is gone. We have our health, and we have each other, which makes us luckier than most."

Kitty wiped at her eyes as the tears fell faster, and then she sniffed and squared her shoulders. "We have twenty-eight hours left to enjoy our family home, and we're darn well going to. We have a wedding to put on. And now that we know we can't save the manor, I'd like everyone to take whatever they want. Caine, would you mind printing off the list for the auction house?"

"Not at all. If everyone would just mark off what they've taken, I'll send a revised list to the auction house tomorrow."

"I have something I'd like to give you, Caine. I know this might sound strange, but for the past few days I've had this feeling that you were meant to have your grandfather's writings and journals. It's almost like a voice in my head whispering to give them to you. I'm sure Ronan would want you to have them." She glanced over her shoulder at her sons, and they nodded their agreement. Then Kitty smiled at Caine. "I'll need to get in there. Your great-grandmother Colleen locked them away in her desk. Your grandfather was very special to her, and I never had the heart to take his papers and journals back when she was alive. I'd forgotten about them until recently."

Hours later in the tower room, Evie rolled over in bed to see Caine going through his grandfather's papers. "Aren't you tired?"

"I'm tired, but someone has decided I don't need my rest," he said, looking around the room.

"Merry Christmas, Colleen." Evie waved.

Caine snorted and shook his head. "Only you would wish my dead great-grandmother Merry Christmas when I tell you she's haunting me."

"What's she saying this time?" For the past week, it had seemed Colleen wanted to ensure that Caine forgave Emily and knew that, regardless of all the bad she had done, she'd loved him. Despite everything going on with Wicklow Developments, Evie believed that was exactly the message Caine had needed to hear. She'd seen signs these last few days that he'd been able to forgive Emily and let go of his anger. But the lightness she sensed in him could also be because the Gallaghers had accepted him into the fold.

"It's something about these papers. She keeps saying *buried*, I think."

"Maybe she means the papers were buried away for a long time and she's glad you have them." Evie's eyes widened at the knock on the door. "Maybe that's her?"

Caine gave her a you-can't-be-serious look, then answered the door. "Clio, it's late. What are you doing up?"

"I'm sorry. I just...I needed to talk to you."

"Come in." He stepped aside, his eyes meeting Evie's.

It was obvious Caine was unhappy with his cousin. He believed she'd leaked the information that enabled Emily to blackmail Mr. Bradford into selling the Savings and Loan.

"Hi," Clio said to Evie. "I'm sorry to disturb you."

For some reason, Evie felt sorry for the girl. Maybe because Caine was practically glowering at her. It took a moment for her to realize why. Clio was holding *The Secret Keeper of Harmony Harbor.* "You knew it was me, didn't you?" Clio said to him.

"It took me a couple days to figure out, but yes, I did."

"But you never told anyone? Other than Evie, I mean?"

"No, and I won't. I saw your face the night my grandmother arrived at the manor. You were sick with guilt, and I didn't want to hurt Kitty any more than she had already been hurt. Your betrayal would have been the last straw." He pulled a check from his pocket and handed it to her. "I appreciated the gesture. But it's of no use to us now."

She looked from the check to Caine. "But it's the money you gave me. Well, minus the thousand dollars I'd already spent."

"Keep it. Use it toward school."

Evie stared at him. Fourteen thousand dollars had been a mere pittance to him before, but with how little he had now, it was a small fortune. As though she understood that too, Clio chewed on her bottom lip, fighting back tears. She handed him the book. "You probably know this already, but Kitty wasn't lying. I marked the place for you."

"I won't be reading it." He walked to the fireplace and tossed the book in the flames.

"No!" Evie cried, jumping off the bed. She grabbed the poker to drag the leather-bound book from the fire.

"Evie, what the hell are you thinking?" he asked as she dragged the comforter off the bed to smother the tiny flame that blackened the cover. "That book has caused no end of trouble."

"I know, but in some ways this is the last link to your great-grandmother. Colleen wrote not only the secrets of her family and friends, she recorded the Gallagher family history and the history of Harmony Harbor. It's important, even more important now that the Gallaghers are losing the manor."

"You're not thinking it should be published?" Caine said.

"Yes, but not as it is now. You should give it to Julia. She's a romance writer. She could maybe make it into a memoir-drama, or something like that. Change names to protect people without losing the history and your family's contribution to the town."

"All right, we'll talk to Julia in the morning. But until then, not a word about this to anyone, Clio," Caine said to the girl who was kneeling on the floor, going through the papers.

She looked up at him, her eyes wide. "I thought it was another one of my da's tall tales, but it was all true."

"What's true?"

"William Gallagher really was a pirate. He buried treasure here. At the manor. In the tunnels." She held up a sheaf of papers. "Read this. Grandpa Ronan was afraid that if they dug where he believed the treasure was buried, it would bring the manor down around their heads. And he was right. But everything has shifted because of the hurricane. The floor has started to come away in this part of the tunnel." She pointed to the map. "That's where the treasure is supposed to be. We should be able to get at it with shovels."

"Caine, that's what Colleen was trying to tell you. *Buried* treasure. It's real, and it's here. What are we waiting for?" Evie said, heading for the door. "Let's go save the manor."

Chapter Twenty-Nine

♥

Colleen had just about given up hope that they'd learn about the buried treasure in time. She peered over Evie's shoulder. She was holding a flashlight, shining it on Caine and Clio while they dug in the dirt. The tunnels were cold, dark, and damp. And like now, every so often the wooden trusses above their heads creaked. Caine put a hand out to stop Clio from digging and cocked his head to listen.

Colleen prayed to every angel and saint she could think of. They needed a Christmas miracle, and the treasure might be it.

"You two get upstairs. I'll do this on my own," Caine said. "It's too dangerous."

"I'm not leaving you," Evie said.

"Neither am I," Clio said as she studied the maps she'd removed from her back pocket. Then she lifted her eyes to the low, rough-hewn ceiling. "We don't have much farther to go."

They went back to digging and then straightened as the tunnel filled with a bright white light. Jasper and Kitty appeared, each carrying a flashlight.

"You shouldn't be down here," Caine said, casting a worried look at Kitty.

"There'll be no dissuading her," Jasper said. "I've already tried. But I imagine we'll have all the help we need in no time. After Simon woke us up and made us follow him to the basement door, he scampered off. No doubt to get the others."

Jasper was right. It wasn't long before the rest of the family joined them. They deferred to Clio and Caine, digging where they said to, stopping when they told them to, just as they had now. Which was why they all heard the loud *clang* when Clio's shovel met metal.

They'd found it. Now, in mere minutes, they'd discover the truth. Colleen wasn't the only one praying as Clio and her male cousins unearthed the treasure chest. It was large and battered, but it didn't fall apart. It took four of them to carry it between them. They'd decided to open the chest in the great room by the fire. Clio and Caine were given the honors of doing so. Caine took a hammer to the rusted lock. Once it broke apart, clattering to the slate floor, he nodded for Clio to lift the lid.

It creaked as she did so, and the firelight danced on the gold, silver, and twinkling gems that filled the chest. They all stood there in shocked silence, all but Clio, who knelt by the chest. She looked up at them, her eyes shining. "This is worth millions of dollars, possibly billions. Greystone is saved."

Colleen pressed her hands to her chest as her family cheered and hugged one another. Once they'd calmed down, Caine crouched beside the chest and held up a coin. "Spanish?" he asked Clio.

"Yes. I'm pretty sure it is," she agreed.

"All right. Clio, come with me. We've got to discover the origin of the treasure and what our rights to it are. Then we have to find someone who will loan us enough money to cover the manor's debt using a few of these gold coins as collateral." Caine glanced at his watch. "Within the next eight hours."

It took almost fifteen hours for the final verdict to come in, and when it did, William Gallagher and his chest of buried treasure had not only saved the manor, but redeemed Clio in the eyes of the family and herself.

Colleen's family was truly whole now, she thought, as she watched Marco and Theia, looking beautiful in their wedding finery. The couple held hands, gazing into each other's eyes as the priest pronounced them husband and wife in front of the fireplace.

They'd been meant to marry in the atrium overlooking Kismet Cove several hours ago but because of the Gallaghers' Christmas miracle, half the town had been invited to celebrate.

"I would say this is the merriest of Christmases we've ever had, wouldn't you, Simon?" Colleen frowned, looking around. "Simon? Now where has he gotten to?" she murmured, trying to ignore the pinch of worry in her chest. He'd been acting strange these past few days. She'd put it down to him picking up on her own mood, her fear that they'd lost Greystone Manor.

She left the room full of people congratulating the newlyweds to look for him in the atrium, thinking he must have gotten his wires crossed, but he wasn't there.

"Simon, where are you?" She put her hand on the glass, searching for him outside in the cold winter's night. "It's too cold for you to be outside."

"But I quite like the cold. I always have. Surely you remember that, my sweet Colleen."

At the sound of her beloved husband's voice, she brought a hand to her mouth to cover her sob, then slowly turned to search the darkened room. "Patrick, is that really you?"

He walked from the shadows with his familiar smile and a twinkle in his Gallagher-blue eyes.

"Oh, Patrick, it is you." She reached up to touch his face when he came to stand in front of her. "You're as handsome as I remember."

"And you're just as bonny as the day we wed," he said, taking her in his arms.

"I feel like I've gone to heaven. How can this be? How are you here?"

"I've been here, by your side, since a week before you died. I'd come to get you, and somehow ended up stuck in the body of a cat."

She reared back. "Simon?"

"Yes, and I'd like to know how you decided on that name. But we'll save that discussion for later. Our time here has come to an end, my love."

"I don't understand."

"You're ready now. You weren't before. You were afraid, but you had nothing to fear. You never did. No one is judged, only loved." He cupped her face and kissed her and then drew back. "And I love you, Colleen Gallagher."

"Oh, Patrick, I love you too." She took him by
the hand and walked to the edge of the atrium to
get one last look at their family. "They're wonderful,
aren't they?"

"They are. We've been blessed."

"We have." She smiled. And like she had done three
years ago, Colleen asked the good Lord to bless her
family by reciting an old Irish prayer, only this time
her husband held her hand and his deep voice joined
hers. "May God give you... for every storm, a rainbow;
for every tear, a smile; for every care, a promise; and
a blessing in each trial. For every problem life sends,
a faithful friend to share; for every sigh, a sweet song;
and an answer for each prayer."

Unlike last time, she didn't worry how her family
or the manor would fare without her. She knew they'd
be fine. Not just because they had the money to save
the manor but because they had one another. And she
no longer worried about what awaited her on the other
side. Patrick was right: The only thing that mattered in
this life and in the next was love.

Her husband smiled. "It's time, my sweet Colleen.
Let's go home." And together they walked hand in hand
toward the warm, golden light glistening through the
wall of windows facing Kismet Cove.

* * *

Evie stood at the bottom of the grand staircase with
half the single women of Harmony Harbor, several of
whom were her friends. They looked up at Theia in

her exquisite white satin wedding gown, with Marco standing beside her in a black tux with a red bow tie.

"Who's Theia making hand signals to?" Mackenzie asked.

"I'm not sure…" Evie turned to see Clio holding up a laptop with Daniel Gallagher's smiling face filling the screen. Evie smiled, raising her hand to wave when she heard a loud whistle. She turned around, just in time to see the red and white wedding bouquet sailing her way. And instead of her friends reaching out to catch the bouquet, they stepped back, and it landed in Evie's outstretched hands. She clutched it to her chest.

"Why didn't you guys try to catch the bouquet?" she asked her friends.

"Because we figured out who Theia was making hand signals at," Mackenzie said, lifting her chin.

Evie turned to see Kitty and Rosa standing arm in arm, smiling at her. "Kitty and Rosa?"

"No. Him."

Evie's eyes met Caine's as he walked toward her, looking gorgeous in his black tux and black bow tie.

"Most men don't want the woman they're dating to catch the wedding bouquet, you know? Especially a woman they've been dating for a matter of weeks. It puts ideas in their head," Evie said, and she should know because she was having ideas of her own.

"I'm not most men, Evie." He smiled and took her by the hand, waving off the teasing comments from his family as he tugged her along after him. He led her to the atrium and the big floor-to-ceiling window that looked onto Kismet Cove, snow glistening in the moonlight.

She looked around. They were alone. "Are you...? Are you proposing to me?" she asked.

He shook his head, his face cast in shadows and moonlight. "No. You were right. It is too soon, and it's Theia's night. I have my man-of-honor duties. But I love you, so think of it as me asking you to save the date." He reached in his pocket and pulled out a sprig of mistletoe, holding it over their heads. "What do you say, Christmas Eve next year, here?"

"Are you leaving Harmony Harbor?"

He lowered the mistletoe with a frown. "No. Why would you think that?"

"Because you asked me to meet you here next year on Christmas Eve, and with your share of the money from the treasure, you'll be rich again." She straightened his bow tie. Not that it needed to be straightened but she didn't want him to see her face when she said, "I thought you might move back to Ireland and try to get Wicklow Developments back."

"A very wise woman told me I should look at what's happened as a fresh start, and I've decided to take her advice."

"Really?" She smiled up at him.

"Yes. Really. I'm not going anywhere, Evie. I've decided to start my own renovation company. Holiday House and Greystone Manor will be my first projects. Free of charge, of course. I'm also going to do some business consulting on the side. And you, my love, are my special project."

"That's really sweet of you, but I'm sure you'll be busy whipping the manor into shape, so—"

"I do have some ideas to improve the manor's bottom line, but you're my priority. We'll start your Evie Christmas line with your candles, stockings, and Scrooge game, and then we'll expand to—"

"I don't have an Evie Christmas line."

"You do now. And once we have it up and running and Holiday House renovated, I have another project for us to work on." He reached inside his jacket and pulled out a white envelope wrapped with a red ribbon. He handed it to her. "Merry Christmas, Evie."

"What's this?" she asked as she opened the envelope to pull out what looked like a bill of sale.

"The town bought back the three empty lots from Wicklow Developments and agreed to sell them to me. The bank in Bridgeport loaned me the money based on my share of the treasure, so you're now the proud owner of the three empty lots beside Holiday House. I thought we'd build your park and the museum you suggested to the council last summer."

"I don't know what to say. This is...It's too much, Caine."

"You know that wise woman I was telling you about? She also said sometimes it's better to receive than to give. I think it's about time you were on the receiving end, Evie. But if it makes you feel better, there is one thing I want more than anything else, and that's your answer. Will you meet me here next year?"

She didn't know if he meant for the proposal or a wedding, but she didn't care and nodded before throwing her arms around him. "I love you, Caine Gallagher."

Her declaration was met with a chorus of gasps, and

she drew back from Caine to look around. They were surrounded by Gallaghers but they weren't looking at them. They were looking up at the night sky.

Her gasp joined theirs. Never before had she seen a Christmas star so bright. It practically filled the atrium with a joyous light. As they stood watching in silent wonder, from behind her Jasper murmured, "Well done, Madam. Well done."

One Night in Christmas

Debbie Mason

After losing her husband, Sophia Dane turned her grief into motivation to open a boutique in the small town of Christmas, Colorado. Ready to start anew and ring in the New Year with her friends, Sophia never expects to come face-to-face with her brother-in-law Adam.

Coming home to Christmas was the last thing that Adam Dane wanted to do. But when he bumps into Sophia—his brother's widow who he's been in love with since...forever—he realizes that making the trip home was fate giving him a second chance.

Keep reading for a bonus story by Debbie Mason!

FOREVER

Chapter One

♥

Snow blanketed the small mountain town of Christmas, Colorado, on the last night of the year. The pastel-painted shops that lined Main Street were decked out for the holidays, their colorful lights blinking through the gently falling flakes.

Sophia Dane couldn't remember the last time she'd been this happy to turn the sign on the door of her boutique, Naughty and Nice, to CLOSED. She'd been run off her feet trying to dress what had felt like half the women in town. They'd begun arriving before eight that morning. She couldn't afford to lose a single sale and had extended her hours of operation for the holidays.

But the women who crowded into her store today were in search of something to wear to the Danes' New Year's Eve party, a hastily organized affair to celebrate both the holiday and their grand reopening. And thanks to the family (of which she was no longer a member) holding their party at the recently renovated lodge, most of her customers had been looking for nice and cozy instead of gold and naughty.

She glanced down at the blush-colored mohair sweater she'd paired with gold-and-silver sequined leggings in an attempt to show her customers glamorous could be just as cozy as flannel and plaid. Her gaze flitted over several still-packed racks of clothing. Her strategy hadn't worked as well as she'd hoped. It looked like she'd be holding a blowout sale of all things glittery and gold this weekend.

"Autumn," she called to the sister of her heart, whose sweet shop, Sugar and Spice, was housed in the same premises as Sophia's boutique. An arched opening in the wall provided access to both stores. Sophia liked to say she was the naughty of their joint venture and Autumn was the nice.

They'd bought the run-down Colonial on Main Street for a steal nine years ago this June. Both their hearts had taken a beating months before they'd decided to go into business together. Autumn's husband, Logan Dane, had asked her for a divorce, breaking her heart and spirit.

Sophia had understood better than most what her best friend was going through at the time. She'd lost her own husband, Logan's brother, in a skiing accident just weeks before Logan pulled the plug on his and Autumn's marriage.

The months of back-breaking work it had taken to get the store in shape had been cathartic. It had brought them back to life just as much as it had the old Colonial on Main Street. And those long hours spent toiling side by side in the dust and heat had served to forge an unbreakable bond between the two friends.

Autumn stuck her strawberry-blond head around the archway. "What is it?"

Sophia's heels clicked on the white marble as she walked to one of the racks. Her gold-painted fingernails flicked through the clothes until she found the gorgeous sequined dress that would be perfect on her best friend's willowy frame. She held it up. "Happy New Year. You can wear this to the Penalty Box tonight."

Even Sophia would admit it was a little much for the local sports bar, but no one would care. They all knew them there. She angled her head in an attempt to read Autumn's expression. It wasn't one of delight or grati- tude; of that Sophia was certain. "You said you *loooved* this dress when it came in, and now you don't?"

"It's not—" The front door's holiday chime of "Auld Lang Syne" interrupted Autumn as a customer walked in.

About to turn and tell whoever it was that they were closed, Sophia instead forced her tired facial muscles into a welcoming smile. After all, the customer might buy an entire wardrobe in glitter and gold, was her hopeful thought, just before she realized it was their friend Ty.

Ty was a former Hollywood hairstylist who'd opened Diva, a high-end beauty salon, in town a couple years before. He'd be all in with the glitz and glamour had she owned a men's clothing store.

Sophia frowned at his army-green parka, plaid flan- nel shirt, and heavy winter boots. "Why are you dressed like that?" She moved her index finger up and down. Until now his wardrobe had reflected his love of all things stylish.

"I know it's small-town-goes-country, but it's all

the rage in chalet-wear these days." He rolled his eyes at Sophia. "I see by your curled upper lip you don't approve. But look"—he stuck a black fedora on his head—"totally elevates the style factor, doesn't it?"

"It would take a lot more than a hat to...Wait, why do you care if it's the rage in chalet-wear? We're not going to the party at the lodge. We're going to the Penalty Box. Like we always do. It's tradition." Sophia did not like change almost as much as she did not like the Danes.

At least some of the Danes. She liked Calder, the family's patriarch, and his second wife, Nell McBride, but Sophia did not like her late husband's brothers, Logan and Adam. Not only had Logan broken Autumn's heart, he'd broken Sophia's too. So had Adam. Her husband's brothers hadn't thought she was good enough for him. They'd tried to talk Bryce out of marrying her, and then they'd blamed her for his death. She blamed herself too.

"Ah, ah, ah, remember what you promised on Christmas Day, Gloria?"

She made an irritated sound at Ty's nickname for her. "I do not look like the *Modern Family* lady, and I do not talk like her either."

"What was that? I can't understand you," he said with a thick Spanish accent, his eyes glinting with amusement beneath his silly hat.

"You are so funny, I cannot stand it." She gave Autumn the side-eye when Ty drew a laugh from her best friend as he walked around the store swinging his hips while flicking his imaginary long hair back with his fingers. His heavy winter boots were ruining the effect. He was usually much better at impersonating Sophia's walk.

His right hand went to the hip he cocked, and he glanced over his shoulder to waggle his eyebrows at her. "And tonight we're going to find you your very own Joe Manganiello to ring in the New Year with."

She was about to say she didn't want her own Joe; she was happy with her life just the way it was. But after one glass too many of spiked eggnog on Christmas Day, she'd caved to Ty's arm-twisting and Autumn's pleading and given her word that she'd get back in the dating game. She was too tired to argue with them now.

"New Year's Eve is the time for making resolutions, and January is a time for keeping them." Or breaking them, as was the case for Sophia and nearly everyone else she knew. "So I will look for my Joe next week. Tonight is all about having fun with my two best friends." She smiled at Ty and went to smile at Autumn, but she'd ducked back inside Sugar and Spice.

"Yes, but what if your two best friends have plans to ring in the New Year with their own Joes?" Ty said.

"Which two of my best friends are you talking about?" she asked, because not only did she have a lot of good friends in Christmas, she'd know if there was a man in Autumn's life. They told each other everything, and they were rarely apart. They not only worked together, they shared an old Victorian house on Holly Lane. They'd bought it last spring.

Ty glanced at the entrance to Sugar and Spice and then motioned for Sophia to join him on the white leather chaise between the fitting rooms. Her stomach took a nervous dip. Ty wasn't often serious, but his demeanor said this was a serious conversation, one which he didn't want Autumn to overhear.

Sophia joined him on the chaise, her shoulders stiff, her back poker straight, as though perfect posture alone would protect her from the bad news she was positive he was about to deliver.

So when he gave her an appreciative look instead and said, "You really are one gorgeous woman," she sagged with relief. She must have misread his expression.

"It's too bad men can't see past your centerfold body and your movie-star good looks to the sweet, caring, and funny woman underneath. If they could, you wouldn't have been alone for so long. But don't you worry. Now that Uncle Ty is on the job—"

"No, I do not need you on the job." Emotion of any kind thickened her accent, and right now fear had garbled the words so badly even she couldn't make out what she'd said. So she repeated them, slowly and emphatically, in English and then in Spanish to make it clear she was serious.

Ty had become as notorious as Nell McBride-Dane for his matchmaking schemes, and his success rate was almost as high as the older woman's. And that was saying something. Nell had a series of books written about the couples she had matched in Christmas. They were shelved in romantic fiction, but everyone knew they were true. At least in Christmas, Colorado, they did.

But Sophia did not need, nor want, another man in

her life. She'd loved and lost and been betrayed in the most horrible way. She wouldn't put her heart on the line again. As both she and Autumn could attest to, love didn't last.

"You do so need me on the job, and do you know why?" Ty took her hand, and she hoped he didn't expect an answer because the sympathy she saw in his eyes had caused her throat to go dry. "Because Autumn has a chance to be happy, and she won't take it unless she knows you have someone to make you happy too."

"That is silly talk. The only person who can make you happy is yourself. And Autumn, she is happy. Happy, happy, happy." Sophia freed her hand from his, waving it in the direction of Sugar and Spice. "Why wouldn't she be? She has a business she loves, a beautiful home...and me. She has me. You too."

"Maybe she wants more, and maybe so do you but you're too afraid to get hurt again and won't put yourself out there."

"I put myself out there."

"Oh, I know you do. You're hands-down Christmas's biggest party girl and flirt. The thing is, I spent a decade in Hollywood with some of the biggest names in the biz and can spot someone acting in two seconds flat, so you don't fool me." He retrieved her hand, giving it a gentle tug to get her to look at him. "I know what you're up to. And one day someone will come along who sees past your act and catches a glimpse of the woman only a few of us are lucky enough to call their best friend, and that man will know you're worth the wait. He'll settle in for the long haul and win your trust."

She pulled her hand from his. "Stop with your silly talk."

"It's not silly talk, and you know it. But while it might take some time before your special someone comes along, Autumn's is already here."

Sophia jumped to her feet. It couldn't be true. "Autumn! Autumn, where are you?"

Ty latched on to her arm. "No! Don't say anything. You'll ruin everything. She told me in confidence."

"Then why did you tell me!"

"Because! When you find out who she's dating, you're going to lose your mind and ruin her chance at happiness. You're as important to her as he is," Ty whisper-yelled.

Sophia briefly closed her eyes and then slowly lowered herself back onto the chaise. Logan Dane. It had to be. He was the only man Autumn had ever loved and the only relationship she wouldn't feel comfortable sharing with Sophia. He'd stopped in at Sugar and Spice over the holidays with his two children. Their mother, his second wife, had died the year before.

Logan had spent the last several months overseeing the renovations at the lodge. Before that, he'd rarely come home. Not since he'd left Autumn. And not once on his infrequent visits to Christmas had he ever stopped by the store. Until this year.

Still, she might be wrong. She sent a prayer to the Virgin Mother. "Logan Dane stopped by Sugar and Spice three times. With his children. Those do not count as dates."

"No, but the two nights Autumn missed our Saturday

Mystery Movie Night do. Remember when she claimed to have car trouble and a late work order? She went out with him instead."

Autumn stuck her head past the archway. "Hey, did you call me? I was taking out the garbage."

"Yes. Yes, I did." Ty pinched Sophia, and she pushed his hand away. She wasn't about to confront her best friend until she knew what she was dealing with. Ty didn't have a clue how badly Logan had hurt Autumn. Sophia did, and she was not about to let her best friend make the same mistake twice. "Ty is being a baby about going to the lodge. So unless we want to listen to him whine all night, we have to go too."

Chapter Two

♥

An hour later, hunched over the wheel of her candy-apple-red Expedition, Sophia drove up the narrow, snow-covered mountain road to the lodge with only the headlights and three-quarter moon to guide her. Out of nowhere, a tree loomed up before her, and she jerked the wheel hard to the left.

"Sophia! You nearly hit that tree."

"It's not my fault it's in the middle of the road!" she yelled at Autumn, who sat in the passenger seat beside her.

"You're not *on* the road!"

"OMG, we're going to die!" Ty cried. "Turn around. Turn around and take us back to town!"

"You be quiet back there. This is all your fault," Sophia said, her nose practically pressed against the windshield as she tried to follow the tire tracks in the snow.

"When are you finally going to admit you need glasses?" Autumn asked.

"Wait. What? Sophia, you told me you had an appointment for laser surgery the week after mine."

She did, but she'd canceled at the last minute after talking to a customer whose surgery had gone wrong. It was all the excuse she'd needed. She didn't like pain of any kind, physical or emotional. "My eyes are fine." She just couldn't see street signs unless she was on top of them.

"You were driving in the woods, not on the road!" Ty protested loudly, and near her ear.

"Stop yelling at me! It is dark, and it is snowing, and you are both annoying. How am I supposed to—"

"Hands! Hands on the steering wheel!" Ty cried.

"It's no problemo. I can drive for miles without using my hands." She wrapped them around the wheel. She had a tendency to talk with her hands. A tendency she should admittedly learn to curb while driving.

"Oh really? So why is your car in Jake's body shop once a month?" Ty asked.

"Because Jake's body is so nice to look at," she said, which was true. The same could not be said about her car's body. There was only so much Jake could do with the multiple dings and dents.

"Look, there's the lodge." Autumn pointed out the lights twinkling through the trees. "The turnoff should be right about…" She thunked her head on the passenger window on purpose. "You missed it."

The only place to turn around with a modicum of safety was the lodge's lower parking lot, and it was a quarter mile down the dark road. It didn't matter if it was ten feet away. Sophia had no intention of going near the lot. The last time she had been there was the morning after her husband died, almost a decade before.

They'd been overcome with shock and grief, and no one had given much thought to the car Bryce had driven to the mountain. A former Olympic skier, he'd been his family's shining star, one of Christmas's favorite sons, and for three years Sophia had been his wife. A good wife, she had thought. And despite how his family had always made her feel, she had taken some comfort in knowing Bryce had loved her as much as she'd loved him. Except everything she'd thought she knew about her husband and their marriage was turned on its head the day she sat in his car in the lower parking lot, reading the letter he'd left behind.

Sophia slammed on the brakes, as much to stop the car as to stop the memories. She'd worked hard to move past her anger and her grief and didn't wish to deal with the emotions tonight. It would be difficult enough being at the lodge without her memories following her there.

Once the Expedition stopped fishtailing, she put it in Reverse and pressed the gas. Lights from an approaching vehicle turned the inside of her SUV heaven-white.

"Sophia!" Autumn and Ty yelled.

She hit the brakes, causing the tires to spin. They kept spinning. Around and around they went, coming to a stop almost bumper to bumper with a monster truck out of a Stephen King movie.

When the driver's door of the black truck opened and a tall, broad-shouldered man stepped out, Sophia gasped. And it wasn't an admiring gasp because the man was so big and so gorgeous; it was a gasp of shock and horror.

Adam Dane was back in town.

"Okay, so I totally forgive you for almost killing us," Ty said, resting his arms on the front seats as he peered out the windshield to no doubt get a better look at the man now walking around the back of his monster truck with his phone to his ear. "What do you think the chances are that our Knight in Sheepskin is gay?"

"None," Sophia and Autumn said at almost the same time.

They used to swoon whenever six-foot-four Adam Dane sauntered into a room, blush and stammer when he deigned to speak to them. They'd spend days, weeks, speculating about his latest romantic conquest while secretly wondering what it must be like to date a man like him. But that was before Sophia had fallen in love with Bryce, before she and Bryce were engaged, before she found out exactly what his older brother thought of her.

"You don't have to sound so definite about it. You could have given me a little...Here he comes." Ty rattled the door handle. "There must be a child lock on this thing. Let me out, bae."

"Do not call me 'bae.' 'Bae' means *poop* in Danish." She felt like poop. She always did in Adam's presence. But it had been years since she'd been within a few feet of him, almost a decade since she'd last spoken to him. At the sound of his boots on the snow, she pressed on the gas, and the engine roared to life.

"No!" Ty, Autumn, and Adam yelled.

The sound of crunching metal cleared up Sophia's why-are-they-yelling-at-me mystery. She'd put the gear into Drive, not Reverse. Swearing in Spanish, she corrected her mistake and put the car in Reverse.

"No!"

The teeth-grating sound of metal meeting metal explained why they yelled at her again. Only this time it was more of a ripping-apart sound than a crunching one.

Her door opened, and Adam leaned past her to turn off the engine and grab the keys, his large body pressing her back into the seat. His jacket was cold where it brushed her cheek. He smelled like suede and fir trees.

"Hey, Red," he said to Autumn in his deep, panty-melting voice, and then he turned his head to look at Sophia.

His blue eyes stood out in his handsome, tanned face. The California sunshine was no doubt responsible for his golden skin and the caramel streaks in his dark brown hair. He worked as a US Marshal in the northern part of the state. She wondered if it was the job or the sun that deepened the lines at the corners of his eyes and the ones that bracketed either side of his mouth. "I see your driving hasn't improved, Dimples."

Sophia's gaze jerked from his mouth to his eyes. He'd stopped calling her Dimples the day Bryce announced their engagement.

Adam straightened to stand by the open car door, and her cheeks warmed like they used to whenever he was near. Even though his big body no longer held her hostage, he made her nervous, and that made her as angry as his dig about her driving. "My driving is not the problem. It's the road. And you and your monster—"

"It's great to see you, Adam," Autumn intervened,

then winced. "I mean, the circumstances aren't great, but it's really nice to see you. Logan and the kids…" She glanced at Sophia, who stared at her, aghast.

Not only was her BFF fawning over Adam like when they were young and stupid and enamored with his rugged good looks, but the way she mentioned Logan and his children told Sophia everything she needed to know and didn't want to. Ty hadn't been exaggerating.

Sophia had ruined her car and her New Year's Eve for nothing. She didn't need to see Autumn and Logan in the same room to know their relationship was more than casual. She could just as easily devise a breakup plan at the Penalty Box as she could at the lodge.

At least if they'd gone to the local sports bar, she wouldn't have to worry about the couple sneaking off somewhere to share a kiss on one of the most romantic nights of the year. And she wouldn't be mere inches from a man she had hoped never to see again. A man she'd once admired and whose opinion had mattered to her more than most.

Autumn continued. "I mean Calder and Nell will be glad you made it."

"I know I am, and you should be too, Gloria, because he is so your Joe," Ty said next to Sophia's ear. Then he leaned the upper half of his body across the seat to offer his hand to Adam. "Hi. I'm Ty. I'm Red and Dimple's—"

"Boyfriend!" Sophia blurted in hopes of stopping Ty's matchmaking before it got started. Then she realized what that sounded like. "Not both of our boyfriend. Just mine. He is my boyfriend."

No sooner had the words come out of her mouth than she realized she'd wasted the perfect opportunity to throw a monkey wrench in Logan and Autumn's budding relationship. She shouldn't have corrected herself. She should have said Ty was Autumn's boyfriend. Except most people in town knew Ty dated men, not women.

Ty and Autumn stared at her. Adam did too, and in such a way that suggested he also knew Ty was gay.

Ty gave Sophia a hug so exuberant it knocked her faux-fur hat off her head. "Good try, but I'm not letting you ruin this," he whispered in her ear. Then he lifted his head to look at Adam. "Isn't she adorable?"

Thankfully, he didn't give the man a chance to respond. The last thing Sophia wanted was for Ty to hear what Adam thought of her. "She's trying to protect my feelings by playing my beard. It's probably that alpha-man vibe you give off," Ty told Adam. "She's afraid you might hurt my feelings if you knew I was gay. And trust me, you don't want to put Gloria between me and a homophobe."

"She knows me better than that," Adam said, then frowned. "Who's Gloria?"

"He did not say *Gloria*. He said—"

Ty talked over her. "You know, Gloria from *Modern Family*? Sofía Vergara?"

The corner of Adam's mouth tipped up. "Yeah, you're right. There's a resemblance."

"Resemblance? They're twins." Ty pulled out his phone. "Here, you have to get the full effect."

Sophia grabbed Ty's phone before he could pass it

to Adam. "He does not have time to watch your silly video."

"Um, are we just going to sit in the car all night?" Autumn asked.

"Yes. Yes, we are. Why? Did you have somewhere you wanted to go? Someone you wanted to see?"

"Why are you mad at me? It was your idea to go to the lodge for New Year's Eve."

"No. It was his idea." Sophia jerked her thumb at Ty, who tried to free his phone from her fisted grip. She tightened her fingers around the gold metallic case. "But you are the reason he had the idea. You"—she stared down her BFF—"and Logan."

Autumn's eyes went wide, and Sophia nodded. "Yes. I know you've been sneaking around with him behind my back."

Autumn turned on Ty, who'd managed to free his phone from Sophia's fingers. "I told you not to tell—"

Sophia cut off Autumn at the same time as she undid her seat belt in an effort to get the phone back from Ty. "You told him not to tell *me*, the sister of—"

The voice of Gloria from *Modern Family* filled the car. "See? Twins, right?" Ty said, holding the phone out of Sophia's reach.

As she practically climbed over the seat to get the phone from Ty, Adam's arms went around her from behind. "Okay, guys, I hate to break up your fun, but the tow truck I called is here." Adam half lifted her from the SUV.

He was exactly like she remembered. Strong, decisive, the first to step forward and take charge of a situation.

He'd been the laid-back, even-tempered Dane. He could defuse a bar fight with a single word or a single look. No one messed with him, and no one had been surprised when he'd ended up in law enforcement.

He set her on her feet beside him, opened the door for Ty, and then leaned in to grab Sophia's white fur hat and purse off the floor. His eyes glinted with amusement as he carefully fitted the hat on her head, his gloved hand brushing her cheek when he tucked away some wayward strands of hair. "You really haven't changed, have you?" he said, handing her the oversize purse.

It didn't matter that the words were said lightly and without sarcasm; they felt like an insult. "You do not know me, Adam Dane. You never did." She turned away, blinking the watery sting from her eyes.

He leaned in to her, his warm, spearmint-scented breath fanning her cheek. "Yeah, I did, Soph. I knew you better than you knew yourself," he said, and then jogged toward the tow truck, which was at that moment sliding off the road.

Autumn and Ty came to stand beside her in the glow of the emergency lights, the three of them watching Adam take control of the situation.

"Please tell me that man has brothers and at least one of them is gay."

"Ty, that's Adam Dane. Logan's...Logan and Bryce's brother."

"Wha-at? Why didn't you tell me?" He wrapped an arm around Sophia's shoulders. "I'm sorry. If I'd known who he was, I wouldn't have teased you or been nice to him. I would have defended you. I'll do that right now."

He tossed an end of his scarf over his shoulder with a flourish and started off in Adam's direction.

"No!" Both Sophia and Autumn grabbed on to an arm and reeled him back. Sophia narrowed her eyes at Autumn. "I know why I don't want him to make a scene. Why don't you?" As the reason came to her, she gave her head a slow, mournful shake. "It's already happening, isn't it? You're protecting Logan, not me, not us."

"Of course not. I love you, Soph." Autumn reached for her hand and gave it a soft squeeze. "I know you're hurt I didn't tell you about Logan and me, and I'm really sorry I kept it from you. It's just that I knew you'd be upset, and I didn't know if anything would come of it."

"Has it? Has anything come of it?" Sophia asked, afraid of the answer but desperate to know.

"Maybe. I'm not sure. It's complicated. There are children involved, so..." She lifted a shoulder, looking up when someone called her name. A man wearing a beige cowboy hat stuck his head out of the open window of a silver Range Rover that idled on the road to the lodge. The cowboy waved Autumn over. It was Logan Dane.

Autumn nibbled on her bottom lip.

"Go," Sophia said, feeling optimistic after Autumn's admission that the children were a complication. To her that sounded like the couple would soon be uncoupling. Besides, there wouldn't be much they could do tonight with the children around. The party was a family affair.

"You and Ty come too. I'm sure Adam called Logan to get us." She nodded at Adam, who'd pushed the tow truck out of the snowbank and was now standing off to the side, guiding the driver, who slowly backed toward the accident scene.

"I can't leave until I know how bad the damage is to my car." She caught Ty gazing longingly at the Range Rover and sighed. "Go with Autumn."

"Really? You're sure?" Before she got *yes* out of her mouth, he hugged her. "Thanks, ba...bunny." He grinned. "It's better than poop, right? And don't worry. I'll keep an eye on Autumn and Logan until you get to the lodge. You are coming, aren't you?"

She glanced from the monster truck eating her bumper to its owner, who'd gotten behind the wheel. "The way my New Year's Eve has gone so far, I think I'll go home and read by the fire."

"Are you crazy?" Ty said, holding up a finger when the Range Rover's horn blasted. "Have you never heard that what happens to you on New Year's Eve is a harbinger of your year to come?"

"No, but—" She was going to say she wouldn't mind spending next year reading by the fire.

Ty cut her off before she had a chance. "I can tell you from personal experience that it's true. And your night has been *Bad* with a capital *B*. The last thing you need or want is to hit repeat for 365 nights next year." As though she didn't understand how truly bad her night had been, he listed the high points for her. "Lousy sales, BFFs lying to you, car crashes, and the first man I decide to match you with turns out to be the meanie from your past."

Since he put it that way...

"Trust me, Gloria. You have to turn this night around, and you have to turn it around fast."

Chapter Three

♥

Adam glanced at the woman sitting in the passenger seat of his truck talking on her cell phone. He was surprised she'd taken him up on his offer for a ride to the lodge. Sophia made no secret of how she felt about him.

She hadn't always hated him though. There'd been a time when her dark eyes followed his every move. When he'd walk into a room and she'd welcome him with a smile that lit up her gorgeous face and showed off dimples that made him smile in return. Smiling, teasing, and keeping a protective eye on her had been as far as he'd allowed the mutual attraction he sensed between them to go. She'd been too young, and he hadn't been ready to settle down.

Back then that was the only future he'd envisioned for Sophia—a house with a white picket fence and kids as beautiful as the girl who'd captured his attention the first time he'd seen her. He'd kept his feelings for her to himself until it was too late to do anything about them.

He'd walked into his grandfather's living room in the middle of Bryce announcing his engagement to Sophia. Overcome with shock and an anger like he'd never felt before, Adam had lashed out. His inability to control his jealous rage had shaken him. He'd said things he regretted to this day. His relationship with his brother and with Sophia had never been the same. As he'd learned, time healed many things, but some things it made worse.

"Were you able to get a loaner from the body shop?" he asked when she disconnected.

"Yes. Jake takes good care of me."

"Boyfriend?" *Brilliant, Dane.* It was none of his damn business who she was dating. It should have been of no interest to him either. She was his brother's widow. Off-limits to him just like she had always been.

She snorted. "I am too old for a boyfriend. Jake is a friend."

He wasn't sure if that meant Jake was her boyfriend or not, but he refused to give in to the temptation to ask. "Thirty-three isn't old."

"You say that because you are old."

He laughed. Classic Sophia. She never did have a filter. Except when she and Bryce were married, he amended. She'd reinvented herself to fit his baby brother's image of the wife his agent, fans, and his family expected. Adam was happy to see the old Sophia back. "Thirty-eight isn't old," he told her.

The irony didn't escape him. At twenty-three, their five-year age difference had felt insurmountable. The thought annoyed him, and he refocused his attention on the winding road to the lodge instead of on the woman beside him. But his mind wasn't on board with his plans. The warm, seductive scent of her perfume filled the truck's cab and his mind with memories. Over the years he'd done his damnedest not to think about her, and now his head was filled with regrets, thoughts of what might have been.

"I thought you were older," she said.

"Thanks a lot."

"I meant when we were young. You were always more responsible than us, more serious."

"You make me sound like an old man. All I did was try to keep you out of trouble. It wasn't easy." She stiffened beside him, and he winced. He'd stepped on a land mine. There were so many between them that it was only a matter of time before he did.

He should have gone with his gut and said no when his grandfather and brother insisted he attend the grand re-opening of the lodge tonight of all nights. With Autumn dating Logan, the likelihood Sophia would be here had been good. The two women were inseparable.

"Oh, yes, I was the wicked, wild woman who was not good enough for your brother. The woman who would lead him astray." There was more than anger in her voice; there was hurt too.

"You know what? It's long past time we got this out in the open." He pulled to the side of the road and put on his hazards.

"There's nothing to get out in the open. I know everything you said about me when you dragged Bryce outside the night of our engagement. He told me after you left. But even if he hadn't, it was obvious how you felt. How your family felt. I'm surprised you didn't all stand up at the wedding and object."

Adam clenched and unclenched his fingers on the steering wheel. He'd had no idea Bryce had told her what he'd said that night. Their mother and Logan had reacted as badly, albeit for different reasons. Unlike him, they'd had no problem sharing their opinion with Sophia. His mother had tried to buy her off the next day. Adam had heard about it secondhand. He'd headed back to California the night they got engaged.

"I'm sorry Bryce told you what I said." Sorrier than she'd ever know. When his brother had taken his own life, it had felt like the ultimate betrayal; this came a close second. At least he'd been able to protect her from learning Bryce's death hadn't been an accident.

From the moment his grandfather had called to break the news of Bryce's fatal *accident*, Adam had begun searching for answers. It didn't make sense to him. He couldn't understand how his brother, a world-class skier, could die on Blue Mountain. A mountain he knew like the back of his hand.

As soon as Adam made it back to Christmas, he headed for the mountain to check out the scene for himself. There'd been no reason for Bryce to be up there after midnight or to crash into a tree. The conditions had been good that night and the runs were clearly marked.

Some people would also say there'd been no reason for Adam to visit the coroner, an old friend from high school, a few hours later. Though the people who knew him best wouldn't be surprised at his need for answers, his need for the truth.

The toxicology report confirmed his suspicions: his brother's blood alcohol was three times over the legal limit, and opioids were found in his system. Still, with no additional evidence and no suicide note, Adam's old friend the coroner ruled it an accident and agreed to keep the findings from the family as a favor to him. Adam spent the days leading up to the funeral digging into Bryce's life, uncovering evidence that served to confirm his suspicions.

Afraid Sophia would blame herself for his brother's suicide, and even if she didn't, his family might blame her, Adam had kept the truth to himself. It was an easy decision to justify. He was protecting Sophia, his family, and his brother's memory. He owed him that at least. After Bryce married Sophia, Adam hadn't been much of a big brother. As a result of his investigation, he'd learned that Bryce had needed him more than he'd ever let on.

It was easier to push back the guilt and regret that accompanied the memories knowing that Bryce had told Sophia what he'd said that night. "I didn't mean for you to hear what I said. Bryce had no business telling you something he had to know would hurt you. I was angry at him, not you."

"You said I would make a terrible wife."

"No. I said you were too young to get married. You both were."

"You said I was a ski bunny and only wanted him for his money and our marriage would never last."

Logan had called her a ski bunny. His mother had called her a gold digger. "I did. I said your marriage wouldn't last."

"Because I was an attention-seeking party girl who couldn't be trusted." Her eyes flashed, and her accent thickened.

"You liked attention, and my brother didn't like sharing the limelight. You liked to dance and have fun, but Bryce was focused on his career. Nothing was more important to him than winning Olympic gold. You were friendly and flirty, but Bryce was jealous and had a temper. You two were a powder keg, one party away from going off."

"I didn't go to parties. I was too busy helping manage Bryce's career. I was a good wife. He was happy. He loved me."

Bryce was far from happy, but it wasn't her fault. And Adam would bet Sophia hadn't been happy either. She'd given up on her hopes and dreams so that Bryce could go after his, only his brother's had ended when he'd shattered his leg and pelvis. Injuries Adam knew without a doubt had contributed to his death. "My brother couldn't have asked for a better wife. He loved you."

"Your family didn't think he did," she murmured, and turned her head to look out the window.

"Who cares what anyone else thinks? All that matters is you know that he did." Adam checked his rearview mirror, turning off his hazards before pulling onto the road. "Have you been to the lodge since...?" He'd been about to say *since Bryce died*, but he didn't want to talk about his brother anymore. There was nothing freeing about rehashing the past. He was still as angry at Bryce as he had been when he'd pulled to the side of the road. Maybe more so. "The renovation?" he said instead.

"No. I can't remember the last time I was here. It was a mistake to come tonight."

"So why did you?" he asked as he turned into the packed parking lot.

"Autumn and Logan. Did you know they're dating?"

Clearly, from the look on her face and from the earlier exchange in the SUV, Sophia was not on board with the couple reuniting. Since Adam was on board with Autumn and Logan getting back together, he thought it best to play dumb. "Uh, I might have heard something about it."

"And...?" She motioned for him to keep talking.

"I'm not sure what you want me to say, Dimples." The nickname slipped out, the way it had earlier. He'd been surprised to see her. Surprised at how little she'd changed. The thing she'd just done with her hands was familiar too. She had beautiful hands—her nails always painted and long. He used to wonder what it would feel like to have her nails dig into his shoulders, score his back..."I don't have an opinion on it one way or another."

At least not one she'd want to hear. And since she wasn't giving him the cold shoulder or yelling at him, it felt like maybe she didn't hate him quite so much after their talk on the side of the road. The last thing he wanted was to give her a reason to.

But before Logan had reunited with Autumn, he'd

been making noises about putting out feelers for other job opportunities. His brother had wanderlust and didn't like to stay in one place for long. If he left, it would fall on Adam to manage the lodge. He had no idea how to run a business and no desire to. But he also didn't want his family to lose the lodge.

A few months back, his grandfather had laid down the law. Either one of them stepped up to the plate, or the lodge would fall into the hands of their second cousin, Rick Dane. Years before, Rick had kidnapped Christmas's sheriff. He'd pleaded temporary insanity and received five years in a mental institution in Pueblo. His five years were up.

"Well, I have an opinion, and your brother, he will hear it tonight," Sophia said as Logan managed to find a parking spot a fair distance from the lodge.

He was going to offer to drop her off at the entrance but decided the walk might do her good. "Come on, it's New Year's Eve. Let it go for tonight and enjoy yourself."

"Enjoy myself? How am I supposed to enjoy myself when my best friend is about to have her heart broken again?"

He pulled into the parking spot and turned off the engine. "I understand where you're coming from. The divorce was hard on both of them. But Logan—"

"Is an asshat."

He laughed. "No, he's..." She lifted a perfectly arched dark eyebrow. "Okay, I'll give you that. Sometimes he can be a jerk. But he's had a tough couple of years. Roxanne, his wife, was sick for a long time before she passed away. He took care of her and the kids. Now he's trying to be both mother and father. He's a great dad. He deserves a little happiness. They both do, don't they?"

"Autumn was happy. We were happy. We have a wonderful life together, and now your brother is going to ruin it."

"It sounds like this is more about you losing Autumn than it is about Logan breaking her heart."

"You don't know what you are talking about." She opened the truck's door.

He knew exactly what he was talking about. She just wouldn't admit it or didn't see it herself. "Hang on a minute. I'll help you out."

"You know what they say about men who drive big trucks?" she asked when he reached her side.

"We have big egos?" His ego was more healthy than big. And his truck was well suited to back-country driving, where he spent most of his days off.

"No, that you're overcompensating for ... you know." She put a hand on his shoulder, and he put one at her waist, or where he imagined her waist would be if she weren't bundled up in an ankle-length fake-fur coat that matched her hat and hid any sign of the lush curves he remembered.

She jumped down, stumbling as she landed. He brought her close to steady her. Looking into eyes the color of melted chocolate, he said, "What do you think I'm overcompensating for, Dimples?"

She stared up at him, her glossy red lips slightly parted, and he thought he should let her go before he forgot she was off-limits and that he had a woman waiting for him back home.

She lowered her eyes and moved away. "I didn't say you were. Other people did."

He decided not to tease her any further, for his own sake as much as hers. "Be careful you don't slip," he warned when she headed for the lodge with a determined, sexy stride. "Your boots aren't exactly made for winter weather."

"Yes, they are." She stopped and hiked up the bottom of her coat to show him a pair of knee-high butterscotch leather boots with gold high heels and decorative gold chains around each ankle.

He dropped his gaze to his rust-colored Timberlands because looking at her in those boots was putting some really bad ideas in his head. "No, these are what you call winter boots."

"No, they are ugly boots, and they are the reason I still have racks of beautiful clothes left." She flounced off, muttering, "You and your boots."

A snowball hit him on the back of the head. "Ow." He raised his hand to check for damage and brush off the frozen flakes. "What the...?" Looking around, he spotted his brother half-hidden behind a fir tree decorated in multicolored lights. Logan waved him over.

Sophia turned. "What's wrong?"

"Ah, nothing. I forgot something in my truck. You okay to get there on your own?"

"No. I'm a helpless woman who needs a big strong man to—"

He held up his hands. "Sorry. Forget I asked."

Her huffed breath crystalized in a small cloud. "No. I'm sorry." She gestured at the lodge with its peaked rooflines, the deck crowded with laughing people, lights ablaze from the antler chandeliers that were visible through the main floor windows. "I'm just...I didn't expect it to be this hard. I don't come here during ski season. I try not to come at all."

"Come on, we'll find Ty and Autumn, and get you a drink," he said as he walked toward her. He took her hand and gave it a comforting squeeze. "Sometimes running away from the pain makes it worse. It lasts a lot longer than it has to, Soph. Sometimes you just have to lean into it."

They didn't get more than a couple feet before Ty and Autumn arrived to take Sophia away. His brother's handiwork, no doubt.

"All right, you can come out of hiding," Adam said when the three of them disappeared behind the wooden doors.

His brother came out from behind the tree. He wore a denim jacket lined with sheepskin over a red plaid shirt. The last few years had taken a toll. Logan could stand to put at least ten pounds on his lean six-foot frame. His dark hair was prematurely streaked with silver, the crow's-feet at the corners of his gray eyes more pronounced. "You had the perfect opportunity to send her back to town, but oh no, my big brother has to play Mr. Nice Guy."

Adam tugged his brother out of the light from the lodge and lowered his voice. "I don't get you. What did she ever do to you?" He held up his hand when the first word out of Logan's mouth was their brother's name. "Don't even go there."

"Whatever. I should know better. You always were her biggest champion. I used to think you loved her more than Bryce did."

Adam kept his face blank. "At least you're finally admitting Bryce loved her. Took you long enough. Then again, you always were a hardhead."

"Yeah, well, all I know is I want a second chance with Autumn, and if Sophia has her way, she'll ruin it for me." He glanced at his watch and then at the mountain. "The show's about to begin. Once it's over, Nell's going to take the kids home with her. I've got plans for Autumn and me. Plans that don't include Sophia dogging our every move. And since you're the one who brought her here, you have to help me."

Since he wanted Logan and Autumn back together, he didn't argue against his brother's misguided logic. "Fine. What do you want me to do?"

"Keep Sophia busy until after midnight."

"After midnight? That's hours away. How am I supposed to keep her busy for that long?"

"I don't care how you do it. Just do it or you might as well pack your bags for Christmas."

"Sophia's right—you are an asshat."

"Whatever. And speaking of the lodge, guess who I saw hanging around today? Rick. He moved into a halfway house just outside of town."

More bad news. But he shouldn't be surprised. It happened every time he came home to Christmas.

Chapter Four

♥

Sophia stood on the deck surrounded by people she routinely hung out with at the Penalty Box, attended book club with at the mystery bookstore, had a skinny latte and cupcake with at the Sugar Plum Bakery, and lunched with at the tea shop.

These were her people. She knew them and liked them, and they liked her. So why was she searching the crowd for a man she hadn't thought about in years? Okay, so maybe she had thought about him. But whenever he dropped into her brain uninvited, she'd push him out because it hurt too much to think about him. His betrayal had wounded her almost as much as his brother's, and despite Adam apologizing and saying all the right words in the truck tonight, she wasn't ready to forgive him.

Yet as she stood around the wood-burning fire pit drinking a dirty snowman and gazing up at Blue Mountain, she was fighting a desperate urge to find him.

It was like she'd reverted back to the girl she used to be. The one who didn't have to worry about guys hitting on her when she danced her heart out at parties because Adam would be there watching out for her. The girl whose heart felt like it would burst if she made him smile or, even better, laugh.

"You were a silly girl," she murmured, deciding she needed something stronger than Baileys with vanilla ice cream, hot chocolate, and whipped cream.

"Where are you going?" Ty called from where he sat on the arm of an Adirondack chair. She'd thought he was too busy with the IT guy from Denver to notice her leave. She raised her empty glass.

"Okay, but hurry up. The show's about to begin."

She'd forgotten about the show. She shivered despite wearing as much fur as a polar bear. That hers wasn't real was probably the reason the cold mountain air cut through the coat, or maybe it wasn't the wind at all.

She went up on her toes, searching for Autumn's pink knit hat with the double faux-fur pom-poms, and spotted her where she'd last seen her, standing at the rail talking to Nell McBride, who wore a tiny Santa hat on a sparkly headband that held back her youthfully cut, dyed red hair. Logan's children were with them, but their daddy wasn't. Sophia said a prayer to the Virgin Mother. Maybe he'd be too busy to join them tonight. She was about to call to Autumn when several other members of the McBride family joined them with their toddlers in tow.

They had the best vantage point for the *show*. So not much chance she'd be able to convince Autumn to join her by the stone fireplace on the main floor.

Or the bar, Sophia thought, nibbling the chocolate

that rimmed her empty glass as she headed for the double doors. Two men walked onto the deck at the exact moment she licked the chocolate from her lips. Logan looked from her to Adam, lifting an eyebrow before turning to walk away.

"Nice to see you too, Logan!" she called to his back. People on the deck stopped talking to turn and stare, including Autumn. Sophia didn't care. It wasn't right for Logan to treat her this way. Though she supposed she was partially to blame. She'd let Bryce's family get away with treating her like crap for far too long.

Logan turned and walked back to her. "Nice to see you, Sophia." His smile was as fake as her fur coat, and he nodded at her glass. "It looks like you got a head start on the night. You might want to slow down."

"I'm just getting started, *mi hermano*." She called him *my brother* because she knew he didn't like it. "But you, you should slow down with *mi hermana*. You broke her—"

"Okay, nice to see nothing has changed between you two. Logan, you go to your corner, and, Soph, you're coming with me."

Adam turned to open the door at the same time music came through the outdoor speakers, signaling the parade was about to begin. A cheer went up from the crowd as everyone turned to look up at the top of Blue Mountain. She hurried though the door Adam held open, relieved at her narrow escape. But just as she was about to walk toward the stairs leading down to the main floor, Adam took her hand.

"Come on, you get a better view of the parade from

over here than down there." He drew her toward a bank of windows to the left of the deck.

She opened her mouth to make an excuse about needing a drink, but the ski instructors and ski patrol had already begun weaving down the mountain with lit torches held aloft. From where she stood, it looked like a ribbon of fire undulating its way around and down the mountain in time to this year's top pop songs pumping through the outdoor speakers.

"Doesn't get old, does it?" Adam said, obviously mistaking her open mouth as an expression of awe.

She pressed her lips together, afraid the sob building in the back of her throat would escape.

"Jeez, Bryce loved this. It was his favorite holiday tradition, even as a kid. As soon as he was old enough to take the lift by himself, he started bugging our grandparents to let him lead the parade. Probably the only thing he hated about being on the circuit was missing out on...Aw, Soph, I'm sorry. I didn't think."

She flicked the tear from her cheek. "He led the parade that last year. You weren't here. Everyone said he shouldn't do it. They thought I should stop him, could stop him, but there was no stopping Bryce once his mind was made up."

She moved closer to the window, pressing her hand to the glass, covering the place she'd met him at the end of the parade, his handsome face aglow in the torchlight. "Do you know, that night was the happiest I had seen him since the accident. He was filled with hope and plans to get back...I should have stopped him. If I had, he wouldn't have..." She swallowed a sob and the truth.

Adam's hand moved over her back in an effort to comfort her. But it wasn't comforting. He wasn't comforting. She didn't know why she'd wanted him at her side earlier tonight. He stirred things up, making everything worse.

"Come on, Soph. There's nothing you could have done. Bryce…Don't blame yourself—"

She turned to face him, causing his hand to fall to his side. "Why not? You did. You all did."

"No. I didn't. Not once. God's truth."

"I saw the way you looked at me at the funeral. You couldn't hide it. Not from me. You were angry."

"I was. But not at you. Never at you. I was angry at Bryce—" He looked away.

She took in the muscle pulsating in his scruff-lined jaw, his hands clenched into fists at his sides. He was angry now. But not at her, at Bryce.

"I'm sorry. You didn't need to do this tonight," he said.

Why would he be mad at Bryce after all this time, she wondered. Why…? "You knew. You know," she said more to herself than to him. The air around them shifted as the door opened and closed, ushering people and a gush of cold inside. But it was like they were in their own private bubble, walking a tightrope between truth and lies. They stared at each other.

"What do I know, Soph?"

She was afraid to say. If she did and he didn't know, or even if he did, it would be like pulling out the one card that would topple the house of cards. But there was something about the way he looked at her that forced the truth past her lips. "That it wasn't an accident."

He brought his hands to his face, moved them up and down, and then looked around. The deck was nearly empty as people walked by, heading down the stairs to the main floor. "We need to talk, but not here."

She didn't want to talk. Her memories of that time were locked away where they could no longer hurt her. Being here, being with Adam, had unlocked the vault and some had slipped out. She needed to leave; that's what she needed to do. "I have to find Autumn."

She searched the crowd and spotted Nell walking down the stairs with Logan's children. Their father and Autumn were nowhere in sight. Sophia hurried to the railing, searching for a black fedora in the crowd. Lines of people stood at the bar and at buffet tables piled high with platters of finger food. A small group gathered at the twenty-foot Christmas tree.

"Ty!" she called out.

He turned from where he stood by the fireplace, looked up, and waved.

"Where's Autumn?"

He frowned, looked around, and then shrugged.

"I know where she is, Sophia," Nell McBride yelled from where she now stood just off to the right of the stairs with Logan's children.

Adam glanced at Nell. "Ah, Soph, I don't think this is a good idea," he said as he reluctantly followed her down the stairs. "Nell's got that look in her eyes."

Sophia stopped to squint at his step-grandmother. "What look?"

"You know, the one she gets when she's up to no good. Don't say I didn't warn you," he muttered when

Sophia walked across the planked floor to Nell, who waved over her husband, Calder Dane.

Adam's grandfather didn't need a wig or a fake beard to play the town's Santa to Nell's Mrs. Claus. Calder looked exactly as Sophia had always pictured the jolly old elf, right down to the sparkling blue eyes.

He winked at Sophia and then pulled a small candy cane from behind each of Logan's children's ears. The little boy and girl, who were subdued only moments before, lit up. They were lucky to have Calder and Nell in their lives. Their uncle Adam too, she thought when he crouched in front of them, pulling two envelopes from his jacket pocket.

They opened the envelopes and withdrew bright and sparkly Christmas cards. Their eyes lit up when they looked inside. "Look! Look what Uncle Adam got us!" They held up identical photos of a puppy with a curly, cream-colored coat before throwing themselves at Adam. "Where is he, Uncle Adam? Where is he?"

"Waiting for you at home." He looked up at his grandfather. "Don't worry. He's in a crate, and I bought everything he needs." He hugged his niece and nephew before standing. "If you guys think of anything else, we'll go shopping before I leave."

"Can we go now? Can we go home now?"

"Yes. Yes," Nell said, making it sound like she was annoyed, but her twinkling blue eyes belied her put-upon voice. Expect they weren't twinkling at the little people. They were twinkling at Sophia and Adam, and it was an uncomfortably familiar twinkle. Although not one Sophia had ever had directed at her.

She shot a panicked glance at Adam, who raised an I-told-you-so eyebrow.

He could tell her so all he wanted, but there wasn't much she could do about it now. And it wasn't like she or Adam were interested in being matched, especially to each other. Even if she were interested in dating again, which she wasn't, she'd never date her late husband's brother.

"I won't keep you, then. I just need to find Autumn," she said to Nell.

"She's with Logan. He wanted her advice on the honeymoon cabin. Calder can take you there."

The excitement on Logan's children's faces at the prospect of seeing their new puppy disappeared in an instant, a flash of resentment in their narrowed eyes. It appeared Sophia would have allies in her bid to keep their father and Autumn apart. So she didn't understand the sudden urge to defend her best friend.

"I'll take Sophia," Adam offered.

She widened her eyes to make the point to Adam that he was playing into the local matchmaker's hands. But his attention was on the phone he'd pulled from his jacket pocket. While he texted someone, she said loudly enough to hopefully regain his attention, "No. It's okay. You take Nell and the children home. I will go with Calder."

"Already have my ride sorted out," Nell said. "Calder has to stick around. He and his dog team are booked up for the night. Lucky for you and Adam, he's got an opening. Better skedaddle."

"Give me five minutes," Calder said, rubbing the

kids' heads and giving Nell a kiss on the cheek before walking toward the exit door.

"No. Adam's busy. Ty will come with me. Ty!" Sophia called, her voice rising on a panicked note because of Nell and her matchmaking eyes.

"Are you the lady on *Modern Family*?" the little girl asked Sophia.

Ty, who must have picked up on the panic in Sophia's voice and rushed over, grinned at Logan's daughter. "They're twins," he told her, and then said to Sophia, "What's wrong, bae... bunny?"

She made a frustrated sound. "Autumn and Logan are checking out the honeymoon suite at the—"

"They actually did it. They set the date." Ty clapped his hands. "This is soo..." He looked from her to the children. "Bad. This is sooo bad."

Once again she found herself torn between wanting to agree it was the worst thing ever and pretending it was the best. Autumn would be an amazing step-mother, and Sophia didn't like the children thinking she wouldn't. But in her heart she knew the worst thing for Autumn would be to reunite with Logan. The Danes were heartbreakers. Even Calder had broken Nell's heart a long time ago.

And the freckle-faced little boy holding up his envelope to Sophia with a gap-toothed smile showed every sign of growing up to be a heartbreaker too. "Can you get your sister's autograph for me?"

"She's not my—"

"Of course she can," Ty said, taking the envelope.

In Spanish, Sophia muttered what happened to men

who lied to little children. Adam glanced up from texting with a half smile. "Soph, the kids are learning to speak Spanish. Lucky for you, you talk too fast for them to keep up. But I can."

She'd forgotten that he spoke Spanish. He used to practice on her when he was first learning.

"And if she can't get you an autograph, I will. What?" Ty said when she shot him a look. "I'm sending a tape of you to Ms. Vergara. You'd make a great stunt double. Don't give me that face. You might need a second career if your sales keep—"

"Ty," she muttered. The last thing she needed was for her customers to think her sales were down. People liked to support winners, not losers.

"Autumn mentioned you girls didn't have a stellar year. I'll make a note to bring it up at the business association meeting next week. Okay, kiddles, looks like our ride is ready," Nell said, zipping up the children's jackets.

Adam tucked his phone away and moved to help with his niece's and nephew's hats and mittens while saying to Sophia, "We should get going too."

"It's okay. Ty will…" Sophia's eyes narrowed at Ty, who was exchanging hand signals with Nell. "What are you two talking about?"

"Nell asked me to stand in for her as hostess with the mostest."

"What does this"—Sophia made the same hand gestures that he had—"have to do with hosting the party?"

"I didn't do that. I did this." He waved, smiled, and pretended to be serving food.

"You did not do that." She waved and smiled. "You did this." She repeated his previous hand signals.

Adam put a hand on her lower back and nudged her toward the door. "Say good-bye, Gloria."

Ty, Nell, and the children laughed.

"You're so funny, I cannot stand it," Sophia said to Adam as she walked to the doors. She didn't have a choice. She had to go with him. Because the last thing she wanted was Autumn alone with Logan in the honeymoon cottage on New Year's Eve.

Chapter Five

♥

Y ou and Ty should take your show on the road," Adam said as he held open the door for her, his smile fading when they stepped outside. "Does he know about Bryce?"

"I don't want to talk about it." Sophia had hoped he'd forgotten or, like her, wanted to. But she should have known better given his earlier remarks.

"I'll take that as a *no*. You didn't tell anyone, did you? Not even Autumn. All these years you've been carrying this on your own."

She slipped, unsure if it was because of the tenderness in his voice or the ice under the snow. He took her arm, tucking it through his.

To anyone who didn't know them, they probably looked like a couple out for a romantic walk under the starry night sky. The Christmas lights that decorated the lodge lit up the path to where Calder's sled and dogs awaited, the sound of music and laughter floating to them on the still night air. No one would guess they were talking about the tragic death of a man they had both loved.

Burying her grief and anger just like she had buried

Bryce had made it easier for her to carry on on her own. "You never said anything to anyone. I would have known if you'd told your family. They would have blamed me." She stopped to stare at him. "You didn't tell them because of me."

Looking away, he shoved his hands in his jacket pockets. "I wanted to save you from spending your nights lying awake asking why, wondering if you could have stopped him. And I wanted to protect his memory and my family." He brought his gaze back to her. "But I didn't deal with it on my own. I told friends, people I trusted. It helped, Soph. I wish I could have been there for you. How did you find out?"

"Autumn brought me to pick up his car. There was a letter addressed to me in the glove compartment. How did you find out?"

He told her about his suspicions, his visit to the coroner, his cover-up of the truth. She wondered what her life would have been like had the truth come out. Now that it was out in the open, even if it was only between the two of them, she felt a slight lightening of the heavy weight she'd carried by herself for all these years. But she had a feeling the easing of her burden was because Adam's first reaction hadn't been to blame her but to protect her. And if he didn't blame her, maybe, just maybe, she could stop blaming herself.

The jingle of bells drew her attention.

Adam lifted his chin to the end of the snow-covered path. "Looks like our ride awaits."

"You don't have to come. I'm sure you have people you want to see tonight."

"I can see them later. I'd just as soon not leave you and my brother to fight without a referee. I don't see Autumn standing up to either one of you."

She ignored him and walked to Calder, casting a nervous glance at the huskies. "Are you sure I can't walk to the cabin?"

"It's quite a hike, and not an easy one with the amount of snow that's fallen. Unless you're up for some cross-country skiing. Nice night for it," Calder said, looking up at the bright three-quarter moon in the star-spangled sky.

Adam laughed. "You do remember who you're talking to, don't you, Gramps? Sophia's allergic to sports of any kind."

Unless you considered dancing a sport, it was true. Another reason why she'd never fit in with the Dane family. There wasn't a sport they didn't love or excel at. All three brothers had been natural athletes.

Calder chuckled and reached for a red plaid blanket. "Sledding it is. Adam, you get on first."

Sophia looked from the six-foot-four, broad-shouldered man standing beside her to the sled. "There won't be any room for me."

"It'll be tight, but we can manage," Adam said, settling himself in.

"No, she's right. Here, Sophia, take off your coat, and we'll put it over you. Adam will keep you warm."

"Ah, Gramps, I—"

"Don't worry. You can tell your girlfriend you had a chaperone."

Sophia gave a little start, surprised by the news,

although she shouldn't have been. There was no way a man like Adam wouldn't have someone special in his life. Though the revelation had her taking a second look at the space they would be sharing.

"Are you sure Autumn and Logan are at the cabin?" she asked Calder, hoping for a way out of this predicament. She pulled her cell phone from her pocket to check if Autumn had responded to her latest text. She hadn't, which was worrisome.

"If Nellie says so, then that's where they're at."

Sophia glanced once more at the tight confines of the sleigh, reminding herself that no sacrifice was too great to make if it meant protecting her best friend from having her heart broken again.

"We better get a move on though. I have another couple booked in twenty minutes," Calder added.

Sophia unbuttoned her coat and handed it to the older man, wrapping her arms around herself against the cold. "I'm not sure this is a good idea," she said with a shiver as she climbed in.

"You and me both," Adam murmured with an odd expression on his face. He looked like he was in pain.

"Sorry," she said, thinking she must have stepped on him.

He tucked the blanket around her. "What are you sorry about?"

"For stepping on you. You made a face."

"Right. It's okay. No permanent damage." He wrapped his arms around her, and the girl she used to be smiled. It looked like she needed to have a chat with the silly girl inside because the man holding her in his arms had a girlfriend, and even if he didn't, the woman Sophia was now wasn't interested. It didn't escape her notice that she'd had to remind herself several times tonight that she wasn't interested in Adam.

Calder lay the coat over the blanket and then tucked both around them. "There, you two look nice and cozy."

With narrowed eyes she followed the older man's progress to the back of the sled. It wasn't until a spearmint-scented breath warmed her face that she realized how close her angled head brought her to Adam's lips. She self-consciously raised her gaze to his. "Do his eyes always twinkle like that, or should we be worried?"

"I'm getting more worried by the minute, Dimples."

So was she, and at that moment, it wasn't the thought they had a matchmaking grandpa and step-granny on their hands that worried her. It was her inability to tear her gaze from Adam's. She was getting sucked into his eyes and the memory of how he used to look at her, how they used to be. Being surrounded by his strong, masculine presence and enveloped in his warm, woodsy scent only served to heighten her reluctant attraction to him.

"Okay, you don't need to come with me. I swear, I won't say anything to Logan. I'll just—" She threw back her coat and the blanket and went to get out of the sled, but the dogs shot off, and she fell back against Adam.

"Hang on!" Calder yelled.

"Your timing's a little off, Gramps!"

Calder laughed, cracking a whip high above their

heads and the dogs. "On Donner, on Blitzen, on Comet…"

"He's not planning to take us back to the North Pole with him, is he? My face is already freezing, and so are my toes."

"You never were much for the great outdoors, were you?" Adam said, a hint of amusement in his voice as he leaned over her to adjust the blanket and her coat. Once he'd tucked her back in, he curled his big body around her.

"She might be warmer if she turned to face you," Calder yelled.

"No!" she shouted above the strangled sound that came from Adam close to her ear. The image of her straddling him must have popped into his mind too. "I'm fine! You just tell Rudolph to pick up the pace or he'll be demoted."

Behind her, Adam snorted a laugh, but she refused to say anything for fear of what else Calder might suggest. She hadn't straddled anyone for a long time, and that was not something she wanted to be reminded about with her girlhood crush doing his best to keep her warm.

She focused on the dogs racing through the snow. In the distance, she heard the low buzz of snowmobiles on the forest trails. They were in a valley, surrounded by the towering Rockies and majestic, snow-laden pines.

Adam was right: unlike 90 percent of Coloradoans, she didn't spend a lot of time in the great outdoors. She didn't climb, cycle, hike, run, or ski. Though, since buying the house on Holly Lane with Autumn, Sophia had developed a passion for gardening. She'd been surprised to discover her thumb was green, not black as she had always believed. But even though she didn't spend the majority of her time outside, she appreciated the beauty of the small mountain town she called home, and thought, as she always did when she was forced to venture off the beaten path, maybe she should get out more often.

She mentally added the idea to her list of New Year's resolutions. But as snow swirled on a fierce gust of frigid air, she sank lower beneath her coat and blanket and adjusted the latest addition to her New Year's resolutions. She'd hibernate for the rest of the winter and come out in the spring.

"Couple more minutes and we'll be there," Adam said close to her ear, pointing to a dark shape on the edge of the woods.

She resisted the urge to snuggle back against him as the wind howled, focusing instead on their surroundings. Which seemed like a good idea until she realized where they were. She jerked upright, clutching her coat. "We're on the lake!"

"Okay, don't panic. The ice is at least eight inches thick."

There was a loud crack, and her heart dropped to her frozen toes. On a panicked cry, she yelled, "We're going to die!"

"We're not going to die. That wasn't the ice. It was a tree." He held her a little tighter, his mouth at her ear. "I wouldn't have let you come if it wasn't safe. Neither would Calder. He's cautious. You can trust him."

A few minutes later, as they got off the sleigh, Sophia had reason to doubt Adam's faith in his grandfather, and so did he.

As she trudged after Adam through the calf-high snow, doing up the buttons of her coat, she heard the jingle of bells. She looked over her shoulder and frowned. Calder appeared to be preparing to leave. Surely he wouldn't...

"Gramps, wait! You can't just leave us here," Adam called from where he stood on the porch step. When his grandfather ignored him and cracked his whip, Adam swore under his breath and took off after him.

"I'll be back after midnight," Calder yelled, tossing a red sack at his grandson. Then the sled took off like a shot, disappearing in a swirl of snow.

"I should have known they were up to something," Adam muttered as he stomped back to the porch, pulling his phone from his pocket. He held it up and moved it around. "No service. Why am I not surprised? This night keeps getting better and better."

"I'm sorry your night is so horrible. Mine isn't any better, you know," Sophia said as she joined him on the porch. She should have kept her mouth closed. There was a decidedly defensive note in her voice, and she didn't want him to think he'd hurt her feelings.

He pocketed his phone, dropping the sack at his feet. "I wasn't talking about you, Dimples. Seeing you again, getting the chance to finally clear the air between us, that's made everything else worthwhile."

"Oh, I . . . Yes. You are right. It has." And even though her car was back in the body shop and her best friend was MIA with Logan Dane, she was glad she'd literally run into Adam tonight. She'd always trusted him, trusted that he would tell her the truth. So to have Adam validate his brother's love for her, to absolve her of the guilt she'd carried around for all these years... Yes, this was one night in Christmas she wouldn't forget.

She glanced at the front window of the dark cabin. She hoped it would be a memorable night because she and Adam had buried the hatchet, not because they'd caught Autumn and Logan in the act.

"Maybe we should knock." She followed through with her own suggestion, banging on the window and calling, "Autumn, get out here right now."

"They're not here." Adam dug around in the sack and then pulled out a key.

Sophia frowned. "How do you know?"

"No tracks, no chimney smoke," he said as he opened the door. He held up the sack when she walked inside. "At least they've made sure we won't go hungry and that you'll be warm and cozy." He pulled out a red plaid onesie and thick wool socks.

"Ty! That's what he and Nell were hand signaling about. But why...?" She gasped when it hit her what they were up to. "They're trying to get me out of the way so he and Autumn can ring in the New Year with their Joes."

Adam's brow furrowed as he handed her the pajamas and socks. "Wait. Autumn's dating a guy named Joe...and my brother?"

She considered saying *yes*. "No. It's another of Ty's silly Gloria jokes. He said he's going to find me my own Joe Manganiello. Sofía Vergara's husband," she said at his blank look. "They don't want to feel guilty for abandoning me to be with their Joes."

"You're not dating anyone?" Adam asked as he walked to the stone fireplace.

"No," she said, looking around the cabin for any signs Autumn and Logan had been there.

The cabin had a rustic charm and was beautifully appointed. The leather couch and chairs had brightly colored fabric pillows decorated with black-bear motifs. The pine end tables and coffee table continued the theme. There was a bathroom to the left of the open-concept living room and kitchen and a set of stairs leading to the open loft where a king-size bed sat in a log frame, neatly made with a fur throw on the end of the dark comforter. Adam was right; they hadn't been here. The honeymoon cabin was a decoy.

Crouched in front of the fireplace, he glanced at her over his shoulder. "*No* as in not dating now, or *no* as in not dating since my brother died?"

He sounded surprised, and maybe concerned. Living in a small town in which people felt compelled to share their opinion about everything, including her lack of a love life, she was well acquainted with the reaction. So she didn't understand why she wanted to lie to Adam. It wouldn't do her any good. He'd always been able to see through her. "I'm not interested in dating."

"Bryce would want you to be happy, Sophia."

"I am happy. I have my business. Autumn and I bought a house last spring, and I have good friends. Well, they were good friends, friends I could trust, until your brother moved back to Christmas."

Adam brushed off his hands on his jeans and stood. Behind him the fire crackled and danced, the smell of woodsmoke permeating the air. "You know, I never understood what it was with you and Logan. It was like hate at first sight."

"He thought I was a bad influence on Autumn." She lifted a shoulder. She might not care now, but there'd been a time when she had. "I thought the same about him, so we're even."

"You know what I think? You were both jealous of how much Autumn loved the other."

She waved her hand as though that was the most ridiculous thing she'd ever heard, even though she suspected he might be right.

"You know I'm right. You just don't want to admit it." He shrugged out of his jacket and lifted his chin at her. "We're here for a couple hours, so you might as well get comfortable."

She dipped her head to hide her reaction to the way he filled out the blue plaid flannel shirt he wore over a black T-shirt. Ty might not be able to pull off chalet-wear, but Adam certainly could. She took off her coat and went to drape it over a chair, turning when Adam made a rough sound in his throat.

"I'll, uh, just put on some water for hot chocolate." He nodded at the fuzzy plaid pajamas and wool socks without looking at her. "You should probably change. You can't be comfortable in…" His eyes met hers, and he gave his head a slight shake, a slow smile curving his lips. "You know exactly what kind of effect you have on men, so I'm not even going to try to pretend

I want you to change so you're more comfortable. Not even sure it would help."

She blinked, surprised. He was right. There'd been a time in her life when she'd dressed to attract attention, but she'd always thought Adam was immune to her. Now she wore clothes that made *her* feel good. Stylish clothes made from gorgeous fabrics that made her happy just to touch and look at them. The fuzzy plaid onesie did not qualify as an outfit that made her happy.

"Trust me, it will help," Sophia said as she gathered up the pajamas and socks. "It will be like sharing the cabin with a lumberjill." He looked like a lumberjack, in a good way. A very good way. She wondered if she should suggest he put his jacket back on. Though, unlike him, she didn't feel comfortable admitting she found him attractive. She wondered if it was because she wasn't only attracted to his rugged good looks. "Maybe we should just walk back to the lodge."

He glanced at her boots. "You're not exactly dressed for a hike, and I'm not comfortable leaving you here on your own."

She looked out the window, not overly thrilled with the idea herself. She'd read too many true-crime stories and thrillers that featured an isolated cabin in the woods. Still, Autumn and Logan were out there somewhere on their own. "Just tell me what to do with the fire and I will be fine."

"Rick being seen hanging around here was my primary concern, but visions of you stoking the fire trump my worries about him. We'll just have to wait until Gramps comes back."

"Rick was released from the mental institution?"

"Yeah. He moved into a halfway house outside Christmas the day before last, and he's been seen hanging around the lodge. Tonight, one of the snowmobiles went missing. Wouldn't surprise me if he took it."

In her opinion, most people could be rehabilitated and deserved a second chance. She didn't feel the same about Rick Dane. "You make the hot chocolate, and I'll change."

Later, as they sat by the fire drinking hot chocolate and eating sugar cookies, she got the feeling Adam didn't think the onesie was an improvement over her mohair sweater, sequin leggings, and boots. Though it wasn't long before they fell into a familiar routine.

She was obsessed with murders and mysteries, and Adam was only too happy to talk about the cases he'd been involved with or give her the inside scoop on current cases in the news. Time passed easily and companionably as they caught up on each other's lives. It only became a little awkward when she asked more about his current girlfriend, the judge.

"She sounds perfect for you." Her smile felt forced. She didn't understand why, because it wasn't a lie. The judge sounded exactly like the type of woman Adam would be attracted to—beautiful, Harvard educated, wealthy, and from a prominent family.

"Yeah, she's great." It didn't sound like a ringing endorsement. His tone was subdued, and Sophia wondered if he was tamping down his enthusiasm because of her. Did he sense that she might be a tiny bit jealous?

Before she could come up with an excuse, there was

a loud *bang* and the dark sky outside the front window lit up. "They must have set off the fireworks early at the lodge." Adam stood and helped her to her feet. From the window, they watched red, white, and blue starbursts light up the night sky.

He held up his cell phone. "They're not early." He looked at her with a smile and slowly lowered his head. "Happy New Year, Dimples."

She inched up on her toes to meet him halfway, placing a hand on his chest for balance. "Happy New Year," she said, just before her lips met his.

His mouth was warm, the taste of chocolate lingering on his lips. A long time ago she'd fantasized about kissing this man, and somehow her body must have confused this moment for then because she leaned in to him, and a kiss that was meant to be friendly and brief became something more.

The *ping* of his cell phone brought her back to reality. Embarrassed, flustered by her reaction to him, she broke the kiss. To hide her heated face, she glanced at his phone while wondering how she'd forgotten he was a Dane and had a girlfriend. Noting the message on his cell phone's screen, she frowned. "I thought there was no…" Her eyes widened as she absorbed what the brief text message from Logan meant. "You were in on it the whole time!"

"Wait, Soph, let me explain."

Chapter Six

♥

T he judge is not happy with you, my friend," said Manuel, Adam's partner in the US Marshals Service.

Adam glanced at the statuesque blonde in the black robes returning to her chambers with the court deputy. "She's going to be less happy if we don't clear her courtroom on time," he said and went back to searching under and around the chairs on the left side of the public gallery.

"She'd be even more unhappy if she learned you dumped her for your brother's widow."

Obviously, Adam shouldn't have shared that with his friend and partner of six years, but he'd needed a sounding board. He'd broken things off with Yvonne a week after he'd come home from Christmas.

One night with Sophia had done a number on him. He couldn't get her out of his head, and it had felt like he was cheating on Yvonne. It didn't matter that Sophia still hadn't forgiven him for New Year's Eve or that he had no intention of moving to Christmas and didn't see her moving to San Francisco. All he knew was that he had to work through his feelings for her before he got involved with anyone else.

"Good thing Zeus's mind is on the job because yours clearly isn't," Adam said, referring to Manuel's K-9 partner, an eight-year-old German shepherd who was at that moment sniffing around the jury box.

The black-and-tan dog had begun his working career guiding the blind, but his personality and talents proved better suited to law enforcement. The ATF adopted Zeus and trained him in explosives and weapons detection. ATF then gave him to the US Marshals Service, and Manuel had been his handler ever since.

His eyes on Zeus, Manuel said, "He knows he has only one more week on the job. He's making the most of it. You're coming to his retirement party this weekend, right?"

K-9 dogs retired when they were between seven and eight years old and were typically adopted by their handlers. That hadn't always been the case. Before 2000, when President Clinton passed Robby's Law, police and military dogs were routinely euthanized when deemed unfit for service. If that were still the case, Manuel would have kidnapped Zeus, and Adam would have aided and abetted. The shepherd and the lanky, dark-haired man with the manicured goatee shared an unbreakable bond.

"Yeah, I—" He broke off at Manuel's command to Zeus. The dog had found something.

Adam called it in as he came to his feet, ordering the courthouse cleared.

It was the beginning of February and the first day of

arraignments for the gang members rounded up in a US Marshals Service's sweep. Word on the street had been an attempt would be made to disrupt the proceedings and to send a message to the jurors. It looked like Zeus had found the message. Now they had to hope there wouldn't be more.

* * *

Sophia sat in the stylist's chair, waiting for Ty. With its chandeliers and black-and-lavender decor, the salon was as high-end as Naughty and Nice. The three chairs beneath the space-age-looking hair dryers were occupied, as were the three other stylists' chairs, which faced oval mirrors framed in black.

Ty stood behind the glass-top reception desk, talking on the phone. "I can't fit you in, Diva. I'm booked solid," he told Chloe McBride, Christmas's mayor and the mother of one-year-old twins. "It's not my fault you have mommy brain and forgot it's Valentine's Day. Trust me, your husband doesn't care what you look like. He adores you." Ty sighed and held up his cell phone. "Ladies, Chloe doesn't believe I'm booked. Smile and wave for the camera."

They did as he asked, and Ty sent Chloe the photo. "See, I told you...No, I can't do that...Fine. Sophia, Chloe has a special date night planned with Easton, and since you don't have plans for tonight, she was wondering if you'd let her take your appointment."

"I can't. I have a date too." Sophia picked up a hunk of hair at her crown. "And this morning I found a gray hair." The other women in the salon gasped. "Oh please, as if none of you had a gray hair at thirty-three. Ty, it is normal, yes?"

"Diva, I have to call you back." Ty lowered himself into the chair behind the desk as though his legs were about to give out. "Sophia has an emergency."

"But it's only one gray hair...Okay, okay, so there were three," she admitted to the women staring at her like they couldn't believe what had just come out of her mouth. "My hair is black, not blond like yours, Dame Alexander and Grace, so you can stop looking at me like—"

"Dimples, we're not staring at you because you have a couple gray hairs. We're staring at you because you're the Merry Widow and you have a date. You haven't had a date for more than a decade. This is not just news. This is a full-out emergency."

She didn't know what bothered her more, Ty using Adam's nickname for her or that they were making a big deal about her going on a date. "Don't call me Dimples."

"Sorry. I forgot how protective you were of that nickname, Gloria." Ty dramatically widened his eyes and slapped his hands to his chest. "Adam is coming home to take you out for Valentine's. Isn't that romantic, ladies? I knew he was her Joe from the moment I saw them together at New Year's. You could practically see the sparks flying off them."

"Oh, yes, there were sparks when I found out he'd been doing his brother's bidding by spiriting me away to an isolated cabin in the woods."

"We've been over this a hundred times. It was Nell's and my idea. Logan just told him to keep you occupied. Adam had no idea it was a setup. You forgave me and Nell like a week after. I'm glad you finally saw the light and forgave Adam."

After their night together, to discover he'd been hanging out with her to fulfill a pact with his brother had been more hurtful than she'd let on. Although Adam might have had some idea she was upset. And while she'd eventually come around to forgiving him, she'd yet to tell him or respond to his texts and e-mails. She should. She owed him her thanks. If it hadn't been for Adam freeing her from the burden of her guilt, she wouldn't be going on her first date in more than a decade.

"But I was right to be worried, wasn't I? Last week, Logan broke Autumn's heart." And if it weren't for finding her best friend crying in her tea the next morning, Sophia would have been dancing for joy.

"You're being dramatic. He didn't break her heart. His kids need time to adjust to the idea their daddy wants to date, that's all," Ty said.

"Really? So if he didn't break her heart, why is she calling her new line of candy Heartbreak Brittle, Fickle Fudge, and Bitter Brownies?" She nodded at the face he made. "I am waiting. I want to hear you say *I am sorry, Sophia. You were right, and I am wrong.*"

"Ty, apologize. We want to hear more about her date," Dame Alexander said. Then the other women chimed in with "Where are you going? What are you wearing? Are you nervous? Are you excited?"

Stella, Nell McBride's best friend and the town's biggest gossip, lifted the hair dryer she sat under to say, "If I were forty years younger, I'd give you a run for your money, Sophia. Adam Dane is hunkalicious."

Sure, but she wasn't going on a date with him. "I'm going to dinner with Jake."

"Wait. Whaaat? You're cheating on Adam?" Ty said.

Stella lifted the dryer next to hers. "Nell's holding out on us again, Evelyn. Sophia and Adam are engaged, only Sophia is cheating on him with Jake."

"But Sophia is such a nice girl." As though just realizing she was there and listening to the conversation, Evelyn gave Sophia a finger wave and whispered to Stella, "You better tell Nell."

"On it." Stella pointed her cell phone at Sophia. "Word of advice: hell hath no fury like the grandmother of a man scorned. You better watch your step, young lady."

"I did not scorn him. I only spent one night with him, and I haven't spoken to him since."

"Hussy."

"Trust me, Stella, I've tried to turn her into a hussy, but no go. And we're going to take care of the Adam situation right now."

"There is no Adam situation. I came to see you about my gray hair, and all you have done is—" Ty shoved a phone at her, Adam's face filling the screen.

The face spoke. "Soph, what's going on? Where are you? And why would you come see me about your gray hair? You haven't returned any of my—"

"Ty!" Sophia shot from the stylist's chair and

headed to the back of the shop, away from prying eyes and ears.

"Okay, I get it now. You're at Ty's salon, and he decided you needed your own Joe for Valentine's Day." He grinned. "I'd like to help out with that, Dimples. But I'm working all night. Ty got lucky and caught me on a break."

Her shock at having Adam talking to her, smiling at her, rendered her momentarily speechless. She shook off her shock. "I don't need a Joe. I have a Jake. And I don't have gray hairs. I have *a* gray hair."

He looked as shocked as she felt, and not just about the gray hair. "You're dating?"

"Yes. Jake Callahan. He owns Callahan Automotive. He takes care of me and my car."

"When are you going to listen to me, man? I told you you should have—" an unfamiliar voice began.

She heard what sounded like arguing, and then a table with a menu and a ketchup bottle filled the screen before a man's face appeared—a handsome man with a goatee. "You weren't kidding; she looks just like Sofía Vergara." White teeth flashed when she made an irritated sound. "Hey, beautiful, do me a favor and give my *amigo* a break. He's—"

There was the sound of a chair scraping, and people sitting at tables flashed past the screen before Adam reappeared. "Sorry about that. I've gotta get back to the courthouse, Soph. But it was good talking to you."

At the drop-a-pin quiet of the salon, she glanced over her shoulder. Ty pretended to be blow-drying Grace's hair, except the dryer was off, and everyone else was looking at their cell phones or intently reading gossip magazines. Sophia ducked into Ty's office and shut the door to the sound of disappointed groans. "I'm sorry I didn't respond to your texts and e-mails. Nell and Ty confessed that they set us both up."

"Does your willingness to forgive me have anything to do with Logan and Autumn taking a break?"

"They're not taking a break. They're over. *Se acabó.*" She told him about Autumn's new candy line.

"We'll see. I really do have to go, Soph. Happy Valentine's Day. Enjoy your date with Callahan."

"Enjoy your Valentine's with Yvonne. And be careful, Adam. I read about the bomb the day of the arraignment. The jury's deliberating on the case against three senior members of MS-13, aren't they?"

He gave her one of his slow smiles. "You keeping tabs on me, Dimples?"

Hours later, sitting across from Jake at an Italian restaurant outside of Christmas, Sophia was having a difficult time getting Adam's last comment and his face out of her mind. Maybe she'd been fooling herself and she hadn't been following the case because of her interest in crime stories but because Adam was involved.

"Your pasta okay, Sophia?"

"It's wonderful. How's your steak, Adam?" She briefly closed her eyes. "I'm sorry. I don't know why I said that."

Jake smiled. He was a handsome man with black, wavy hair and a square jaw. "It's the second time you have. What's up? You don't seem like yourself."

"I'm sorry. I shouldn't have agreed to go out with

you, Jake. I'm a terrible date. I don't think I was ever a good one."

"You're not a bad date. And don't be sorry. You gave me bragging rights. I'm the first guy who asked you out that you said yes to. Now all you have to do is say yes to the right guy."

"But I like you."

"I like you too. And maybe that's the problem. I'm safe, and you're safe. We were probably always destined to be friends, not lovers." He laughed. "Your mind never even went there with me, did it?"

"No, but don't be offended. My mind doesn't go there with any man."

"Not even Adam?"

Before she'd fallen in love with Bryce, it had. In the beginning, she'd felt guilty about once lusting after her husband's older brother. But since lusting after Adam Dane had been the favorite pastime of the majority of single women in Christmas, she'd given herself a pass. And now her phone provided her with another one. "Sorry," she said at the sound of the alert. She glanced at the update on her phone, and her breath caught in her throat.

"Sophia, what is it? Are you okay?"

"There was a shooting at a San Francisco courthouse. Two US Marshals were critically injured. I...I think one might be Adam."

Chapter Seven

♥

It had been weeks since the shooting at the courthouse in San Francisco. Adam had thankfully recovered from his injuries, but his friend and partner had died. Sophia had contemplated visiting Adam at the hospital in San Francisco, but she knew his family wouldn't want her there. Besides Nell and Calder, of course. He'd also have his girlfriend and many friends at his side, and Sophia hadn't been sure what she was to him anymore. So instead she sent flowers and chocolates and get-well wishes. She hadn't heard from him and wrestled with whether to text or e-mail, but she'd been preoccupied these last few days.

Spring had finally sprung in Christmas. The blue-birds warbled, the grass grew, wildflowers bloomed, and the breeze that wafted down from the Rockies carried with it a sweet, earthy fragrance. But there was something more than the smell of spring in the air, and it worried her.

This past week, she had seen the undeniable signs that love was in the air in Christmas. Actually, it was sitting right beside her on the couch in the house on Holly Lane, hugging a bowl of popcorn.

Autumn, the only person Sophia trusted to help her bury a body if the need ever arose, was keeping secrets from her again, and Sophia was very much afraid the secret was a renewal of her love affair with Logan.

Staring blindly at the sixty-five-inch TV screen hanging above the whitewashed brick fireplace, Sophia debated what to say. So far her tentative queries had left her with more questions and concerns than answers. Anytime Sophia mentioned Logan, Autumn would abruptly change the subject or pretend she didn't hear her.

Sophia squared her shoulders. No more pussyfooting around. She'd lay her evidence on the table and get a straight answer even if that answer would force her to have a come-to-Jesus conversation with her best friend.

She shifted on the black sectional and opened her mouth.

Autumn glanced at her with a grin. "I knew you couldn't keep the killer's identity to yourself. Go ahead, tell me. You've ruined every Saturday Mystery Movie Night for the past five years. Why should this one be any different?"

Because lately everything had been different. "I couldn't ruin the last two. You were with Logan, remember?"

"No, I—"

"Yes, you were." She cleared her throat of what had sounded like petulant anger instead of what it actually was, hurt. Then she made a concerted effort to slow down her normally fast-paced speech to ensure Autumn understood the jig was up. "I know it wasn't Ty who put that I-had-sex glow on your face two Saturdays ago. And maybe that is why you're not thinking straight. Logan broke your heart three months ago." When Autumn opened her mouth to no doubt deny what Sophia had seen, she pointed her long, cherry-red painted nails at her eyes. "He made you cry! Just like he did before. Just like he always does."

Autumn stared at the television screen. "It's not the same. You don't understand."

The background music became suspenseful, signaling the killer was about to be revealed. "It's the FBI agent," Sophia said, unable to let the moment pass.

She typically solved the crime within the first ten minutes of the movie. It was her special talent. Sometimes she thought she'd missed her calling. She should have gone into law enforcement. As if on cue, there was a *bang* and then a *gasp*. The FBI agent shot herself in the thigh before turning the gun on her partner.

Sophia returned her gaze to Autumn. "How? How am I supposed to understand when you lie to me?" She patted her chest. "Me. Your best friend. The sister of your heart."

"We've had this conversation before. I knew how you'd react. But it doesn't matter anymore. I can't do it. Logan and I can't make it work."

Sophia made the sign of the cross and then pressed her bunched fingertips to her lips, blowing a kiss to the Virgin Mother. Her prayers had been answered.

Beside her, Autumn sighed. "I guess I should be

grateful you're not cheering or dragging me to the bar to celebrate."

"I would never do that. I can see you're sad, but it could have been worse. You could have been dating for months instead of weeks." She pulled Autumn in for a hug. "It's for the best, you will see." She rocked her in her arms. "We'll have fun, just you and me. We'll put a pond in the backyard like you wanted and refinish the stairs and railings in that gray stain you loved." The stain Sophia hated. She wasn't a fan of the pond or the goldfish Autumn wanted either.

"It doesn't matter. Nothing—"

"A dog! We'll get a dog."

"You hate dogs."

This was true. But she was willing to put up with animal drool, hair, and piddles on the white shag area rug if it made Autumn happy. "We'll get a little one. It can come to work with us. We'll dress it up."

Autumn's lips twitched. "You'll bling it out."

"Of course." She loved bling, but what she loved even more was seeing the hint of a smile on her best friend's face. "It's too late to go to the shelter tonight. We'll go first thing in the morning."

Sophia smiled and settled back on the couch, reaching for the popcorn container. Over the past week, the worry that Logan had sucked Autumn in again had ruined her appetite.

After devouring a handful of popcorn, she made a face and shook the red-and-white-striped container at Autumn. "It tastes like cardboard. You forgot the butter and the salt."

"No, I didn't. I just didn't drown it in butter like you do."

Sophia got up from the couch and headed for the recently renovated kitchen. A short hall off the adjoining living and dining room led to the kitchen at the back of the house.

"You're thirty-three. You have to start watching what you eat," Autumn called after her.

"I went for my annual checkup in January, and Dr. McBride, he said I am the picture of health," Sophia called back as she entered the kitchen with its white-painted brick walls.

Dr. McBride had actually said her blood pressure was higher than he would like and recommended she start exercising to help manage her stress. Autumn's news that she and Logan were once again *terminado* the week before Valentine's Day had taken care of Sophia's stress.

After shaking salt onto the popcorn, she opened the kitchen cabinet for the butter. In the living room, Autumn's cell phone rang, and she answered. There was something in her best friend's voice that caused Sophia to turn her head and listen. She strained to hear the conversation, but Autumn had lowered her voice.

Sophia turned on the microwave. The noise would enable her to sneak back undetected and listen. She turned on the fan above the stove for added coverage and then tiptoed across the kitchen and down the hall, wincing when the hardwood creaked.

"I have to go. No, I…Okay."

Peeking around the corner just as Autumn ended the

call, Sophia noted the rosy tinge to her best friend's usually pale skin. Despite Sophia's heart beginning to race at the telling sight, she walked casually into the room. "Who was that?"

Autumn frowned and held up her cell. "You mean on the phone? It was a wrong number."

Unless a phone-sex operator had called her best friend by mistake, there was only one explanation for Autumn's glowing skin and sparkling eyes. Sophia swore she felt her blood pressure rising. Logan Dane would be the death of her.

Autumn gave an exaggerated yawn and made a show of stretching before standing. "You know, I think I'll go to bed."

"It's nine o'clock."

"I want to get up early and head to the store. I have some ideas for Easter that I want to test."

The holiday was less than a month away. "Good. I will come with you, and we can coordinate ideas for window displays."

Years ago, the Christmas Business Association had voted that stores would close on Sundays. Some shop owners had balked, but Autumn and Sophia were all for it. Although lately Sophia wondered if being open the extra day would help boost their sales or just spread them out. Things hadn't picked up since the holidays. She was pinning her hopes on her new spring and bridal lines.

Autumn laughed. It sounded like a nervous laugh to Sophia. "When I say early, I mean early as in six a.m., not noon. We can talk about it tomorrow night when I come home."

Sophia crossed her arms, positive her BFF's plans didn't include testing Easter candy recipes. "What time will you be home?"

"Around eight," Autumn mumbled, walking past her.

* * *

Birds chirped outside Sophia's bedroom window, and the sun shone directly on her face. She squinted at her bedside table, looking for her cell phone. It seemed awfully bright outside for five in the morning. She'd been positive Autumn would sneak out early, so she'd set her alarm accordingly. She planned to follow her BFF to see what she was up to.

But Sophia's phone wasn't on her bedside table. She sat up and spotted it lying faceup on the floor. She squinted, trying to make out the time. It didn't help. She leaned over to open the bedside table drawer and pull out the pair of cheaters she'd hidden there. She fitted them on her face and read the now-clear numbers on her screen.

"Ten!" She shot out of bed, stuffed her feet into her slippers, and then raced down the hall. She threw open the door to Autumn's room with its rich wood furnishings and blue-and-cream accessories. Her bed wasn't as neatly made as usual, so Sophia had a feeling she'd also slept in. Which made her feel slightly better.

Still, she ran out of the room, down the hall, and down the stairs, grabbing her car keys off the console table. She caught a glimpse of herself in the mirror and made a face. She weighed the consequences of taking the time to change out of her pajamas, brush her hair and teeth, and put on makeup. Too much time had passed for her to take the risk. She wasn't going to see anyone anyway. But to be on the safe side, she grabbed her trench coat out of the hall closet and a piece of gum out of the console table drawer.

She stepped outside into the bright Sunday-morning sunlight, her flower beds catching her eye. Pink tulips, white crocuses, and yellow daffodils were poking through the garden soil. The bucolic sights and fragrant smells of spring were everywhere, and she felt the stirrings of gardening fever. But instead of indulging in the feeling, she had to go chasing after her best friend, who had the other kind of spring fever. The kind that would get her in trouble.

Sophia hurried to her SUV and got inside, her eyes lifting to the Victorian and the cluster of cherry trees on either side. She'd never thought she'd be house proud, but she was. She and Bryce had lived a nomadic life and had kept only a small apartment in Christmas for when they were home.

After she and Autumn had bought the house on Main Street, they'd moved into the two-bedroom apartment above the stores. Now they rented it…Sophia swore. The apartment was empty. A new tenant was taking over the lease at the beginning of April, which was ten days away. The perfect love nest in which Autumn could once again lose her heart to Logan.

Sophia put the car in Reverse and stepped on the gas, nearly taking out their neighbor and his dog. She lowered the window, yelling *sorry* as she put the car in

Drive and headed down Holly Lane. She turned onto Main Street, driving at a crawl as she searched for signs of Logan's Range Rover on the street. She wouldn't put it past him to park several stores away from Sugar and Spice.

A car honked at her and then another one did. She waved them on, edging toward the side to give them room to pass as she continued scanning the cars and trucks lining the road.

A black monster truck parked in front of the sheriff's department caught her eye, and she blinked in surprise. But not half as surprised as when a car plowed into her from behind.

Chapter Eight

♥

As soon as Adam walked into the office of Christmas's sheriff, Jill Flaherty-Anderson, he knew he'd been set up. Which was why, before he'd even sat in the chair across from her, he said, "The answer is no."

Jill pretended to be surprised, but she was fighting a smile. "All I said was it's good to see you."

"Right. And it's good to see you too. Congratulations on your very obvious pregnancy. I hope you've got a replacement lined up, because it won't be me."

His grandfather and Nell had been after him to move home to Christmas from the moment his eyes had opened after surgery. So when they'd called him two days ago, professing their fear his cousin Rick was up to no good and begging him to speak to Jill on their behalf, he had a sneaking suspicion they were playing on his protective instincts. Now he had evidence they were sneakier than he'd given them credit for.

Jill tapped on her keyboard and turned the monitor. On the screen was an application with his name on it. "I figured it was too good to be true. But you got the job, in case you're wondering." She filled him in on the compensation package. "I'm only taking four months off, if that makes it more palatable."

"I appreciate your confidence in me and the offer, but trust me, I'm not small-town-sheriff material, Jill. I've put down roots in San Francisco."

"Nell thought you could use a change of scenery after the shooting. I'm really sorry about your partner, Adam." She nodded at Zeus, who lay by the door. "Nell mentioned you adopted his K-9 partner. How's he doing?"

He didn't have a choice. On his dying breath, Manuel had exacted the promise from him. At the time, Adam hadn't known if he himself would make it. He'd taken a bullet to the stomach; Manuel had taken one to the chest. They'd just gotten back to the courthouse. Manuel had been teasing him about Sophia seconds before all hell broke loose.

Adam glanced at the dog, who didn't react to Jill's voice. Lethargic and despondent, he barely did anything but sleep. "He's not good. It's like he blames himself— and me—for not saving Manuel."

Zeus was the reason Adam had finally given in to Nell and Calder's plea to come to Christmas. He thought the change of scenery might do the dog good. "So, do you have legit concerns about Rick? Or was that just an excuse to get me in here?"

"It's more Nell and Calder's concerns than mine, but given Rick's history, there is a possibility they are legit. I just don't have enough evidence to confront Rick or to talk to his parole officer." She smiled. "And full disclosure, I may have mentioned you were better suited to handle this than me. You're the expert at this end of the justice system."

He was decidedly less confident in his abilities since the shooting. He blamed himself for not locating the shooter before he got off a round. In his defense, the area had been crowded, with multiple places to hide. But he'd eventually taken the shooter out before he hurt anyone else.

"Full disclosure on my end, I've been keeping tabs on Rick since he was released," Adam said. "I've checked in with his parole office and the halfway house before he moved into the apartment on Main Street. As far as they're concerned, he's doing everything by the book. He would though. Rick is a smart guy and happy to bide his time to get what he wants."

"And what does he want?"

"His share of the lodge. He believes my side of the family stole his inheritance. So, in his eyes, the snowmobile that went missing, the ski equipment, and the petty cash are rightfully his. Nell mentioned that he has a YouTube channel, and she thinks he's beginning to make some cash, so that's a step in the right direction. He was always motivated by money, and it's not like he'd have an easy time finding a job around here."

"Yeah, I've had some complaints about his channel. It's called *The Truth Behind Small Towns*. Sounds like he's airing Christmas's dirty laundry, only he's changing the names of the parties involved."

"He wouldn't happen to be blackmailing anyone with their dirty laundry, would he?"

"You see, that's exactly why you would make a great sheriff. I—" A knock on her office door interrupted Jill.

Suze, the dispatcher, opened the door and poked her head inside. "Sheriff, you're needed out front. Sophia—"

From the outer area came a torrent of Spanish curse words. "It is not my fault he rear-ended my car!"

As Adam and Jill came to their feet, Zeus lifted his head from his paws.

"She stopped in the middle of the road!" an unfamiliar man's voice said.

"I pulled to the side and put my flicker on."

"What the hell is a *flicker*?"

"A flicker, you know." She made the sound of the signal light.

Jill moved past Adam, who stood stunned in the doorway after catching his first glimpse of Sophia. She had serious bedhead and looked librarian-sexy wearing a pair of glasses, but her fuzzy bunny slippers paired with a pink trench coat took the look to laugh-out-loud territory. And given her current mood, he didn't think she'd appreciate him laughing. He did though. He hadn't felt like laughing since before the shooting.

He leaned against the doorframe, crossed his arms, and settled in to watch the show. The heavyset bald man stared at her, gave his head a slight shake, and then looked at Jill. "What are you people thinking, issuing this woman a driver's license? She's wearing bunny slippers."

Adam felt a warm weight against his leg and glanced

down. Zeus had come to stand beside him. It was the first time the dog had moved without being told, and even then, he took his sweet time.

"Yeah, but on the other hand, she got herself a pair of glasses. They look good on you, Soph. Now, why don't we take this…" Jill trailed off.

Adam looked up from Zeus to catch the moment Sophia clued in to his presence. Her face softened, and her eyes got shiny behind her glasses. "Adam," she whispered just before rushing over to throw herself into his arms. "I was so worried about…*Ack*," she squeaked and shuffled backward. "What's that?"

"Okay, I see how it is. Her boyfriend is a deputy, so everyone looks the other way."

"He's a US Marshal, and he's not her boyfriend. He's her brother-in-law," Jill informed the guy.

"Is that right? Well, her husband might want to borrow her glasses because it's obvious there's something going on—"

Jill, who, like Adam, was watching the interaction between Sophia and Zeus with interest, said, "Suze, can you take the gentleman's statement, please?"

The guy muttered something about suing and preferential treatment as he followed Suze to her desk.

"Soph, this is Zeus. He won't hurt you." Adam reached out to stop her from backing into the corner of a desk. "Come here. Let him smell your hand and get to know you."

"It's okay. He knows me. He licked me."

"Yeah, and trust me, that's a pretty big deal for him. I think your accent reminds him of his handler, Manuel."

"That's nice. Can you put him away now?" Zeus moved toward her, and Sophia stumbled in an effort to get away from him. "Adam," she said, a tremor in her voice.

"Zeus, *sitz*." Sit. He walked over and crouched beside the dog, who had yet to make up his mind if he was going to listen to Adam. "Sorry. I was so intent on Zeus, I didn't realize you're really afraid of him. This is the most interest he's shown since Manuel died. He was his K-9 partner. They were together twenty-four seven for years."

"Manuel, was he your friend, the partner who died in the shooting? The one who took your phone on Valentine's Day?"

"Yeah, that was Manuel."

"I'm very sorry for your loss, Adam. Yours too, Zeus." She leaned in to gingerly pat the dog on the nose. When she pulled back her hand, Zeus nudged her. Sophia dutifully patted him again. Though when she stopped for the second time and ignored the dog's insistent nudge, Zeus stood up on his hind legs, put his paws on her shoulders, and licked her face. "Adam."

He was so stunned at the change in Zeus that it took him a moment to react. "Sorry. Zeus, *plaz*." Down. Once again the dog took his sweet time doing what he was told, but eventually he sat at Sophia's feet, staring up at her adoringly.

"Damn pregnancy hormones," Jill said, wiping her eyes. "The poor dog was in a deep depression before he met you, Sophia. Now he's happy and in love. Looks like you might be staying in Christmas after all, Adam."

"You're moving to Christmas?" Sophia asked while inching away from Zeus, who inched along with her.

"No, I'm not, and I have to get going. Can I take you home? It sounds like your SUV is headed back to the body shop." Then he remembered who her boyfriend was and tamped down the same flare of jealousy he'd felt on Valentine's Day. "No doubt Jake is coming to get both you and the car, so I'll—"

"Why would he? The tow truck is taking my SUV to Jake."

"I thought you guys were dating?" Adam wondered if Sophia and Jill heard the hopeful note in his voice. He prayed they didn't.

Jill snorted. "She went on one date with him. Her first and last date of the next century. Isn't that what you told Ty, Sophia?"

"Yes. Dating is for young people." She wouldn't look at him and tried not to look at Zeus either.

"Right, 'cause you're so old. And just FYI, rumor has it that Ty put up a profile for you on Match, and he's been fielding your requests. You've had forty so far, but none of them have been Ty-approved," Jill told her.

Sophia made an irritated sound, and Zeus stood at attention. Eyes widening behind her glasses, Sophia took a step back. "What's wrong with him?"

"He's reacting to the sound you just made and looking for a threat."

"I am looking for a threat too. His name is Logan Dane."

"What's my brother done now?"

"He has arranged an assignation with Autumn, and

I am going to catch them in the act...Not *that* act. I don't want to catch them in *that* act. I want to confront your brother once and for all and tell him how much he's hurting my best friend with his games. But I slept in, and I'm running late, so I have to get going."

"Okay, so that explains why you look like you do. I was actually a little worried about you," Jill said.

"Soph, where are you going?" Adam called to her when she went to walk away with Zeus following after her.

"To Sugar and Spice," she said over her shoulder. Catching a glimpse of Zeus behind her, she quickened her pace. It didn't do her much good, as the dog did the same.

"Zeus, *heir*." Come here.

"Uh, Sophia, you do remember you have bunny slippers on your feet, right?" Jill said. "And I'm almost afraid to ask, but you do have clothes on under that trench coat, don't you?"

"Of course I have clothes on," Sophia said, clearly ticked off because the words rolled off her tongue and into one another. She unbelted her trench coat and held it open.

"Whoa, you definitely have the *naughty* in Naughty and Nice down. Can you maybe put a pair of those pj's away for me for after I have the baby?" Jill glanced at him. "You might want to close your coat before Adam has a heart attack."

Chapter Nine

♥

Sophia opened the door to her house, and the dog and Adam followed her inside. "Are you sure Nell doesn't know where Autumn and Logan are?" she asked him.

After the truck towed away her SUV, Adam had driven her to Sugar and Spice. Autumn wasn't there, and there was no sign she had been. She wasn't in the apartment upstairs either, nor was she answering her cell. Sophia couldn't shake the feeling there was more going on than an early-morning booty call.

"Nell swears she doesn't know where they are. Gramps says the same, and so did the kids. And it's not like there was a reason for them to lie. I said I was checking in because we had plans to go fishing." Closing the door behind him, he looked around. "Nice place, Soph. Might be a good idea to lock the door when you go out though."

"I usually do, but I was in a hurry." She lifted a slippered foot as evidence, and the dog came over to sniff it. She would have preferred he stayed in the truck while she changed, but she felt sorry for him. As sorry as she felt for his new owner.

The loss of his friend and his own near-fatal injury had taken a toll on Adam. He was pale, the angles of his handsome face more pronounced, but it wasn't just the physical changes that concerned her. His reflexes were off. In the past, he would have been between her and Zeus before the dog had taken a step in her direction. She didn't think his surprise at how Zeus responded to her explained it away. There was more going on than he let on.

"I won't be long." Sophia pointed to the kitchen. "If you want something to eat or drink, the kitchen is in there, and the living room is that way. You can sit on the couch, but you stay on the floor," she told the dog as she removed her trench coat. Catching a glimpse of the look on Adam's face as she hung it in the closet, she rolled her eyes.

Ty had given her the adorable pj's as a joke gift when he'd found out about her brief stint as a Playboy Playmate. She'd been Miss January. A job the Danes had never let her live down. Still, she didn't allow herself to regret the decision. The money had paid her college tuition after all.

But it wasn't like she was parading around in a merry widow and a thong. The lingerie set was hardly risqué. The pink camisole imprinted with the Playboy logo and pink tap pants decorated with tiny bunny ears covered all her parts.

"Some women would wear this outside in the summer, and no one would bat an eye."

Adam scrubbed a hand over his beard-stubbled jaw. "Pretty sure you're not one of those women, Dimples."

Suddenly conscious she wasn't wearing a bra, she turned and walked to the stairs. "Go to Christmas's Facebook page and ask if anyone has seen Autumn and Logan."

"To do that, I'd have to be on Facebook, which I'm not."

She glanced over her shoulder. "Twitter?" He raised an eyebrow. "Instagram?" He raised the other eyebrow. She sighed and gave him her Facebook log-in information. "I'm an administrator on Autumn's page, so you can access hers through mine. Check Instagram too. Autumn posts all the time. But be careful who you like or respond to. People will think it's me."

"Got it. I promise not to try to pick up hot women."

"If you do, I'll tell Yvonne."

"You'll have to do better than that. Yvonne and I ended things in January."

The girl she used to be cheered, and so did the woman she was now. Although she wished she'd known sooner. Yvonne was the reason she'd stayed away from San Francisco. She'd been afraid the judge would see through her. She'd pictured them laughing at his brother's silly widow and her pathetic crush. "I'm sorry. She seemed perfect for you."

"Yeah, well…Zeus, *heir*. Come here."

Sophia bowed her head at the clicking of nails on the hardwood floor. Adam called the dog again, but the clicking continued unabated.

"What is it with you and this dog?" Adam said as he came to get Zeus.

"Typical male. They always want the woman who doesn't want them." She shouldn't judge. She was a silly woman lusting after a man who'd never wanted her. "It's okay," she relented when Adam tried once again to get Zeus to come, feeling some empathy toward the animal, who now bounded up the stairs ahead of her. "But you're not coming in my bedroom."

"I promise I'll get him out of there so you can change. He just needs to make sure you're safe before he can relax."

"Okay." She stood beside Adam outside her bedroom, watching the dog at work. "I didn't get a chance to make my bed."

"This isn't the same setup you had when you were married to Bryce, is it?" he asked in a tone of voice that made his thoughts on her overly feminine room perfectly clear.

"No. I decorated it for me, and I love it." Her gaze moved fondly over the mirrored bedside tables and dresser, gray velvet headboard and bedframe, and pink bedding and chandelier. "It makes me smile every time I walk in my room."

It was true. Though, ever since New Year's, she'd been fantasizing about Adam standing right where he was now, looking at her bedroom with that same half smile on his face. Only in her fantasy, he didn't lean on her doorframe for long. He swept her into his muscular arms, carried her into her room, tossed her on her bed, and then covered her with his big body.

"I'm glad it makes you happy, Soph." He held up his phone. "I should get on this."

"You're not pretending to help like last time, are you? You really are trying to find Logan and Autumn?"

"Like I told you at New Year's, I agreed to keep you occupied but never got a chance. Nell, Ty, and my grandfather took care of that all on their own. Couldn't pretend then and can't pretend now that I'm mad at them for setting us up though. I enjoyed spending New Year's with you."

"I enjoyed spending it with you—" She broke off when the dog jumped on her bed. "Zeus, down. Now." He got off immediately and came to her side, sitting at her feet. "I wish all men listened as well as you. Okay." She waved both the dog and Adam off. "I'm getting changed."

"You have anything casual?" he asked as he glanced doubtfully in the direction of her open closet. "Jeans, maybe? I have a feeling my brother took Autumn on an adventure, so we'll be taking one of our own if you want to find them."

"How adventurous?"

His mouth lifted at the corner. "Horseback riding, hang gliding, white-water rafting. That kind of thing."

"Oh, I thought you meant something really adventurous." She waved her hand like she took part in activities such as those all the time and then shut the bedroom door in Adam's laughing face.

While Sophia searched her closet for something outdoorsy to wear, Adam updated her on the activity on her Facebook account.

"Soph, when was the last time you checked Facebook?"

"A couple of days ago. Why?"

"Because there's a bunch of guys thanking you for accepting them, and you sound, ah, really friendly."

She growled low in her throat and heard an answering rumble on the other side of the door.

"Relax, Zeus," Adam said. "Stop pacing. She'll be out in a minute. Zeus, *sitz*."

At Adam's frustrated sigh, she said, "Zeus, sit," and then picked up her cell phone to call Ty. It went straight to voice mail. "Just because you have spring fever doesn't mean I do, Ty. Stop pretending you are me on my Facebook page and stop screening your calls. Autumn is missing."

"Don't worry. He won't get on your account anymore. I took him off as an administrator. I also got rid of the guys he accepted. I'm on Autumn's page now. She hasn't updated her status in a couple days..."

"What? What do you see? Don't pretend you don't. I can hear it in your voice."

"It's not what she says. It's some of my brother's recent comments. He's been messaging her too. Okay, I'm not really comfortable with this, Soph. But I will tell you that there's no doubt they're dating. And I know you don't want to hear this, but it sounds like they're serious."

She whipped open the door. Adam, who'd been sitting on the floor leaning against her door, fell on his back at her feet. He stared up at her and gave his head a slight shake. "Next time, do me a favor and wait until you're fully dressed before opening the door."

She looked down at herself. She had on a long-sleeve

cream thermal top, a faux-fur vest, and a thong. She turned, ignored his groan, and went to grab the black jeans off the end of her bed. "You can't say things like that to me and expect me not to react."

"And you can't parade around in your underwear and expect me not to react."

"I'm not parading around in my underwear," she said, hopping with one foot in her jeans.

"Can you stop that, please? I'm already having trouble thinking straight."

She stopped to stare at him. "You're worried. Don't try to deny it. I can see it on your face. You get a line here." She rubbed her index finger between the bridge of her nose and right eyebrow. He couldn't fool her. She'd studied his face for years, mostly searching for some sign he liked her as much as she liked him.

He walked into her room with the dog on his heels. Zeus skirted around him, reaching her first. He sat at her feet. All but positive Adam was about to deliver bad news, Sophia slowly lowered herself onto the edge of the bed. Adam joined her there, which caused the flutter of nerves in her stomach to increase. The girl she used to be cheered, *Adam Dane is sitting on my bed!*

"Okay, I could be wrong, but I do think something's going on, and that's why Nell and Calder came up with this story about Rick to get me home this weekend. I tried to push them off to next weekend, but they were insistent."

He'd filled her in about Rick when they were driving around Christmas looking for Autumn and his brother. "Not five minutes ago you said you believed them when they said they didn't know where Autumn and Logan are."

"I don't think they do. But I do think they know what they're doing wherever they are."

"Even I know they are having sex, Adam."

"That's not what I'm talking about. Trust me, the two of them having sex is the least of our worries."

Because they were sitting on the end of her unmade bed and talking about sex, it took a moment for Sophia to stop thinking about Adam naked in her bed. Once she did, her eyes widened. "You think he's proposing to her?"

* * *

Adam stood on the back deck of his grandfather's log house nursing a beer as the sun slowly sank behind the Aspen trees. He'd been right. Logan had taken Autumn up to the top of Blue Mountain at sunrise and proposed to her. She had said *yes*. Around the time Sophia had been getting rear-ended on Main Street, the newly engaged couple were at the Rocky Mountain Diner with his niece and nephew. About ten minutes after Adam had shared his theory about the couple with Sophia, Autumn arrived home to break the news.

Only she hadn't shared where the couple intended to spend their life as man and wife. Logan asked Adam to keep the couple's plans for their future to himself for at least a week. They wanted a chance to slowly ease Sophia and the family into the idea of them moving halfway around the world.

He lifted the beer bottle to his mouth and took another deep pull. Before the night was over, he'd need something a lot stronger than a bottle of beer. So would Sophia. He couldn't keep Logan and Autumn's plans from her. He'd tell her tonight.

As he'd suspected, Nell and his grandfather had wanted him home for a reason. They knew damn well Logan planned to propose this weekend, no matter how hard they tried to deny it. His evidence: the *impromptu* engagement party they were hosting tonight at seven. Nell assured them only close friends and immediate family would be there, but it sounded like half the town had been invited.

A rustle in the undergrowth and the snap of a branch brought Adam's head up. His grandfather's house was on an isolated part of the old mountain road, and it wasn't uncommon for a big cat, bear, deer, or elk to end up near the place. He glanced back at Zeus, who lay practically comatose at the back door. Neither his tail nor his ears perked at the sounds coming from the bush.

Adam had made the mistake of thinking Sophia had somehow gotten through to him and the Zeus he remembered was back. Sophia had worked her particular brand of magic on both of them. Adam had felt better today than he had in weeks, but now the feelings of guilt returned, weighing him down. He'd failed Manuel the day of the shooting, and now he was doing it again.

His mood darkened, which might have been why he growled, "You've got two minutes to show yourself or I shoot."

A wild animal wouldn't be as noisy as whoever was in there. A dark-haired man wearing camouflage stumbled out of the woods with his hands up. "Don't shoot."

"What are you doing, Rick?" Adam asked his cousin at the same time he checked on Zeus. The dog didn't lift his head, but his eyes followed Rick from the woods to the deck.

Rick held up a camera. "I heard the news about Autumn and Logan and wanted to offer my congratulations."

"Try again."

There was something about the defensive lift to Rick's chin that reminded Adam of his baby brother. There was no denying the strong family resemblance. "Does no one remember I'm family? I didn't get an invitation. That hurts, you know. I'm a changed man, and I'm trying to get back on my feet. It's not easy around here. All anyone does is throw my past in my face."

"Maybe that's the problem, Rick. You should have gone somewhere where no one knows you. Start over with a clean slate."

"How? I have nothing. The Danes are real good at helping everyone else, but I haven't seen any of you offering me a hand up."

"Is that why you stole the snowmobile, ski equipment, and petty cash?"

His face flushed, but his chin once again went up. "You know as well as I do that the lodge is as much mine as it is yours and Logan's."

"I know that's what you believe, but that's not what the judge ruled. You have to move past this, Rick." Adam reached in his back pocket for his wallet and pulled out a couple hundred-dollar bills. "This isn't the time for it now. I'll talk to Gramps and Logan in the morning. I can't make you any promises, but if you give me your word that you'll clean up your act, there might be a job for you at the lodge."

"Doing what? Lift operator? I'm a Dane. I—"

"And that's your problem, Rick." Zeus came to his feet and began whining at the back door. Adam frowned. No one was expected for at least a couple hours. It had to be Sophia. "Look, I can't deal with this or you right now. Drop by tomorrow. I'm sure there will be leftovers—"

"I don't want your handouts. I want what is due to me." He stormed off the deck and into the woods.

And not a moment too soon. The back door opened, and Sophia stepped out. She wore her pink trench coat and shiny black boots that disappeared under the hem of her coat. Her hair was disheveled, her glasses askew, and he couldn't help but wonder what she had on under her coat. When images of her in her Playboy Bunny pj's filled his mind, he had to fight the urge to walk across the deck and check for himself.

"Hello, Zeus," she said to the dog dancing at her feet. Her voice sounded like she'd been crying for a week. She surprised him by kneeling beside Zeus and throwing her arms around the dog. "I'm so sorry I wasn't kinder to you. I forgot what it was like to lose your best friend, and now I remember."

If she was this bad off because Autumn was marrying his brother, he didn't want to think what she'd be like when she learned the truth.

"Come on, you're going to get your coat dirty." He went to help her up. Zeus looked like he wanted to tear him limb from limb. *Totally get where you're coming from, pal*, he thought. But he couldn't let the dog's reaction go. He repeated the Spanish phrase Manuel used when he wanted to remind Zeus who was the alpha in the partnership. And there was the problem—Adam and Zeus weren't partners. As though aware of the battle for dominance playing out around her, Sophia waved Adam off and gave the dog one more hug.

Just when Adam was thinking he wouldn't mind taking Zeus's place, Sophia rose to her feet and walked to him. Wrapping her arms around his waist, she sobbed her heart out. He guided her to a wooden rocker and sat down, pulling her onto his lap. Zeus sidled over and put his head on her knee.

"You're worrying me, Dimples. Zeus too."

"They're leaving Christmas, Adam. Logan has a job opportunity in Switzerland, and they're leaving in six weeks."

"How did you find out? Logan said they weren't going to say anything for at least a week."

"Oh, but he tells you. He doesn't think his fiancée's best friend, her business partner, the woman she owns a home with deserves to know that he's about to upend her life completely?"

"I wouldn't let you be blindsided, Soph. I planned to tell you tonight. Is there any chance you can buy Autumn out of the house and business?"

"No. And Autumn will need her equity from the

house and the business if she plans to open an online candy store."

"What did she say when you talked to her about this?"

"She doesn't know I know."

"How did you find out?"

"I knew she wasn't telling me everything, so I followed the crumbs they left on social media." She looked at him through fogged-up glasses, her face splotchy and tear-stained. "What am I going to do?"

"We're in this together, Soph. I don't want them to move any more than you do. If they do, I have to take over the lodge or Rick will inherit, and that would kill my grandfather."

Chapter Ten

♥

"Why do you get to be best man and I get to be *matron of honor*? I should be best woman. *Matron of honor* makes me sound old and boring," Sophia grumbled from the passenger seat of Adam's truck.

They were on their way to the lodge for Spring Fling, the final weekend of events before the ski runs were closed for the season. It was also the weekend they put Operation Happy Ever After in Christmas into action. Sophia's idea, not his. She said they needed a code name for their plan. At that point, he'd been ready to agree to just about anything to get her to stop crying.

"You are the best woman, a gorgeous best woman, but right now we have more important things to think about. Like how we're going to convince Autumn she loves you and her friends and Christmas too much to leave. And—"

"You think I'm gorgeous?" she asked with a teasing smile, because the woman was nothing if not confident in her looks. All she had to do was look in the mirror or go to her Facebook page for confirmation. Today she

was stunning in a body-hugging, cream-colored ski suit
with a pink vest and pink fur boots.

"Yeah, and I think you know I do. You always did,"
he said, his eyes on the narrow mountain road. Traffic
was heavy as everyone made their way to the lodge for
the cardboard box race. Tonight they'd be dining under
the stars with live music.

He glanced at Sophia when she didn't say anything.
She was staring at him. He frowned. "What?"

"I didn't know you thought I was gorgeous back
then. I didn't know you looked at me that way."

"Come on, you had to know. And how was I supposed to look at you? I was a guy. You were a girl."

"I didn't know, Adam. If—" She broke off and
looked out the window.

"You had to know I was attracted to you, Soph. All
the guys were."

"I didn't care about all the guys. I only cared what
you thought about me."

"I thought you were beautiful and incredibly sexy
and funny and sweet, but I was enjoying being single
and free, and you were too young for me."

"And now?"

He wasn't sure how to respond. He was as attracted
to her as he'd always been, maybe more so. But there
was a part of him that still thought of her as his brother's
wife. And even though Bryce had been gone, and gone
a long time, Adam found it difficult to get past that.
"I still think you're the most beautiful woman in all of
Colorado."

"You know that's not what I meant."

"Yeah, I do." He reached for her hand, brought it to his mouth, and brushed his lips over her knuckles. The same hand that had worn his brother's ring. He lifted his gaze to hers, and the thought must have shown in his eyes because she nodded and drew her hand away. "Soph, look at me."

"It's okay. I understand. I don't know if I can get past it either."

"We'll talk, okay? But right now we have a job to do."

"Yes, convince Autumn and Logan that they belong in Christmas, not Switzerland."

He'd returned to San Francisco the day after Logan and Autumn's engagement party to get cleared for work, so he and Sophia had done their strategizing by phone. They were planning to show the couple that not only would Autumn miss Sophia and her friends, but that his brother and Sophia had things in common and could get along. Then they'd pull out the big guns Easter Sunday. They'd show his brother what his kids would be missing if he took them away from their extended family.

"If they're anything like Zeus, that shouldn't be hard. He missed you this week." If he was honest, so had he. Even though he'd talked to her every day, sometimes twice a day.

"I missed you too."

He thought she was talking about him and was just about to admit he'd missed her too when he glanced over and realized she was talking to Zeus. "Hey, stop feeding him," he said when she gave the dog an iced cookie. "You can't give him human food, Soph. It's not good for him."

"He's skinny, and I'm not stupid." She dug a Sugar Plum Bakery bag out of a purse the size of a suitcase. "Grace is making doggie cookies now."

"Okay, but don't overdo it with the treats." Adam pulled into the parking lot. It was filled beyond capacity, so he drove around to the back of the lodge to take advantage of family parking.

"I'm sorry for thinking you didn't know what you were doing, Sophia." She mimicked a man's voice. "I should have known that just because you have big hair and big boobs doesn't mean you're a bimbo with no brains."

"I don't sound like that, and trust me, I know better than anyone that behind that big hair and body lies a devious little mind."

She cocked her head.

"A mind as big as your other assets." That earned him a look from both her and the dog. "Okay, I'm sorry. I know you'd never do anything to endanger Zeus."

But an hour later, the same could not be said for Operation Happy Ever After in Christmas. From Logan's expression, his brother definitely did not feel like he had anything in common with Sophia...or Ty.

"Adam, I'm not sure putting Logan on Team Diva was a good idea," Autumn said, glancing to where Sophia and Ty were hard at work blinging out the pink car they'd fashioned out of cardboard while his brother stood watching them with his arms crossed. Twenty-five vehicles—cars, boats, tanks, planes, and trucks—

fashioned out of cardboard had been entered in this year's race. Prizes would go to the best-looking and the fastest time down the bunny hill.

"Yeah, Soph kinda forgot to mention their entry's theme," he told Autumn.

"It's Sophia and Ty. What did you think they'd be entering in the race?"

He laughed, and then he saw Zeus. "What's he doing over there? He's supposed to be on our team." Autumn, Jill, Nell's nephew Gage and his wife, Madison, were on his team. Since three of them were law enforcement, they'd made a police cruiser three times the size of Sophia and Ty's car. Zeus was their mascot. Just five minutes before, he'd been wearing a vest with a badge and sheriff's hat, which had been replaced with a pink tutu and crown.

"Soph, you stole my dog. And in case you forgot, his name is Zeus. He's—"

"Stop while you're ahead," Gage warned Adam as he affixed a cardboard headlight to the front of their cruiser.

"Did the dog tell you its name was Zeus, Adam? No, I didn't think so. Just like I don't think it told you its gender identity," Ty said.

"The—" Adam was about to point out what did identify Zeus as male when Gage said, "Geezus, don't go there."

And maybe because Sophia also could tell where he'd been going, she decided a distraction was in order. "I did not steal your dog, Adam. I cannot steal that which is already mine." She gave him a smug smile and Zeus a cookie.

She'd added a pink fur hat to her outfit and looked so adorable that all he could do was smile back at her like an idiot. Well, he was smiling until Ty decided his brother didn't fit the Diva theme and sprinkled him with pink glitter.

Autumn yelped and ran over to save the day, but not Adam and Sophia's plan. At least not the part in which his brother and Sophia became lifelong friends. Autumn suggested she and her fiancé change teams.

Logan managed to crack a smile when Team Diva came barreling down the hill, Zeus in the front of the pink cardboard car with what could only be described as a doggie grin, while Autumn, Ty, and Sophia were hugging one another and laughing hysterically behind him. They didn't win for best-looking car or fastest down the bunny hill, but that didn't stop them from celebrating as if they had.

Logan wasn't smiling several hours later as they stood by the outdoor bar, watching Sophia, Autumn, and about ten of their girlfriends, including Ty, dance to live music under the stars.

Adam had finally had enough. "I don't get it. What is it about Sophia that you don't like?"

"Everything," his brother muttered, and Adam wanted to punch him.

Instead, he tightened his grip on his glass of soda. He was the designated driver tonight.

Logan must have sensed Adam was ticked because he rolled his eyes. "Start thinking with your other head and put yourself in my shoes for a change. I've loved Autumn since we were in grade school. There was no one else for me but her, and she'd always felt the same. Until she went off to college and met Sophia. Every weekend she came home, Sophia tagged along with her. So instead of hanging out together like we used to, the two of them were the life of every party."

They were the life of the party again, Adam thought. He glanced at Zeus, who paced the perimeter of the outdoor dance floor, keeping a watchful eye on Sophia.

"But you married her, so obviously you guys worked through it."

"I thought we had. And then about a week after Bryce died, I got the offer for my dream job. Travel, great money, everything we had talked about, but she wouldn't go. She wouldn't leave Sophia."

"So you left her."

"I was tired of coming in second." He glanced at Sophia and Ty, who were now performing in the circle of their clapping and laughing friends. "Soon I won't have to." His brow furrowed, and then he pointed at the man videoing the women on the dance floor. "What's Rick doing here?"

He'd had a feeling today might be a bust and had a backup plan. "You're leaving, and like I've been trying to tell you, I'm not taking your place. Which means, if Gramps won't step in, Rick will."

He wouldn't let it go that far, and he certainly hadn't broached the idea with Rick. His cousin had come to him the morning after the engagement party with a business proposition. Rick had once owned the town's local newspaper and had an interest in photography and videography. He'd proposed offering it as a service to the lodge's guests. Adam had been impressed that Rick had gotten his ego in check and wasn't asking for a handout. He also believed in second chances and that family should help out family when they could. So he'd decided to give him a trial run, albeit with security keeping an eye on him.

"Good try, but I know you too well. And this is an offer of a lifetime that I can't afford to pass up. It'll be good for the kids. It's the chance for a new beginning for the four of us. Please don't stand in my way, brother." He looked at the two women hugging and laughing on the dance floor. "And maybe you can make Sophia understand that if she loves Autumn, she has to let her go."

"Maybe if you gave her a chance and sat down and talked to her, explained where you're coming from, she would. But from where she's standing, her best friend, business partner, and co–home owner is moving to the other side of the world with a man who is an asshat."

"I'm not an asshat."

"No, not to most people, but you are to Sophia, and it ends now."

"That's how it is, is it? Can't say I'm surprised. I always thought you'd end up with her. But then you went to California and Bryce came home." He looked up at Blue Mountain. "If he were still here, we wouldn't be having this conversation. He was always Gramps's first choice to manage the lodge."

Sophia's too, he thought, no matter what his brother said. No matter what he once believed.

"I'm going to take Autumn home. You mind sticking around?"

"No. I'll look after things here. Soph's with me, so you'll have a couple hours before she gets to the house."

"You're a big boy, so I won't warn you to be careful. Besides, if anyone can handle her, it's you. She was too much woman for our little brother." He raised his hand. "Okay, I'll shut up."

"Yeah, you do that. And for the record, Bryce loved her, and she loved him. You know it, and so do I."

"You weren't around. Things weren't good after the accident. Bryce—" His brother glanced at the people waiting for drinks and must have realized it wasn't the time or place for this conversation. Adam would be just as glad to never talk about it again. "I better go get Autumn. Appreciate you closing up for me, Adam," Logan said before walking toward the dance floor.

Adam was keeping an eye on Sophia when he felt someone watching him from the other side of the bar.

The guy was about six foot one with dark hair and tattoo sleeves. "You Adam Dane? US Marshal who got shot in San Fran?"

"I am. Who's asking?"

"Jake Callahan. Callahan Automotive."

"Ah, the man who keeps an open bay just for Sophia." He smiled and offered his hand as he sized up her Valentine's date.

"Right, and you're the guy who ruined my shot with the woman of my dreams." He grinned. "So, you heard of me. Good. At least it's not one-sided."

"You've lost me, man."

"She's in love with you. Thought she might be when

she called me Adam a couple times during our date. Knew it for sure when she got word you were shot." He glanced to where Sophia danced by herself. "You going to stand here all night, or are you going to dance with the woman?"

Adam moved to put his glass on the bar and then clapped the other man on the shoulder. "I'm going to do something I should have done a long time ago."

Jake lifted his beer bottle. "Good luck."

Adam thought he might need it when Sophia saw him coming and stopped dancing. "It didn't work, did it? Your brother still hates me."

"We have Sunday. But I don't want to talk about Autumn and Logan right now."

"No." She looked down when he put his hands on either side of her waist and drew her toward him. "What are you doing?"

"I was hoping to dance with you."

She smiled like she used to, and he smiled in return, fighting the urge to kiss her adorable dimples.

"I didn't think you could dance. You never did. All you did was watch," she said as she moved into his arms, looping hers around his neck.

"You were fun to watch, but I don't want to watch anymore. I'm tired of sitting on the sidelines." He glanced over his shoulder at Jake, who saluted him with his beer bottle, and then Adam looked into Sophia's eyes. "I'm afraid if I do, someone else will come along, and I'll lose out on my chance with you."

"That would never happen."

"It did, Soph. It happened more than a decade ago."

"I . . . I don't know what to say."

"You don't have to say anything. It's time to let go of the past. Nothing we do or say will change anything."

"I can think of something that will change everything."

"What's that?"

"Dance with me, and then kiss me."

"Happy to." But as they began to move to "The Keeper of the Stars" by Tracy Byrd, Adam knew he couldn't wait and bent his head to kiss her. Almost from the moment his mouth closed over hers, he knew it was nothing like the kiss they'd shared at New Year's. It wasn't friendly, and it wasn't brief. It was deep, and it was real and hot and tinged with regret for all the years lost. There was also a hint of nerves, because this kiss felt like a promise.

Chapter Eleven

♥

The first real kiss Sophia shared with Adam would be a moment she'd never forget. The kisses that followed in the past twenty-four hours were equally memorable and wonderful. So wonderful that they changed everything, just like she'd predicted.

Only she didn't know what to do about it. If Operation HEA in Christmas succeeded, her life would stay pretty much the same. She'd have her best friend in town, their business partnership would remain intact, which would enable Sophia to work out a deal for the house, and Adam would return to San Francisco and his job as a US Marshal.

But if Operation HEA in Christmas failed, Autumn, Logan, and the children would jet off to Switzerland. And not only would she lose her best friend, the house would have to be sold, and eventually her business unless she found another partner. Only in this scenario, Adam would remain in town to run the lodge or risk losing it to Rick, something she knew he would never do no matter how much he might want to. Either way she lost, and she didn't want to choose.

She stood at the top of the bunny hill on Easter morning, watching Autumn help Logan's children hunt for the hidden plastic eggs. Last night, Sophia had volunteered to help fill the colorful eggs—all twenty-five hundred of them—with chocolate and candy. It was their biggest hunt ever, and half the town had shown up.

Her volunteerism seemed to have won her some brownie points with Logan. Though having Adam at her side might have been the reason Logan hadn't sent his usual pointed barbs her way.

Sophia spotted one of the special giant eggs with prizes inside that had been donated by local businesses. As Chloe and Madison McBride arrived with their children in tow, Sophia texted Autumn the location of the giant egg in an effort to win her best friend some brownie points with Logan's children. With that done, she decided the McBride women needed a distraction. "Madison! Chloe! There are lots of eggs under the deck." Both women looked from her to Autumn. "Follow Autumn," Chloe said.

"Go! Ski, ski!" Sophia cheered Autumn and the kids on.

Logan, who'd been talking to Madison's husband, turned. Immediately catching on, he sprinted toward his family, scooped up his kids, and followed Autumn's pointed finger to the egg. His daughter scooped it up seconds before Chloe swooped in. The egg was filled with Easter treats from Sugar and Spice. As Sophia had known they would, the Dane family generously shared their winnings.

And while Sophia stood on the hill watching her best friend and her new family-to-be, it hit her that Autumn was the one person who would understand exactly how it felt to be torn between your best friend and the man you loved. Though she might also be a little ticked if she heard about Operation HEA in Christmas. Sophia wouldn't blame her.

She wanted the best for Autumn. And as she continued watching them together, she noticed something. Her best friend looked different. She looked…happy, really and truly happy. She looked like the girl who used to talk endlessly about her boyfriend back home. The boy she wanted to marry. Sophia was just about to shout *Go, go and be happy* to her best friend when a man wrapped his arms around Sophia's waist from behind.

"Why are you looking so sad, beautiful?" Adam nuzzled her neck, poles in his hands, his skis on either side of hers. He'd never raced professionally like Bryce, but he was an excellent skier and volunteered with ski patrol whenever he'd been home.

She turned her head and kissed him, wondering what he'd say if she told him. They'd known each other for what seemed like forever, and it felt like they'd had feelings for each other for almost as long. And maybe that's why she said "I love you" without meaning to.

She closed her eyes, wanting to cry. She did love him. Some part of her always had. But she hadn't meant to tell him. Not yet. Not now. Not here. And from the expression on his face, she thought maybe he wished she hadn't told him either.

"Is that what's making you sad?"

She nodded and blurted out how torn up she was about him and about Autumn. She didn't want anything between them. She'd kept her secrets about Bryce, and she'd made herself a promise at New Year's. No more secrets or lies, to herself or anyone else.

Adam didn't say anything, just wrapped an arm around her waist and skied her to the bottom of the hill. He didn't have to. She knew his answer. Which was why, when Zeus bounded over, she crouched to give him a hug, burying her face in his fur so no one would see her tears.

"Soph, don't cry." Adam released his boots from his skis and then hers, drawing her to her feet. "Come on. I'll grab us a couple hot chocolates. We'll go for a walk."

"I can't. I promised Nell I'd help with the baby bunny race."

"Okay." He wiped away her tears and then gave her a tender kiss. "This doesn't have anything to do with you. I want to be with you, but I don't want to take over management of the lodge. I love my job, Soph. I've put down roots in San Francisco. I've got a great place, and I've got really good friends."

"I understand." She wished she didn't, but she did.

"No, I don't think you do." He framed her face with his cold hands. "I love you too. I do. But the idea of moving here—"

"Sophia!" Nell waved her over to the front of the lodge.

"I'd better go." Zeus went to follow her. "Stay, Zeus. I'm sorry. I'd take you if I could, but there will be babies crawling in the snow." And no matter what Adam said, Zeus should probably get used to not seeing her. Adam was returning to work in less than a week.

When she reached Nell, the older woman's eyes narrowed at her. "Maddie and Chloe, do me a favor and get the parents and babies in a line. You, come with me." She took Sophia by the arm, stopping at a secluded spot near a fir tree decorated with brightly painted Easter eggs.

"All right, what did my step-grandson say to make you cry?"

"It wasn't him. It's me, Nell. I thought…" She lifted a shoulder. "It's okay."

"You're in love with him, aren't you?" She waved a hand when Sophia didn't answer. "You can tell me. Despite what everyone thinks, I can keep a secret. But if you don't think everyone knows how you feel about Adam after Spring Fling, you're mistaken."

"I thought you and Calder might be upset because he's Bryce's brother."

"You've been on your own for too darn long, if you ask me. Both you girls have. Get your happy wherever you can find it, and don't let anyone stand in your way."

"Like I'm standing in Autumn's?"

"I figured it'd take you a week or two to come around, but in the end, I knew you'd do what's best for your girl. You don't have to worry about her. He loves her. It'll be good for them, being on their own, having to depend on each other. And it might be good for you too."

"I don't see how. I have to sell the house, and I have

to find someone to partner with or I'll lose the business too. I—" Spotting Rick Dane a few feet away with his camera, she hurriedly wiped her eyes.

Nell followed her gaze and waved Rick away. Then she said to Sophia, "Don't work yourself into a tizzy. I know it's a lot to take in, but you don't have to do it alone. We're all here for you, girlie. We'll put our heads together and figure something out." A slow smile spread across her face. "I think I've just come up with the perfect solution for everyone. Bryce might have died, but you're still Calder's granddaughter by marriage. How would you feel about managing the lodge? You've got a degree in business and lots of experience."

"Yes, but I love my store and..."

"So, move Naughty and Nice and Sugar and Spice into the lodge. You should be able to get a good price on your place downtown. Enough to buy Autumn out of the house, I'd imagine." She put her hands on Sophia's shoulders. "Change isn't always easy, but it's good."

Chapter Twelve

♥

Adam grabbed two hot chocolates and went outside looking for Sophia. The baby bunny races had ended five minutes ago in a tie. Madison's son and Chloe's daughter were the official winners. Adam walked over to the ski rack and set the hot chocolate on the nearby bench, pulling a cookie for Zeus from his jacket pocket as well as his phone. Just as he was about to call Sophia, he spotted her on the deck with Autumn.

After watching their heartfelt and tearful exchange, he sat heavily on the bench. "That's it, boy. Sophia just threw herself on her sword for her best friend's happiness." There was a *swoosh* of an incoming text, and he looked at the screen. Good news travels fast, he thought. Logan wanted to see him in his office. "This day keeps getting better and better," he murmured, thinking about Sophia. In the early days, if they'd admitted they loved each other, it would have been a whole lot less complicated than it was now.

Catching sight of Sophia leaving the lodge at the same time Adam did, Zeus shot off in her direction, his cookie forgotten. She offered the dog a weak smile and gave him some love before continuing on her way without giving Adam a passing glance.

He stared after her. What the...? "Soph, hold up. Where are you going?"

"Back to town. I have things to do."

"You don't have a car." His cell rang. It was his brother. "Just give me a minute. I have to see what Logan wants, and then I'll take you home. We need to talk." He was pretty sure he knew what his brother wanted, so the conversation would be brief.

"It's all right, Adam. I can't get into it now, but Nell has come up with a solution to your problem. If Calder agrees, no one will expect you to leave the job, town, and people you love. Least of all me. I'll be too busy building a wonderful life."

"If it's so wonderful, why do you look like you're holding back tears?"

"Because you're taking Zeus from me!"

"Adam!" his brother yelled from the lodge.

"Soph, come on. Just give me two minutes." She ignored him and walked toward the parking lot.

"Adam, get in here now!"

He looked from Sophia to his brother, who appeared to be having a breakdown. "Come on, Zeus." He gave the whining dog's collar a light tug. "It's okay. We won't be long. She won't get far."

By the time he made it inside the lodge, his brother was nowhere to be found, so Adam headed for Logan's office on the third floor. He opened the door to see his brother standing at the window that overlooked Silver

Lake and the mountains. Logan turned, holding up his phone, his face pale, his eyes stricken.

"What's going on?"

"Someone texted me this." He walked over to hand Adam the phone. "I don't know who, but it can't be true. It can't be. Bryce would never do this."

Adam knew before he even looked at the screen what the message would read. It didn't make sense though, not after all this time. Two people knew about his brother's suicide, though the coroner might have guessed.

Adam looked at the screen. He was wrong; he hadn't expected this. "This is bullshit. Sophia is not to blame for Bryce committing suicide. She did nothing wrong."

His brother stared at him. "But Bryce...Are you saying it's true? It wasn't an accident? Bryce took his own life?"

Adam nodded and then proceeded to tell his brother everything he knew about their baby brother's state of mind leading up to the suicide.

Logan sank into a chair. With his elbows on his knees, he lowered his face into his hands. "I knew he shouldn't have married her. I knew she'd bring him down. Things were great when he was riding high, when the royalties were coming in from the endorsements, but after the accident, when the money dried up—"

"Stop. Just stop. Bryce was self-medicating for the pain. He got hooked on opioids."

"Whose fault is that? She wanted him back in the game, and she didn't care how hard she pushed him. She—"

"Isn't to blame. Sophia—" Adam broke off as the office door opened.

"Sorry. Am I interrupting something?" Autumn's smile faded when she got a better look at his brother. "Logan, what—"

His brother lifted his head to look at her, his eyes accusing. "Did you know?"

"Know what? What's going on?"

"My brother's death wasn't an accident. Bryce killed himself. He killed himself because your best friend didn't get him the help he needed."

"Don't start with that again, Logan. I—" Adam began, but Logan was beside himself with grief and anger and kept going.

"Because she couldn't stand that he was no longer earning the big bucks, she pushed him, and when they wouldn't let him back on the circuit, he killed himself. He killed himself because of her!"

Autumn stared at her fiancé as if she couldn't believe he was the same man she loved. "How dare you! How dare you speak about Sophia that way. You have no idea what you're talking about. She did everything she could to help Bryce. She loved him, and he loved her."

"If he loved her so much, then why did he kill himself?"

Her color high, Autumn got in his brother's space. "If you loved me so much, why did you leave me? Sophia never did. She's always been there for me, Logan Dane. She's the best friend I could have asked for. She's losing everything, everything because of you and me. And do you know what she did? She told me to go and be happy. That's the kind of woman she is."

The door opened, and Nell walked in. "What the Sam Hill is going on here?"

"I'll tell you what's going on, Nell. The wedding is off!" Autumn pulled off her engagement ring and threw it at Logan.

"Autumn, wait!" Logan called after her, bending to retrieve the ring from the floor.

Nell shut the door. "The two of you sit down." When Logan protested, she added, "Now."

As though sensing he'd have to bodily move Nell out of the way, Logan returned to the chair, his shoulders slumped. "You have no idea what's going on here, Nell."

"Oh, I think I do. Probably better than the two of you."

"No, you don't." Logan glanced to where Adam stood by the window. "Give her the phone."

"No, I won't. Because it's a lie. Whoever—"

Nell walked over, took the phone, and read the text. "That's a lie. Sophia did everything in her power to help Bryce. Who sent this?"

Adam frowned, confused by her reaction. "Wait. You knew Bryce committed suicide?"

"Just like your grandfather, I suspected it. Most of the folks in town did. We were here. We saw what was going on. Tried to help where we could, but your brother…" She lifted a shoulder. "You can't force someone to get help or to accept it."

Crossing her arms, she looked from him to Logan. "Now I've got some advice for the pair of you, and I suggest you take it. Until you boys got involved with Sophia and Autumn again, they were happy. They'd made wonderful lives for themselves. They might not have had a man in their lives for a good long while, but as someone who spent decades on her own, I can tell you, you can be perfectly happy without one. In fact, with men like the pair of you, they'd be better off single."

Adam opened his mouth to defend himself and then, remembering Sophia's face earlier, closed it.

"What are you talking about? Autumn—" Logan began, but Nell cut him off.

"I'll tell you exactly what I'm talking about. You expected Autumn to give up everything because of you and your dreams. Bryce did the same to Sophia. And you"— she pointed at Adam—"aren't willing to give up anything for her." She held up her hand. "Don't give me the *we just started dating; it's new* bull crap. You love her, and she loves you, and you're not getting any younger. Either one of you. But you can't build a life or a relationship living nineteen hours apart. You have to take a risk, do the work, make the sacrifices."

She pointed at Logan. "So do you. Stop thinking about yourselves and start thinking about them. If you can't, leave them alone and move on because they don't need the two of you to be happy. There. I've said my piece. And just so you know, Calder doesn't need either one of you to manage the lodge. Sophia's going to take it over, and she'll do a damn fine job."

Someone knocked on the door. Adam was all for not answering. Logan appeared to feel the same. But

Ty opened the door, sticking his head inside. "Happy Easter…" He looked at each of them in turn. "Okay, so not so happy. Sorry to disturb you, but I'm looking for Sophia. Everyone said she left, but I can't get her on her phone."

At the mere mention of her name, Zeus's ears perked, and he sat up. Nell's attention perked too, and the last thing Adam wanted to do after her lecture was admit that the last time he'd seen Sophia, she was heading for the parking lot, no doubt looking for a ride home. "I'll, uh, see if I can find her," he said.

Adam barely held back a groan when someone else knocked and stuck their head in the office. It was Jill. "Sorry to interrupt, but I think we might have a problem. Have any of you seen Autumn?"

Logan avoided looking at Nell. "She left here a few minutes ago. Why?"

"Okay, I don't want anyone to panic. It might be nothing. But her car door was open and…there are signs of a struggle. Her purse is on the ground, wallet's gone, but her phone is there. No one I've spoken to has seen her. Gage has organized a search of the grounds."

"I can't get Sophia on her phone," Ty said.

Adam, who'd been trying to call her, said, "She's not picking up for me either. She left about fifteen minutes ago. I asked her to wait, but she was upset. Last time I saw her, she was heading across the parking lot."

"I've got people searching the lot and the surrounding area." Jill's cell phone rang.

"Zeus, *heir*. I'm going to look for Sophia. Let me know—"

"Adam, wait." Jill held up a finger. "Okay, yeah, we need to interview anyone who might have seen either Sophia or Autumn. Put it out on all social media channels with the timeline. Our best information will come from people leaving the parking lot in the last thirty minutes."

"What did they find?" Adam asked the second Jill disconnected. He had to work to keep his panic under control, trying not to go to worst-case scenarios. Trying not to see the hurt on Sophia's face before she walked away from him.

"A secondary location was found in the parking lot. There are signs of a struggle. Sophia's hat was found at the site but nothing else. There's a faint tire imprint. We're having it analyzed now."

Adam was racking his brain, trying to figure out who would take Sophia and Autumn and why. "Logan, give Jill your phone."

"Why . . . ? What—" Logan began.

"Because I don't believe in coincidences," he told his brother, then returned his attention to Jill. "Logan was sent a text within ten minutes of Sophia leaving. It implicated her in my brother's suicide. It's connected. I'm sure of it. I just don't know how. We need to find out who sent the text."

"But why would they take Autumn if they blame Sophia for Bryce's—"

"They don't blame Sophia," Adam told his brother. "They want you to. Which begs the question—why? What did they have to gain from you blaming her? I'd say them knowing Bryce killed himself might be a clue, but from what Nell implied, a lot of people in Christmas had come to the same conclusion. But you're right. Autumn is somehow connected."

His frustration grew as he tried to connect the dots, to see a pattern. He took Autumn out of the equation and focused on Sophia and the text. What did the person stand to gain with Sophia out of the way? What had happened within the last hour to trigger…? "Nell, did you tell anyone else that Sophia was going to take over management of the lodge?"

"Just you boys, and Calder knew, of course. Why? What are you—"

He held up his finger and called security. "Is Rick on the grounds? When was the last time you saw him? Okay, and…"

Nell tugged on his arm. "He was there. Rick. I shooed him away, but he might have heard me talking to Sophia about the lodge."

"Jill, put out an APB on a 2010 Buick, black. Best they can remember, Rick asked one of the staff to borrow it twenty-five minutes ago." He moved to the door. "Zeus, *heir*." As though he sensed that Sophia was in trouble, Zeus responded immediately.

Chapter Thirteen

♥

Sophia woke up in the dark. As she waited for her eyes to adjust to the lack of light, she tried to remember what had happened. The last thing she recalled was hearing heavy footfalls behind her and then a soaked rag was pressed over her mouth and nose. It smelled sickly sweet. Chloroform. She'd struggled and tried to call out, but the person was strong. She remembered thinking it was a man because of his height, his size. Within moments, she'd lost feeling in her legs and arms. Then her vision and hearing dimmed. She couldn't remember anything else after that.

She went to move, only to discover her hands were taped behind her back. There was also duct tape on her mouth. She wasn't alone. Someone else was with her in the small, confined space. She smelled gasoline and heard the rumble of an engine. A trunk. They were trapped in the trunk of a car. Her heart began to race, and she began to shake. *Your mind can't work if you panic*, she told herself. *Listen. Think.*

The road was bumpy. Too bumpy for a paved road.

Either backwoods or off-road. She heard tinny music, a man singing along. Middle-age, something familiar about his voice. The car hit a rut, and she bounced, rolling into the other person. Her back was to their front. She smelled perfume, and panic once again set in when she recognized the familiar feminine, powdery scent. Autumn!

Sophia wiggled deeper into the trunk until she had room to lie flat on her back and then turned to face Autumn. Her eyes were shut. There was blood near her temple.

Hands. She had to get her hands free. On Saturday Mystery Movie Night a month before, a woman had freed herself from duct tape. Her mind reminded her it was a movie. Anything could be done in a movie.

She shut out the negative thoughts. There was no room for pessimism. Besides, once her hands were free, she could easily open the trunk. She'd tried it after reading one too many books where the kidnap victim had been trapped inside. There should be a release by the latch. But the car was moving too fast. She'd have to wait until he reached his destination.

Wiggling to put as much distance as possible between herself and Autumn, Sophia then pulled her knees to her chest. She should have taken yoga, she thought, as she arched her back and then moved her shoulders down in an effort to get her bound wrists under and then over her feet.

After several tries, she knew it was futile. But if she could just…She stabbed the tape between her wrists with the heel of her boot. On the third try, it went through. As the tape began to give, Autumn awoke. Her eyes went wide as she took in their surroundings.

Seeing the fear and tears in her best friend's eyes, Sophia stabbed through the tape with renewed strength caused by fury at the man who had done this to them.

She wrenched her wrists apart and then tore the duct tape from her mouth, stifling a pained yelp. It felt like the tape had ripped the skin off her lips. "It'll only hurt for a second," she whispered to Autumn, biting the inside of her cheek as she went to rip the tape off her best friend's mouth. "Are you okay?"

Autumn nodded, her gaze darting around the space. "Why would Rick do this to us?"

"Rick? Rick Dane?"

"Yes. I...Logan and I had a fight. I ran to my car. Rick was just closing the trunk of a black car. He was angry. He asked what I was looking at. I said nothing. And then he asked why I was crying. I told him the wedding was off. Then he bent down and held up your hat. I went over to get it, and he..." She touched her temple. "He slammed my head against the car."

"I'm sorry he hurt you, and he will pay for that. But right now we don't have time to worry about his motivation. Our only job is to get free and be ready when he opens the trunk. Unless he stops and leaves us alone and we can get away without him seeing us. But I don't think that will happen. Turn so I can get the tape off your hands."

While Autumn rolled to her stomach, Sophia looked around. She smiled and reached for her purse. "It's a good thing Rick isn't very bright." Though she didn't share with Autumn that even stupid kidnappers could be dangerous. If they had a gun.

The car slowed, and the road grew bumpier. "We're getting closer," she whispered in Autumn's ear as she took a small pair of scissors from her purse and cut through the tape.

Once Autumn was free, Sophia began pulling anything that could be used as a weapon from her purse. The benefits of being a mystery-loving, true-crime junkie and a fan of oversize purses were that she was well equipped to deal with situations such as this. She had Mace (thank you, Madison), a Taser (thank you, Jill), a pink switchblade (thank you, Chloe), and a deep faith that the man and the dog she loved were out there searching for them right now. The thought of Adam and Zeus on the job buoyed her spirits. The situation also helped put everything in perspective. As long as he loved her, they could figure it out.

The car stopped. *Be ready*, Sophia mouthed as she handed Autumn the Mace, pointing at her eyes. Then, with hand signals, she laid out the plan. Autumn would strike first with the Mace, and then Sophia would use the Taser on his chest. She would be in the ideal range of seven feet. She just had to ensure the prongs made contact with his chest.

A car door closed. There was no sound of traffic. They were somewhere isolated. No one to help them. Yet.

"Now!" Sophia yelled as soon as the trunk opened.

Rick's eyes went wide, his hand reaching up to slam the trunk just as Autumn sprayed the Mace in his face. He screamed, brought his hands to his eyes, and stumbled backward. Sophia lunged, half in, half out of the trunk to press the prongs to his chest. She activated the Taser, maintaining contact while she climbed out of the trunk. She wouldn't stop until he was unconscious. His body contorted, his screams becoming guttural and weak. Finally, he dropped to the ground.

Her hand fell weakly to her side as she walked back to the trunk. She returned the Taser to her purse before helping Autumn out of the trunk, her eyes narrowing on her best friend. "You're dizzy. Here, lean against the trunk. I'll take care of everything."

Once she'd zip-tied Rick's hands and feet (thank you, survivalist.com) it took twenty minutes for her to access his phone (no password protection made it easy) and look through his latest communications to ensure he'd acted alone, as well as establish that the small, well-provisioned hunting cabin was safe. She got Autumn settled with a cup of tea on the bed, and then went back to the car, grabbing some rope from the trunk before dragging Rick inside the cabin. He began to stir as she tied him to a chair.

She dragged her purse and her tired self to the bed, crawling in beside Autumn.

Her best friend smiled, looking better than she had an hour earlier. "I'm so glad you're addicted to mysteries and murder." She glanced at Rick in the other room, still half out of it, or at least pretending to be. "Why do you think he kidnapped us?"

"The lodge. It's always been about the lodge for Rick." She told her about Nell's idea and surmised Rick had overheard and wanted to get rid of her. "He must have worried that you had seen something you shouldn't or he thought if the wedding was off, Logan wouldn't leave Christmas. Why did you call off the wedding?"

Autumn reluctantly told her about the text, which Sophia had seen when she checked Rick's phone looking for a partner in crime, and Logan's reaction to it. She was surprised to learn Autumn had guessed the truth all those years before. She hadn't had to carry it around on her own after all.

"Don't call off the wedding because of how he reacted to the text, Autumn. He was shocked, angry, hurt at discovering Bryce had died by suicide. I felt the same. It's natural to want to blame something or someone. And Rick made sure Logan blamed me."

"But if no one other than you and Adam knew for sure, how did Rick know?"

"Why don't you ask me?" Rick turned his head to look at them. There were streaks of dirt on his face, and his eyes were bloodshot. "I'll tell you. I can even tell you what was in the letter he wrote Sophia. I can tell you because I was there. At the last minute, he was going to back out. He was afraid you'd blame yourself. But I wasn't going to let that happen. I wasn't going to let him ruin my best chance to get the lodge. It was mine, not his, not theirs. Mine."

"It was you. You were getting him the drugs, weren't you?" Sophia said, her throat tight with tears and fury. Her hand shook as she dug in her purse for the Taser and her phone. She left the phone on the bed and wrapped her trembling fingers around the Taser.

"Well, someone had to help the poor boy. You

wouldn't, and he was in so much pain. He would have killed himself someday. I just helped him along."

"What are you doing?" Autumn asked when Sophia got off the bed and walked to Rick. There was a nervous hitch in her best friend's voice.

Sophia pressed the prongs to his chest. "Then maybe I'll help you along too."

"Sophia, don't!" Autumn cried.

"I wonder what a full charge does at this close range. Autumn, video this. I'm sure people would want to know how…" She looked down at the puddle forming on the floor.

Eyes wild, Rick strained at the ropes. "Stop her, Autumn. Stop her!"

"Did my husband beg you to stop, Rick? Did you push Bryce off the mountain? Tell me, what did you do?" She pressed the prongs as hard as she could against his chest.

"Please," he gasped. "I'll tell you everything. Just stop pushing that thing into me."

She released the pressure. But as he relayed the last hours of her husband's life and the part he had played in excruciating detail, her grip on the Taser caused her fingers to ache, her hand to shake.

"I told you everything. You can't kill me. It was his choice, just like I told you. I didn't push him. I didn't give him the pills or the booze that night."

"No, you just made sure that he felt like his life no longer had any meaning, that he was a burden to me and his family." She put the Taser down, and he sagged on the chair.

Exhausted both emotionally and physically, Sophia picked up the roll of duct tape, cut off a piece, and then taped his mouth shut. "Death is too easy. I want you to suffer. I want you to spend the rest of your life in jail. A real prison this time."

Autumn, who'd moved to stand beside her as Rick recounted the last moments of Bryce's life, took Sophia in her arms and held her tight. "I wish there was something I could do or say that would make this better."

Sophia drew back. "All we can hope for now is that Rick will pay for the part he played, but in the end, nothing has changed."

"As long as you know there wasn't anything more you could have done for Bryce."

"Don't worry. I will not carry this burden. This is Rick's to bear. I'm just grateful we made it out alive and I'm here, with you." From now on, she would not take one more moment of her life for granted. She'd live it to the fullest. She put an arm around Autumn's shoulders. "I could use a cup of tea. How about you? Do you want another one?"

"Um, sure, but don't you think we should let everyone know we're okay?"

"There's no cell service, and I don't feel like hiking through the woods. Besides, Adam and Zeus will find us soon."

* * *

They'd gotten a break early in their search. Someone had spotted the Buick turning onto one of the back roads north of the lodge. But their good luck didn't hold. Rick had gone off-road, and his wasn't the only vehicle to do so.

"I know you don't want to give up, but we're losing light, Adam." Jill had stayed with him, along with Logan and a couple of volunteers. Gage and his brothers had followed other leads in case the information they'd been given didn't pan out.

"You go, Jill. Zeus won't stop, and neither will I." He couldn't make Zeus stop if he wanted to. The dog was as sharp and as focused as when he'd been in his prime. And he was working as well with Adam as he had with Manuel. "We could use a little help, my friend," he murmured to Manuel in heaven.

He wouldn't lose hope. Rick had pulled this before with Gage, and Gage had escaped. Adam clung to that.

"If we get them back, I'll do whatever Autumn wants. Stay, go, I don't care as long as she loves me. I don't care if she marries me, as long as she lets me be in her life. Nell's right. I've been an asshat. In the past and now."

"It's Soph who thinks you're an asshat. And there's no *if* about it. We will find them, and they'll be okay. Trust me. Soph wouldn't let anyone hurt Autumn."

"I know. She's kinda scary. In a good way," he said when Adam gave him a look. "I will never say another negative word about her... What is it?"

"Zeus found something." He ran to the dog, who sat still as stone. It was a coffee cup. Adam held it up. "Must be Rick's." He walked a short way and found tire tracks. They were fresh. "Zeus, *such*." Track.

"Thank God for that dog."

"Look. Around the bend. There's the Buick. Zeus, *heir*." Come here.

After a brief and heated exchange, Jill let him take the lead. She was an excellent sheriff, but she knew as well as he did that she should be on desk duty at this stage of her pregnancy, which was no doubt why she acquiesced. Adam crouched low and ran to the window, inching up on an angle to get a look inside. He shook his head with a laugh.

"What's going on?" Jill joined him at the window to peek over the ledge. "I should have known." She rose to her feet with a hand at her lower back. "Honestly, if you don't take the job as sheriff, I'm offering it to Sophia."

Logan's voice came from behind the Buick. "I'm dying here. Would someone please tell me they're okay?"

"Unless Rick tied himself to a chair and duct taped his own mouth, they are." Adam opened the door to the cabin.

Rick made noises behind the tape, jumping the chair forward as though they were coming to save him and not the two women, who were sitting on the bed. Autumn was drinking something from a cup, and Sophia was doing her nails.

"No one move," Jill yelled, pulling out her cell phone. Once she'd taken several pictures, she said, "Okay, go ahead. You can kiss and make up now."

Logan pushed past Adam to rush to Autumn's side, and Zeus beat Adam to Sophia. She smiled, put her nail polish on the bedside table, and then moved to sit on the edge of the bed to give Zeus a cuddle.

"I knew you would find us." She looked up at Adam with nothing but love shining from her eyes. No fear at the ordeal she'd just gone through and no anger at him for putting his job and his life in San Francisco ahead of her. But then she turned those gorgeous dark eyes on Rick, and they flashed with fury.

"He killed Bryce, Adam. He fed his drug habit. He told him to kill himself."

Adam stared at her, stunned. "Say again." She repeated the exact same words he'd thought he'd misheard, and he slowly turned his head. He stood rooted to the spot, afraid of what he'd do if he got any closer to Rick. Putting Sophia and Autumn in danger had been bad enough, but this... Adam walked over and ripped the duct tape from his cousin's mouth.

"It's not true. Don't listen to them. They're setting me up," Rick cried.

"I don't know why everyone thinks I'm a bimbo with no brains." Sophia held up her phone, and Rick's voice filled the room as she played the recording of his confession.

"That's inadmissible. You can't tape someone without their consent."

"You heard me tell Autumn to video you. You didn't object."

"I thought you were going to Taser me to death!"

"Get him out of here before I do," Adam said to Jill.

"No problem. We'll give you a couple minutes." She looked over at Sophia. "Good job with the Taser, girlfriend."

"Thank you. And you would have been proud of Autumn. She handled the Mace like a pro."

Jill frowned. "Mace?"

"Um, I meant bear spray."

"Sure you did. You might want to check her purse, Adam. It wouldn't look good for the acting sheriff's girlfriend to be packing illegal weapons."

"Call me an optimist, but I'm hoping, when I take over for you, she'll be my fiancée, not my girlfriend," he said to Jill, and then went down on one knee in front of Sophia. Zeus moved in beside him and put a paw on her knee. Adam laughed, and Sophia stared at him. "You're going to take over for Jill? You're moving to Christmas?"

"Yeah, but did you miss the other part? The reason I'm down on one knee in front of you? Or are you pretending you didn't hear me so I didn't just embarrass myself? Don't say no, Dimples. I know it's fast, and I know I messed up earlier, but I love you, Sophia Vergara Cortez, and I'll do whatever I have to to make you happy. Please say you'll marry me and my dog?"

"Yes. Yes, I will marry you." She threw herself into his arms and kissed him until his brother groaned and Zeus barked. She laughed and leaned over to hug Zeus. "I love you too. You are mine as much as Adam's." She waved a hand at Autumn and Logan. "Now it's your turn to make up."

"No, it's my turn to make up to you, Sophia." Logan took her hand. "I'm sorry for being such a jerk to you over the years. There was no excuse for it."

"You were jealous of me. It happens." She winked at

Adam, but then she grew serious. "I was jealous of you and overprotective of Autumn and didn't always make your life easy. For that I am truly sorry. But I know you love her. You have my blessing."

She reached for Autumn's hand and placed it in Logan's. "Marry him. You always wanted to travel, to see the world. I've done that and then some. Now's your chance to do it with the man you love. We've made a nice life for ourselves here, but I think we got stuck and our dreams got too small. Go chase the dreams you used to have, and when you've done all you wanted to do, come home. We'll be here."

"And if I'm happy here?" Autumn asked his brother.

"Then I will be too," Logan said.

"What if I want a double wedding?"

Logan looked from Autumn to Sophia. "You two have already talked about this, haven't you?"

"A little bit when we were waiting for Adam and Zeus to find us." Sophia looked at him. "But it was just a dream. I didn't know if you would want to marry me."

"Wait a minute," Autumn said. "Adam called you Sophia Vergara Cortez. You're not really related to Sofía Vergara, are you?"

She sighed. "Yes. She is my second cousin. But don't tell Ty."

"How are we supposed to keep it from him? We promised he could be in the wedding party if we ever got married again. He'll see your name when we sign the papers."

As the two women walked away talking about the

wedding, Logan looked at Adam. "I'm beginning to think their dream wedding might turn into our nightmare."

"No, the real nightmare would be if we weren't the men they were marrying."

Epilogue

♥

Five weeks later.

Ty, you have taken over my wedding. I will not let you take over my new store," Sophia said, pushing the rustic-looking wooden counter back where it had originally been.

"You really do have to learn to share, bunny. It's our store, remember? Menswear to the left, ladies' wear to the right. And this is where my display is supposed to go," he said, pushing the counter out of the way.

"I don't know why I ever agreed to go into partnership with you," she said, now in a tug-of-war over the counter.

"You went into partnership with me because your best friend is moving to Switzerland and you bought her out of the house on Holly Lane. Besides that, other than you, I'm the only person in this town who has an eye for fashion. Not to mention, I'm your other best friend, and you need me. You're manager of the lodge now, remember? You can't do it all."

"Why not? You do. You own Diva and a catering business too."

"Yes, but unlike you, I have staff. Which you would have if you just hired the woman I found for you yesterday."

"I don't trust her. She has shifty eyes."

He sighed. "You said the same thing about the woman Autumn hired to run Sugar and Spice."

Logan had signed a two-year contract with the company in Switzerland, so Autumn decided to move Sugar and Spice to the lodge instead of closing. Though their new locations were half the size of the old.

The Colonial on Main Street sold three days after the FOR SALE sign went up. But the sale was dependent on an early-May occupancy. Since Autumn wanted to leave with Logan and the children and it was a good offer, they accepted. Between their upcoming wedding, moving locations, and overseeing the construction of the new stores at the lodge, not to mention learning everything she had to about the management of the place before Logan left, there weren't near enough hours in the day.

Suddenly too tired to fight, Sophia sprawled across the counter. "Fine. I will hire the lady. If she ends up being a serial killer, I will sue you."

"If she ends up being a serial killer, we'll both be dead."

"If you're talking about the woman who applied for the job yesterday, she's a con artist, not a serial killer," said a familiar deep voice.

Sophia lifted her head to smile at her husband-to-be, who looked breath-stealingly gorgeous in his sheriff's uniform. Zeus looked to Adam for permission. At his head nod and smile, the dog bounded to Sophia's side. But Adam wasn't smiling when he joined him there.

He lifted her chin with his knuckle. "You look beat. You gotta take a break, Dimples."

"I can't. There's too much to do. We want the stores up and running on the first day of June. Then there's the wedding and—"

"Ty, I thought you were handling the wedding stuff for her."

"So did I, but your fiancée has control issues."

"I don't have control issues, I just want it to be special for you. It's your first wedding. I want it to be special for Autumn, too, and the children."

Adam frowned. "Wait a sec. What about you?"

"I'm marrying you. That's special enough for me."

"No. Do not even think about it, Adam. She doesn't know what she's saying. She wants a wedding, a big splashy affair with lots of bling. And pink. She loves pink."

Sophia narrowed her eyes at Ty. "Fifteen minutes ago, you told me to think garden-party-goes-country."

"Well, what was I supposed to do? It's a double wedding, and everything you liked Autumn didn't, and everything Autumn liked, you hated. So I had to make an executive decision."

Adam smiled. "You thinking what I'm thinking, Dimples?"

She walked into his arms. "I hope so," she murmured against his chest.

He bent his head to whisper in her ear. "Paperwork is done, so we'll head to the courthouse and see if the judge will marry us right now. And then we'll spend the next two days at the honeymoon cabin on Silver Lake. Sound good?"

She tipped her head back. "Sounds perfect. I love you, Adam Dane."

"I love you too, Dimples. Now, let's get this done."

"Hey, you two, get back here right now. This is not funny. Sophia? Adam?"

About the Author

Debbie Mason is the *USA Today* bestselling author of the Christmas, Colorado and the Harmony Harbor series. Her books have been praised for their "likable characters, clever dialogue, and juicy plots" (RTBook Reviews.com). When she isn't writing or reading, Debbie enjoys spending time with her very own real-life hero, their three wonderful children and their son-in-law, and two adorable grandbabies in Ottawa, Canada.

You can learn more at:
AuthorDebbieMason.com
Twitter @AuthorDebMason
Facebook.com/DebbieMasonBooks

Fall in love with these charming contemporary romances!

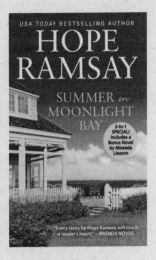

SUMMER ON MOONLIGHT BAY
by Hope Ramsay

Veterinarian Noah Cuthbert had no intention of ever moving back to the small town of Magnolia Harbor. But when his sister calls with the opportunity to run the local animal clinic as well as give her a break from caring for their ailing mom, he packs his bags and heads home. But once he meets the clinic's beautiful new manager, he questions whether his summer plans might become more permanent. Includes a bonus novel by Miranda Liasson!

WISH YOU WERE MINE
by Tara Sivec

When Everett Southerland left town five years ago, Cameron James thought it was the worst day of her life. She was wrong: It was the day he came back and told her the truth about his feelings that devastated her. Now she's having a hard time believing him, until he proves to her how much he cares. But with so many secrets between them, will they ever find the future that was always destined to be theirs?

Find more great reads on Instagram with @ReadForeverPub.

ALL I WANT FOR CHRISTMAS IS YOU
by Miranda Liasson

Just when Kaitlyn Barnes vows to get over her longtime crush on Rafe Langdon, they share a sizzling evening that delivers an epic holiday surprise: Kaitlyn is pregnant. While their off-the-charts chemistry can still melt snow, Rafe must decide if he'll keep running from love forever—or if he'll make this Christmas the one where he becomes the man Kaitlyn wants...and the one she deserves. Includes a bonus novel by Annie Rains!

SNOWFALL ON CEDAR TRAIL
by Annie Rains

Determined to give her son a good holiday season, single mom Halona Locklear signs him up for Sweetwater Springs' Mentor Match program. Little does she know that her son's mentor would be the handsome chief of police, who might know secrets about her past that she is determined to keep buried. Includes a bonus novel by Miranda Liasson!

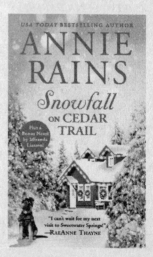

IT STARTED WITH CHRISTMAS
by Jenny Hale

Holly McAdams loves spending the holidays at her family's cozy cabin, but she soon discovers that the gorgeous and wealthy Joseph Barnes has been renting the cabin, and it looks like he'll be staying for the holidays. Throw in Holly's charming ex, and she's got the recipe for one complicated Christmas. With unexpected guests and secrets aplenty, will Holly be able to find herself and the love she's always dreamed of this Christmas?

CHRISTMAS IN HARMONY HARBOR
by Debbie Mason

Evangeline Christmas will do anything to save her year-round Christmas store, Holiday House, including facing off against high-powered real-estate developer Caine Elliot, who's using his money and influence to push through his competing property next door. When her last desperate attempt to stop him fails, she gambles everything on a proposition she prays the handsome, blue-eyed player can't refuse. Includes a bonus novella!

THE AMISH WEDDING PROMISE
by Laura V. Hilton

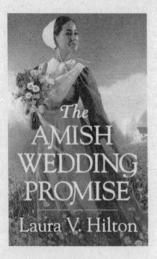

After a storm crashes through town, Grace Lantz is forced to postpone her wedding. All hands are needed for cleanup, but Grace doesn't know where to start—should she console her special needs sister or find her missing groom? Sparks fly when the handsome Zeke Bontrager comes to aid the community and offers to help the overwhelmed Grace in any way he can. But when her groom is found, Grace must decide if the wedding will go on...or if she'll take a chance on Zeke.

MERMAID INN
by Jenny Holiday

When Eve Abbott inherits her aunt's inn, she remembers the heartbreaking last summer she spent there, and she has no interest in returning. Unfortunately, Eve must run the inn for two years before she can sell. Town sheriff Sawyer Collins can't deny all the old feelings that come rushing back when he sees Eve. Getting her out of Matchmaker Bay when they were younger was something he did for her own good. But losing her again? He doesn't think he can survive that twice. Includes a bonus novella by Alison Bliss!